ALWAYS&
FOREVER

OTHER BOOKS AND AUDIO BOOKS
BY CANDIE CHECKETTS:

Another Chance

ALWAYS & FOREVER

a novel

Candie Checketts

Covenant Communications, Inc.

Covenant.

Cover illustration *Orchid* © Kay Spatafore.

Cover design copyrighted 2004 by Covenant Communications, Inc.

Published by Covenant Communications, Inc.
American Fork, Utah

Printed in the United States
First Printing: June 2004

10 09 08 07 06 05 04   10 9 8 7 6 5 4 3 2 1

ISBN 1-59156-505-7

Dedication

This book is dedicated to my children—
Chad, Alex, Kimberly, and Ryan
without whom, life would be pretty dull.

Acknowledgements

I would like to say a special thanks to Angela Colvin,
my editor at Covenant, for her patience, faith, and guidance,
and for her many hours of hard work.

CHAPTER ONE

"You can't marry Maren, Dad! You *can't!*" I watched with a sinking feeling as the seven-year-old version of Jake stamped his foot and hollered at his father. Our other three children observed the scene with wide eyes, but I wasn't surprised that Jeff had chosen this moment to throw another tantrum. He'd become a completely different child in the weeks since Jake and I had announced our engagement. I glanced at the clock, wondering exactly how long it would take Jake's parents to pick up their rental car, and how soon they would arrive at my house. I prayed that perhaps there'd been a delay on the freeway that might keep them a few minutes longer.

"Jeffrey!" Jake said.

Jeff ignored the warning and shouted, "And I'm not gonna be good when Grandma and Grandpa come! I'm gonna ask them to take me back to New York with them, so I can see my mom!"

Jake's eyes went wide at the suggestion, and Jeffrey took advantage of the obvious weak spot. "I don't wanna live with you anymore! It's your fault that Mom left. You keep making her leave, and I hate you, Daddy! I wanna live with Mom!" Jeff shot his father a ferocious look and marched out of the room.

The expression on Jake's face was a combination of shock, anger, and worry. I moved to touch his arm just as the doorbell rang. He glanced down at me and placed a reassuring hand over mine before pulling away to answer the door. Apprehension rushed through me, and I silently prayed that the evening might somehow go smoothly.

Jake greeted his parents with warm embraces and invited them in. The Jantzens were just as I'd remembered them from my months of dating Jake at BYU, albeit a few years older. Jarold Jantzen was a mature reflection of his son, with stately streaks of silver threaded through his black hair, and deep laugh lines near his eyes and mouth. Beverly Jantzen's coloring was similar to my mother's, but her chestnut hair was cut shorter and styled more sleekly. They were generous and refined people who looked younger than their years.

"Maren!" Jake's mother greeted me warmly after she'd kissed Elizabeth's cheek. "We're so happy to finally have you in the family."

I accepted her hug and thanked her.

"You're just as pretty as you were the last time we saw you," Jake's father said as he hugged me too. Then they both turned their attention to my children. Jarold held his hand out for Trevor to shake, but my four-year-old son apparently decided to give him five, and slapped his hand as hard as he could instead.

"Trevor!" I chided him.

Jarold just laughed and said, "Wow! That's quite an arm. Are you a baseball player?" I suspected he already knew that because Trevor and Jeff had played T-ball together, and I knew that Jake's parents spoke to their grandchildren frequently over the phone.

"Yep!" Trevor answered enthusiastically.

"How was the plane ride?" I asked Jake's parents, trying to be polite.

"Just fine," Beverly answered. "And this cooler Utah air is certainly a refreshing change. It's been a warm autumn in New York. The humidity there is terrible."

Jeffrey reappeared then, looking disgruntled, but he obediently walked toward his grandfather's outstretched arms. Beverly went to introduce herself to Rebecca, which left Elizabeth a little lonely. She threw her arms around my legs and chanted a new favorite expression, "Mommy Maren, Mommy Maren!"

That made everyone laugh, except Jeff, who turned to scowl at her and mutter, "Maren's not our mom, Lizzy."

"Jeffrey," Jake said with a quiet note of caution, "we've already talked about this. Elizabeth can call Maren 'Mom' if she wants to, just like Rebecca and Trevor can call me 'Dad.'"

"Well, I'm not gonna call her that," Jeff insisted.

"You don't have to," Jake responded. "You can still call her Maren, just like you always have. But you do need to be respectful to her."

I felt a bit flustered, but over the past few weeks I'd learned that the best way to handle Jeffrey's negative comments was to ignore them. "Dinner's ready," I announced pleasantly. "I just need to get everything on the table."

To my relief the meal went quite smoothly, with only one glass of punch being spilled, and only a few quiet reminders to my children about table manners. Thankfully, Jeffrey ate in silence. It was during dessert that Jake's parents finally brought up the wedding. "So, I guess you kids are getting excited about the wedding, eh?" Jake's father asked the children jovially. "It'll be twice as fun with all four of you living in one house, won't it?"

"Except that I don't get my own room anymore," Rebecca complained.

"You'll get to share a room with Elizabeth, Becca," I politely reminded my daughter with a warning glance. "And you'll get to have bunk beds. I think you'll like it."

She gave me a pouty look but didn't say anything else. Jeffrey filled in the ensuing silence with, "Well, I won't like it."

"Why wouldn't you like it, kiddo?" Jarold asked in surprise. "You have a great time with Trevor."

"Yeah," Jeffrey admitted slowly. Then, as if testing his grandparents for a response, he added, "But I still don't want my dad to marry Maren."

I forced the bite of food I'd just taken past the lump in my throat and looked at Jeffrey, not knowing how to react. *Why does he have to behave this way in front of Jake's parents?* I thought.

Beverly tried to smooth over the moment by saying, "But you love Maren, Jeffrey! You talk about her all the time when we call you or come to see you."

Jeffrey picked at his food sullenly, ignoring her comment.

"It'll be all right, Jeff," Jake said as he reached across the table to rest a hand on his son's arm. "I know it's going to take a little getting used to for all of us, but we all love each other and everything's going to be okay."

Jake's mother graciously changed the subject by asking her son brightly, "You said the wedding's on November eighth, didn't you, dear?"

"That's right," Jake answered, sitting up to smile at her.

"And where are you getting married?" she inquired.

"Well, we're going to have an open house at the church afterward for our family and friends. We'll have lunch and maybe dancing." He winked at me.

"Will the wedding be there, too?" she asked.

Jake gave her a confused look and answered slowly, "No . . . We're getting married in the temple, Mom."

A look of dismay fell over Beverly's face. "But you already did that once!" she protested.

I tried to disguise my alarm as I waited for Jake's response.

"Mom," Jake said with a touch of humor to his voice, "we're Mormons. We're getting married in the temple."

His attempt to lighten the mood failed. Beverly's poise faltered as she objected meekly, "Surely you're not going to leave us out of your second wedding too, Jacob?"

Jarold reached for his wife's hand and explained gently to Jake, "That was very difficult on your mother the first time, son. Maybe you could do things a little differently this time."

"But they *have* to get married in the temple!" Rebecca argued with seven-year-old intensity. "That's how families are forever!" She looked thoughtful for a moment, until something she apparently hadn't considered before came into her mind. "Mom?" she asked me. "What about Daddy? How's he gonna be with us forever if you marry Jake?"

I thought through my response carefully before saying, "Sweetie, if Daddy and I both do what's right, then you can be with both of us. You don't need to worry, okay?"

"But then what about Jake?" she asked. "Don't you want to be with him?"

"Yes, Becca, I do . . . We don't understand everything here, honey. We just have to have faith that if we do what's right, Heavenly Father can work it out so that we're all happy. He will, I promise." I wished that I felt as certain about everything as I was attempting to sound. The matter was still a complicated one for me.

"Okay . . ." she conceded a little hesitantly.

"Why don't you all go play downstairs?" Jake suggested to the children. "We won't even make you help clear the table today, how's that?"

"Okay!" Trevor said as he jumped up and ran for the basement. Elizabeth was close behind him, and Rebecca and Jeffrey followed a little more slowly.

There was a long, awkward silence before Beverly said quietly, "I guess I just don't understand, Jacob, how you can leave us out of your wedding again."

Jake's face fell, and he looked toward me. In a gesture of support, I took his hand and waited for him to answer her. "I'm sorry I didn't clarify this sooner," Jake finally said to his parents. "I just assumed that you knew we'd be getting married in the temple. I know it's difficult for you to understand, and I don't want to hurt either of you. I wish you *could* come to our wedding. Nothing would make me happier. But the temple is the house of the Lord. It's a beautiful and sacred place, and worthy Church members are admonished to get married there. I can't imagine getting married anywhere else."

Jarold sighed and shook his head, but there was a glimmer of admiration in his eyes as he said to his son, "You certainly are committed to this religion of yours, aren't you?"

"Yes, Dad, I am."

Beverly dabbed at her eyes with her napkin. I couldn't imagine how difficult it must be for her, not being able to attend her son's wedding. And even though we could technically get married outside of the temple, since we couldn't be sealed yet, I agreed with Jake that I simply couldn't fathom having it anywhere else. I also wanted our children to understand the importance of temple marriage, and felt like I would be letting them down if I didn't set a proper example.

"Maybe if you took the missionary discussions," Jake began carefully, "it would help to give you a better understanding of our religion and why—"

His mother cut him off with a mild look of disgust. "For heaven's sake, Jacob," she protested. "Do we have to hear this every time we see you?"

"We've told you many times, son," his father added. "If being a Mormon makes you happy, then we're glad for you. But we're God-fearing people with Christian values. We live a good life, and we simply don't see the need for organized religion."

"I'm sorry," Jake answered a bit sheepishly. "I just . . . wish that I could share it all with you. I won't say anything else."

"Thank you," his mother replied pointedly.

After a few moments of awkward stillness, Jake changed the subject by saying, "I'm sorry about Jeff. He's having a hard time adjusting to all of this."

"Well, we know he loves Maren," Beverly seemed compelled to say. "He's always said wonderful things about her."

"Funny how Elizabeth seems so excited, and Jeff seems so upset, isn't it?" Jarold observed thoughtfully. "Especially since Maren's been babysitting them for the past year and a half."

Jake shrugged. "Jeff's two years older than Elizabeth. He's old enough to have some vague memories of when his mother left the first time. And this time . . . well, having Tess leave again has been very difficult for him. I don't think it's really Maren that he has a problem with. I think it's his mother."

I mulled over Jake's words. His ex-wife had moved to Utah nearly a year earlier in order to be near her children. I knew she hadn't been much of a mother to them even then, but they'd still gotten attached to her—the recent abandonment had been very difficult for both of them. It had only been a month since she'd made the decision to return to New York again and move back in with her boyfriend.

Beverly shook her head in dismay. "What kind of mother could leave her children like that—not only once, but twice?"

"Well, in her own words," Jake muttered bitterly, "she's 'no kind of mother.' But she won't have the opportunity to do it a third time—I made her sign away her parental rights before she left."

"You did?" Jarold asked in surprise. I was a little surprised myself to see that Jake hadn't already informed his parents of that.

"I certainly did," Jake answered unapologetically. "This coming-and-going business has got to stop. It's killing Jeff and Lizzy. I told Tess she needed to either stick around and be some sort of mother, or stay away for good. She chose the latter. That's part of the problem, actually. I told Jeff and Lizzy she wasn't coming back."

"You did?" Jarold asked again.

"Do you think that was wise, dear?" Beverly questioned timidly.

Jake met her gaze and said softly, "I don't know, Mom. I didn't have a lot of options. I agonized over what to tell the kids, but I finally decided that it would be better for them to go through the grief process and get it over with, once and for all, rather than hold out false hope forever. At least they know they can depend on me to be here and to be honest with them."

The Jantzens exchanged a concerned look, but they both nodded in silent understanding.

In an effort to escape another uncomfortable moment, I stood and began clearing the table. As I was loading the dishwasher, the doorbell rang. "Could you get that, please?" I asked Jake.

Jarold and Beverly came into the kitchen to help, but I insisted that they sit down in the great room. "Just relax and make yourselves at home," I told them. "I'll clean up."

Jake walked back toward me and whispered, "Ted's at the door. He didn't look too happy to see me."

"Please tell me you're joking," I said.

"I'm afraid not," Jake muttered under his breath. "Does he make a habit of showing up uninvited whenever he feels like it?"

I gave him an exasperated look before I moved around him to go to the door, but Ted had already walked inside. I felt anger welling up inside of me that he would just walk into my house when we'd been divorced for nearly a year and a half. He took in Jake's parents sitting in the great room, and Jake and me in the kitchen.

"Hi." I tried to greet him politely, for the sake of my future in-laws if nothing else. "I'll come and talk to you outside."

"Oh, no need," he answered casually. "I just came by to see if I could borrow the kids for a while."

I was totally taken off guard. He'd never just shown up and asked to take the children before. In fact, he'd only recently had his visitation rights restored with no supervision required. "Uh . . ." I stammered. "Actually, it's not a very good time right now."

"Why not?" he challenged.

I softly said, "Could we please discuss this outside?"

"I just want to see my kids, Maren. They're having an anniversary party for my parents tonight. My whole family's going to be there, and I want to take my kids. Is that so much to ask?"

"You could have called," I told him quietly.

"I didn't think it would be that big of a deal," he answered defensively.

I glanced over at Jake's parents, who were watching us curiously, and felt an overwhelming urge to shove Ted out the front door. Instead, I explained, "Jake's parents are here, Ted. They came to see us this weekend. They're flying back to New York on Sunday morning, and I'd like the children to stay here. It is my weekend, you know."

"Came to see you?" Ted asked, as though they weren't sitting right there listening. "Why would they come to see you?"

I knew this whole thing must be some kind of terrible social faux pas, but I had no idea how to redeem myself. I decided that not making introductions at this point would be more blatantly rude than making them. I turned to Jake's parents and said, "Mr. and Mrs. Jantzen, this is my ex-husband, Ted Saunders. Ted, Mr. and Mrs. Jantzen."

Jake's mother smiled politely at Ted and then said to me, "Call us Jarold and Beverly, Maren, please."

"Or Mom and Dad," Jarold added cheerfully. "Whichever you prefer."

Ted's look turned suddenly sharp. *"Mom and Dad?"* he sneered at me.

I had known that I was going to have to tell him about my engagement before his next weekend with the children, but I'd planned to do it over the phone so I wouldn't have to take the heat face-to-face. I could see that Jake's parents looked distressed, and Jake stepped closer to me in a protective gesture.

"I'll talk to you outside," I whispered to Ted and headed for the front door.

He followed me onto the porch, where I closed the door behind us. "What's going on?" he asked heatedly.

"I'm engaged to Jake," I informed him.

"So you were thinking you wouldn't have to tell me, or what?" he demanded, his voice going up a notch.

"I was going to tell you, Ted," I answered quietly, "even though it's really none of your business."

"None of my business?" he hollered. "You left me for that jerk and you don't even have the decency to tell me you're—"

"Ted!" I interrupted him. "I did not leave you for him! I divorced you *a year and a half ago* because I couldn't live with alcoholism and violence any longer! I stayed with you for ten years, and I tried everything I could think of to help you, to make our marriage work. *You* chose not to change, Ted. Jake didn't even live in this state until after you and I were separated, and my relationship with him was nothing more than friendship for months after our divorce was final. Don't you dare accuse me of something you know I would never do. This has nothing to do with you any—"

"Nothing to do with me?" he asked incredulously. "I couldn't care less what you do with your life, Maren, okay? But if you think you're gonna move my kids in with that jerk, you just *made* it my business! What if I refuse to allow that?"

I was furious and completely forgot about Jake's parents on the other side of my door as I hollered back at him, "Refuse to allow it? This is my life, Ted! You chose your path, and now I'm choosing mine. You're out of my life!"

"My kids are not going to be raised by your wimpy boyfriend, Maren!" Ted shouted. Then he pushed his face into mine, threatening, "I'll fight you tooth and nail. I'll take them away from you."

I fought back the fear that was beginning to seep into me and stood firm. "Ted," I tried to say calmly, "you've been in recovery for months. Please don't start this again. It will only—"

He grabbed my upper arms and said viciously, "You quit running my life the day you kicked me out, Maren! I will do whatever I want, and you'll shut up about it! You got it?"

"Let go of me," I warned.

The door flew open before Ted could respond. He released his hold on me and took a step back. Jake stepped onto the porch and glared at Ted, pulling the door shut behind him. "You know something, Ted?" he said with barely controlled fury. "There's a big difference between being a wimp and maintaining some degree of self-control. If you *ever* lay a hand on her again, you'll find that I am anything but."

"You're quite the hero, aren't you, Jantzen?" Ted spat. "You really think you scare me?"

I'd never seen Jake look so angry. I didn't even think he had it in him. He was slightly taller and more muscular than Ted, but his nature was simply calm and mild. "I realize it takes a lot of guts to terrorize a woman, Ted," Jake answered with cool sarcasm. "Especially when you've got an advantage of seven inches and at least sixty pounds. But I *will* scare you if you force me to it. That's a promise."

Ted's expression turned to ice as he hissed, *"I want my kids."*

"There's no way those children are leaving with you in your present state of mind," Jake replied smoothly, moving slightly to position himself in front of the door.

Ted took a step toward Jake, putting himself only inches away from him. "My kids are none of your business, Jantzen!"

"Will you *stop?*" I pled. "Just stop it, Ted! It's not your weekend, and you're obviously over the edge! Go home and mellow out." I wanted to tell him that Jake had been a better father to his children over the past year than he'd ever been, but I bit my tongue.

Ted glared at me, and Jake leaned closer to him. I hadn't seen Ted so upset in several months, and I was immensely grateful that Jake was there, but I was fast becoming afraid that this might turn into a fist fight. "Do yourself a favor and leave," Jake warned him.

"Who do you think you are?!" Ted hollered back at him.

"I'm Maren's fiancé, and I'm Rebecca's and Trevor's soon-to-be stepfather," Jake replied dryly. "You really ought to learn to put your children before yourself and control your temper. But if you can't be man enough to step up to the plate and protect your children, Ted, then I will."

I watched Jake's cheek twitching and the look of fury on Ted's face. Ted finally backed away, but before he left, he leaned close to whisper in my ear, "Watch your back, baby."

Jake apparently heard him. He moved so fast that his fist connecting with Ted's jaw was only a blur. The next thing I knew, Ted was sitting on the sidewalk, touching a hand to his bloody lip and staring at Jake in apparent shock.

I could only gape at Jake myself, wondering how he could have possibly done something so completely out of character for him. I didn't think he had a drop of violence in his blood.

Jake looked momentarily stunned as well, but then he pointed a finger at Ted and warned, "Don't you *ever* threaten her again! . . . Beat it." He opened the door and nudged me in ahead of him before he closed and locked it.

I was totally unaware of his parents sitting on my couch as I still just stared at him.

"What!" He finally threw his hands in the air.

"How could you do that?" I questioned.

The anger in his expression fled quickly, and he looked almost ashamed. "I don't know," he muttered.

I turned to see Jarold and Beverly Jantzen watching us with concern. "I'm sorry," I told them before I hurried down the hall. I locked myself in the bathroom and tried to regain some degree of composure. It unnerved me to see Ted's old patterns of violence re-surface after several months of sobriety and calmer behavior, though I supposed I should have expected it, but Jake's reaction to it had shaken me even more. I told myself to calm down and took a deep breath before I opened the bathroom door and went back out to finish cleaning up. Jake and his parents had already cleared the table when I arrived in the kitchen. "I'm very sorry about all of that," I apologized again, as I began to wipe off the counters.

"Don't worry about it, dear," Beverly said gently. I felt completely humiliated though, in addition to feeling frustrated and upset.

When everything was back in order, Jarold and Beverly headed downstairs to spend a few minutes with the children. I suspected they'd left Jake and me alone intentionally.

When they'd gone, Jake said quietly, "I'm sorry for getting so angry."

"I just can't believe you did that," I mumbled.

"What do you think I should have done instead?" he asked genuinely.

I shook my head. "I don't know, Jake. It was just so completely out of character for you. You're usually so gentle and calm."

Jake sighed and defended himself, "I don't think Ted understands 'gentle and calm,' Mar."

I felt a spark of anger as I spouted off sarcastically, "Why don't you just stoop to his level, then?"

"I didn't stoop to his level, Maren," Jake insisted. "If I wanted to stoop to *his* level, I would've had to deck *you.* "

The anger diffused and I conceded quietly, "You're right . . . I know you'd never hurt me."

"No, I certainly wouldn't," he answered resolutely. "And I'm not going to let anyone else hurt you either. I'm not going to watch Ted bully you, or threaten you, or anything else. And you can't send Rebecca and Trevor with him if he's going to behave that way, Mar—"

"I *won't* send Rebecca and Trevor with him if he behaves that way," I said firmly.

He forced himself to calm down and answer, "I know you won't. I'm sorry. To be perfectly honest, I'm a little surprised myself to find I had that in me," he admitted. Then he said more heatedly, "But I can't just stand there and let him treat you like that, Maren. I can't! And I can't understand . . ."

When he didn't continue I finally probed, "You can't understand what?"

Jake considered me for a moment before he confessed, "I can't understand how you married him in the first place, let alone how you stayed there for ten years."

I leaned against the counter, feeling emotionally exhausted. "Jake, he wasn't like that when I met him in college," I said tiredly. "He was ambitious, and fun, and attentive. I believed that he had a strong testimony, that he honestly wanted to live the gospel . . ." I let my voice trail off and thought about things for a minute before I confided, "You know, he apologized to me a few weeks ago."

"How impressive," Jake muttered, shoving his hands in his pockets.

"Jake, I don't want to argue with you, okay? I have no desire to defend Ted. He's done some awful things that are inexcusable. But he did tell me some things that day that gave me a better understanding of him and his behavior."

I paused for a minute, and Jake asked carefully, "What did he tell you?"

"He doesn't come from the healthiest family," I explained dully. "They don't communicate at all. I think his parents probably did what they thought was best, but they're 'letter of the law' people. They're piously religious and very controlling. Ted felt like he couldn't even admit to them that he had a problem, let alone that he needed help to overcome it. He started drinking when he was a teenager—I didn't know that until a few weeks ago—just to prove that he could do what he wanted to, I guess. His parents were in complete denial about the whole thing. Finally, he decided to pull his life together after high school, with the help of his bishop, so he could go on a mission.

"When we got married, Ted had been sober for over three years and apparently thought he was on the downhill slope. But we were both pretty young, and marriage was a bigger adjustment than either of us ever imagined it would be. Ted said he felt overwhelmed with stress because he was working, going to school, and trying to take care of a wife. He didn't know how to talk to me. I knew something was wrong, but I didn't know what it was or how to help him. He finally turned to alcohol to help him cope with everything, and got hooked again. When I got pregnant and added another level of stress to his life, he really went off the deep end. That was when it became too hard for him to hide the drinking. I freaked out about the whole thing, not knowing how to handle it, and we started to fight all the time.

"Ted told me that his violent outbursts were more a result of his anger at himself than at me," I continued. "I'd pretty much already guessed that, but it didn't make them any easier to cope with. So, losing his family finally made him hit rock bottom and seek help. He's been sober for a few months now. I can't remember exactly how long he told me it's been, but it's huge progress for him. He's been much better to deal with . . . until today."

I sighed deeply and took a moment to think before adding, "And as for staying in it for ten years, I've already explained that, Jake. I lost all my self-esteem, I blamed myself for everything, and I felt frantic about holding on to Ted and trying to help him. There were good times here and there that gave me hope, but those hopes were always dashed eventually. I also felt confused and upset because I'd made an eternal commitment to Ted, and I didn't take my temple covenants lightly. I wanted to do the right thing. I felt like I had to give him every chance that I could. I thought it was my duty to try to work through things with him." I paused, thinking. "Eventually, I realized that I was in an unimaginably low place, and I had to get myself and my children out . . . so I did."

Jake nodded slowly and leaned against the opposite counter, not saying anything. I felt a twinge of irritation as a thought struck me, so

I prompted, "And now that I've told my story to you, do you want to tell me how a man as generous and kind as you are managed to marry a woman who was so self-absorbed and heartless that she would abandon her own children?"

Jake bit his bottom lip and looked thoughtful for a minute. "I've asked myself that question a thousand times, Maren," he finally admitted. "And I'm still not sure I have an answer."

"You must have some idea," I insisted.

Jake considered me carefully for a moment, and I was surprised to see a hint of fear in his eyes. "Are you afraid to tell me?" I asked him cautiously.

"No," he answered too quickly. "Why do you ask that?"

I shrugged.

He hesitated again before saying, "I suppose that I thought Tess needed me . . . and I wanted to be needed. I'm not sure why." He blew out a long breath and added, "But she didn't need me. She wanted my money—or rather, my family's money—I didn't have any money at the time. She wanted me to spoil her and coddle her . . . It just wore me out. I told you I jumped into it way too quickly, without taking time to get to know her like I should have. And she was so . . . not you."

"What do you mean by that?" I asked.

A flicker of hesitation appeared in his eyes again. "Maren," he began slowly, "I was largely at fault for the problems in my first marriage."

"Why would you think that?" I asked in surprise. "Your wife had an affair, for heaven's sake! And you're so kind and good and—"

He cut me off. "I *was* largely at fault, Mar. Like Ted, Tess's actions were inexcusable, but unlike you—I may have deserved it."

"Jake!" I protested. "Nobody *deserves* to be cheated on by their spouse!" I was shocked that normally self-assured Jake could even entertain such an idea. "Why on earth would you think such a thing?"

An unfamiliar guardedness rose in his expression as he replied, "I don't know . . . I don't want to talk about it."

"Well, maybe you *should* talk about it."

Jake watched me quietly for a few seconds before he glanced at his watch and said, "Oh my gosh! I didn't know it was so late. I'd better get the kids home and in bed. And I'm sure my parents are exhausted—with jet lag and the time change and everything . . ." His voice faded as he hurried downstairs, leaving me wondering and a little concerned.

CHAPTER TWO

On Sunday morning after his parents had left for the airport, Jake came to pick us up for church. We got a lot of strange looks, mischievous grins, and raised eyebrows as we walked together down the hall toward the chapel. Most of the ward knew we were close friends, but not many people were aware of our engagement yet.

After church, Elizabeth insisted that she had to go to the bathroom, and couldn't wait. I told Jake that I'd take her and then meet him and the other three children at the car. I checked my appearance in the mirror while I waited for her, pulling myself up to my full five and a half feet, and smoothing the wrinkles out of my dress. I noted that my carefully curled, blond hair had grown out almost to my shoulder blades again, and wished that I had worn it up—the day had turned hot for September. I looked into my pale blue eyes and smiled to myself as I thought about all that I had to look forward to.

My thoughts were interrupted when Lydia Workman walked into the rest room and came up beside me. I had met her when I'd started going to the single-adult activities more than a year earlier, but I still didn't know her especially well. She'd always been a bit cold toward me for some reason. I knew she'd started attending the regular ward several months ago, instead of the singles ward, which seemed a bit strange to me at the time. I guessed that she was close to my age—somewhere in her early thirties. I'd continued to attend the family ward after my divorce because I had children, but I knew that Lydia didn't have any. Still, I'd figured it was her own business which ward she preferred to attend and I hadn't given it much thought. I wondered about it again, however, as she was standing right next to me.

Lydia didn't even look at me as she pushed her face close to the mirror and applied a fresh coat of shimmery peach lipstick. I wondered if it could be my imagination that she seemed unfriendly toward me, and decided to test my theory. "Hi, Lydia."

"Hi," she answered coolly, still not looking at me.

Elizabeth appeared, and I scooted over to make room for her to wash her hands. I was suddenly very bothered by the tension and awkwardness that I was feeling around Lydia. "So, how are you?" I asked her, thinking that things might feel a little more comfortable if I started a conversation.

She froze, then carefully put her lipstick back in her purse before she looked at me. She seemed to be studying me for a minute, and in that moment I noticed she was quite pretty—tall, with wavy, ash-brown hair and intriguing hazel eyes—and I wondered if she was just snobbish. "Fine," she answered at last. "You?"

I gave her a strange look, surprised at her brusqueness. "I'm fine," I replied haltingly.

She gave me a stiff smile and said, "Great," as she brushed past me to leave the room.

I took Elizabeth's hand and led her out to Jake's car, still wondering about Lydia.

"What's up?" Jake asked me on the way to his house.

I was surprised that I'd been distracted enough for him to notice. "Nothing," I told him.

After Sunday dinner, the children went outside to play. Jake rolled up his shirt sleeves and took off his tie. Then he finished clearing the table, while I loaded the dishwasher. I glanced over at him a couple of times and smiled to myself, thinking how natural it felt to be working in the kitchen with him like this. The thought of having a husband who worked alongside me was refreshing. After I closed the dishwasher, I just stood watching Jake for a minute, admiring the whole six feet and two inches of him, and feeling affectionately amused at the perfectly straight part in his black, wavy hair.

Jake seemed to be momentarily lost in his own thoughts until he finally looked up to meet my gaze with intensely blue eyes. "Well, I guess we survived the weekend with my parents, anyway," he joked, as he finished wiping off the table. "At least Jeffrey didn't ask them to take him back to New York to find his mother." His voice still held a touch of humor, but I could sense the concern behind the comment.

"Do you think we should wait a while to get married?" I asked him, voicing a thought that had crossed my mind more than once recently. "Maybe it would be easier for Jeff."

Jake lifted his eyebrows in surprise and then cracked a smile as he answered firmly, "No."

I smiled back, and he continued, "My mom and dad love you, by the way."

I felt a slight flutter of nerves. "Even though I didn't marry you the first time?" I asked, only half teasing.

"Yep," he said simply.

I held up my left hand and said teasingly, "And even though your dad paid for my ring twelve years ago?"

Jake pointed a finger and remarked comically, "He probably doesn't even remember that. He's getting senile, you know. Just don't remind him."

I laughed, and he continued, "I told you I had that ring paid off years ago, before I left on my mission."

I looked at the exquisite arrangement of diamonds and platinum and said in awe, "I can't believe you really paid for it and kept it all that time, even after I married Ted."

"Well, I did, Mar," Jake replied more seriously. Then he added, almost under his breath, "Even though maybe I shouldn't have."

"What do you mean?" I questioned, looking up at him.

He glanced at me and shook his head. "Nothing," he said. "I told you I thought about taking it back, but I just couldn't make myself do it." He paused before smiling slyly and changing the subject. "So, do you still think you can leave your house to move into mine?"

"I'm not sure," I answered almost seriously. Of course it made more sense, but the thought of leaving the only home my children had ever known was a little painful. I hadn't yet mustered the courage to put it up for sale.

"We'd have a lot more room . . ." Jake let his voice trail off and looked at me pointedly with a mischievous grin.

I narrowed my eyes at him and asked suspiciously, "Room for what?"

His grin broadened. "Oh . . . I don't know," he said, his eyes sparkling now as he took hold of my arm, then waist. "Perhaps—the tango?" With that Jake spun me around the kitchen floor and finished with a sudden dip.

I returned his impish grin and responded a little breathlessly, "Well, that was a surprise. I thought you were implying that we might have one or two blue-eyed children, after all." My mind flashed back thirteen years earlier to the months that Jake and I had dated in college. *You know we'd have beautiful, blue-eyed children, Maren,* he used to joke. I smiled at the memory, noting that none of our four children had blue eyes.

Interrupting my thoughts, Jake laughed and said, "Who knows? Maybe we'll have room for that, too."

He went to call the children in then, so we could play a game with them and spend some "family time" together. We answered the typical battery of questions regarding our upcoming arrangements, then sent the kids off to play for another half hour before it was time for Rebecca, Trevor, and me to go home.

Jake leaned back on the couch and put his arm around me. I rested against his shoulder and sighed contentedly. My pleasant thoughts were abruptly interrupted when Jake sat up and asked, "Hey, I almost forgot—what happened at church?"

"Nothing," I responded automatically.

"Something was bothering you on the way home," he said matter-of-factly.

I dismissed it with a wave of my hand. "Nah . . ."

Jake looked at me and insisted, "Maren, something obviously happened to upset you. Why don't you just tell me about it?"

"I wasn't really upset . . . I was just thinking about something. It was silly—nothing important."

I could hear the frustration in his voice as he muttered, "Your communication skills have really taken a beating over the past twelve years, haven't they?"

Annoyed, I responded, "Look, Jake, it has nothing to do with you, okay? I'm sorry if I was a little distracted earlier. I was only thinking—it's no big deal. Now can we please just drop it?"

"Fine," he said coolly as he stood up and walked away.

The children came running in then, all four of them arguing fiercely over who could play with what. It had been a wonderful afternoon up until the last few minutes, but I suddenly felt very tired. "Becca and Trevor, get your things," I said firmly. "It's time to go home."

Jake kissed me good-bye, although he remained slightly aloof.

***

Ted called on Monday and said, "I'm sorry, Maren."

"You are?" I asked in surprise.

"Look, I said I'm sorry and I am. Don't push it."

"Yeah, okay. Thanks for the apology," I retorted sarcastically.

He sighed loudly. "Okay, I know I . . . lost it a little," he confessed. "I just didn't expect you to get married again . . . so soon."

"It's been a year and a half, Ted," I reminded him.

His tone was one of defeat—another surprise—as he said softly, "I know that. I guess I didn't let myself think about this possibility. I should've known better. I suppose it's . . . a little difficult for me. I mean, just to think about my kids being raised by someone else and . . . well, it was unexpected, that's all. And just so you know, I didn't go get drunk or anything."

"I'm glad, Ted," I responded sincerely. "And thank you. I appreciate the apology."

He hesitated before saying, "I'll be fine with the kids this weekend, Maren. I'm not going to take my frustrations out on them. I know you worry, but I don't want to lose my visitation rights again. I love my kids."

"I know you do," I admitted a little warily. "You understand that I have to protect them, though. If I have any reason to think they won't be safe with you, I won't let them go."

"Yeah, I know," he muttered with a hint of bitterness. "That's why I'm apologizing and telling you that I didn't start drinking again, that I'll take care of them."

"Are you sure, Ted? You seemed pretty angry, and your past record isn't great—"

"Maren," he interrupted me, sounding irritated. "You hit me with some pretty big news in front of Jake *and* his parents, no less, and then—"

"That was your own fault, Ted. You just showed up over here and walked in—"

"I know! Okay? I know, Maren. I screwed up. I should've called. I shouldn't have yelled at you. I *really* shouldn't have touched you, and I didn't mean it when I threatened you. I was just so annoyed with that jerk . . . Anyway, he cuffed me a good one, so I guess we're even."

"I'm sorry about that," I said quietly.

He gave a dry laugh and answered, "Yeah, well, maybe I deserved it. I'll see ya later."

"Bye." I hung up very relieved. I'd been afraid that Ted would start back down his path of anger and violence and wind up drinking again. It sounded like maybe he was genuinely in recovery, after all.

***

Jake didn't pressure me any more about our conversation on Sunday. In fact, he seemed to have forgotten about it by the time he arrived at my house on Monday night to pick up Jeff and Lizzy, although he did look tired. "Rough day at the office?" I asked.

He shrugged. "Just the usual—taking care of sick kids all day."

I tried to lighten things up by teasing, "Yeah, I hear that's what pediatricians do."

He laughed and admitted, "I'll still take my job over yours."

"A wise decision," I agreed. "I can't wait to go to work on Wednesday so you can take a turn with these four little monsters."

He laughed.

Later, that Wednesday after work, Jake looked more flustered than usual when I went to pick up Rebecca and Trevor.

"How did it go?" I asked him.

He sighed and leaned against the wall. "Fine, except for Jeffrey," he told me. "His bad attitude seems to grow in direct proportion to the nearness of our wedding day. But the more I try to talk to him about it, the more closed off and defiant he becomes." Jake shook his head and muttered, "I never should have allowed this to happen. I should've made Tess sign away her parental rights when she left the first time."

I touched his arm. "She's their mother, Jake. You did what you thought was best. Anyway, if you'd tried to stop her from seeing them when she came back here, you could have ended up in a long, drawn-out court battle. That wouldn't have been good for them either."

"True," he admitted, then changed the subject. "How about if I take you out on Friday night? I'm in desperate need of a break, and I can't even imagine how badly you must need one."

I moved closer to him and reached up to kiss him. "That would be wonderful," I agreed.

Jake stood up straight, looking in slightly better spirits, and said, "I'll see if I can get a babysitter. Do you have any recommendations? Four kids is a lot to handle."

"It'll only be two kids," I reminded him. "It's Ted's weekend with Rebecca and Trevor."

A look of surprise crossed Jake's face. "You're going to let him take them?" he asked. "After the way he behaved on Sunday?"

"They'll be all right," I assured him. "Ted called me to apologize."

"That was big of him," Jake retorted.

"I really have no choice," I reminded him. "The judge determined that Ted's made enough progress to have his visitation rights restored—unsupervised. You know that. Ted's doing everything he's supposed to in order to comply with the judge's orders. If I keep the children from him, I'll be the one in trouble."

"What if he's not safe?" Jake challenged.

I just watched him, not saying anything. For a moment, I questioned my own judgment. I wondered if perhaps I shouldn't send the kids with Ted. Then I felt angry that I'd allowed a man to make me doubt myself again, however briefly. I wasn't going to lose myself in another relationship. "Rebecca and Trevor will be fine," I insisted.

He looked closely at me for a moment and then shrugged. "I guess that's your call then, isn't it?"

"Yes, Jake. It is."

***

When Ted dropped Rebecca and Trevor off on Sunday night, they both seemed a little reserved. Ted was calm and polite, but after he left I asked, "Did everything go okay with Daddy?"

"Yeah," Rebecca answered hesitantly. "Only . . ."

"Only what?" I prodded.

Trevor looked at her, apparently bewildered. When Rebecca still didn't answer me I started to feel panicked. "Did he get drunk, Becca?" I asked her.

"No." She shook her head firmly.

I felt relieved to be reassured of that. I would have felt horrible if I'd misjudged Ted and let him take the children, only to have him drink while he had them. "Was he mean to you then?" I asked.

Both children shook their heads in the negative.

"So, why are you worried?" I asked in confusion.

"I didn't like what Daddy talked about on the way home," Rebecca confessed.

"What did he say?" I asked, trying to think what he could have said to them that would be so upsetting.

Trevor's face perked up as he apparently realized what Rebecca was referring to. "Dad said Jake was a jerk," he announced. "And I told him I like Jake, but he said he's still a jerk."

I sighed. "Was your dad nice except for that?" I asked them, feeling concerned but relieved.

"Yeah!" Trevor told me enthusiastically. "We went to the park, and played baseball, and rented videos, and made popcorn."

"Really?" I commented.

They both nodded.

"Well, I'm sorry Dad said that, you two. I guess it's a little bit hard for him to see me in a good relationship when he's alone. He still shouldn't have said it, though. And you both know that Jake's not a jerk."

"Is Daddy gonna be mad if we live with Jake after you get married?" Rebecca asked me cautiously.

I didn't know how to answer her. After thinking for a minute I finally said, "He won't be mad at you, Becca, or at you, Trev. It might be difficult for him at first, but he'll get used to it. You both know why Daddy and I got divorced. It was the best thing for both of us. Your dad's finally making the changes he needs to make in his life, and I've made some improvements myself that make me happy. I'm sure that it will be an adjustment for all of us after Jake and I get married. But we're all going to be fine. You don't need to worry about Daddy. He's not mad at the two of you. He wants you to be happy, just like I do."

"Are you sure?" Rebecca asked me.

"Yes, honey, I'm sure," I promised, as I resigned myself to discussing this with Ted.

CHAPTER THREE

The following weekend, Jake and I took the children and went to stay with my parents in Idaho. My family had known Jake well during the year we'd dated in college, and they were thrilled with the recent news of our engagement. My parents had also become acquainted with Jeffrey and Elizabeth during visits to my house over the last several months. They greeted us with open arms and enthusiastic smiles. My mother made a special effort to make Jake's children feel welcome, telling them how happy she was to include them as her grandchildren. I'd told her over the phone about some of the difficulties we werc having with Jeffrey. She'd assured me that it was probably just normal, and advised me to give it time.

My brother and sister came over on Saturday with their families. My younger sister Natalie was seven months pregnant with her first baby and could barely contain her excitement over the prospect of motherhood. "Jake!" she exclaimed when she saw him. "Welcome to the family!" She threw her arms around him, and then pulled back to observe, "You're just as adorable as you were before."

Jake grinned. "I'm surprised you remember me. You've grown up since then."

"Of course I remember you! You were always so sweet to me when Maren was dating you." She smiled and added conspiratorially, "And I always did like you better than Ted."

"Natalie!" I chided her, but Jake only laughed.

She laughed too, then pushed her husband forward to introduce him. "This is Doug."

I studied Douglas for a minute. He wore tasteful, wire-rimmed glasses, and his appearance was neat. He and Natalie could almost pass for brother and sister, with the same thick dark hair, light brown eyes, and unblemished olive skin. But their personalities appeared to be vastly different. Douglas was friendly, but not overly outgoing. He seemed to be much more quiet and reserved than Natalie. I dismissed my thoughts about my sister's husband as we all crowded into the kitchen to help with dinner.

By that evening, the children were so exhausted that they actually wanted to go to bed. I asked Mom and Dad to keep an eye on them while Jake and I went for a walk, and they were happy to oblige. We donned our jackets, and I pulled Jake out the door into the magical fall night. "Wow, the stars are amazing out here, aren't they?" he noted as we started down the street.

"I know. When I was a teenager, I used to dream of walking down this road at night with the love of my life," I confessed to him.

"Really?" Jake asked. "What was he like?"

"Well . . ." I began thoughtfully, "He was always tall, dark, and handsome. He was sweet, caring, kind, spiritual, fun, responsible, talented . . . I forget all his redeeming qualities, there were so many."

"Did you ever find him?" he asked curiously, gazing up at the stars.

"Oh yes, but it took a long time."

"How long?"

"Oh, I finally figured it out after about . . . thirty years or so." I smiled at him before admitting, "I only worry about one thing . . ."

"What's that?" He raised an eyebrow at me as I slowly backed away from him.

"I'm not sure if he's fast enough to catch me!" I called as I climbed a split-rail fence and leaped over it. I heard Jake laugh before I took off across the pasture. The night breeze billowing through my hair, the smell of ripening apples and sweet new hay, and the familiar muddy terrain brought back fond memories of my childhood and teenage years. There was such freedom and power in jumping fences and running forever with no traffic, no roads to stop you. If you weren't afraid of the occasional bull, it was absolutely exhilarating.

I could hear Jake running behind me, but the footing wasn't familiar to his city-boy feet. I wondered if there was ever any room to run in his native New York City, or if there was just a sea of too many people to fight through. Out here, I felt like I owned the world. I ran hard and fast, and when I jumped the next fence, I fell quickly to the ground and lay perfectly still, flat on my stomach. I remembered as children how we used to play tag in the dark like this. It was next to impossible to find someone lying in a pasture. Your eyes would play tricks on you, so you had to use your other senses to pick up tiny whispers, almost imperceptible giggles, hard breathing, a feeling of someone watching you, the ground quivering under your feet . . .

I saw Jake's silhouette running toward the fence I'd just jumped. He stopped and looked around. He was breathing hard, but not too hard. He was in good shape. "Maren?" he whispered. "Come on, love. You're scaring me." I could see his straight white teeth as he grinned in the moonlight. He seemed to consider which way to go, and then looked toward the spot where I lay hidden in the grass. My heart beat faster as I began to wonder if he could feel my eyes on him. I couldn't risk it. I jumped up and ran again.

He was a pretty impressive fence-jumper for a city boy. He hopped over them easily with his long legs. I ran for quite a while and then stopped suddenly. I couldn't see Jake behind me anymore. I couldn't hear him either. I looked at all the dark shadows of trees and horses that loomed nearby. I had no idea where the road was and started to feel a little spooked. I didn't want to give in, but I was so tempted to whisper Jake's name. I knew he must be close by. He wouldn't leave me out there all alone. Besides, he'd never find his way back. I was sure he didn't know how to follow the fences. Suddenly a toad croaked, and I nearly jumped out of my skin. Then Jake caught me from behind. I screamed and tried to pull away, but he held me tight. I turned toward him and fell against his chest, half laughing, half crying. "You scared me to death!" I accused him.

He kissed the top of my head and held me until my racing heartbeat slowed down. "Caught you," he finally said, laughing softly.

I wrapped my right ankle around his left, then pulled. He fell into the grass and dragged me down with him, laughing again. Then he rolled onto his back and looked up at the sky. "I can't believe this," he breathed.

I rested my head on his arm and looked up too. "It's like magic, huh?"

"Yes, all of it." He squeezed me closer to him.

We lay gazing up at the expanse of bejeweled velvet sky until the world started to spin and I got dizzy just looking into it. I closed my eyes. There was nothing like the smell of autumn in the country. Jake's clean, masculine scent mingled with the earth and air to make me shiver. "I wish we could stay out here forever," I whispered.

"I *would* stay out here forever," he joked. "But your dad might come looking for me with a shotgun." Then he stood up and extended his hand to me. I took it, and he pulled me up and kissed me. "No wonder you're you, Mar, coming from this magical place," he said softly.

I looked for the mountains to mark the east, then followed the fences that ran north and south until we reached the road. We walked back to the house holding hands.

***

At dusk the following evening, we piled four reluctant children into the van after everyone had hugged and kissed them. Jeffrey even smiled and waved good-bye with the others. I was glad that Jeff and Lizzy had seemed to feel comfortable and even loved, though Jeff still wasn't thrilled with things.

Jake and I took advantage of the long drive home to talk about some things after the children had fallen asleep.

"So, are you going to want to keep doing design after we're married?" Jake asked me.

"I don't know," I responded hesitantly. "I know you said that you wanted Tess to stay home with your children when they were little. But they're older now. The kids are all gone three afternoons a week. How do you feel about it? Do you want me to work?"

"That's up to you, my dear." He gave me a quick smile.

"Do I need to work?" I asked him, watching carefully for his reaction.

"No, Mar, you don't. But I want you to do whatever makes you happy. If you want to work because you enjoy it, I'll support you in it. I can still watch the kids on Wednesdays, as I've been doing, and I can help you at night and on the weekends. If you want to stop, though, that's all right too. We'll be fine. I told you I'd take care of you."

"I don't want you to suddenly feel all the pressure of a wife and two extra kids wearing you down," I returned, voicing my concern over the issue. "I don't want to fight over money or be a burden to you."

He glanced away from the road to look at me. "Maren, you'll never be a burden to me. Your children will never be a burden to me. If I had to work three jobs to take care of you, I'd do it cheerfully. I'm very blessed, though, and I don't have to do that. We won't fight over money, Mar. What do *you* want to do?"

I took a moment to consider my feelings. I did enjoy design, but I was getting tired of all the stress that came along with it. The thought of being able to just relax and focus on the kids for a while seemed a welcome release. "I think I'd like to quit working and stay home with our children, if that's really all right with you," I admitted carefully.

Jake smiled and reached for my hand. "I'm glad. I think it'll be better for our children to have you home with them while they're adjusting to all of this. We'll get to spend Wednesdays together, too. Why don't you just finish whatever jobs you have going, and then quit? I'll make sure you have whatever you need."

I let out a happy, relieved sigh, feeling a huge burden being lifted from me as I leaned back against the seat.

"And I mean that," Jake continued. "I gave you a checkbook. If Rebecca and Trevor need clothes or anything for school, or if you—"

"I know you mean it, Jake," I answered, turning to smile at him. "But I'll manage just fine until we're married. You see, I babysit for this very handsome, very generous doctor. He pays me rather well, and I think I can scrape by for a few more weeks."

Jake lifted his brow and glanced at me to ask, "How handsome is he?"

"Very."

"And he's generous, you say?"

"Very."

"Well, that's nice to know. Tell him if he doesn't mind his manners, I'll have to beat him up."

I gave him a teasing punch on the shoulder and he laughed.

"So, love," Jake started again after a few more silent moments, "what do you think about our family planning?"

"What do you mean, exactly?"

"Well, we talked about having a baby. I think it might be best if we wait a year or two to give the children and us time to adjust to everything."

"That's fine," I agreed. I thought wistfully of Natalie's bulging tummy. Although I didn't envy her the nine terrible months of pregnancy, I did ache for another baby. It had been so long. "I want to have two more children, Jake. The other kids will be so much older. If we have two close together, then they'll have each other to play with."

"Two?" he repeated.

"How do you feel about that?"

He looked thoughtful for a moment before saying, "I think I could handle that."

I suddenly felt compelled to explain my feelings to him. "Remember when we went on that river run with the young men and young women and I almost drowned, and I had that dream?"

"Yes," he replied quietly. It had been over a year ago. He'd saved my life.

"I saw two children in that dream . . . and I think they're supposed to be mine."

He took his eyes from the road for a moment to look at me. "You did?"

"I did."

"All right then," he agreed. "But we wait at least a year, okay?"

"Okay." I smiled at him.

"Where do you want to go on our honeymoon?" Jake changed the subject.

"Are we going on one? What will we do with the kids?" I wondered aloud.

"My parents will stay with them after they come for the wedding," he said. "I already asked them."

I thought about it for a minute. "You know, I think I'll see if Mom and Dad will take Trevor and Becca home while we're gone. I think it might be easier if they all stay with someone they know well, and if they start out life together with us, rather than with someone else."

"Ah, my brilliant wife. Future wife, I mean." Jake grinned at me. "Correct, as usual."

I humored him with a smile.

"So, where do you want to go, Mar?"

"I don't know—Where do you want to go?"

"I couldn't care less, as long as you're there. Won't it be wonderful to have a week to ourselves?" He dropped my hand to reach up and rub the back of my neck.

"Yes. Fabulous." I felt shivers run up and down my spine at the thought. "Let's go to Disneyland," I suggested on impulse.

He laughed. "Are you serious?"

"It's the most magical place on earth."

"Then Disneyland it is," he announced theatrically.

I leaned over to kiss him as he drove.

As night settled in around us and the miles passed in comfortable silence, I thought of how much my life had changed in the past two years, of how much it was still going to change. Although I was filled with eager anticipation at the prospect of becoming Jake's wife, I hoped the transition would be a smooth one, especially for Jeff. Then I thought of my own children, and how Ted's negative comments about Jake had upset them a few days earlier. I knew I had to talk to Ted, and I prayed that I would know what to say. I wanted my children to be able to enjoy the blessings that Jake brought to their lives without fear of reprimand from their father. I couldn't help feeling a twinge of sadness on Ted's behalf, even though he'd brought pain on himself because of his own poor choices. I hoped the progress he'd made since we'd divorced would continue, and that he would find peace and happiness for himself someday.

Then I wondered why I was even thinking about Ted. After pondering on that, I realized that somewhere inside me, a little seed of guilt was festering . . . *Well, that's just ridiculous, Maren,* I told myself. *You have nothing to feel guilty about.* I shook all thoughts of Ted from my mind and reached over to kiss Jake's cheek.

CHAPTER FOUR

I called Ted on Monday afternoon while the children were at school, not wanting them to hear a fight if that was what it came to. "Ted, I need to talk to you," I said.

"Okay, what?"

"I'm going to put the house up for sale. The children and I will be moving in with Jake."

He didn't say anything.

"I'll be taking some of the kids' things, but we won't need most of the furniture. Do you want any of it?"

He finally answered me quietly, which caught me off guard. "Maren, do you really want to do this?"

"What do you mean?"

"There's still a chance we could work things out, you know? I'm doing better. I still love you. The kids should have both of us."

I felt sad for Ted, but that was all. I felt no doubt when I answered him. "That's just not possible, Ted. I love Jake and he loves me, and this is the right thing for me."

He got angry then. "For you? What about your kids?"

I felt some anger at him too, for all he'd put me through, but I said calmly, "This is also the best thing for them. They love you. You'll always be their dad, and nothing will change that, but they love Jake too." I paused before adding, "And it's very difficult for them when you bad-mouth Jake in front of them. You don't have to like him, Ted, and you don't have to like the situation. But it only confuses and upsets your children when you voice those opinions to them."

"They should have us both, Maren," he insisted. "They shouldn't have to adjust to a stepfather."

I tried to keep the anger in my voice in check as I replied, "Maybe that's something you should have considered twelve years ago."

There was a long pause before he shot out, "You have to give me half of whatever you make on the house, you know."

"I'm aware of that, and it won't be a problem. I'll need to stay in the house for a few more weeks until our wedding. I'd like to keep the furniture until then. You're welcome to anything you want after that."

"All right," he finally sighed, the anger apparently gone. His voice sharpened a bit, though, as he challenged, "So, I suppose you think I'll still pay you every month?"

"For next month, yes. You can stop paying alimony in November, but I *am* expecting you to still pay child support for your children."

"Or what?"

"Oh, for heaven's sake, Ted! You know you need to contribute something for them. That's not unreasonable."

Ted was quiet for a moment before he finally said, "Call me when you move in with your boyfriend, and I'll come get some of the furniture. My apartment's pretty bare."

"I will—but for the record, you know I won't be moving in with him until he's my husband."

"Yeah, of course, Maren. See ya."

"Bye." I breathed a sigh of relief that the conversation was over.

Ted seemed relatively calm when he picked up the children on Friday evening, for which I was grateful.

***

On Sunday I hurried into Relief Society too quickly, trying not to be late. I bumped into Lydia, who was on her way out. To my surprise, she was carrying a baby and a diaper bag. Several toys spilled out of the bag, as well as a handful of pictures she'd been carrying.

I hurriedly bent down to pick up the items I'd caused her to drop, but she stooped to get them too. "I'm so sorry," I told her.

"It's fine," she answered tersely. "I can get them."

"No, let me help you. You're holding a baby."

As if on cue, the baby began to cry. Lydia only hurried faster in an effort to recover the scattered items. "Do these need to go back to the library?" I asked her, referring to the assortment of pictures. "I'd be happy to take them for you."

She still didn't look at me as she crammed toys back into the diaper bag. The tiny little girl she held was making such a racket by then that several people were turning around to see what was going on. "That's okay. I've got it," Lydia muttered quickly.

"Let me take the baby, then," I offered, recognizing her as Michelle Rose's daughter.

Finally, Lydia looked up at me and said in a harsh whisper, "Look, I said I've got it, okay?"

Slightly taken aback, I mumbled, "Okay . . . Sorry." I handed her the pictures I'd retrieved and headed in to find a seat.

Michelle Rose was setting up props for the Relief Society lesson she was apparently going to teach, but seemed distracted. When she saw me sit down, she hurried toward me and whispered, "Is Sarah okay?" She'd evidently seen me bump into Lydia and heard her baby crying.

"She's fine," I assured her. "I think she was just startled."

She nodded gratefully and went to finish her preparations, leaving me in silent contemplation for the duration of her lesson.

Relief Society got out five minutes late, so I left the room to find Jake waiting in the hallway for me, Jeffrey and Elizabeth in tow. Lydia was standing nearby, still holding a now-happy baby Sarah, and laughing. Jake was shaking his head and chuckling. "Well, it sounds like you've got your hands full," he said to Lydia. "I don't do kittens. Kids are enough for me."

Jeff and Lizzy ran to greet me when they saw me. Jake looked over at me and smiled. I glanced at Lydia, wondering whether I should attempt to talk to her again. The smile on her face had been erased by a blank stare, so I opted to ignore her and sidled up next to Jake. "See you later," he told Lydia as he took my hand.

"Bye, Jake."

"What was that?" I asked him on the way to the car.

"Oh, Lydia was just telling us about her new kittens," Jake explained. "Elizabeth asked her if that was her baby she was holding, and she said no. I guess Lizzy looked a little disappointed, so Lydia told her she had baby kittens."

"Yeah!" Elizabeth cut in enthusiastically. "Can we get baby kittens, Daddy?"

Jake gave her an exaggerated smile and replied, "Not today, sweetheart."

"Someday?" she asked hopefully.

Jake scooped her up and hugged her. "Maybe someday," he agreed.

***

Suddenly it was mid-October, less than a month until our wedding, and Jake and I were in a whirlwind trying to get everything ready. I put the house up for sale with a Realtor and started packing things up. I took a lot of things to Jake's house, gave some away, and saved some things to see if Ted wanted them first.

Rebecca, Trevor, and Elizabeth were growing more excited about the wedding and looking forward to living in the same house. They were even getting used to the idea of sharing bedrooms. But Jeffrey remained angry and resistant. In fact, he seemed to grow more and more sullen as our wedding day drew nearer. I finally decided to attempt a one-on-one conversation with him and caught him alone for a minute when he was at my house. He'd come upstairs for something while the other children were playing in the basement. "Jeffrey, I'd like to talk to you," I said. "Why don't you come sit on the couch with me?"

He hesitated, but then reluctantly trudged over to sit on the far end of the sofa. "Jeff," I began, wondering how to approach this, but feeling that I had to say something, "your dad and I are both concerned about you. We love you a lot and want you to be happy. I know your dad has tried to talk to you many times, but you haven't felt like talking to him. Since it seems to be me that you have a problem with, I thought maybe you and I could talk about it."

"I don't wanna talk about it," he grumbled.

"But you need to, honey," I insisted. "Your dad and I are going to be married in less than a month. It's already been a month since we told you that we were getting married, and you seem to be getting more upset all the time. I know you miss your mom, and I've told you that I'm not trying to replace her . . . If you just told me what was bothering you, buddy, maybe I could do something about it. I promise I won't get mad at you if you just tell me, Jeffrey."

He glanced over at me warily and then looked down at the floor. "It's just bothering me that you're marrying my dad," he said cautiously.

"*Why* is it bothering you?" I prodded gently.

When he made no response, I attempted to guess. "Is it because you're going to have to share your bedroom with Trevor?" I questioned.

"No," he answered.

"Do you think your dad won't have enough time for you if he marries me?" I asked him. "Are you afraid that Rebecca and Trevor and I will take too much of his attention away from you?"

"No," he said again.

"Are you just worried that it might be hard because it's something different?" I suggested.

"No." He sounded like a broken record.

"Jeff, I really want to help you to feel good about this whole thing," I told him honestly. "But I can't do that if you won't talk to me or tell me what it is that you want me to do."

He looked up at me and considered me carefully for a moment. "You promise you won't get mad at me?" he asked.

"I promise," I said, feeling a tiny glimmer of hope. "And I'll always love you, Jeffrey, no matter what."

His eyes suddenly welled up with tears and I saw the little boy I'd known for so many months reappear for a moment. "Maren, please don't marry my dad," he pled. *"Please* don't marry him."

I scooted toward him and put an arm around him. "Why, honey?" I asked gently. "Why don't you want me to marry your dad?"

"I just don't!" he insisted fiercely, the hardness returning to his face.

"Jeff, please—" I began, but he jerked away from me and ran downstairs before I could finish. I sighed and covered my face with my hands, praying that he would somehow come to accept this. After a few moments in silent contemplation, I finally decided that maybe things would improve after the wedding. Maybe after we all moved into the same house together and started life as a real family, Jeffrey would realize that it wasn't as bad as he'd thought it would be. Perhaps it was just the prospect of a change that frightened him. Or maybe he simply needed time to adjust to the fact that his mother was gone for good. That was certainly understandable. I resigned myself to being calm and patient with him, and hoped that time would allay his fears and soothe his heart.

***

Jake and I went to a harvest dance in the singles ward the week before Halloween. "Do you think they'll throw us out?" I asked jokingly.

"They can't," Jake replied with confidence. "We're not married yet. Besides, the regular ward never has dances, and I want to take you dancing."

Even though I'd been dancing with him several times by then, I was still astounded at his skill. He'd never liked to dance in college, and I never would have believed that he had enough natural ability to learn to do it so well. I knew that Tess had convinced him to take lessons, and that he'd had ten years away from me to practice, but it was still a pleasant surprise every time we went. He knew almost as many steps as I did, and I'd been dancing my whole life.

Several numbers into the dance, Jake asked teasingly, "Aren't you going to tell me how astonished you are that I learned to dance? You haven't said that even once this entire evening."

I smiled. "I was under the impression that you were beginning to find it insulting rather than complimentary."

He grinned back at me. "Actually, I think I've become so accustomed to your constant astonishment that I've come to rely on it. I was beginning to be afraid that I might not be living up to your expectations tonight."

"I thought you'd gotten tired of hearing it," I told him. "But if you'd like me to reassure you, I will." I drew a deep breath and spoke with a southern accent to imitate Scarlett O'Hara. "You do dance divinely, Dr. Jantzen."

He started laughing, and it made him miss a step, but he pressed a firm hand to my back and caught up with the next one. "Is that all the alliteration you can come up with?" he teased. "Four words?"

I laughed and kissed him quickly, saying, "I'll work on it."

When the last song of the evening came on, Jake pulled me close to him. I rested my head on his shoulder and relished the moment. I loved getting lost in his familiar scent of cologne mixed with shaving cream and soap.

"Well," Jake observed with exaggerated disappointment, "I suppose this is our last singles dance. By the time they have another one, we'll be old married people. No more living it up, no more free spirits, no more single parenthood, no more lonely nights . . . Will you miss it, Mar?"

I pulled away to smile up at him. "Not even for a second. Will you?"

He answered me with a kiss, then rested his forehead on mine and whispered resolutely, "No."

As we resumed moving together to the music, I glanced over at the sidelines and saw Lydia standing a few feet away from us. She seemed to be staring right at me with an icy glare. I looked away from her.

After the dance, I helped take down decorations in the gym while Jake fought the crowds in the hallway, looking for our coats. As I was tugging on the end of a crepe-paper streamer, Mandy, a friend from the singles activities, came up behind me. "You and Jake put on quite the floor show," she said jokingly. "I didn't know you were so talented."

I turned around and smiled. Her straight blond hair was pulled up on the sides, and she appeared to be her usual vivacious self. "Hi, Mandy. How are you?"

"Good. So, how long have you two been an item? I mean, I saw the sparks months ago, but it seemed like nothing was ever going to come of it. I haven't seen you around much lately. I think I missed something."

I gave her a conspiratorial grin and held up my left hand.

She gasped and took hold of my hand to study my ring more closely. "Ohmigosh! *Ohmigosh!*" she squealed. "When did this happen?"

"A few weeks ago," I told her.

"A few weeks ago? And you didn't tell me? I can't believe it! Congratulations!" She hugged me. "Oh, I'm glad for you, Maren. He is so sweet. You deserve to be hap—" She cut herself off mid-sentence because Lydia had come to an abrupt halt a few feet in front of us. Mandy tilted her head to smile at Lydia. "Hi," she said cheerfully.

Lydia looked almost pale as she mumbled, "Hi," and hurried toward the door.

A tall, blond man named Glen walked quickly after her. "Hey, Lydia!" he called. "Can I give you a ride home?"

She didn't respond before she disappeared into the hallway.

I stood watching after her thoughtfully for a minute before I asked Mandy, "Is it my imagination, or does she hate me for some reason?"

Mandy gave me a strange look and replied, "I don't think she hates you."

"She just seems so cold," I observed. Then I shrugged and said, "Maybe she's that way with everybody. She wasn't too nice to Glen just now, and he's a good guy. He's not bad looking either. Is she just a snob?" I was aware of the fact that Mandy knew Lydia better than I did, but I wasn't really expecting her to answer me.

"She's had a rough life," Mandy responded.

"Who hasn't?" I remarked without thinking.

Mandy shook her head. "I mean she's had a *really* rough life, Maren. I think she's just afraid of getting close to people. She does a lot of good things, but she's quiet about it. I'm guessing it was a little hard for her when she heard us talking just now."

I gave her a bewildered look.

"Well, c'mon Maren," she said a bit defensively. "You know she's got a thing for Jake, and she was probably holding out hope—until now."

I was stunned for a moment, but then realization slowly seeped in.

Mandy must have been bothered by my prolonged silence because she said, "You already knew that, didn't you?"

I shook my head and muttered, "I suppose I should have." I remembered Lydia asking Jake to dance at some of the singles dances we'd both been at. I'd seen her talking to him occasionally . . . I guessed I'd even seen her attempting to flirt with him, if I stopped and thought about it. But she hadn't seemed to throw herself at his feet like many of the other women did. The issue of other women in the singles ward had concerned me for a while once I'd discovered I loved Jake, but didn't know for certain how he felt about me. I remembered talking to my best friend Ann about it on one occasion. But she'd told me that Jake had confessed to her husband Tyler that several women had asked him out and that he always turned them down. After that, I hadn't given it too much thought.

"Well, anyway," Mandy started again, "Lydia always kinda liked Jake, I think. And after he took her out a couple of times, I guess she hoped there was some reciprocation. She's never admitted it, but I think that's why she started going to the family ward a while ago."

I felt my cheeks growing hot as she rambled on. ". . . and I wasn't sure what to think. I mean, I'm friends with both of you. Jake just seems like a generally nice guy, so I would've been happy to see either one of you end up with him. And like I said, I saw sparks between you and Jake from the beginning, but it just never seemed like anything was going to come of it. I'm not sure what the deal was. But he's obviously in love with *you,* so I guess things are cleared up for everybody now."

Oh yeah, I thought sarcastically to myself. *Things are real clear for everybody.*

"So, I guess you're the lucky one," Mandy finished happily.

"Yeah . . ." I agreed slowly. "Well, I'd better run. Jake's waiting for me." I just wanted to get out of there and talk to Jake.

"Oh. Okay. Tell him congratulations too. Bye, Maren!" Mandy disappeared into the crowd, as I hurried toward the hall.

I pushed my way through the hoards of people, feeling increasingly agitated. I thought I was making my way toward the exit, but couldn't see anything for all the bodies in front of me. I suddenly bumped into a hard chest and tried to push my way around it, feeling embarrassed. "Sorry," I mumbled without looking up.

Someone caught my arm and said humorously, "Where you going, love?"

The familiar voice was comforting, but a bit disturbing as well.

"Come on." Jake took my hand and led me through the crowd, making a path for me. Just outside the doors, we were met with a freezing gust of wind. Jake paused and held up my coat, which I gratefully slipped on.

As he pulled out of the parking lot, I reached over to turn down the radio and got right to the point. "Jake? What's up with you and Lydia?"

He glanced over to give me a puzzled look and said, "What do you mean?"

"You've seen how rude she is to me," I assumed.

"No," he answered slowly. "I don't believe I have."

I felt irritated that he seemed to be defending her, but tried to control my rising emotion. "Why didn't you tell me that you went out with her?" I demanded.

I saw his jaw muscle tense as he replied, "I don't recall your giving me an inventory of all the men you dated over the last few months."

"That's different, Jake! You knew I was dating then! It was just to get out and do something. I was totally in love with you, but you couldn't seem to get your feelings straightened out. I was confused, and lonely, and tired of putting my life on hold—"

"I know all that, Mar," Jake cut me off. "I felt the same way."

"But why didn't you tell me you were dating her?" I protested.

"For one thing," Jake responded, "I wasn't 'dating' her. I went out with her twice. And for another thing, you never asked me! I didn't realize it was such a big deal."

"Well, it is, Jake! Here I've been trying to figure out why she gives me the cold shoulder, and what I did to offend her, and it wasn't even me! It was you! And you must have done something to give her the wrong idea, because she just overheard me telling Mandy that you and I were engaged, and she looked like she was going to faint. Mandy said Lydia even quit going to the singles ward to go to *your* ward!"

Lines of concern were deepening on Jake's face as he seemed to be thinking hard.

"So, what did you do?" I finished heatedly, throwing my hands in the air for emphasis.

Jake continued to watch the road ahead, gripping the steering wheel with both hands as his jaw muscle grew increasingly tighter. He appeared to be pondering something before he finally glanced over his shoulder, and then pulled off to the side of the road. A nearby street lamp illuminated his face as he turned to look at me. I just watched him expectantly for several tense, silent moments.

Finally, Jake seemed to force away his anger to ask me quietly, "Do you trust me so little, Maren?"

"I . . . Well, Jake, you—" I struggled for words, and finally gave up. I looked down at my hands in my lap and felt suddenly ashamed. "I'm sorry," I whispered.

"Remember when we went to the opera last spring?" Jake asked me after another moment's pause.

I nodded.

"And when I took you home . . . I guess you were trying to tell me that you loved me, but I mistook what you said for rejection."

"Yes," I mumbled, wishing we'd cleared up all the confusion between us months before we had.

"Well, shortly after that I had a medical convention to attend, and there was a dinner that night that I was obligated to go to. I thought I'd scare you away permanently if I asked you on another date so soon, so I asked Lydia to go with me instead. A few weeks later she invited me to her company picnic, and I figured I ought to return the favor— so I did. That's it, Mar. That's all there was. The end."

"Did you kiss her?" I asked hesitantly.

"No! For heaven's sake, Maren! I didn't even hold her hand!"

"Why Lydia?" I questioned. "Why did you ask her?"

Jake laughed at the irony and answered, "Partly because she seemed to be like you in some ways."

"Like me?" I asked in surprise, looking up at him. "How?"

"Well . . ." he started, " . . . she appeared to be a kind and compassionate person. And I think she's pretty talented, but I've only heard things from other people. She's not proud, and she doesn't flaunt things . . . and she's fun to be around, once she warms up a little."

I just watched him, wondering if those things were true of Lydia.

"And the other reason I asked her," Jake continued, "was because I thought she would realize that it was simply a friendly thing, and not get the wrong idea. If what you said is true, though," he added, seeming perplexed, "maybe that was a bad call on my part. Did

Mandy really say that Lydia started coming to our ward because of me?"

"She said that she thought that was the reason, but Lydia had never admitted it to her. Mandy also said that Lydia's had a thing for you ever since you moved here, and that after you took her out a couple of times, she hoped the feeling was mutual."

Jake let out a long breath and muttered, "Oh boy . . ."

"Maybe you should talk to her, " I suggested reluctantly.

"No." Jake shook his head firmly. "I don't think that's a good idea."

"Why not?"

He looked at me as though it were obvious. "Because I'm engaged to you, Mar. I shouldn't be having conversations like that with other women, no matter what the circumstances. If she did get the wrong idea, I feel terrible, but I can't think of anything I did that would have given her any indication that I felt more than friendship toward her. It's obviously clear to her now—maybe Mandy's just reading into Lydia's behavior. She told you herself that she was just making assumptions."

"She's not seeing things that aren't there," I told him decidedly. "It's so obvious now that she's told me that I can't believe I didn't see it sooner. I can't believe *you* didn't see it. But I guess there's not anything I can do about it either."

Jake still looked troubled, so I added, "I'm sorry for jumping to conclusions and getting mad at you."

He shrugged and gave me a wistful smile as if to say, *Oh well.*

In an effort to patch things up, I leaned forward to kiss him. He was a bit hesitant at first, but then pulled me close to him and returned my kisses with fervor.

"Does that mean I'm forgiven?" I asked playfully.

Jake touched his fingers to his lips and gave me a vacant look. "Forgiven for what?" he asked.

I laughed and leaned in to give him one more brief kiss before he took me home.

CHAPTER FIVE

Some of my friends from the singles ward threw a surprise bridal shower for me the Saturday before our wedding. It was well attended, and I was touched by their efforts. As the party was winding down, I pulled Mandy aside and asked, "I know this sounds kind of stupid but . . . have you talked to Lydia? She's okay, isn't she? She's not too upset or anything?"

Mandy smiled and patted my arm. "You're giving yourself quite a guilt trip, aren't you? Don't do that, Maren. That's silly. Just be happy."

"I'm happy," I told her honestly. "I've just thought about her quite a bit over the past few days."

"She's fine," Mandy assured me. "She's been through much worse than this and come out fine. Don't worry about her."

"What has she been through?" I asked curiously.

Mandy shrugged. "I know her mother left when she was still little, and her grandmother disowned her after she joined the Church. She pretty much grew up in dire poverty, I think. And she's had rotten luck with men. But you've seen her. She's pretty, she's talented, she's certainly committed to the gospel . . ." Mandy paused thoughtfully before continuing, "It's funny the way life works out sometimes, isn't it? It just doesn't seem to make sense."

"Yeah . . ." I agreed.

Mandy bounced back to her bubbly self then and hugged me. "I'm sorry, but I've got to run. I have a date to get ready for."

"Really?" I asked with a teasing grin. "Who are you going out with?"

"Oh, he's not from the singles ward. He's from work. I've been trying to get this guy to ask me out for weeks, and he finally did, so wish me luck!"

"Good luck," I told her. "And thanks for coming, Mandy."

"Hey, I wouldn't miss it. I guess I'll see you at your open house next week, if I don't see you before then."

As I watched her leave, I decided that I felt better about things with Lydia. I realized there must be a lot more depth to her than I'd imagined. Thoughts of Lydia were soon forgotten, however, as I told the last guests good-bye, and then went home to get ready for my own date that night.

Jake and I had planned to go out, since all of our children were gone. Jeff and Lizzy had gone to spend the night at their grand-mother's house. Tess's mother loved her grandchildren and tried to spend time with them regularly, even though her daughter wasn't around. Rebecca and Trevor were supposed to stay with their father, but our plans changed when Ted called and said that he had to leave right away for an emergency business trip. He brought Rebecca and Trevor home just in time for me to get them into bed. When I tele-phoned Jake to fill him in, he offered to go rent a movie and bring it over to my house instead. Anxious to be with him, I agreed. When he arrived, he was wearing a black leather jacket over a gray sweater. I pressed a hand to my chest and whispered dramatically, "Be still, my beating heart."

He laughed. "Happy to see me, my love?"

"You'd better believe it. I don't think I can take much more of you in that jacket, though. Here, let me hang it up."

"Never!" He smiled wickedly.

"What are you trying to do to me?" I demanded. "You're so darn handsome I can't stand it."

Jake's eyes sparkled with mischief as he leaned close to me and whispered, "Am I?" He tried to kiss me, but I moved away from him.

"Oh, no you don't," I warned. "Look, I'm serious, Jacob. Hand over the jacket, or I'm going to have to ask you to leave." I held out my hand and tried not to smile.

He gave an exaggerated sigh and rolled his eyes. "What I won't do for you . . ." he muttered as he took the jacket off and tossed it to me.

Then he winked at me and said, "If it's that powerful, maybe you'd better keep it here until after the wedding."

Trevor heard his voice and yelled from the bedroom, "Can Dad come and tuck me in?"

I smiled at Jake. "I guess that's you. Thank heaven for a distraction."

He laughed and walked down the hall.

When he finally came back to the great room ten minutes later, I'd made popcorn and lemonade and was turning on the dishwasher. "I'm glad to see you," I told him. "I thought you'd fallen asleep back there."

He leaned on the bar and touched the tip of my nose. "I listened to Trevor tell me about preschool and rocket ships for five minutes, so Becca demanded equal time," he explained.

"You're a good man," I told him as he came around the counter to kiss me. I wrapped my arms around his neck and accepted his display of affection eagerly. His kiss started out gentle, but then he pulled me into a strong embrace as he kissed me more and more deeply. When I pulled away and met his gaze, his eyes were brimming with warm affection.

"I love you, Jake," I whispered.

He smiled and stroked my cheek with one hand, still holding me close with the other. "I love you too," he whispered back, then added after a moment's hesitation, "And *that* is why I'm going to go home now."

"What?" I asked in surprise. "But you just got here! The kids are in bed, and we're going to watch a mov—"

Jake touched a finger to my lips and shook his head firmly. "I'm not sure what I was thinking when we planned this," he said. "But suddenly I don't think that snuggling up on your couch a week before our wedding to watch a two-hour movie, unchaperoned by children, is a good idea. Do you?"

"No," I admitted reluctantly. "But I don't want you to go."

"I know," he said sympathetically. "And this is taking everything in me, believe me." He gave me one more quick kiss before he moved toward the door. He paused with his hand on the knob to turn back and suggest, "Let's say a prayer together before I go home."

"All right," I agreed.

We knelt on the great room floor, and Jake took my hand in his as he prayed for strength and discretion in the coming week. He thanked God for our many blessings, especially each other, and asked for the continued health and safety of our families. He prayed that our children would adjust quickly to the changes in their lives, and that Jeffrey, especially, would be comforted. I felt peace fill me as I listened to his humble prayer.

When he finished praying, Jake stood and pulled me up with him. He pressed a tender kiss to my lips and whispered, "Good night, Mar."

I gazed up at him with admiration and echoed, "Night."

He walked to the coat closet to get his jacket, then paused to grin at me before he put it on.

I shook my head and waved a hand at him as I said teasingly, "Get outta here."

He laughed and pulled the door shut behind him.

***

We met with Bishop Rowley later that week to get our wedding recommends. After we'd each been interviewed and received the required piece of paper, the bishop talked to us together. "I'm very happy for you," he told us. He'd seen both Jake and me through many of the trials that we'd each faced over the previous year and a half, and I sensed his relief and joy on our behalf. "Now, is there anything else I can help you with?" Bishop Rowley added.

I was about to shake my head in the negative when Jake responded, "Well, yes, actually. As long as we're here we might as well find out how to start the process of getting Maren's sealing to her first husband canceled. We plan on being sealed in a year, of course."

I felt my mouth drop open, but closed it quickly, hoping that neither of the men in the room had noticed. Jake glanced at me sideways for a moment, but then turned his attention back to the bishop, who seemed unaware of my surprise.

Bishop Rowley nodded and smiled. "I thought you might say that. There are some forms that Maren will need to fill out. Then we'll send a copy of them to Ted's bishop, who will give him the opportunity to respond. I request a letter from Tess, and I write a letter myself. After that, we submit everything to the First Presidency and wait for their reply." He rummaged through a file drawer and handed the papers to me when he'd found them. I accepted them numbly.

Jake glanced at me again before he said, "Thank you, Bishop. We'll see you at the wedding, then?"

"I wouldn't miss it for the world."

As we left his office, a feeling of dread settled in my stomach. How was I going to confront this? I'd reassured my children that God would take care of things, but in truth, I hadn't really let myself think about it. The weight of such an eternal decision was simply too overwhelming. I thought back over the past twelve years of my life and was tempted to wish that I'd done things differently. Then I reminded myself that there was no good in that and tried to just concentrate on the prospect of becoming Jake's wife. We could talk about it later, I decided.

Once we were in the car, Jake started the engine to get the heater going and then turned to face me. "Maren, what's wrong?" There was an urgency in his eyes.

So much for talking about it later, I thought. My hope that he hadn't noticed my response in the bishop's office was obviously in vain. I tried to dismiss it lightly as I shrugged and forced a smile. "Just pre-wedding jitters, I guess."

Jake shook his head. "It's more than that."

I sighed and looked out the window. "Let's discuss this later, Jake. Please. We can talk about it after the wedding."

"You're still planning on the wedding then?"

I snapped my head back around to face him. "Of course I'm still planning on the wedding!"

"But you don't want to be sealed to me?" The hurt was evident in his expression, as he shook his head in bewilderment. "I don't understand, Maren. I mean, I just assumed . . ." He searched my face deeply. "You do love me . . . don't you?"

I took his hand and answered gently, "Of course I love you."

He leaned closer to question earnestly, "Then *what's wrong?*"

I searched for a response and chose the simplest one. "Jake, I'm sealed to Ted. You're sealed to Tess. It's even."

He narrowed his eyes at me. "Maren, the choices that Tess made voided the commitment we shared years ago, and in my opinion, Ted's actions did the same. Getting your sealing officially annulled is just a formality."

"Then why do it?" I said quietly.

The pain in his expression deepened. "Because I want to be sealed to you. I want to know the ordinances are in place so you're mine after this life, too."

"And what if Tess shapes up?" I challenged. "And you're also sealed to her?"

The hurt changed to exasperation as he protested, "Oh, come on, Maren. Tess and I wouldn't want to be together even if that was an option. The divorce was the best thing for both of us, just like it was for you and Ted. I believe in the Atonement, and I believe that Tess could change her life and earn forgiveness if that was what she chose to do—though I'm sure it wouldn't be easy. But you and I both know that priesthood ordinances in and of themselves are no guarantee of anything. The promises behind them are contingent on our obedience. The whole point is that if we live worthily, God will work everything out so that we're all happy. I'd like to see Tess happy, Mar, but I love *you*. I want to be with you."

When I didn't respond, Jake finally said, "Surely you know all that, Maren. You believe it."

I nodded slowly and agreed, "Yes . . . I know you're right, Jake. But the whole Tess thing still just bothers me. And what about our children?"

"God will work that out too, Mar. If we all live right, we'll all be together. You've said that yourself. Our children will be adults by then, and be sealed to their own spouses anyway."

"Except for Ashlyn," I reminded him quietly. "Did you forget that my first baby died when she was only a few hours old? I have a daughter to raise in the next life, Jake, and I don't want to give up that opportunity."

His look changed to one of empathy. "Of course I didn't forget," he said gently. "But God will also take care of that."

I nodded as I choked back tears, angry with myself for getting so emotional.

Jake wrapped his arms around me and held me to him, brushing my hair with his lips. "I'm sorry," he told me. "I didn't mean to upset you, love. You're right. We can deal with this after the wedding, when things are a little calmer. We'll talk about it then, okay?"

I breathed a sigh of relief as I pulled back to look at him and smile. "Okay," I agreed before I reached up to kiss him.

When Jake pulled away, the anticipation gleaming in his eyes was only slightly clouded. "Three more days, Maren," he whispered. "After all this time—only three more days, and you'll be mine."

CHAPTER SIX

On November eighth I woke before it was light outside. I tiptoed into the kitchen quietly, trying not to disturb my children or my family sleeping downstairs. If I didn't make myself eat something then, I knew I wouldn't eat at all. I was too excited. I choked down some yogurt and then went back to my room to take a shower.

I was meticulous in getting ready, sweeping my longish blond hair into an elegant updo and putting on just a little more makeup than usual. I wanted to look perfect that day. After my family came upstairs, Natalie checked the back of my hair for me. Then she smiled at me, teary eyed. My always-optimistic little sister rarely cried. "Maren, I hope you've finally found the happiness that you deserve. I love you so much."

I hugged her and said, "You hush, Nat, before you make me cry and mess up my face." We laughed together.

Jake came to get me at eight o'clock. Our families would be meeting us at the temple with the children, and Jake's parents had agreed to watch the kids in the temple waiting room during the ceremony.

My almost-husband was wearing a black suit, and he smiled at me in my baby blue dress. "How did you find a dress to match your eyes so perfectly?" he said teasingly.

"You must be the most handsome man in the world." I smiled back, kissing Becca and Trevor good-bye before I followed Jake to his car.

"How's Jeff doing this morning?" I asked him as we started down the road.

"Better than my mother," Jake muttered. "I left them both bawling."

I reached for his hand as I said, "Oh, Jake, I'm sorry."

He lifted my hand to his lips and kissed it. "They'll both get over it," he told me, though there was a twinge of sadness in his voice. Then he gave me a gentle smile and said, "We're doing the right thing, Mar. I suppose a little opposition is to be expected. My mom understands that I'm committed to the gospel. She's sad, but she'll be all right. As for Jeffrey, I'm just hoping and praying that once we all start living together he'll adjust and come to accept things."

"I hope so too," I agreed.

"We knew it wouldn't be easy when we started down this road," Jake pointed out. Then he smiled and added, "Now, let's quit worrying and enjoy our wedding day."

I leaned over to give him a brief kiss.

Walking up the hill to the Provo Temple, to go inside together after all these years, made me cry. "Hey, sweetheart, I hope that mascara's waterproof," Jake said tenderly as he brushed away my tears and hugged me. "Can you believe it, Maren? We're here!"

I shook my head in amazement and followed him through the front doors.

Mom and Natalie met me in the bridal dressing room a few minutes later. I remembered how hopeless I'd felt watching Natalie dress for her wedding, and now I was bursting with joy. My hair had done exactly what I wanted it to for once, and my eyes just sparkled with happiness. I looked in the mirror, and for the first time in forever I thought, *Wow. I actually look pretty.*

Natalie's reflection in the mirror caught my attention, and I looked toward her. She had a faraway, almost wistful look in her eye. I turned around and asked, "Are you okay, Nat?"

She snapped out of her reverie quickly and gave me a bright smile. "'Course I am," she said quickly, if not a bit defensively. There was only the slightest pause before she added jokingly, "I'm just losing my big sister again, that's all."

I smiled, then hugged her and my mother before I went to meet Jake.

I tried so hard to listen to the words of the ceremony as Jake and I knelt together at the altar, but I was lost in his eyes. I studied his chiseled chin, smooth lips, tiny endearing laugh lines, and dark, wavy hair. He was the most remarkable thing I'd ever seen, even after all this time.

I felt the sting when the officiator pronounced us married for the period of our mortal lives instead of sealed for "time and all eternity," but I pushed the thoughts away. I couldn't let anything take away from my happiness.

We stood to look in the mirrors together afterward, both of us smiling. Then we exchanged rings. I was so thrilled to finally slip that band onto Jake's finger. I'd chosen one to match mine. It was simple and masculine, with a band of brushed platinum on top, and a band of shiny platinum on the bottom, separated by a fine black line. "Do you like it?" I asked him quietly.

He held his left hand next to mine to look at our rings together and smiled. "It's perfect, Mar."

"You're mine now. You can't change your mind," I whispered to him.

He chuckled softly and kissed me.

We hugged everyone there before we left the sealing room. "Well, it's about time," Tyler remarked as he embraced me and Jake. "I didn't think you two were ever going to figure it out." He smiled, but I didn't miss the moisture in his eyes. Tyler's wife Ann was the best friend I'd ever had. They had lived across the street from me for three years before Ann lost her battle with breast cancer and passed away. After she was gone, Tyler said he couldn't stand the emptiness and moved to St. George.

"Thanks for coming so far to be here for us," Jake told him, grasping his hand warmly. He and Tyler had grown close as well.

"As if I could miss this," Tyler said with a grin.

I felt a pang of sadness and voiced what I guessed we were all thinking. "I only wish Ann could have been here, too."

I was surprised at the peace in Tyler's expression as he smiled and leaned closer to say, "I'm pretty sure that she was."

I just hugged him again, profoundly sad for his loss, and yet filled with gratitude at the assurance we had of a life beyond this one.

We greeted our children when we got back to the waiting room. "Did you really get married?" Jeffrey whispered hesitantly.

"Yes we did, buddy," Jake replied as he hugged him. Jeffrey let me hug him too, but I wished that perpetual look of concern would leave his little face. I supposed that I should just be grateful that he didn't yell and make a scene in the temple waiting room.

Jake's mother wiped discreetly at her tears with a handkerchief before she stood to embrace us. She put on a bright smile and asked, "Well, how was it?"

I saw the hint of sadness in Jake's expression when he answered her. "The ceremony was beautiful, Mom. Simple, but beautiful."

Her eyes welled up again, and she hugged Jake quickly to disguise her emotion. My heart ached for both of them. I wished desperately that Jake's parents would accept the gospel, for his sake as well as theirs.

The day was warm for November, but a rainstorm came up just as we got to the church to celebrate. Jake and I ran in together, under the cover of a large black umbrella. We took dozens of family pictures with all of us smiling in front of a blue and white background. I wanted the happiness of that day to last forever.

My brother Clayton came running in just before we sat down to eat. "Come out here!" he called to Jake and me. "You guys have *got* to see this!" He caught the photographer, who was just about to start packing away his equipment. "You too," he ordered excitedly. "We need you out here."

I didn't know what could be so interesting that it would warrant going out into the rain in my wedding gown, but I obediently followed my older brother, pulling my husband along with me. Nearly everyone else came along also, out of curiosity I supposed. As we approached the glass doors, I was grateful to see that the rain had let up. Clayton pushed them open, and we stepped outside. I looked around, but didn't see anything special. "What, exactly, are we looking for?" I asked him skeptically.

He just smiled and motioned for everyone to follow him around the corner to the other side of the building. A hush fell over the crowd as we looked up at the eastern sky. There was a huge arc of color painted clear across the brilliant blue background on the far side of the storm clouds. "How's that for a photo backdrop?" Clayton grinned.

The photographer hurriedly set up his camera and had us pose in front of the rainbow for more pictures. On impulse, Jake suddenly dipped me down and kissed me. The photographer got that too.

The excitement wore off as the colors began to fade back into the clouds and it started to sprinkle again. Everyone went inside, but Jake took my hand and held me back. We stood looking at the dissipating rainbow for a few moments alone. "So, I guess this means that Ann was here, huh?" I mused aloud.

Jake laughed and kissed me before he led me back inside. He turned back once to call to the rainbow, "Thanks for coming, Ann! And hey, you were right—she loves me!"

I shook my head, but then humored him with a smile. Ann would have laughed at him, I was sure.

Everyone ate and danced into late afternoon. Jake finally pulled me discreetly into the hallway to wrap his arms around me and kiss me. He was simply striking in his black tuxedo with his black and silver vest and tie. He traced the outline of my collarbone with his fingers, then ran them up my throat, around the back of my neck, and into my hair.

"Jake?" I whispered.

"Hmm?" he said, with a vague flicker of amusement in his eyes.

I smiled back and asked a bit shyly, "Are you as happy as you thought you'd be?"

He pulled me to him tightly, and I put my arms around his neck and clung to him. I felt more love and passion than I'd ever believed possible. He pulled away and seemed to be looking into my soul as he answered gently, "Maren . . . do you really have to ask that?"

I shook my head, feeling overcome with emotion.

"And what about you?" he whispered with a trace of humor. "Are you happy, Mrs. Jantzen?"

I laughed softly. "Say that again."

He grinned. "All right. Let's get out of here, *Mrs. Jantzen*. We have a plane to catch."

Jake and I changed our clothes, hugged and kissed our children, and left them in the care of their grandparents for a week. They threw rose petals at us as we ran down the sidewalk—that must have been Natalie's idea—and got into Jake's toilet-papered car. We left to hoots and hollers all around to begin our life together.

We went straight to the airport and flew to California. Then we drove a rental car to our hotel on the beach. Jake wanted to be near the ocean because he thought it would be more romantic. It was definitely beautiful. The view was breathtaking, but all I cared about was being with him.

It was night by the time he finally carried me over the threshold and kicked the door shut behind him. He didn't put me down at first, just held me and kissed me for a long time. When he did set me down, I suddenly felt nervous butterflies flitting around inside me. I tried to ignore them as I whispered, "I'll be out in a minute," and went into the bathroom to change into a shimmery, pale pink nightgown.

When I returned, Jake was sitting on the bed, wearing black pajamas. He just stared at me for what seemed like forever, making me even more tense. "What?" I finally whispered, ready to run back into the bathroom and close the door.

"You . . ." he breathed. "Maren . . . you're the most beautiful thing I've ever seen."

I looked away, afraid to meet his eyes again. Could he really mean that?

He came slowly toward me and reached out to pull me to him. I rested against his chest for a moment, and then stretched up to kiss him. He pulled back to look into my eyes, and I felt calmer when I met his adoring gaze.

"You're trembling," he whispered gently. "Are you nervous?"

"Very nervous," I admitted.

Jake smiled back and asked, "You want to know a secret?"

I nodded and watched him expectantly.

"I'm nervous too," he whispered in my ear.

I laughed and said, "I love you, Jacob Jantzen."

He cupped my face in his hands and kissed me softly, saying, "You're finally mine, Maren. Only mine." He kissed me again and again. "Everything I have . . . everything I am . . . is yours." Everything else drifted into oblivion with his words.

Our wedding night was so different from what I had known before. It was all beauty and love and tenderness, nothing selfish or cold. For the first time in my life I felt completely one with my husband, completely cherished, completely adored, completely loved, and completely full of love for him.

Far into the night I sighed contentedly in Jake's arms and tried to nestle even closer to him, burying my face in his neck. He squeezed me to him tightly and kissed the top of my head. "Love you, Mar," he whispered sleepily. It was all so new and wonderful, and yet it felt like I'd been there forever. I was finally where I belonged.

When I woke up in the morning, Jake was leaning up on one elbow, watching me. I stretched and smiled at him. He smiled back, but didn't say anything. He just continued to gaze at me with a familiar look of adoration.

"What're you doing?" I finally asked softly.

He smiled a dreamy smile and said, "Marveling."

"Marveling?"

He nodded.

"At what?" I wondered.

"At you. At how beautiful you are. At the fact that you're here with me. You have no idea how many times I've dreamed this, but I always woke up and you were never there."

I traced my fingers up his arm and across his shoulder to his face.

"Most of all, I'm marveling at the fact that you're my wife. Aren't you the girl I just met in English class yesterday?"

I leaned up on my elbow too, and answered him. "Ah, yes. That's where I know you from. You're that incredibly handsome man from my critique group, the one who took my breath away with your amazing intellect and insight. And you had such impeccable manners and good taste."

"You were impressed with me right off, then?" he asked teasingly.

"Absolutely." I smiled. "I thought I'd never been so fortunate as I was to come into your life." I stopped to wrestle with my rising emotion. "But then I walked into this fog, away from you. I lost you for a long, lonely time, didn't I?" I suddenly felt an ache for all the time with him I'd given up, to think that I could have been feeling this way for the past twelve years. I shook the thought from my mind.

Jake brushed my hair back from my face with his fingers and whispered, "It's all right, love. I found you again."

"Yes, you're here now," I agreed. "That's all that matters."

CHAPTER SEVEN

I still felt like I was floating on air when we returned from our honeymoon. As soon as we pulled into the garage, Jake gave me one more long, passionate kiss in the car. "That was the most wonderful week of my life," he whispered.

"Mine too." I sighed. "So, I guess we get to go face reality together now, huh?"

He laughed softly. "Maren, we've been facing reality together for months. Now we have our marriage to lift us up. It's going to be easier, not harder."

I squeezed his hand and agreed, "I guess you're right."

My parents had driven down with the kids to meet us that morning. All four children came running to greet us. We gave them little packages that we'd brought for them and hugged and kissed them all. We hugged both sets of parents too, and thanked them profusely.

By that night, everyone was gone except for our little family. We said family prayer together, read a bedtime story together, and Jake and I tucked the children in together. Jeffrey was still a little sullen, but not openly defiant. When Trevor hugged me he whispered, "Mommy, are you and Jake going to get divorced someday, too?"

My heart hurt to hear him voice such an awful fear. I sat on his bed and ruffled his hair. "No, sweetheart, not ever." I smiled up at Jake.

"But what if Jake starts getting drunk like Dad did?" I thought for a minute, trying to know what to say. I didn't want him to think I'd put up with that ever again. But how could I tell him that I knew

Jake would never do that, when I hadn't been able to predict it with Ted?

Jake knelt by Trevor's bed and cut in. "Trevor, I would never, *ever* do anything that might make me lose your mom or this family. I promise you that."

Trevor threw his arms around Jake's neck and said, "I love you, Dad."

To my surprise, the tender exchange between my new husband and my nearly five-year-old son seemed bittersweet. Although the scene touched me deeply, it also made my heart ache for Ted. I couldn't look at Trevor without being reminded of his father—He reflected everything beautiful and good that I'd ever seen in Ted. My eyes filled with tears of joy for all that I'd been blessed with, and tears of sorrow for all that Ted had thrown away.

***

I embarked on my new life with a hopeful heart. Jake got up early in the mornings to go make his rounds at the hospital before going into the office, and he usually made it home by five or so, leaving us two or three hours of family time before the children went to bed.

Despite the occasional arguments, Rebecca, Trevor, and Lizzy seemed to be adjusting fairly well. I was still met with quite a bit of resistance from Jeffrey, most often in the form of comments like, "You can't tell me what to do 'cause you're *not* my mom!" I did my best to remain calm and patient with him, but my nerves were wearing thin. I spent a lot of time on my knees, praying for patience and direction, and trying to have faith that Jeff would eventually adjust to the changes in all our lives. Jake and I talked a lot at night about the problems Jeff was having and how to handle them. I was thankful that I wasn't doing everything alone anymore.

The first couple of weeks seemed almost too good to be true. Jake and I both put a big effort into making the transition as smooth as possible, but sometimes I almost wondered if he was trying too hard. He always kissed me before he left and after he came home. He asked how my day was, he helped me with dinner dishes, and cleaning up, and with the children. He called during the day just to tell me that he loved me. He often came home with flowers, and once in a while I'd find a sweet note that he'd left for me. I knew he worked long, hard days caring for his patients, and often told him to sit down and take a break when he got home, but he always refused. Occasionally, I'd find him studying me intently, as if gauging my reaction to something he'd done. I finally decided that maybe his devotion simply seemed exaggerated in comparison with Ted's. I knew that my perception of what marriage should be was likely distorted, due to the ten years I'd spent in misery, and advised myself that rather than question Jake's motives, I ought to just appreciate all that he did.

I tried to put everything I could into the marriage as well, both by doing things for Jake and by trying to show gratitude for the things he did for me. Although I had to admit that I was happier than I'd ever been, something in me made me wary. I sometimes wondered if I was only dreaming, if Jake would suddenly vanish in a poof, and I would wake to find him gone. Or more likely, I worried that one day he might snap from the effort of trying too hard and simply walk away.

***

The first time that Ted came to pick Rebecca and Trevor up from Jake's house, he stepped into the foyer and looked around. He tilted back on his heels, gazed up at the crystal chandelier, and let out a long, low whistle. Jake walked in from the kitchen, then, and Ted grinned at him like the Cheshire cat. "This is quite the place, Jantzen," he observed with dramatic grandeur. "I can see why Maren went for you . . . after turning you down the first time, I mean." He stared up at the ceiling again and said thoughtfully, "It's a definite move up for you, isn't it?" Then he looked directly at me with cold, green eyes.

I should have tried to say something to diffuse the situation; instead, I let my quick tongue get the better of me and replied, "It certainly is."

"Oooh," Ted said with a delicious shudder. "Married—what? A couple of weeks now? And you're already getting feisty?" He shoved his hands in his pockets and gave Jake a curious look. "You put up with that, Jantzen?" He grinned and lowered his voice to say, "Or maybe I should call you *Doctor* Jantzen. Maren says it upsets the kids when I don't give you the respect that you deserve. Of course, she never worried about it upsetting the kids when she didn't give me the respect that I des—"

"You're in my house now, Ted," Jake said icily. "Put a lid on it."

Ted laughed and remarked, "You're getting a little hostile yourself, aren't you?" He waved a hand through the air and said, "Don't worry about it, though—I understand. Marriage has that effect on a guy."

Ted hadn't been so cold and sarcastic in a long time. All I could think was that it must have been very difficult for him to see me married to Jake.

"Do you think you're up to having your children this weekend?" Jake asked Ted pointedly.

"As a matter of fact, I've never been better."

"Ted—" I started, but he cut me off with an annoyed look.

"Just get the kids, okay, Maren? And I'll leave you and 'lover boy' here alone."

I knew that Ted still had to report before a judge regularly to prove that he was continuing to take anger management classes, going to counseling, and attending the Church-sponsored substance abuse program that he'd enrolled in. I also knew that if he messed up, he could be forced to go back to having only supervised visits with the children, or lose his visitation rights completely. Despite his treatment of me, Ted had never threatened or hurt the children—though that was no guarantee of anything. However, the fact that I knew the state was keeping a close eye on him brought me some peace of mind.

"Don't tell her what to do, Ted," Jake ordered quietly.

Wanting to keep peace, I touched Jake's arm and said, "It's all right. I'll get the kids."

Rebecca and Trevor were glad to see Ted. They ran to greet him, and he actually stooped to hug them. I kissed them both and watched them leave with him, saying a well-worn prayer in my heart for their happiness and well-being.

Jake stood silently watching after them for several moments before he said, "You think they'll be all right?"

"They have been so far—I'll call them later to make sure."

He nodded and agreed, "Good idea." Then he turned to look at me.

When I'd had all that I could take of his silent appraisal, I finally asked, "What?"

"Maybe we should think about getting some family counseling to help us all . . . adjust," Jake suggested carefully.

I felt the past few days of utopian matrimony crumble around me, and narrowed my eyes at him.

He shrugged defensively. "Weren't you seeing a counselor before anyway? After you and Ted separated?"

I nodded, knowing full well that he was perfectly aware of that. In fact, it had only been a couple of months since my last visit. I'd quit going shortly before I got engaged to him.

"So, what do you think?" Jake prodded.

"I went to counseling to recover from the effects of living in an abusive relationship for ten years," I responded. "I needed to find my own strength again. I needed support to help me go through with the divorce, and advice on how to help my children through it. I needed to learn to trust myself again, and open up enough to trust someone else, too. I feel I'm past that, Jake. I've come a long way."

He nodded in agreement. "Yes, you have come a long way."

I folded my arms across my stomach and stared at him before I finally said, "We've been married three weeks, and you already want to go to counseling?"

"Exactly," he replied. "We're certainly having a rough time . . . with . . . Jeff, and maybe it would help us all get through the transition a little more smoothly. Why wait until things are worse?"

"Worse than what?" I asked defensively.

"I don't mean that things are bad, Mar," Jake responded quickly. "I just mean we're all going through some big changes here, and I thought it might be a good idea, that's all." He looked suddenly worried, and held up his hands in defeat. "Forget it," he said quickly. "I'm sorry. It was a dumb idea."

He hurried away, and I thought about his abrupt change in demeanor. What had I said to cause that? Or had it simply been my imagination?

My thoughts were interrupted when I heard something and glanced over to see Jeff scurrying out of the nearby dining room. I wondered how much he'd heard.

I forgot about Jeff's eavesdropping as the days passed, and soon we drove up to Idaho again to spend Thanksgiving with my family. As soon as we came back, I went into a flurry of getting ready for Christmas. I decorated, baked, shopped, sewed, and did everything that I hadn't had the time or energy to do for the last two years. The prospect of Christmas approaching seemed to cheer even Jeffrey a bit.

I sold my house the first of December. I was shocked that it sold so quickly, and chalked it up to just another one of the many blessings in my life. The children and I walked through our house one last time to say good-bye. I knew I was really saying good-bye to Ted, too. It was sad for me. I felt a wistful kind of ache remembering the happy times we'd shared there. I tried to forget the bad ones. But when I walked out the front door and Jake put his arms around me, I knew I'd found my real home.

***

On the morning of December fifth, Natalie called me. "Guess what?" she said brightly.

"You can't possibly have had your baby!" I gasped. "You sound way too energetic."

"Oh, Maren! Not everyone has as hard a time as you do. I did have my baby, and I feel great!"

"You did? Natalie, congratulations! I'm so happy for you!"

"Thanks."

"Well, tell me about him!" I said excitedly.

She laughed and proceeded to give me the details. "We're going to name him Nathan," she said.

"Oh, how fun, Natalie! I'm jealous."

"Guess what else?"

"There's more? Don't tell me you had twins!"

"No," she giggled. "We're moving to Salt Lake next month."

"What?" I gasped. "That's only a twenty-minute drive on the freeway from here!"

"Yep. Douglas is going to do a master's program at the U."

"Oh, my gosh! You're really going to live by me? I can't wait!"

"Neither can I."

"Well, you get lots of rest. Tell us when you're coming, and we'll help you move."

"I'll do that. Bye, Maren."

"Bye, Nat." I smiled when I hung up the phone, excited by all the good news in our lives, and caught myself smiling often over the next few days until Ted came to return the children that Sunday. "I've changed my mind. I want the kids for Christmas," he told me.

"What?" I protested, looking over my shoulder to make sure that Rebecca and Trevor had disappeared from earshot.

"Why should you get them for Thanksgiving *and* Christmas?" Ted demanded.

"Because that's what we agreed to, Ted."

He chortled and said with a grin, "I must have been drunk at the time."

"That's not even funny."

He shrugged. "Maybe not. But neither's this—I want the kids for Christmas, Maren."

"Why?" I asked. I felt close to tears, and fought to hide my emotion.

"Don't you think you're being a little selfish here?" Ted challenged. "You have a husband and two stepchildren. If I take the kids, you still have a family to spend Christmas with. If *you* take the kids, who do I have? No one."

"That's not true, Ted," I argued. "Your parents are only half an hour away, and you have three brothers who are always in town with their families. You know darn well that you won't be alone—unless you *choose* to be."

Ted leaned close to me, and I took a step backward. "Whatsa matter, baby?" he questioned, obviously amused. "You scared of me?"

"No—I'm not," I answered firmly. But then I wondered if I was trying to convince him or myself.

"You got Thanksgiving," he reiterated, turning abruptly serious again. "I get Christmas. That's fair. Ask the judge, if you want."

"But, Ted, we agreed—"

"You got that in writing?" he asked snidely. When I didn't respond he said, "I didn't think so. I'll pick them up on Christmas Eve. You can have them back on the twenty-seventh—I have to go to work . . . Wouldn't want to get behind on any child-support payments."

I narrowed my eyes at him. "Are you threatening me?"

Ted scoffed at the idea. "Really, Maren. Grow up." He glanced down at his watch then and announced, "Oops. Gotta run. See you in a couple of weeks." He gave me another patronizing smile and hurried away.

***

"*What?*" Jake asked incredulously when I told him about my conversation with Ted. "He can't do that! We simply won't let them go."

"If it goes to the judge, Jake, he'll order me to let them go . . . Ted's right," I added sadly. "We had the kids for Thanksgiving—he should get them for Christmas."

"That's not what he agreed to," Jake insisted.

I felt upset and frustrated, and shot back caustically, "Yeah, well, I don't have that in writing, Jake."

Jake's eyes went wide. "Is that what he told you?" he demanded.

"Look," I said wearily, "I have to think of what's best for Rebecca and Trevor."

"And that would be letting their poor excuse for a father manipulate you?" he asked with blatant irritation.

"I have to maintain some degree of peace, Jake," I said in my defense. "If I turn it into a war, my children are the ones who will suffer."

Jake shook his head and looked away. Then he sighed and sat down on the back of an armchair, putting himself at eye level with me. "Maren . . ." he started carefully, "you don't recover from an abusive marriage overnight, you know? If you don't want to go to counseling together . . . well, maybe you could still benefit from going yourself occasionally." He looked worried after he'd said it, and added hastily, "I mean, you already have a counselor who you know and trust, and you've said yourself that he's done a lot to help you recover your own strength and everything . . ." When I made no response he finished quietly, "Maybe you could just think about it."

I felt annoyed, and a little angry with him, but I forced myself to think rationally. In truth, intermittent counseling sessions had benefited me immensely for many months, and I had to admit that they likely still could. I wasn't even sure why I felt bothered by his suggesting it. "I'll think about it," I finally agreed. "After Christmas. It's too hectic right now."

Jake looked mildly relieved, but I wasn't sure whether it was because I'd agreed to think about it, or because I didn't blow my top like he appeared to be fearing I would.

***

I woke up one terrible morning in the middle of December with a horrible churning in my stomach. I felt like everything inside of me was going to turn inside out, and I ran into the bathroom to throw up. A few minutes later I brushed my teeth, splashed my face with cold water, and went back to bed.

"Are you okay?" Jake asked.

I shook my head. "I think I have the flu."

He stayed home that day and took care of the kids. I felt better later in the afternoon, but the next morning I found myself throwing up again. "Must be the forty-eight hour flu," I muttered. "Go ahead and go to work. I'll be all right."

"Are you sure?"

"Yes."

When he came home that night, I was feeling better again.

By the third morning, I knew. I squeezed my eyes shut tight, trying to stay asleep. *No,* I thought. *I can't be. I just can't be.* This would be the definitive end of our wedded bliss, after little more than a month. I walked calmly into the bathroom and managed to turn on the shower—so Jake wouldn't hear me—before I threw up.

The romance came to a screeching halt after that. Besides being sick, my whole body was so sore I couldn't stand to have Jake touch me. I told him I was just fatigued. "Is everything all right, Maren?" he asked, a look of concern in his eyes. "Have I done something wrong, or hurt you in some way? Is there something you want to talk about?"

I shook my head and put on a smile. "No, not at all, Jake. I'm just tired. It's the stress of Christmas and the kids and everything." I tried to make it sound trivial. "Just give me a few days." He didn't bother me or pressure me like Ted had, but he seemed to wonder.

Christmas was very different that year. It was wonderful to be married to Jake. I didn't feel the despair and loneliness that I'd felt the year before, but I had a different kind of ache because Ted got the children. I knew that he would be taking Rebecca and Trevor to stay with his parents in American Fork, and that they would be surrounded by cousins close to their ages. But the thought of spending Christmas without my children was heart-wrenching.

Jake made it clear that he thought I should fight Ted on the issue, but I stayed firm in my resolve to keep peace for the sake of my children. "All right, Mar," Jake finally conceded. "But you can't let him think that you'll give in to all of his demands just to keep peace."

"I won't," I assured him. After that, we considered how to best handle the holiday, and finally decided to have a small celebration with all of our children before Rebecca and Trevor left on Christmas Eve. We gave them our gifts and told them that we'd save the things Santa brought them until they got home.

I forced a cheerful smile when I told them good-bye, but my tenderhearted seven-year-old squeezed my neck especially tight and whispered, "You'll be okay, won't you, Mommy?"

Unbidden tears rushed into my eyes at her innocent perceptiveness, so I held her close to disguise them. "Of course I will, Becca," I promised. "You have fun with Daddy, and I'll see you in a couple of days, okay?"

"Okay." She pulled away and smiled.

Jake, Jeff, and Lizzy hugged Becca and Trevor too, and we all stood at the door waving after them.

"Is Mommy gonna come see *us* for Christmas?" Elizabeth asked with five-year-old innocence.

Jake picked her up and hugged her. "No, sweetheart," he told her.

She didn't say anything, but Jeffrey glanced up at me uneasily. I put an arm around his shoulders and smiled at him. He smiled back, just a little.

After we read the Christmas Story and tucked Jeffrey and Elizabeth in on Christmas Eve, I sat on the couch wrapping presents, and Jake sat on the floor putting things together. "It's so wonderful to be married to you, Mar," he said. "Such a change from the loneliness of last year."

I smiled in agreement, trying to focus on the positive and push away how much I missed Rebecca and Trevor, and how ill I felt because of my condition. "We did come over at Christmastime last year," I reminded him. I waited for his response, then continued, teasing, "After we went sledding . . . you made us hot chocolate . . ." Exasperated, I added, "I sat on your couch with you . . . You kissed me for the first time in eleven and a half years . . ."

He gave me a blank stare, but then I saw the twinkle in his eye as a staged look of enlightenment came over his face. "Was that you?" he asked. "I couldn't quite recall which ravishing woman I'd kissed on my couch last year."

I threw a pillow from the sofa at him. He laughed and came to kiss me.

The next morning was filled with giggles and shrieks of delight. Although I missed Trevor and Becca, I couldn't help but be caught up in Jeffrey's and Elizabeth's enthusiasm. "It's certainly good to see him happy, isn't it?" Jake commented, nodding toward Jeff.

"Yes, it is," I agreed. "I'd almost forgotten what it's like to see him this way."

Ted brought the children home on December twenty-seventh, and we had another mini celebration of sorts. Rebecca and Trevor were obviously happy to be home, but they were also bursting with excitement over the festivities they'd shared with Ted's family. I felt a little envious, but then told myself to just be grateful that they'd enjoyed themselves, and that they had so many people who loved them.

The next morning, Jake woke me with a good-bye kiss and left for the office. I willed my stomach into submission long enough to hear him start down the stairs, then ran for the bathroom. Angry at being sick, I brushed my teeth fiercely and tried not to cry. As I mentally tallied up the days, I realized that I'd been feeling like I wanted to die for nearly three weeks. I prayed that the children would sleep in—My only desire was to go back to bed and sink into oblivion. I walked out of the bathroom to find Jake standing in our bedroom. I jumped and said, "I thought you'd left!"

"I know," he answered softly.

I just looked at him, trying to appear casual.

"Is there anything you want to tell me, Mar?" he asked.

I shook my head. All I could think about was Ted's reaction every time he found out that I was pregnant. Even though it took "two to tango," it was somehow always all my fault. The first time had been the worst. He was angry the whole nine months. When our daughter died shortly after birth, part of me blamed him for a long time because he hadn't wanted her.

Jake just stood there in his shirt and tie with his hands in his pockets, watching me. That piercing gaze unnerved me. I couldn't look into his eyes. I looked down at the floor, thinking hard. I didn't want this marriage to be like the first one. I had to be honest with him. I tried to tell myself that I wasn't sure. I hadn't taken a test yet.

I didn't need to. I knew. This was my fourth pregnancy. I always knew before I took a test because of the blasted morning sickness that plagued me almost from conception. Anyway, I was nearly two months late now. There was no mistaking the obvious symptoms. I braced myself for Jake's reaction and felt a familiar defensiveness rise in me. I met his gaze with determination, as though daring him to challenge me, and said with a trace of defiance, "I'm pregnant."

He seemed surprised by my attitude as his eyes searched mine. There was an almost wounded look in them. I felt my defenses weakening as I suddenly realized that I hadn't been fooling him. I was shocked that he'd managed to figure it out so quickly, but I could tell from the look on his face. "You already knew," I said slowly. "Didn't you?"

"I was definitely suspicious. I've been waiting for you to tell me, but you haven't. Why didn't you tell me?"

I didn't know how to respond. The fact that he was so aware of me was a bit unsettling somehow. I wasn't sure what to expect, and it frightened me. I felt the threat of tears pressing in with the confusion and looked away quickly. I had to keep my guard up, just in case.

"What's wrong, Maren?" Jake asked gently. "You don't want the baby?"

I was immediately back on the defensive. "I never said that!" I snapped. "You're the one who said you didn't want a baby."

He looked both surprised and hurt again. "Did I?" he asked with a touch of cynicism.

"All right," I conceded. "You said that you wanted to wait a year or two."

"Well, it obviously isn't going to work out that way, is it?" he observed.

I narrowed my eyes at him, feeling increasingly upset. "Are you saying that's my fault?" I challenged him.

Jake furrowed his brows for a moment, as if trying to solve a puzzle. "You're putting words in my mouth, Maren," he said quietly.

Another wave of nausea prompted me to sit down in a nearby armchair. The harsh reminder of what lay ahead combined with memories of the past to make me feel suddenly overwhelmed with oppression and fear. "I can't do this again, Jake," I told him wearily. "I can't go through this alone again—I can't."

"Go through it alone?" he asked, then stood silently with his jaw clenched. After a pause, he looked down and chuckled dryly, as though he'd just discovered something. When he met my gaze again, he said with quiet control, "You won't have to go through it alone, Maren." He softened then, and his lips twitched upward just a bit as he added, "Correct me if I'm wrong, but I'm pretty sure I was there at the time. That makes me at least fifty percent responsible, maybe more."

I felt my eyes go wide at his unexpected response.

"You're the one who's suffering, not me," he pointed out. "Are you always this sick?"

"I'm afraid so," I answered softly.

He cracked a smile and breathed an exaggerated sigh of relief. "Well, I'm relieved to know why you haven't wanted me anywhere near you lately."

I humored him by smiling back, but confessed to him seriously, "Jake, I really want this baby."

"Are you sure?" He grinned. "It might look like me."

I laughed that time and gave a helpless shrug. "Oh, well. The poor little thing will probably grow on me eventually—you did."

He laughed with me as he pulled me up and into his arms. "If it's a girl," he whispered as he kissed me, "I hope she doesn't look like you. I wouldn't be able to stop myself from spoiling her rotten."

I smiled coyly, but didn't get a chance to comment. He was kissing me again and didn't stop.

CHAPTER EIGHT

Natalie and Douglas moved to their new apartment in Salt Lake the first of January. Jake and I went to help them move, and I announced my pregnancy to my sister. She was ecstatic at the thought of Nathan having a cousin close to his age, and I told her how glad I was to have her nearby.

The following day was Sunday, and I wondered about Lydia again when I saw her at church. I had thought that she might start attending the singles ward again after Jake and I were married. If I was honest with myself, I had to admit that maybe I'd even hoped she would. But she didn't. I supposed she'd likely just gotten used to the neighborhood ward and didn't want to change again. Whatever her reasons, I felt even more uncomfortable around her than I had before. I felt sorry for her too—especially after the things Mandy had told me—which made me a little angry. It was her own fault for reading things into Jake's simple friendliness, and she certainly seemed to have plenty of other men who were interested in her. For a while, I tried to make a point of telling her hello when I saw her, but her coldness toward me only intensified. I finally developed somewhat of a "suit yourself" attitude and resigned myself to ignoring her. I told myself that I had enough to worry about, with nurturing a new marriage, taking care of four children—one of whom was still very rebellious—dealing with a disgruntled ex-husband, and suffering the physical and emotional side effects of an unplanned pregnancy. Lydia Workman was the least of my concerns.

***

When Jake came home one night during the second week of January, he walked up behind me in the kitchen, put his arms around me, and kissed my neck. He rested his warm hand gently on my stomach and kissed my neck again. I turned around to hug him and say, "Mmm, that was a nice greeting."

"Yeah . . ." He grinned. "So tell me how the most beautiful woman in the world spent her day?" He waited for my answer, still holding me close to him.

"Oh, you know, the usual," I replied. "Cleaning the house, cooking, taking care of the kids, doing laundry, throwing up, and dreaming of you."

He laughed. "Was it the throwing up that made you dream of me?"

"Well, maybe indirectly."

"Why is it so quiet?" he asked suddenly. "Where are those four little angels of ours?"

"Angels?" I raised my eyebrows at him. "Playing downstairs. Thank heaven for new Christmas toys. Jeff's even stayed pretty happy the last couple of weeks."

"Maybe he's finally coming around."

"I hope so."

"What can I help you with?" he asked.

"Nothing. Why don't you just sit down and relax for a minute? I've already set the table, and I'll have dinner out in just a second."

"Should I go get the kids?"

"That would be great." I smiled at him. I was getting used to having help, and it was very nice.

Jake walked to the top of the stairs to call down to the children, and they came running when they heard him. I watched with a feeling of contentment as they all threw their arms around him and began chattering excitedly about their day. He crouched down to listen to them while I put the vegetables and rolls on the table, and his eyes caught mine, making my heart flutter.

I told the children to go wash their hands, and they scampered away to the bathroom. Jake stood and came over to wash his hands at the kitchen sink. He was taking off his tie when I opened the oven door to get the casserole. I held my breath and told myself that I could do this, but as soon as I set it on the counter and caught a whiff of it, I dropped the oven mitts and ran upstairs. After I threw up, I brushed my teeth and leaned over the sink, splashing cold water on my face. I rested my head on my arm and moaned. Why did it have to be so hard to bring a baby into the world?

Jake knocked on the bathroom door and opened it without waiting for me to answer. He rubbed my back with one hand and asked, "Are you all right?"

"I'd forgotten how bad it is," I mumbled without looking up at him.

"Tess never got sick," he remarked, as he seemed to be thinking out loud.

"How nice for her."

"I'm sorry. That was a stupid thing to say." He tugged gently on my arm to pull me up and hold me.

I pushed away from him. "I have to lie down," I said, heading for the bedroom. I didn't know why I suddenly felt resentful toward him.

Jake sighed and went back downstairs. I heard Rebecca ask, "Where's Mommy?"

"She's sick, sweetheart," he answered. "Who would like to say the blessing?"

"She's sick a lot," Elizabeth pointed out. I guessed they'd noticed more than I thought.

Trevor agreed with her. "Yeah. How come she is?"

It was too early to tell the children. Seven months was forever to a child. I wouldn't show for several more weeks, and I wanted to go to the doctor and make sure everything was okay first. "Well . . ." Jake apparently paused to think. "Mom's going to be sick for a little while, so we all need to help her. She can't do everything she usually does. I need you guys to be really good for her during the day while I'm at work, okay?"

I heard tension in Jeff's voice as he asked, "What's wrong with Maren, Dad?"

"We'll tell you about it later, bud. She just doesn't feel well. You don't need to worry."

"Does she have . . ." Jeffrey's voice trailed off.

"Does she have what, Jeff?" Jake prodded.

He squeaked out the words with a hint of foreboding. "Does Maren have cancer?" It sounded like he'd started to cry, something he didn't do very often anymore. "Ann was sick all the time when she had cancer. That's why we had to go with Maren to take care of her every day. Is Maren gonna die too, Daddy?"

My heart sank. Jake's little children had been through far more than their fair share of pain. Their mother had only been gone for a few months, and I knew that watching Ann suffer and finally pass away had been very difficult for all of our children. They had all loved her very much. I felt terrible to think that Jeff was worried about that. I held my stomach as I got up and went quickly down the stairs. Jake had gone over to hug him and was saying, "No, no, honey. Maren's not going to die. She's going to be fine."

"Mommy!" Trevor greeted me. "Are you still sick?" I couldn't help smiling at the thought of being cured that quickly, but I nodded.

I kissed Jeffrey's head and put my hand on Jake's shoulder. When he looked up at me I said, "We'd better just tell them. I don't want them to worry about that." I sat down in my chair at the table, and Jake came to sit next to me. I nodded for him to tell them. I was afraid to open my mouth, and tried not to look at the chicken and broccoli swimming in front of me.

"We were going to wait a while, but I guess we'll tell you guys now," Jake began. Jeffrey wiped his eyes with the back of his hand and watched his father expectantly. The other children were looking at us curiously. "We're going to have a baby," Jake announced as he put his arm around my shoulders.

Rebecca's eyes grew wide and she sprang from her chair to come and hug me. "A baby! You're going to have a baby, Mom?"

I smiled and nodded at her.

Trevor scrunched up his face and observed, "You don't look like you're going to have a baby, Mommy. Where is it?" Elizabeth stood up to look at my stomach and waited for my answer too.

"It's in my tummy, Trev. The baby starts out really tiny and grows until it's big enough to be born. It takes a long time. That's why we were going to wait a little while to tell you."

"But why are you sick?" Lizzy asked.

"Sometimes you get sick when you're pregnant," I answered. "My body has to work really hard to give the baby everything it needs, and it makes me feel sick sometimes. I'll feel better when my body gets used to being pregnant again."

"Is it a boy or a girl?" Rebecca questioned.

Jake answered this time. "We don't know yet."

"You're sure you don't have cancer?" Jeff asked again, nervously.

"I'm sure, Jeff." I smiled at him. "I'll feel sick for a while, and I need you all to help me. I can still take care of you, though, and I'm not going to die. I'm going to be fine—I promise." He nodded like he understood.

For the next few days, the children seemed to make more of an effort to help me. Jeffrey, especially, was on his best behavior. However, I wasn't surprised when they gradually returned to normal.

It was a couple of weeks after we'd given the children the news before I had another really difficult day with them. After I broke up what seemed like the hundredth scuffle of the afternoon, I said in exasperation, "My gosh, can you guys just get along? You're driving me crazy!"

Jeffrey gave me a hateful look and said, "Why are you having another baby if you don't even want *us?*"

I sighed and told him, "I love *you,* Jeff, but I sure don't like the way you're behaving."

He glared at me for a moment and then rushed out of the room.

It was frankly a relief when Tess's mother called the following day and asked if she could take Jeff and Lizzy overnight. Apparently eager for a break themselves, the kids were excited to go, so Jake consented. It happened to be Ted's weekend with Rebecca and Trevor, which would leave Jake and me alone for a night. He asked me if I'd like to go out to dinner, but I told him I'd rather not. I didn't think my stomach could take it, and I hated to waste money on something that I knew I'd likely throw up. We decided to rent a movie and stay home instead.

Ted came first to get Rebecca and Trevor, and we kissed them good-bye. It was the first time since I'd married Jake that Ted was actually agreeable. "Are you sick?" he asked when he saw me. I realized that I probably looked a little under the weather, but I was shocked that he would notice.

"I'm just tired," I told him.

"Well, I guess that's understandable," he joked, but the smile he gave me was genuine. "You've got double the kids now."

I returned his smile and replied, "I guess I didn't think about that."

When Mrs. Brulett came to pick up Jeff and Lizzy a short while later, they welcomed her with delight. She hugged and kissed them, happy to see them. Jake introduced me to her and she greeted me coolly, but at least she seemed to love her grandchildren.

"Guess what, Grandma?" Lizzy asked, and without waiting for a response she burst out, "We're going to have a baby!"

Mrs. Brulett's eyes darted to Jake's face in alarm. He only smiled at her and put a protective arm around my shoulders. Her look turned to mild disgust, but when she realized that Elizabeth was watching her expectantly for a response, she forced a slight smile and replied, "How nice, honey."

"We'll see you two tomorrow," Jake promised as he hugged Jeff and Lizzy. I hugged them too and watched them leave with their grandmother.

"They'll be all right with her, won't they?" I asked Jake.

"They'll be fine. She's never been overly friendly with me either, but she's good with the kids and they love her."

"Well, in that case, what are we going to do with an entire night to ourselves?"

"For starters . . . come here," he said, pulling me into the kitchen on a sudden impulse. He turned on the stereo in the family room. A slow, romantic song was playing and he held his arms out to me, "Would you care to dance?"

I slid my arms around his neck and replied, "I'd love to. I should tell you, though, I'm married."

"No!" Jake gave me a look of shock as he started leading me to the soft music. "A pretty young thing like you—already married?"

"Oh, yes." I smiled. "And pregnant, too."

"Pregnant? You can't be!" he said with dismay.

"Oh, but I am."

He shook his head in disappointment, eyes glittering in the soft glow of the family room lamps. "Ah, well . . . I suppose I'll just have to dance with you anyway. I don't believe I've ever seen a more beautiful, married, pregnant woman."

I laughed and laid my head against his shoulder, nuzzling into his neck. I breathed in his clean, masculine scent and sighed. He held me close as we moved together slowly across the tile kitchen floor.

"You certainly did learn to dance," I remarked.

He chuckled before he answered me. "Well thank you, my dear, but it was for purely selfish reasons. I only wanted to impress you and have a good excuse to hold you close."

"It worked," I murmured. "You know, this is much nicer than watching a movie."

He squeezed me tighter and laid his cheek against my hair. "I couldn't agree more . . . Too bad you're married," he commented with a sigh. "And pregnant," he added.

"Yes, too bad." I laughed softly against his throat.

"Because *I'd* like to marry you," he whispered, giving me a mischievous grin.

"Oh, you scoundrel!" I punched him lightly on the chest, making him laugh. Then he slowly leaned down to kiss me, and I kissed him back, filled with both relief and delight that I could kiss him all I wanted to now. I suddenly broke away, giggling, thinking of his recent remark.

He feigned hurt as he asked with more than a touch of drama, "What? You find my passionate kisses amusing, madam?"

"Very much so." I leaned against him, giggling still.

He let out a long, patient sigh and said reluctantly, "Alas, dear lady, you leave me no choice but to teach you a thing or two." Then he lifted me into his arms and carried me up the stairs slowly, shaking his head. "I can't believe you force me into this, but I must make you see just how serious I am."

I laughed again as he set me down gently, and once more when he suddenly dipped me back to kiss me theatrically. "Do my ears deceive me, or do you mock me still, m'lady?" he demanded.

I stared at him with wide-eyed innocence until he finally said, "That's it!" He chased me into our room, where I fell on the bed, screaming and protesting as he tickled me. When he stopped we were both breathless. He leaned over me and whispered, "You have such beautiful eyes . . . for a married, pregnant woman, I mean."

I raised a fist to punch him playfully, but he caught my wrist and held it to his chest as he kissed me.

***

When Ted brought Trevor and Becca back on Sunday afternoon, I hugged them before they ran to find Jeff and Lizzy. Ted was obviously not in the agreeable mood he'd been in on Friday night, as he looked me over sullenly. "The kids told me you're pregnant," he said.

"Did they?" I looked him in the eye.

He waited for me to say more, and when I didn't, he finally asked, "So, are you?"

"Am I what?"

"Are you pregnant, Maren?" he said, exasperated. He flipped back the lock of sandy hair that hung over his eyes.

I wanted to tell him it was none of his business, but I knew it was futile. He saw my children at least twice a month, and this was a pretty exciting thing for them.

"Yes, Ted, I am," I answered coolly.

I couldn't tell if it was gloating, or disgust, or maybe even pain that I saw in his expression, as he asked cockily, "So, how did old Jake handle that news?"

Jake came up behind me just then and rested his hands on my shoulders. "I'm thrilled with the news, actually, Ted," he remarked cheerfully. I felt the tension in his hands as he added, "So thrilled in fact, that I've actually been *nice* to my wife."

Ted's look challenged him as he asked, "What's that supposed to mean, Jantzen?"

"Your comment seemed to imply that no husband would be happy with this news. On the contrary, I look forward to loving and supporting my wife through this pregnancy, and I can't wait to have our baby."

Ted shook his head and chortled, "Yeah, right."

"I don't doubt that you'd find it hard to believe," Jake answered, moving to hold the door open. "Thanks for bringing the kids back, Ted. See you later."

Ted gave him a dirty look as he turned to go. He paused in the doorway before turning back and saying to Jake, "Since you and Maren are going to have a kid of your own, maybe you could quit trying to take over mine."

"Excuse me?" Jake said, lifting his brow.

"I think you have some nerve telling *my* kids to call *you* Dad," Ted clarified.

Jake opened his mouth to respond, but I cut him off. "They asked him if they could call him Dad, Ted. Truthfully, we were worried about your reaction. But I decided that it was more important for Rebecca and Trevor to feel secure and comfortable than it was to protect you from consequences you've brought on yourself."

"I didn't bring this on myself, Maren!" Ted argued, his voice rising. "*You're* the one who got married again."

I felt the old familiar anger brewing inside me as I shot back, "Yes, I am! And *you're* the one who treated me like garbage for ten years before I finally left! I can't even count how many times in those ten years you told me that you never wanted the kids in the first place, Ted. It's great that you're finally getting your life together, and it's certainly a good thing for the kids. But it doesn't change the fact that you were never there for me or for them in the decade we spent together. Rebecca and Trevor love Jake, and he loves them. And if you're any kind of a father, you'll recognize the good he's brought into their lives and be grateful for it. They don't have to hate Jake in order to love you. They can love you both."

Ted gave me an icy glare, and Jake repeated pointedly, "We'll see you later, Ted."

Ted spun on his heel and left, slamming the door behind him.

Trevor and Becca hurried into the entryway. "What happened?" Trevor asked.

"Nothing," I told them.

"The door slammed," Trevor observed. "Did Daddy slam the door?"

I let out a slow breath before I admitted, "Yes." I saw the uneasiness in my children's faces, and it made me even angrier at Ted.

"Is Daddy really mad?" Rebecca questioned.

"Not too much," I replied. "Don't worry, sweetie. Everything's fine."

She hesitated, but then said, "We made him mad, huh?"

"Who's we?" I asked her.

"Me and Trevor. He got mad 'cause Trevor said something about Jake on the way home, and he called him 'Dad.' He said that Jake's not our dad and we shouldn't call him that."

I swallowed my fury and forced myself to ask calmly, "And what did you guys say when Daddy said that?"

Trevor piped up, "Rebecca told Daddy that Jake's like our dad too, and that he said we could call him that if we wanted to."

"You can," Jake assured them.

"But if we do, then Daddy will be mad," Rebecca said.

"I'll talk to your father," I reassured my children. "The two of you have a right to be happy. You shouldn't have to worry about upsetting Daddy. I know you love him, and I know you love Jake too, and that's fine. All right?"

They nodded, albeit reluctantly.

"Did anything else happen?" I asked them.

"No, just that," Rebecca answered.

"Yeah. We had fun with Daddy til he got mad at me on the way home," Trevor volunteered. "He didn't yell at me, but he said he doesn't want me to call Jake that."

"You can call Jake 'Dad' if you want to, Trev," I insisted. "I'll take care of it, don't worry."

"Okay," he mumbled. "I'm goin' to find Jeff. We're gonna build a road for our cars."

He left, but Rebecca lingered. "What's up, Becca Bug?" I asked her.

"Well . . . if you tell Daddy that we can call Jake 'Dad,' will he yell at you?"

"I don't think so, sweetie. He's—"

Jake interrupted me with a firm, "No, he won't, Rebecca. It's not okay for your dad to make you and Trevor feel afraid, and it's not okay for him to yell at your mom. As long as he's nice to you and your brother, and as long as you want to go see him, you can. But if he's mean to you, we won't let you go with him. And I won't let him be mean to your mom, either."

She looked at him in surprise, but nodded slowly. Jake softened and seemed compelled to add, "I do think your dad is making some good changes, Becca, but there are still things that he needs to change. Everyone gets mad sometimes, and I'm sure it's difficult for your father to hear you call me 'Dad,' too. It's okay for him to tell you that it makes him feel sad, or even that it makes him feel angry. But it's not all right for him to be mean to you because of it, or to make you feel afraid. If he does that, you need to let your mom and me know so that we can do something about it."

"Okay," Rebecca agreed. She watched Jake silently for a moment before she left the room.

Jake clenched his hands into fists and said with gritted teeth, "What is wrong with him?"

"Jake, calm down," I said gently.

"Calm down? How can he threaten his own children like that?"

"He didn't threaten them," I pointed out as I laid a hand on Jake's arm. "He was disturbed by it, which is understandable to a degree. His behavior upset the kids a bit, but it's not like we're always perfect parents either. I'll talk to him. It'll be fine."

"Do you hear yourself?" he demanded, pulling his arm from my grasp. "I can't believe you're still defending him and justifying his behavior!"

"Jake—" I began.

He held his hand up and waited a few moments, apparently trying to get his emotion under control. "You're right, Maren, okay?" he finally told me. "You're right. It just makes me so angry to have him come to our home twice a month and think he can treat you with such disrespect. His whole arrogant attitude—" Jake looked at me and sighed. "I'll keep myself in check next time. I don't know what's wrong with me lately," he added, more thoughtfully than defensively. Then he told me firmly, "But I won't put up with him being mean to you, or to the kids."

"I know you won't. I won't either. And I know he's infuriating sometimes. Actually, it's kind of nice to have someone be protective of me for a change." I stretched up to kiss his cheek.

"It's too bad I wasn't there to be protective during your other three pregnancies," he muttered in disgust.

"Do you want to talk about something?" I asked carefully, touching his arm again.

"I just can't stand thinking of you living with him, Maren. It makes me sick to think of the way he treated you all those years. I can't believe the way he treats you now. I just—" He looked into my eyes and looked down again, shuffling some imaginary particle of something across the tile with the toe of his shoe. "I should have been there to take care of you," he finished softly.

"It wasn't by your own choice that you weren't," I admitted. "Anyway, you're here now."

His eyes met mine for a lingering moment before he turned to leave the room, and I wondered what else he was thinking.

"Dad?" I heard Jeffrey ask warily as soon as Jake walked into the kitchen. It startled me a bit since I'd thought all the children were playing downstairs.

"Hmm?" Jake responded, but he seemed distracted.

"Are you and Maren fighting?"

"No, buddy," Jake told him, sounding more focused then. "Everything's fine."

CHAPTER NINE

In February, I noted that Natalie had called me at least two or three times a week from the day she'd moved to Salt Lake. I was happy to have her close by, but I got the feeling that she was a little bored and lonely. I tried to go see her or take her to lunch at least a couple of times a month, but I had a lot more going on than she did, and I still wasn't feeling well. I thought she probably realized that, and hoped that she didn't feel neglected. I figured that she had her own family to attend to and keep her busy as well, so I didn't worry too much about her. As outgoing as Natalie was, I expected her to make friends with half the apartment building by the end of the first month.

Also that month, I got a new visiting teaching assignment. I glanced down at it and felt my heart drop. My partner was Ruth White, an elderly sister in the ward who I knew was in failing health and not likely to accompany me very often. We were assigned to visit two sisters—Hannah Maines, another young mother with whom I knew I could enjoy talking, and Lydia Workman. I closed my eyes and questioned silently, *Why me? Is this some sort of joke?* I almost laughed at the miserable irony as I shoved the slip of paper in my purse, and the assignment to the back of my mind.

Later that week, I went to my first doctor's appointment. I'd scheduled it on a Wednesday so Jake could go with me, although I'd been stunned when he'd suggested it. I thought back to our conversation.

"Why don't you make your appointment on a Wednesday, Mar, and I'll come with you?" he'd said.

"You want to come with me to the doctor?"

He'd looked up from the drawer where he was putting silverware away. "Yes. Unless you'd rather I didn't. I'm trying to be a support, not a nuisance."

"I'd love for you to come. I just didn't even think about it. I just always—" I'd stopped myself and changed what I was going to say. "Thanks," I'd told him with a smile.

He'd smiled back and offered, "I know a couple of good doctors if you'd like a recommendation."

"Thank you. I think I would. The doctor I had before was in Provo—I should find someone closer to home."

Now, as we walked toward the doctor's office hand-in-hand, I was still in awe at how involved Jake wanted to be, but I was happy to have him there. On the way down the hall, I told him, "One ground rule. No looking at the scales, the whole nine months. Never."

"What? You think you could get fat enough to chase me away?"

"Maybe," I said seriously. "But I'll try not to."

"I was only teasing," he said. "You have to gain weight when you're pregnant. It's not the same as getting fat. Even if you ever did get fat, I'd still love you."

I sighed. "I should still be going to the gym, but I'm just too tired and sick to get up and go in the mornings."

"The gym's been good for your self-esteem, hasn't it?" he observed.

"Yes. It's been very good for me, physically and emotionally."

"What equipment do you use when you go?" he asked.

"Usually just hand weights and the treadmill."

"What if we got those things at home? Would you feel like using them there?"

I hadn't even considered that possibility. "Probably. Actually, it would be very nice to just be able to work out at home when I feel like it." I looked up at him.

"I'll see what I can do," he said.

"You're a gem, you know that?" I squeezed his arm.

"You know you have me wrapped around your little finger, Mar. I'd give you anything you wanted if I could." He grinned.

"Anything?" I teased.

"Almost." He winked at me, and I laughed.

"I'm just grateful to have *you*," I said. "You're very sweet and perceptive. I hadn't even consciously realized how much going to the gym had boosted my self-esteem, but you did. That happened long before we were married too."

"I try to pay attention." He stopped outside the door to the doctor's office before going in and kissed me.

I sat down in the waiting room with a stack of new-patient paperwork. I always cringed when filling in the column titled "complications" under my first pregnancy: *Baby died shortly after birth, presumably due to complications resulting from a shortage of oxygen.* I tried to write the words mechanically and not let myself feel them.

Jake sat with his arm around me, his right ankle resting on his left knee. "How does it feel to have to take a turn sitting in the waiting room?" I teased, as I checked boxes regarding my health history.

He smirked. "Actually, it's a refreshing change—especially since I'm not the one seeing the doctor."

I elbowed him in the ribs.

When I met Dr. Stewart, I liked him right away. He shook Jake's hand. "Jake! Good to see you!" Then he turned to me. "So this is Mrs. Jantzen. It's a pleasure to meet you, Maren. I guess I don't need to tell you what a good man your husband is."

I smiled. "No, I've known that for quite some time."

When we heard the little whoosh-whoosh sound of the baby's heartbeat, Jake squeezed my hand and smiled at me. This was our baby, Jake's and mine, and there was the little heartbeat to prove that it was true. I felt my eyes grow misty as I smiled back at my husband.

Dr. Stewart said that everything looked good, gave me a prescription to help with the nausea, and told me that he'd see me in a month.

"Aren't you going to give me the due date?" I asked.

"Oh, didn't the nurse tell you? Let me look it up here. I guess you're anxious to start counting down the days, eh?" he chuckled.

"It helps," I agreed.

He looked at my chart and announced, "August second."

A startled look crossed Jake's face as Dr. Stewart left the room.

"What?" I asked him.

"Nothing." He shook his head.

"What was that look for then?"

"What look?" he asked innocently.

"You suddenly looked like you'd seen a ghost. Why?" I demanded, feeling uneasy.

He bit his bottom lip.

"And now you're biting your lip, which you only do when you're nervous," I pointed out, and then insisted again, "Why? Is something wrong?"

He smiled and reassured me, "No, Mar, nothing's wrong. The due date just surprised me a little. I don't know why. It's no big deal, just a weird coincidence."

I raised my eyebrows and waited for him to continue.

After a pause, he shrugged and said, "August second is Tess's birthday, that's all."

"My baby is due on your ex-wife's birthday?" I asked.

"Strange, isn't it?"

I felt annoyed at first, and then I felt sick again. I didn't even want to think about Jake being married to someone else, having children with another woman. It had never bothered me as much as it did at that moment. I'd also been married before, after all. "Did you go to her doctors' appointments too?" I said sarcastically, letting the thought slip off my tongue before I realized what I'd done.

Jake folded his arms on his chest and watched me quietly for a minute, that muscle in his jaw twitching again. "If you must know— no, I didn't," he finally admitted. "I was too busy with my residency at the hospital. I made mistakes the first time around that I'm trying not to duplicate." He added with a hint of sarcasm that defied his usual nature, "Maybe it's a good thing you turned me down the first time after all, Maren. You might've ended up married to a real jerk." I saw the pain in his expression, and felt the sting of his words as he walked out of the room.

I didn't know why I felt so distraught about Tess. I was finally married to Jake, pregnant with his child . . . *A child that might not be sealed to him,* the thought struck me. I told myself that I knew better than that, but I suddenly felt ill and ran across the hall to the bathroom. Even after I threw up, I couldn't stop the dry heaves. There was nothing left in my stomach, but I just felt sick. Jake still looked frustrated when I finally made it out to the car, but he said calmly, "I'm sorry, Mar. I shouldn't have even said anything about the due date. It's irrelevant. It just caught me by surprise." He cleared his throat and looked out the front windshield. "And I'm sorry for saying what I did. That was just a hurtful thing to say."

I was surprised that he was apologizing to me, and was struck with a wave of guilt. "I'm sorry too," I responded. "I guess I asked for it. I certainly have no right to resent your first marriage."

"But you do resent it," he observed quietly as he turned to face me. "Don't you?"

I shrugged and looked out the window.

Jake sighed and said, "You know, this prying-everything-out-of-you business is beginning to wear me out."

"Then don't pry," I snapped.

"And what's going to happen if I don't?" he challenged. "Are you ever going to talk to me at all? Or are you just going to keep stuffing everything deeper and deeper inside until you start to resent *me,* too?"

I just looked at him, wondering what was happening to us after only three months of marriage.

Jake softened his voice and asked genuinely, "Am I so difficult to talk to, Maren?"

I considered him for a moment before I confided, "All right, Jake. I do resent your first marriage. And that makes me angry with myself because I know it's not fair. I admit I saw some humanity in Tess before she left, and it surprised me. I even felt empathy for her situation after I listened to her explanation of it. But I still feel angry with her for being cold and selfish, for breezing back into her children's lives to replace me after I'd grown to love them, and then leaving them empty. Jeff hasn't been the same since she left, and I think he directs that anger at me. I'm so frustrated with him that I don't know what to do. He's like a completely different child. And it does make me sick to think of you spending seven years of your life with her, having children with her—I just wish your first wife's shadow wasn't always over everything."

Jake was quiet for a minute before saying, "Tess's shadow isn't over anything, Mar. I love *you.* And it doesn't matter when the due date is—it's *our* baby."

I felt angry with myself for even worrying about Tess at all. Jake never made me feel like I was in second place. I did all that to myself. When I didn't respond, Jake considered me carefully for a long time before he spoke again. "It seems that you're afraid to let me love you, Maren." He cut right into my heart. "That's all I've ever wanted to do."

After a few quiet moments, when I still didn't answer him, Jake looked away from me and put the car in gear.

On the drive home, I willed myself to think logically. There was no reason to let Tess bother me, I realized. I knew that God would work everything out in the hereafter. And we'd neither seen nor heard from her for several months now. I decided that perhaps I needed to pray for peace on the matter, and felt better at the thought. I reached for Jake's hand and squeezed it.

He let his eyes dart from the road just long enough to smile and give me a brief kiss.

That weekend, Jake bought me weights and a treadmill and we set them up in the basement. "I know you've already been working out for the past several months," he told me, "but just take it easy, will you? Remember, you're pregnant."

I raised my eyebrows at him. "How could I forget?"

"Funny, Mar," he said. "Very funny."

I laughed and kissed him. "Thank you."

"You're welcome."

***

Over the next few days, I sincerely prayed for help to accept the issue of Jake being sealed to Tess. Logically, I knew that I had nothing to be concerned about, but I asked the Lord to help my heart catch up with my head. I began to feel a serenity that I hadn't before; and for the most part, I was finally able to let the subject drop from my mind.

I also did a lot of thinking about the conversation I'd had with Jake after my doctor's appointment. I finally shared my thoughts with him. "Honey? I've been thinking, and . . . well, maybe continuing with a little counseling wouldn't be a bad idea."

Jake cracked a smile and quipped, "Whatever you think, love."

I smirked, but told him, "I'll make an appointment. You want to come with me?"

"Absolutely."

I scheduled an appointment for the following week with the marriage-and-family counselor I'd seen for several months by myself. Since I hadn't spoken with him for a while, I informed him of my recent marriage, and explained a few details over the phone. "Well, it's good to see you again, Maren," he told me with a genuine smile when Jake and I arrived at his office.

"Thanks." I smiled back, though a little guiltily. "This is my husband, Jake Jantzen. Jake, my counselor, Miles Wilson."

Miles extended his hand and said, "Pleasure to meet you, Jake."

Jake looked a bit nervous as he replied, "Yes, you too."

We spent the first session mostly filling him in on our relationship, telling him about the children, and describing a few of our struggles. We also told him about the difficulties Jeffrey was having.

Miles nodded thoughtfully, tapping a pen on the notebook he held in his lap. "A few family therapy sessions might be beneficial," he said. "Although the children are still quite young . . . Perhaps I could talk with Jeffrey alone sometime. Of course, I'd want him to come in with both of you and get to know me a little first. I try to be very careful with children. He'd need to feel comfortable with me before I could get him to open up at all."

Jake and I sat quietly thinking for a minute.

"Why don't we concentrate on the two of you and your relationship for a bit?" Miles decided finally. "It's only been three months since you were married, and especially with all of the other disruptions you've told me about in your son's life, an adjustment period is certainly to be expected. If he continues to struggle, however, you should consider bringing him in."

"That sounds reasonable," Jake agreed.

"Good then," Miles finished. "I'll see you in a month. And I'd like to commend your efforts, by the way. Second marriages are typically more challenging from the beginning, and a little counseling can go a long way in helping any marriage succeed."

"Thanks, Miles," I told him.

"Thank you," Jake echoed. As we left the building, Jake said, "Well now, that wasn't so painful, was it?"

I laughed at him. "You certainly look relieved, anyway. You've never done this before, have you?"

"Nope." He shrugged. "It's not so bad though. It'll probably be a good thing for us."

"Well, it certainly helped me before," I agreed. "I'm sorry I was a little stubborn about coming back, but I'm glad you suggested it."

Jake just smiled and took my hand.

***

As the month wore on, I started feeling immense pressure from my conscience to do my visiting teaching. I finally succumbed to guilt and called Sister White. "Oh, I don't go out in the winter, dear," she explained in a patient voice. "Too hard on my brittle bones. I get to church when I can, but I'm too old to go visiting. Why don't you just go ahead without me?"

So I did. It wasn't hard to visit Hannah. I found her home the first time I called and went to see her a couple of days later. I took her some cookies, summed up the visiting teaching message, and chatted with her for a few minutes. "Do you need anything?" I asked the standard question, but was relieved to get the standard response. "Oh, no." I was still feeling poorly a good deal of the time, and didn't know if I could handle any extra burdens.

I left three messages for Lydia. I tried sounding bright and cheerful, quiet and humble, and businesslike. None of my approaches worked. She never called back. I figured she probably had caller I.D. and purposely didn't pick up when I phoned. I finally left a plate of cookies outside the door of her basement apartment, with a note saying that I'd stopped by. I went in the middle of a weekday afternoon, telling myself that it was a good time because the children were all in school. The fact that Lydia was at work was simply a coincidence.

***

The beginning of March marked two years since Ted and I had separated. I was surprised that I noted the date with a twinge of sadness. It seemed like so long ago. So much had changed. Jake and I went to the temple together that weekend. We tried to go at least once a month. Sitting in the celestial room next to Jake, I whispered, "It's so nice to be here with you." I'd sat there alone countless times, aching to have my husband's arm around me and whisper quietly with him like the other couples I saw all around me.

He squeezed me to him and kissed my forehead.

In the car in the temple parking lot, Jake turned toward me and said, "Can we talk about something, Mar?"

Some of the peacefulness I'd felt in the temple turned to hesitation at the underlying seriousness in his tone, but I forced a smile and replied, "Sure, honey."

"We've been married nearly four months now," he started. "I know we still have adjustments to make, but things have settled down somewhat, and with you being pregnant and everything, I thought . . . well, maybe now would be a good time to turn in your request for a sealing cancellation."

My mind drew a blank, and I could only stare at him. "Uh . . . huh," I stammered slowly. "I guess maybe . . . it would be. Or maybe we should wait a bit until I'm feeling a little better and then—" I stopped myself abruptly as electrical currents from his eyes ripped into me.

"What's holding you back, Maren?" Jake demanded. *"What?"*

"You're . . . sealed to Tess, Jake," I mumbled softly.

"Yeah," he replied with cool sarcasm. "So?"

"All right," I finally conceded. "I'll get started on the paperwork. I'm just a little . . . overwhelmed with it all right now, I guess." I wondered why I felt hollow.

Jake turned away from me to look out the window for several contemplative moments. When he turned back, I couldn't tell . . . Was it anger brewing in his eyes? . . . Or fear? I braced myself for his rebuke, but his voice was even. "That's something you should do because you want to," he decided quietly, "not because you feel forced to." He rested his elbow on the steering wheel and rubbed his eyes with a thumb and forefinger for several tense seconds. When he at last met my gaze, he looked utterly dejected, but he told me softly, "I'll wait until you're ready, Mar."

I narrowed my eyes in confusion, trying to weave his words and his body language together to get a clear picture. But the image was blurred by an all-too-familiar fog that swirled around me and threatened to envelop me every time this subject came up.

CHAPTER TEN

When Natalie and I went to lunch that week, I told her about my dilemma. "So, I think Jake's pretty upset," I finished, after explaining everything to her. "And understandably so. I just feel so . . . guilty, Natalie. I don't know what to do."

"Are you crazy, Maren?" she demanded, leaning across the table toward me. "What do you mean you 'don't know what to do'? You cancel your sealing to the guy with the capital 'L' tattooed on his forehead, and get sealed to the man who loves you and has the maturity to handle life."

I gave a humorless laugh and said, "It's not that simple, Nat."

She rolled her eyes. "Oh, for heaven's sake, Maren! Life *is* simple. People like you make it complicated."

I looked at my sister and wished that I hadn't been desperate enough to pour my heart out to her. I should have realized that she wouldn't understand. I resisted the urge to snap back at her, reminding myself that she was inexperienced. In that moment, I missed Ann desperately and wished that she had been there to talk to instead.

"Maren," Natalie said more quietly. "Jake loves you. He takes care of you, he's good to the kids, he lives the gospel . . . This is obviously killing him." She paused thoughtfully and then told me, "Maybe you still have that masochistic thing going. Have you thought about that? I mean, you seemed to have really found yourself after you finally got up the guts to kick Ted out. But maybe . . . Maybe you haven't completely recovered from living in a nightmare for ten years, you know? Ted had you convinced that you were worthless. Do you think that you could possibly still believe that in there somewhere? Just a little bit?"

"I'm not sure what your point is," I told her, feeling more than a little irritated at being raked over the coals by my little sister. *She's a baby,* I thought to myself. *She has no idea what she's talking about.*

"My point is that maybe you're still punishing yourself," Natalie stated bluntly. "Maybe you still think you don't deserve a righteous husband who really loves you. Maybe the thought of wholeheartedly diving into this marriage terrifies you—because of your trust issues."

By then, I felt myself gaping at her as I sat in stunned silence.

Natalie shrugged. "You took college psychology, right? You've heard of that 'self-fulfilling prophecy' thing? If you keep shoving Jake away, maybe you'll eventually shut him out completely. And then where will you be? Coexisting in a lifeless marriage, doing everything yourself, and feeling emotionally shut down? Maybe that's still your comfort zone after living that way for so many years, Maren. Look, you know I love you, and I'm telling you this for your own good— This is your own life you're sabotaging now. You'd better be careful."

I thought about Natalie's words all the way home. I wanted to believe that there was no truth to them, but something deep inside prevented me from completely convincing myself.

I went looking for Jake as soon as I walked into our house. It was Wednesday, so I knew he was there somewhere. After checking everywhere else, I finally headed downstairs to his office. I paused outside the door when I heard him talking to someone on the phone.

"I'm just so completely frustrated," he was saying. After a pause, he replied, "Of course I love her. You know that." There was a longer pause, and then Jake laughed a little. "Yeah, you're great at playing the devil's advocate . . . Things are going all right then? . . . I'm sure you do," he said quietly, after listening for a few moments. "It's gotta be rough . . . All right, I'll tell her. Give us a call when you get up here next . . . Yeah, you too. Good to talk to you."

I waited a few seconds before knocking on the door and pushing it open. Jake was sitting at his desk, looking contemplative. "Hi," I said.

He glanced up and smiled tentatively. "Hi."

"You working on something?" I asked him curiously.

"Nah . . . Just talking to Tyler. He says hello, by the way."

I sat on the corner of Jake's desk and inquired, "How's he doing?"

"He sounds pretty good, actually. A bit lonely, I guess. But then you'd know that. Ann hasn't been gone that long."

"Seven months," I responded, still feeling the ache of my best friend's absence. I couldn't imagine how badly Tyler must be hurting. "Is he coming up anytime soon?" I asked, nodding toward the phone.

Jake shook his head. "Doesn't sound like it. I don't think he can stand the thought of coming back here yet. At least in St. George he's not constantly surrounded by memories."

I nodded in understanding, though I wished Tyler would come for a visit. I missed him almost as much as Ann, and I knew that Jake did too.

I'd wanted to talk to Jake about my conversation with Natalie, but I felt apprehensive suddenly. I knew the subject was touchy, and I guessed from what I'd heard that maybe he'd been discussing it with Tyler. I decided to leave it alone for a few days while I considered Natalie's observations and my own inner motives—to honestly compare them to my behavior.

***

That weekend Rebecca and Trevor were more eager than usual to go with Ted. "Why are you guys so excited to go with Daddy?" I asked them casually as we were packing their backpacks.

"'Cause it was really fun there last time," Trevor said. "Daddy has a basketball court at his apartments, and he took us there."

"Yep," Rebecca agreed. "And to the playground, too. He lets us go down the slide, even when there's snow on it."

"Really?" I asked, trying not to sound too critical.

My daughter gave me a bright smile and said, "Uh-huh. Daddy's just nicer now, Mommy. He's fun to be with."

"I'm glad, sweetheart," I told her, but I couldn't help questioning Ted's progress. In fact, I wondered about it all weekend. By the time Rebecca and Trevor arrived home on Sunday afternoon, I'd resigned myself to giving Ted the benefit of the doubt, and truly hoped that his progress was genuine.

I was glad that Ted had brought the children back in time for dinner since we'd invited Natalie and Doug over. We were just finishing the meal when the telephone rang. Jake hesitated, but then got up to answer it. I heard him talking quietly in the kitchen for a minute, though I didn't pay too much attention to what was being said. "Who was that?" I asked with only mild interest when he returned to the table.

"I'll tell you later," he answered quietly. His response heightened my curiosity, but I let it drop when I saw the anxiety in his expression.

Once dinner was cleaned up, Jake asked my sister and her husband discreetly, "Do you guys have time to stay with the kids for a little while? Something's come up that Maren and I need to attend to."

"Sure," Natalie agreed after glancing at Doug for confirmation. "Is everything all right?"

"Yes," he assured her, but I felt uneasy. "And I promise to return the favor."

"We'll hold you to it," Doug responded with a grin.

Jake told the children that we had an appointment and that we'd be back soon. "Be good for Aunt Natalie and Uncle Doug," he instructed. We left them playing happily on the family room floor with Nathan. I hoped they'd stay that way until we got back.

"What's up?" I asked as soon as we were in the car.

Jake rested his hand on the back of my seat and looked over his shoulder as he backed out of the garage. His cheek twitched when he answered me. "That was Tess on the phone."

"What?" I asked in disbelief. "What does she want?"

"She's in town visiting her mother—she wants to talk to us while she's here."

"Oh, no," I muttered, pressing a palm against my forehead. "Jake, you can't let her do this again. She's been gone for six months. She signed away her parental rights. Jeff still isn't back to normal. You can't let her see Jeff and Lizzy. You *can't!*" I was feeling increasingly alarmed and tried to keep it out of my voice.

"Calm down, Mar," Jake answered, though his voice didn't sound terribly calm either. "I *absolutely won't* let her do this again."

"Why did you even agree to see her?" I asked, feeling annoyed.

"I figured it would be easier for all of us if we could settle things peacefully," he responded. "I'd like to avoid a nasty court battle if I can." He took my hand and let his eyes dart from the road to my face for a moment. "But don't worry—I'll go to court if I have to."

I sighed, feeling a degree of relief in his conviction.

Tess answered the door at her mother's house, looking just as I'd remembered her. Her long, sleek, auburn hair hung straight down her back. She wore more makeup than I did, and more jewelry. Everything about her looked expensive. She *was* beautiful, but I was surprised to note that I didn't feel the least bit intimidated by her anymore. I was suddenly reminded of the peace I'd recently had regarding Tess, and her marriage to Jake, and felt immensely relieved that she no longer seemed a threat. Tess actually appeared to be nervous, but she managed a smile as she greeted us. "Hi."

"Hi," Jake answered her curtly, unconsciously tightening his grip on my hand.

"Come in," she invited us, holding the door open.

Jake and I sat on the old-fashioned brocade sofa Tess motioned us toward. The house she'd grown up in wasn't what I'd expected. It was modest and only relatively tasteful. There were several pictures in the room. Many of them were of Jeff and Lizzy. Some were of Tess during her childhood and teenage years.

Jake glanced around and then asked outright, "Where's your mother?"

"Ward choir practice," Tess answered from a nearby chair. "That's why I thought this would be a good time."

Jake raised an eyebrow at her but said nothing.

"So, I hear you're going to have another baby," Tess volunteered. Her attempt at small talk completely threw me for a loop. In my experience, she was a straight-to-the-point person, bordering on harsh.

"Yes, we are," Jake answered matter-of-factly.

"When's it due?" Tess questioned.

When Jake only furrowed his brows, I responded with a slight smile. "August second."

"Really?" Tess looked surprised.

"Really," Jake answered with obvious irritation.

Tess glanced at me then, and said with apparent sincerity, "Well, you look great, Maren. I don't know how you do it. You're not even showing yet."

I tried to hide my shock at the compliment by answering smoothly, "Thank you."

"Are Jeffrey and Elizabeth excited about the baby?" she asked hesitantly.

"Yes," Jake said simply.

"Yeah . . . of course they are." Tess seemed almost to be talking to herself. "So, how are they?"

"They're struggling," Jake informed her coolly. "Jeff's had some very rough months."

Tess looked mildly alarmed, and then sad. She didn't ask any more questions. "Well, I appreciate the two of you taking time to come over. Did you say Maren's sister was there to stay with the kids?" she asked Jake.

He only nodded.

"That's nice. Anyway, thanks for agreeing to see me. Look, I guess I could have told you this over the phone. Actually, I probably didn't need to tell you at all—Bishop Nelson said he was going to send you a letter. I guess I just felt like since I was here anyway, I ought to make the effort to tell you in person."

"Tell us what?" Jake asked skeptically. He looked as confused as I felt. When Tess hesitated to respond, Jake voiced my silent question. "What does a letter from Bishop Nelson have to do with the children?"

"The children?" Tess asked, looking a bit confused herself. "Well, nothing, really. Or everything—depending on how you look at it, I guess."

Jake considered her carefully for a minute before saying, "Tess, I can't let you see them. I'm sorry, but I just can't. It's been six months, you know. That's forever to a child. And after all they've been through—"

Tess cut him off as understanding seeped into her countenance. "Jake, I don't want to see the kids."

"What?" he asked.

"I mean, I *want* to see them. I miss them. I . . . ." Her eyes grew misty as her words evaporated. Then she snapped out of it and explained, "I signed them away, I know. I gave them to you. As much as I'd love to see them, I know it would only hurt them in the long run because . . . well, I'm not staying. You know that."

"You mean, you didn't call us over here to try to back out of our agreement?" Jake asked in surprise. "You're not going to ask to see the kids?"

"No!" Tess exclaimed, as though she couldn't believe he would suspect such a thing. "Of course not."

Jake looked completely baffled for a moment before his expression changed, and he asked slowly, "You want money?"

"Oh, for heaven's sake, Jacob!" Tess rolled her eyes and looked completely disgusted. I didn't think the assumption was that far-fetched, considering her history, but I kept my mouth shut.

"I signed that away too, I know," Tess clarified. "And I don't need your money."

"Vance is keeping you in the lifestyle you want then?" Jake asked with only a trace of sarcasm.

"Yes, actually," Tess responded. "Things are going very well."

"But you're still not going to marry him?" Jake inquired. I wasn't sure if he was asking out of curiosity, concern, or disapproval.

"No, I'm not," Tess stated firmly. "That would simply ruin a good thing. I've decided I'm just not the marrying kind."

"I'm glad you finally discovered that," Jake muttered almost under his breath.

Tess looked at him long and hard. "You're not making this very easy."

Jake sighed and leaned back against the couch, looking tired all of a sudden. "I'm sorry," he answered. "I suppose I got a little worked up, thinking you were going to insist on seeing the kids, and that I was going to have to fight you to protect them. I'm relieved to find that's not the case, but I'm afraid I don't see the point of all this. Why, exactly, are we here, Tess?"

Tess hesitated, but then ventured, "Before I tell you, I just have one question. I know it's none of my business, and I'm pretty sure I know the answer anyway, but I just want to know if . . . well, the two of you are still happy, right? I mean, you still love each other, and you want to be together and all of that, don't you?"

I couldn't help wondering about her motives as Jake glanced at me and squeezed my hand. "Yes," he answered resolutely when he turned back to Tess.

"Good." It floored me to see her smile before she went on. "So, you know that Bishop Nelson kept threatening to call me back in for another Church court hearing," she started to explain to Jake. "After the first one, I mean," she clarified, "when they disfellowshipped me."

"Yes," he answered hesitantly. "Although I didn't really think it was a threat. It was more a word of caution, something for you to take under advisement."

"Of course." She smirked. "So, you remember?"

"I remember the bishop discussing that with us once or twice," Jake agreed.

"Well, he finally called me back in," Tess explained. I just watched her, wondering what on earth this had to do with Jake or me. "I won't bore you with the details," Tess went on, "but the bottom line is that the bishop pretty much told me I had to change my life. He was nice, and fatherly, and compassionate, and all of that. But I told him that my life is exactly what I want it to be, and that I'm not going to change it. He asked me about my testimony. I told him that I didn't have one, and that I'm not sure now if I ever did." Tess sighed before confessing, "So Bishop Nelson told me that I've lost the guidance of the Spirit in my life because of my continuing poor choices. He asked me if I would be willing to pray, to read the scriptures, and to ask God if it's true."

When she paused, Jake asked quietly, "And what did you tell him?"

"I told him no," Tess answered simply. "I told him that I don't want to know if it's true. As I said, I'm living the life I want to live, and I don't want anyone to tell me that I can't. Then the bishop asked me if I would at least marry Vance—he wants me to quit living in sin, though he didn't actually say that—but I told him no way. As soon as you become a wife, it's all over for you. Your husband quits trying to impress you, forgets about you, gets too busy for you, expects you to have his children, and then puts them in front of you." She paused to shake her head and decided, "Let's not go there again. The point is, when I became a wife, that was my first step down a road I didn't want to be on. Then I became a mother, and I almost forgot who I was completely. I far prefer to be a girlfriend. Men don't forget their girlfriends. They don't take them for granted because they know they could walk away in a split second and never look back."

I felt overwhelmingly sorry for Tess as I listened to her. I knew that she and Jake had experienced their share of difficulties. Jake and I had been through plenty of challenges already as well. But I knew that the joy and security to be found in a solid marriage with a committed spouse were so much more fulfilling than anything she was describing.

Jake looked hard at Tess and said, "I'm sorry."

"What?" she asked, apparently bewildered. I looked at him in astonishment myself.

"I'm sorry," he repeated. "For all the mistakes I made when we were married. I'm sorry for hurting you. I'm sorry for giving up, for not working on things like I should have. I'm not saying that I'm sorry the marriage is over. I love Maren, and I think you and I are both better off. But I've come to realize that I made many mistakes, and I ought to ask your forgiveness."

I sat in stunned silence as Tess's mouth dropped open. *"You're* apologizing to *me?"* she asked Jake.

"I am."

She laughed and shook her head. "You always were too good to be true. Yeah, you messed up here and there, Jake. Nothing like what I did, but there were little things . . . Look, I know I was a spoiled brat, and you were trying to get through a residency, and be the mom as well as the dad, and . . . Well, you had the patience of Job. You should've left me long before I left you, ya know? So if it makes you feel better, I'll forgive you. But if you're thinking that my mistakes or my viewpoint are somehow the result of something you did, you're wrong. If I couldn't be happy married to you and trying to live as a good Mormon, then I know I couldn't do it with anyone else. You're one of the few decent men in the world. It wasn't you. It was just the whole marriage and family and religion thing—It's simply not for me."

Jake looked surprised, but then nodded and prompted, "Well, now that I got that off my chest, go on with your story. You said the bishop called you in."

"Yes." Tess nodded. "After we talked, Bishop Nelson said that it was with regret that he was going to have to recommend another bishop's court, but that it was for my own good. I told him I wasn't going to come, but that he could go ahead and do whatever he thought was best."

Jake actually looked concerned as he said, "Tess, even if it wasn't my fault, there's so much more to it than what you've described. The gospel and eternal marriage are part of God's plan for our happiness. Is this really what you want for your life? You're short-changing yourself in a big way. I know it's none of my business, but I can't help feeling—"

Tess interrupted quickly, almost as though she feared what he was going to say. "You can't help feeling what, Jacob?" she asked, then continued without waiting for a response. "Responsible? Well, you're not—I just told you that. My choices are my own. You made a valiant attempt to save me when we were still married, even after you found out what I'd done. I just didn't want to be saved."

"But, Tess, surely on some level you still know the gospel is true—"

"I told you, Jake, I don't *want* to know. I don't want to have to wrestle with my conscience every day."

"But if you *have* to wrestle with your conscience every day, then you must know—"

"Jake!" Tess protested. "Bug off, okay? I didn't call you over here to preach to me, or to try to send you on some kind of guilt trip. You're not responsible for me. You're right—this is none of your business. This has nothing to do with you, especially now. Which is what I've been *trying* to tell you . . . They excommunicated me."

"What?" Jake asked, looking dazed.

"Are you really so surprised, Jake?" Tess responded quietly. "You must have known that it was only a matter of time."

Jake evidently picked up on the bitter edge to her voice as he began carefully, "Tess, the purpose of excommunication isn't to punish someone. It's to give them an opportunity to repent, to accept the gift of the Atonement and change their lives—"

"Yes, Jake, I know all that. Bishop Nelson made it all very clear. You know me," she said flippantly, though I suspected there must be pain in there somewhere, "I'm not very patient. I'm far more concerned with here and now than I am with some abstract concept of forever."

Jake opened his mouth, but Tess held up her hand to stop him. "I know, Jake, okay? I'm well aware of the strength of your testimony. I know you believe the gospel with everything in you. I know you're completely committed to it. But there's nothing you can say. There's nothing you can do. I'm simply not your concern any longer, in any sense of the word." She gave him a slight smile before she waved a hand at me and commanded, "Now, take your wife home to that houseful of kids and live happily ever after. I'll see ya around."

After a long pause, Jake finally stood, pulling me up with him. He looked at Tess once more, but she only waved us toward the door.

"Good luck, Tess," I said, feeling like I ought to say something.

"Thanks," she responded. "You too, Maren." She hesitated before adding with a shaky voice, "Take good care of my kids, will you?"

Her comment hit me with a huge conglomeration of emotions, but I only said, "I'm doing my best."

She nodded and smiled as a trail of tears escaped down her face. Jake led me to the door without looking back.

In the car, I observed aloud, "She's changed."

"A little," Jake conceded as he shook his head sadly. "But not enough." He started down the street, but then pulled over in front of a park a few blocks away. He just sat in silent contemplation for a few moments.

I finally decided that maybe he needed to talk about it and asked, "So, how do you feel about all of this?"

He shifted his gaze to search my face. "I feel deeply sad for Tess," he admitted. "She's denying the truth to herself and giving up eternal blessings for temporary thrills. But I don't see that the bishop and his counselors had any other choice, really. She's an endowed member of the Church, who knowingly committed a terrible sin, and continues to, and she's not sorry. She broke up a temple marriage, she violated the covenants she's made . . . The bishop tried to help her, and she did finally move out here. But then she went to New York again and moved back in with the guy." Jake paused to shake his head. "She did tell me once that she loved him, you know. But as you just heard for yourself, she doesn't want to marry him. That's too much commitment for her. She thinks it would just ruin a good thing."

"I'm sorry, Jake," I said softly, not knowing what else to say.

"So am I," he agreed. "For Tess. But she's right, there's nothing I can do. She has her agency. And if the Church court determined this was best for her, then I'm sure it must be."

I just sat quietly watching him. I knew it must be painful for him to see Tess on a self-destructive path, with no desire to change. I could definitely relate to some of that feeling firsthand with Ted. I realized that I could also relate to some of the guilt that he was apparently feeling, even though I knew that Tess's problems weren't his fault.

"To tell you the truth, Mar," Jake admitted slowly, "it's a relief in many ways. I don't have to worry about her anymore."

I nodded, though I didn't understand the intensity in his expression.

"I love you, Maren," Jake whispered with fervor.

I smiled and echoed, "And I love you."

He slid his hand around the back of my neck and threaded his fingers through my hair, watching me all the time. I felt my brows furrow slightly in question before he kissed me tenderly. "I love you," he whispered again, as his lips brushed my face.

I didn't get a chance to question the source of his exaggerated ardor before he kissed me once more. I decided it must just be the result of too many emotions running together, and let myself get lost in his affection for a moment.

When Jake finally broke away, he gave me a breathless smile. He threw his head back to laugh at the ceiling, and then hugged me tightly.

"You're certainly in a good mood," I observed in a bewildered voice.

He seemed oblivious to my confusion as he answered happily, "Yes, I am. Now, I guess we'd better go rescue your sister from my son."

"I guess so . . ." I agreed slowly as he pulled back onto the road and headed for home.

CHAPTER ELEVEN

Jake's upbeat mood lingered for several days. It seemed a little off to me, but I finally just dismissed it as apparent relief that he no longer felt responsible for Tess.

Toward the end of the following week, I was feeling better than usual one evening. At that moment, all four children were playing contentedly downstairs. I impulsively turned on the radio and danced while I made dinner. An Enrique Iglesias song came on, one that I loved. I wiped off the counters as I danced to it. I heard Jake come in, but I didn't hear him come up behind me. When I reached a hand into the air, he took it from behind, startling me. Then he wrapped his other arm around my waist and pulled me tightly against him.

He moved right into the step that I was doing, then twirled me around to face him, still dancing with me. He took the dishcloth from my hand and threw it toward the sink as he led me slowly around the kitchen floor. I laughed softly and laid against his chest as I listened to the words of the music: *I can be your hero, baby. I can kiss away the pain. I will stay right here forever. You can take my breath away . . .*

When I looked up at Jake, he kissed me tenderly, but didn't stop moving to the music. After the song ended, he put his cheek next to mine and whispered, "I'm not going to be so presumptuous as to go for the hero thing, but I *am* trying to take away your pain . . . and I'll absolutely be here forever."

I smiled and kissed him. "You definitely take my breath away. You know, I always dreamed of my husband doing that."

"Taking your breath away?" He raised an eyebrow at me.

I laughed. "That, too, I suppose. What I meant, though, was that when I was young and hopelessly romantic, I used to dream that my husband would come home and just take me in his arms and dance with me like this in the kitchen."

He grinned as he resumed twirling me across the floor to the next song and remarked, "Really? That's funny, because he does. That dream was certainly easy enough to make come true . . . Do you have any others?" He leaned close to me to whisper, "I *still am* hopelessly romantic."

I touched his cheek and answered him seriously. "You're more than I ever even dreamed, Jake. I still . . ." I stopped to fight away the emotion that rose without warning.

Jake stopped moving and just held me. "You still what, love?" he asked gently.

I shook my head. "I still can't believe this is my life, after all these years. You won't stop loving me . . . will you?"

"Nope," he answered resolutely. "Loving you is just a fact of my existence, Mar."

I suddenly had another unsettling thought and voiced it, "Did you ever come home and dance with Tess like this?"

Jake laughed, but then sobered up when he saw my expression. "No, sweetheart, I didn't. She would've told me I was being silly—or more likely, she'd have just turned away and ignored me. She was never in the kitchen, anyway."

I couldn't help smiling at the look of amusement on his face. He became more serious then and said, "I swear, Maren, I'm going to find you. I know that self-assured girl I fell in love with in college is still in there somewhere. Somehow I'm going to make you believe that I love you completely."

I stared at him in awe for a moment before I pressed a hand into his hair and kissed him. "I can't even tell you how I love you, Jake," I said softly when I pulled away from him, feeling completely at a loss for words.

"Then show me," he whispered back with a teasing smile. He swept me into his arms again and kissed me dramatically. Then I laughed and turned to check on dinner. As I pondered the things Jake had said, several different thoughts began swirling in my mind. I thought about the conversation we'd had with Tess a couple of weeks ago, and a few unanswered questions began nagging at me, intruding on the serenity I'd felt. Determined to put them to rest, I resolved to talk to Jake right away.

However, it was much later that night when I finally had an opportunity to talk to him again. "Could I ask you about something?" I said, after we'd finished reading scriptures together.

Jake had been reaching over to turn off his lamp, but sat back up to look at me. "Depends on what it is," he replied.

I smiled inwardly at his return to more typical behavior, and gave him the look of mild annoyance that I was sure he was expecting. He positioned himself to give me his full attention, then commanded, "Shoot."

I became more serious as I asked him the questions that had been bothering me since our conversation that afternoon. "What mistakes did you make in your first marriage? . . . And why did you apologize to Tess?"

Jake sighed and leaned back against the headboard. He was silent for several moments, his brows furrowed in thought.

"You don't have to tell me if you don't want to," I finally remarked a little defensively.

Jake looked at me then, and I caught a glimpse of fear in his expression. "I'll tell you if you want me to, Mar," he said. "I was just thinking . . ." He blew out a long breath and began, "To be perfectly honest . . . I think I put you on a pedestal to some extent. I told myself that I'd put you out of my mind, but then when things got difficult, I started comparing Tess to you—which wasn't fair. I was gone a lot, and although I did what I had to do for the children when I was home, I virtually quit making any effort at all to work on the marriage. I tried to hold on to Tess and felt terrified of losing her, but I didn't even cry when she left. I felt sad, and guilty, and empty . . . but most of all, I felt relieved. It was one less thing I had to worry about . . . And I did things that hurt her," Jake continued cautiously. "Even though I may have been in denial about them at the time."

"How did you hurt her?" I asked.

Jake considered me carefully before admitting, "Well . . . I don't want to hurt *you* by saying this. . . but the first thing that comes to mind is that I probably shouldn't have kept the ring I bought for you. Tess found it once and asked me about it."

"Did you tell her the truth?" I asked uneasily.

"Yes, but it was hard, and I felt pretty guilt-ridden."

"What did she say about it?" I probed, wondering if I really wanted to know, but sensing that Jake needed to confess it.

"She said that she was certainly glad I hadn't given it to her, that it was far too simple for her taste. She picked out her own ring—some horrible gaudy thing." Jake paused to rub his eyes. He suddenly looked exhausted.

"Well . . ." I said. "That's not great, but it doesn't sound too terrible."

Jake looked miserable and finally confided, "She also found a letter with the ring—a letter I wrote to you and never sent."

"What did the letter say?" I asked him slowly.

He gave a humorless laugh and looked away, evidently attempting to hide his emotion. Then he stared down at the bedspread and touched his fingertips together. After a few moments in silent contemplation, he confided, "I went through a whole lot of grief after you left me, Mar. For a while there, I doubted whether I was going to make it through."

I felt a knot forming in my throat, and rested a hand on his knee.

Jake concentrated hard on pressing his fingers together as he continued. "I finally wrote you a letter expressing everything I felt—love, passion, anger, pain, betrayal, helplessness, hopelessness . . . It was a rather lengthy letter, but it allowed me a degree of closure. I sealed up what I'd written, put it in a box with the ring, and kept you tucked away there for a long time."

Jake looked at me then and said, "Tess confronted me with it. I apologized to her for keeping the letter and threw it in the fireplace. It killed me, though, Maren. I didn't want to do it. Then I told her that I'd get rid of the ring if she wanted me to. She said she didn't care, that it didn't make a difference, that she had old boyfriends too . . . But I realize now that she probably did care. She seemed not to care about a lot of things, but maybe that was just a defense mechanism. I convinced myself that it wasn't that big of a deal at the time, that your ring was just another token from my youth, that holding onto it was harmless, that I'd never opened the letter since I'd written it . . . I told myself that you were long gone, just a poignant memory. I justified my behavior by thinking that I loved my wife, and that I would have let the ring go if she'd wanted me to, but that since it didn't bother her, there was no harm in keeping it. How could that not have hurt her, Maren? A part of me is glad that I had it to give to you now . . . but for the sake of my marriage back then, I should have let it go."

I nodded, and he asked carefully, "Is it hurtful for you to hear that?"

"Not really," I answered, and was grateful to find that I meant it. My concerns had been alleviated by discussing them with my husband, and the peace I'd felt earlier returned.

Jake looked relieved and admitted, "I was selfish too, in many ways. And there were other things . . . little insignificant everyday things that added up to a whole lot of neglect and hurt over the years."

We both sat in silence, absorbed in our own thoughts for several moments. Then Jake touched my face and added gently, "Thanks for listening to my confession and for loving me in spite of myself . . . You do still love me, don't you?" I was surprised at the vulnerability in his eyes, but didn't ask him about it. I figured he'd spilled his guts enough for one evening. I didn't want to give him cause to close off.

"Yes, Jake, I still love you."

There was a timid knock on our bedroom door then, and Jeff pushed it open.

"What's up, buddy?" Jake asked him.

Jeff looked uncomfortable for a minute before he said hesitantly, "I had a bad dream."

"Oh, you did?" Jake asked him sympathetically, though he didn't look totally convinced of his son's excuse for being out of bed. "Come on," he instructed as he stood up. "I'll tuck you back in."

***

By the second week of March I could no longer squeeze into even my baggiest jeans. I stood helplessly in front of our bedroom mirror, trying not to cry when the buttons wouldn't stretch across what used to be my waist. Jake came out of the walk-in closet and sauntered toward the mirror to finish tying his tie. He saw my dilemma and his reflection smiled at mine. He wrapped his arms around me and rested his hands on my swelling stomach. "Good morning, Mrs. Jantzen." He kissed my neck and put his cheek next to mine to smile at me in the mirror again. "Would you look at that blossoming evidence of our deep love and affection?"

I couldn't help laughing, as I reached up to rest my hand on the back of his neck. "Proud of yourself, are you?" I teased.

"Very much so, my love." He kissed my shoulder.

"But I shouldn't be showing already, Jake. I'm only four months pregnant."

"Most people start showing by the time they're four months pregnant, don't they?"

"I don't. I'm supposed to fit into my jeans still," I argued.

"This is your fourth pregnancy, Mar. Your body can only resist for so long."

I turned to slug him playfully on the chest. "You hush up, Dr. Jantzen. You did this to me. You've completely spoiled my girlish figure."

He wrapped me in his arms and purred into my ear, "I like your new womanly figure, too."

"Well, I'm glad one of us is happy, because I don't have anything to wear."

He chuckled and said, "Then I guess you'd better go shopping, my dear."

"You're too good to me." I smiled at him.

"I am, aren't I?" he teased. I pushed him away and tried to run across the room, but didn't get very far before he caught me and kissed me again.

I went shopping for maternity clothes that week, and comfort won out over vanity as I resigned myself to wearing them.

***

Later that month, Jake and I went to another counseling appointment. Miles asked us how Jeff was doing. "About the same," I responded. "Still a little obstinate, but no major problems."

"Good," he said.

We discussed working on our communication skills, told Miles about our conversation with Tess, and talked about how the surprise pregnancy had impacted our marriage. At the end of the session, he observed, "You both seem happy."

I smiled up at Jake and said honestly, "Yeah . . . I guess we do."

"So things are going fairly well then, overall?" Miles asked us.

We both nodded. Jake put an arm around me and squeezed my shoulders. "The whole thing with my ex-wife is really a big relief," he admitted. "It's made a lot of things easier." He looked at me after he'd said it, like he was waiting for me to say something, too.

"Ted's also been better to deal with lately," I volunteered, assuming that was what Jake was thinking about. "The children actually look forward to their weekends with him now. He seems to be making progress." When I looked back up at Jake, he gave me a strange look. "Wouldn't you agree?" I questioned awkwardly, suddenly wondering if his perspective regarding that matter was different than mine.

He didn't move his arm, but he did pull back just a little. "What does any of that have to do with us?" he asked me, obviously annoyed.

"Well, his attitude affects our life . . ." I looked to our counselor for help, feeling trapped.

"How does his attitude affect your life?" Miles asked me.

I shrugged. "It certainly affects our children. If Ted's agreeable, and the children are happy to go with him, it makes it much easier to send them. I don't feel so much pressure to keep peace all the time. And I hate the tension when he appears angry or upset . . . It just seems like things go more smoothly when Ted's doing better."

Jake pulled his arm from behind me and leaned forward to rest his elbows on his knees, holding his head in his hands for a moment.

"Do you want to talk about what's bothering you, Jake?" Miles asked.

Jake looked back over his shoulder at me. His eyes sparked with electricity, but then turned cool and still. "No," he said as he sat up and looked at the counselor. "I don't."

"When you don't feel like talking about something," Miles suggested carefully, "that usually means you *need* to talk about it."

"Thanks for the advice," Jake told him evenly. "But it's just . . . not the time." He glanced at the clock and added, "Besides, our hour's up."

I thought about confronting Jake on the way home, but he seemed content to let the issue die, so I followed suit. I had no desire to bring up another conflict when things had been going so well.

As the day wore on, though, Jake grew more and more sullen. When we finally went to bed, I couldn't stand it any longer. "Do you want to tell me what's bothering you now?" I asked him.

Jake looked at me for a moment with an almost icy expression.

"Look," I finally asserted myself. "I'm not going to sit here and be silently punished, when I don't even know what I'm being punished for. You say you have to pry everything out of *me*—Well, what's this? It's ridiculous, Jake."

I waited for a moment with no response, and finally lost patience. "Fine!" I hollered at him as I stood up. "Sit in here and suffer in silence. Pout all night if you want to! But don't expect me to stick around for it." I marched out of the room.

"Maren, wait—" Jake caught me in the hall. "I'm sorry," he told me. "I just . . . Well, I feel mad."

"Yeah, I think I picked up on that."

Jake took hold of my arm and said, "Just come talk to me about it, okay?"

"Okay." I sighed, feeling tired suddenly. I followed him back into our bedroom and sank onto the bed again.

Jake sat down on his side of the bed and began, "Things have been going great, Mar, you know? I've felt so much relief, and I've felt happy . . . and I think you have too."

"Yes . . ." I agreed tentatively.

"So, I was talking about all of that at our counseling appointment," Jake explained, as though it were obvious, "and then you suddenly burst in with Ted and how great *he's* doing."

"Well, Jake! My gosh, you turned the happiness thing into a conversation about Tess, and then looked at me like you expected me to say something too, so I assumed we were discussing the impact our ex-spouses have had on us."

"But, that's not the same thing!" Jake protested.

"Why not?" I asked, feeling completely annoyed.

"Maren, I wasn't talking about Tess to talk about Tess. I was just describing the impact of her getting excommunicated on our lives."

"So, Tess has gone further off the deep end, and Ted's improving—and we can talk about her, but not him?" I asked in complete confusion. Surely that wasn't what he was getting at.

"No, no, Mar . . ." Jake looked annoyed now too. "We still have to deal with Ted on a regular basis. I know Tess has left her mark on Jeff, but at least she's completely gone now, and the relief is immense. It's ironic, and like I said, I feel guilty that her downfall has brought me so much happiness . . . But it's not that, of course. It's just the fact that it's made things so much easier for you and me."

I gave him a baffled look.

"We've both felt so happy," he went on, sounding like a broken record.

"About Tess's excommunication?" I asked. I could see how he felt some relief that his ties to her had all been cut with finality, but I didn't see cause for celebration here.

"No, about *us*, Mar!" Jake clarified in exasperation. "Are you tired or what?" He shook his head, but then smiled at me. "I know you felt uneasy with Tess being sealed to me, even though I also know you realized it was a situation that would be remedied in the hereafter. And I understood that you needed some time to work through your feelings on that, but now . . . Well, with Tess's ordinances being voided out, you don't have to worry about that anymore, so there goes our roadblock to being sealed."

I felt my mouth go dry.

"Now it's simply a matter of getting your sealing cancellation, and they've got to grant that . . . Anyway, I just felt a little angry that I was describing this whole situation and you brought up Ted. I can see how you were confused, though, so I'm sorry." Jake grinned at me, as the elation he'd displayed for days returned to his expression. "I just feel so wonderful," he told me gently. "I don't want to fight with you . . . Have you turned those papers into Bishop Rowley yet?"

I shook my head numbly, wondering what was wrong with me. Why hadn't any of this registered before? And now that it had, why didn't I feel anything? I told myself that perhaps it was because I'd already come to terms with Jake being sealed to Tess, and the fact that he no longer was didn't make much difference as far as our relationship was concerned. But then what was preventing me from being sealed to him? I felt confused and angry with myself, but even more than that, I felt empty and afraid.

"Maybe you should get on that, sweetheart," Jake suggested. "Maybe we could still push it through in time to get sealed right after our first anniversary."

"Yeah . . ." I mumbled. "Okay."

Jake didn't actually say anything more about getting sealed, but I could almost see the aura of hope and happiness around him, and that was even worse. It plagued me for days. I finally took out the paperwork the bishop had given me and looked it over, but then put it away again. I told myself I'd get to it eventually.

CHAPTER TWELVE

Sister White declined to go visiting teaching with me in March also. Finally, I made a bold move and cornered Lydia at church. "Hi, Lydia." I forced myself to greet her cheerfully when I stopped her in the hall. I didn't wait for a response, but got right to the point. "I guess you know I'm your new visiting teacher. When could I come by and see you?"

"Well . . ." she stammered, probably searching frantically for an excuse that would cover the entire month, I assumed. "Uh . . . Saturday's usually the best day, I guess."

"Great! So would this Saturday work?"

"I guess so . . ."

"What time's good for you?"

She shrugged. "I don't know . . . Maybe around ten thirty?"

"Okay, I'll see you then," I told her.

She hurried away with no further comment. No one answered the door on Saturday. After knocking and ringing the bell for a good five minutes, I looked heavenward and thought, *What do you want me to do here, Lord? I mean, you've got to realize this is an impossible situation. I'm open to any direction you might want to give me.* I left when I received no heavenly counsel.

I was still feeling troubled off and on over the Lydia situation when the phone rang on Thursday morning. "Maren?" Natalie asked when I answered.

"Hi, Nat. How are you?"

"Okay . . ." She paused before asking, "Can I come over there? I'm going to go crazy if I have to stay locked in this tiny apartment for another day."

"Come anytime," I told her.

"Thanks. I'll see you in a few minutes."

Trevor answered the door a while later and called to me in the kitchen, "Mommy! Aunt Natalie's here!"

"Tell her to come in!" I called back.

Natalie appeared in the kitchen, and I greeted her warmly. "Hi. Do you want to sit down in the family room? I just have to finish putting these dishes away."

"Okay," she agreed. She took Nathan out of his car seat and proceeded to peel off his snowsuit.

Elizabeth bounded into the room and asked, "Can I hold the baby, Aunt Natalie?"

"Sure, sweetie," Natalie answered her absently. "Come sit down."

I finished my task and smiled at the scene in front of me. Lizzy was holding Nathan, a look of pure delight on her little face. He was smiling up at her, waving tiny fists and gurgling. Trevor came in to observe also, and announced, "He's trying to talk! Huh, Nathan? You're trying to talk. We're gonna have a baby too. Then you'll have a friend."

Lizzy giggled and agreed, "Yeah!"

Natalie flopped down on the couch next to Elizabeth and pulled Trevor onto her lap. "So, what have you guys been up to?" she asked.

"I'm learning a new dance in my class!" Elizabeth announced. "*Two* new dances—a tap one and a ballet one."

"Are you still going to be a dancer like Mommy?" Natalie asked her, giving me a knowing look.

"Yep! Wanna see me dance?"

"I'd love to." Natalie smiled at her.

"Do you wanna see tap or ballet?"

Natalie glanced at me, and I suggested, "I think ballet might be a little better for the floor, Lizzy."

"Okay. I have to get my shoes. Here, Mommy." She tried to hold Nathan out to me, and I took him quickly.

Elizabeth flitted up the stairs, and Natalie turned her attention to Trevor, who was still on her lap. "And what are you doing today, Trev?" she asked.

"I was making a spaceship with Tinker Toys in my room, and then I was gonna play store with Lizzy 'cause she wants me to. But you came, so we didn't play it yet."

"That sounds like fun," Natalie commented. "Do you like to play store?"

Trevor shrugged. "It's okay. Lizzy said if I play store with her, then she'll play astronauts with me."

"Wow," Natalie told him. "It sounds like you guys are really good at cooperating."

"Yep," Trevor answered proudly. Then he added, "Except when we fight."

"That pretty much sums it up," I remarked, and Natalie and I both laughed.

After Elizabeth had danced and received enthusiastic praise from her aunt, she and Trevor ran upstairs to play.

"So how're you doing?" I asked my sister absently as I made faces at Nathan.

When she didn't answer right away, I looked up to see tears in her eyes. "What's wrong, Nat?" I thought something must be dreadfully wrong if it could bring my almost annoyingly upbeat sister to tears.

"Everything's wrong, Maren!" she said despairingly, as she pressed a hand over her eyes and began to cry.

"Like what?" I prodded.

"I hate it here!" she wailed. "I hate living in Salt Lake up by that awful university! When we were at BYU-Idaho, there were lots of little families and hundreds of married couples. Here, no one's married, no one has little kids . . . I guess there are a few people in my apartment building who do, but they all work. I seem to be the only mother in the world who stays home, and maybe I shouldn't. The money's so tight, and I know Douglas resents me since I had Nathan and quit working. I hate that dark, dingy apartment. I hate being locked in there every day with nowhere to go and nothing to do. I've never been so bored, Maren! I love my baby, but I can only hold him for so long. There has to be more to life than diapers and house-work."

"Have you talked to Douglas about how you feel?" I asked her.

She wiped at her face as more tears spilled. "Yeah, but it doesn't do any good. He goes to work all day, and then goes to school all night, and then has homework besides. He's going crazy too. He never helps with anything. We never go out—there's not enough money to do anything. He doesn't even have time for me anymore, Maren. I'm not even sure if he still loves me."

"He loves you, Natalie," I reassured her.

"I don't know, Maren." She shook her head. "I'm starting to wonder if I made a big mistake."

"What do you mean?" I asked her slowly.

"Doug and I are total opposites," she said matter-of-factly. "I guess that 'opposites attract' thing is really true. When I first met him, he seemed calm, and steady, and responsible. Now he just seems boring, cold, and unfeeling. He used to think that I was fun and exciting, and now he thinks I'm spoiled and immature. It's just . . . not what I thought it was going to be."

I felt a little stunned, and struggled with what to say to her. "I think a little disillusionment is normal," I said cautiously. "When you're dating it's all new and fun, but then after you're married, you take on a whole new set of responsibilities. And then when you have children . . . I know it's hard, Natalie, but it's also an opportunity to grow. Babies are a lot of work, but hasn't Nathan taught you a new level of love, and given you reasons to become better, and made you think more about what's really important?"

"Yes," she admitted softly. "I wouldn't trade my baby for anything. "And I love Doug, but . . ."

"But what?" I prodded, when she didn't continue.

"Wasn't that part of the reason that you and Ted had so many problems?" she asked. "Because you were too different from each other?" Then she added without waiting for a response, "And you and Jake are a lot alike. Doesn't that make it easier?"

I sighed. "Yes, and no. Being married to someone who's different from you isn't necessarily a bad thing. You could probably learn a lot from each other. And maybe you can offer your children a more balanced view of the world. As long as you're both committed to the gospel, and to each other, and to making things work, I don't think the other differences matter that much." I paused before clarifying, "Ted started drinking and getting violent, Natalie. That's not the same as being stressed out, or over-whelmed with work and school and family life."

She was quiet for several moments before admitting softly, "I just didn't realize it was going to be this hard."

"I know," I responded with empathy. "I remember starting a family and trying to get through school, and it wasn't fun."

"Well, you're certainly happy enough now," she muttered.

"Sure I'm happy, Nat, but . . ." I stopped myself, realizing that she probably just needed someone to listen to her, not lecture her.

"But what?" Natalie asked.

"Nothing." I shook my head. "So, tell me how else it's hard."

"Now you're just patronizing me," she mumbled, leaning her head back against the couch cushions and closing her eyes. "What were you going to say? Don't tell me you and Jake are having problems now. You guys had me convinced that things were just rosy between you. If you and Jake aren't happy, then there's definitely no hope for us." Natalie suddenly opened her eyes and sat up quickly. "Oh, geez, I almost forgot," she said. "Are you still being wishy-washy over the sealing thing? He's gotta be upset over that."

I sighed and admitted, "A little. We haven't talked about it much lately. There are other things, too—that's all that I was going to say. Our struggles are different than yours, and we *are* happy . . . but it's not like it's all just smooth sailing now."

"What struggles are you having besides that?" she asked with a combination of curiosity and skepticism.

"Well, there's Jeff, for one thing," I told her. "He's still really angry that we got married, and I don't know why. All the kids have little arguments and tussles constantly. They don't have major fights too often, but the little things still wear on me. We're all going through a big adjustment trying to learn to live together. And I got pregnant sooner than we'd planned, so I'm sick a lot. We have Ted to deal with, and his relationship with the kids. And Rebecca and Trevor feel caught between Ted and Jake, I think. Ted doesn't want them to love Jake, but they do. Even though Tess isn't around, we still live with the repercussions of her choices. Jake and I both have baggage to work through . . ."

Natalie furrowed her brows. "I guess I didn't think about all of that," she said quietly. "But you and Jake still love each other, right? You're still happy?"

"Yes, for the most part," I answered honestly. "Some days are harder than others, but we're trying to work through things together, with a whole lot of help from the Lord. Jake and I both made mistakes in our first marriages that we're trying to learn from and avoid making again. We'll be all right. We're both committed to making this marriage and this family work."

"Wow . . ." Natalie blew out a long breath and leaned back against the couch again. "So, when does it get easier?"

"That's what I kept asking myself too," I replied. "In fact, I finally asked Mom."

"Really? What did she say?"

I gave her a wry grin and admitted, "She said that Grandma told her it never gets easier, and that she supposed it was for the best, because if it got easy we'd quit growing."

"Great," Natalie muttered, but she cracked a smile. Then she said with sarcastic humor, "Thanks, Maren, I feel a lot better."

We both laughed for a minute before Nathan started getting fussy. Natalie sighed and took her baby from me to feed him.

I just watched her for a few minutes, wandering back in my thoughts and remembering how difficult things had been when I was at that stage of life. I had to admit that I'd done a lot of growing, but I was grateful that it was behind me. I could only be thankful for where I was then. I decided I preferred my struggles over hers, and felt a little guilty thinking it. I took notice of the dark circles under Natalie's eyes. She looked completely exhausted. "Is he sleeping through the night yet?" I asked her, nodding toward Nathan.

"Nope. He's up every three hours, like clockwork."

A thought suddenly came to mind, and I chastised myself for not offering weeks earlier. "Why don't you drop Nathan off tonight, and you and Doug can go out to dinner?" I suggested. "If you came in and nursed him right before you left, you could be gone for at least a couple of hours and have a break."

"I know you don't feel good, Maren," Natalie argued. "And you have four kids of your own."

"I'm your sister, Nat. You obviously need a break. I'd love to watch Nathan—and besides," I suddenly remembered that Natalie and Doug had watched the kids when we went to talk to Tess, "Jake owes you."

She grinned. "He does, doesn't he?"

"Yes," I assured her with a smile. "And in the future, don't be afraid to call and ask for help . . . Do you need any money?"

"No." She shook her head firmly. "Like I said, things are tight, but we'll make it through. You did. And Clayton did. It's just my time to struggle with this."

"If you need help, Natalie, please ask. Jake and I are probably in a better position to help out a little here and there than Mom and Dad are."

"Thanks, Maren," Natalie said genuinely. "But we're all right." I was surprised at her humble demeanor. Though I was sorry to see my sister struggle, I had to admit that I could see some growth in her already. I felt very concerned for her, though, and hoped that she and Doug would be all right.

I filled Jake in on Natalie's visit before she and Douglas arrived to drop off Nathan. "We should've offered our babysitting services before now," Jake commented in a tone of self-chastisement. "I forgot I'd promised to return that favor."

"Thanks for being so sweet," I told him, as I gave him a quick kiss.

"Do they have any money to go out with?" Jake asked.

"I doubt it."

"Do they even have any money for groceries?" he questioned. "Or diapers? Or anything else?"

"I asked her if she needed money, and she said they're all right," I responded. "But I'm sure they're struggling."

He sighed and muttered almost bitterly, "Of course they're struggling. Getting through school with a family is a nightmare."

We were cleaning up the kitchen when Natalie and Doug arrived. Natalie went upstairs to feed Nathan, and the kids pulled Douglas into the family room to wrestle. Jake gave me five twenty-dollar bills from his wallet and nodded toward Natalie's purse on the table. "Put that in your sister's purse," he instructed.

I quickly obeyed to avoid being caught and then wrapped my arms around my husband. "You're a good man, Jacob Jantzen," I told him.

He smiled and replied, "Just as long as you think so."

A couple of days later, Natalie called to ask, "Do you know anything about an anonymous money order for a thousand dollars arriving at my house by certified mail?"

"No," I answered honestly.

"Are you sure, Maren?" she asked suspiciously.

"Cross my heart, Nat. I know absolutely nothing about you getting a money order. I'd say just chalk it up to a blessing and be grateful. Unfortunately, a thousand dollars doesn't go that far, but you can probably put it to good use."

"That's exactly what we're going to do," she said humbly. "You know we didn't apply in time to get loans for this school year. Doug's been working overtime, but we still haven't saved enough for his spring-quarter tuition. We thought he was going to have to take some time off from school and drag this whole ordeal out even longer . . . Now he won't have to do that."

"I'm glad, Natalie."

"It *was* you, wasn't it?" she insisted. "I know you put that money in my purse the other night, so you might as well admit to this, too."

"Natalie, it *wasn't* me! Do you think I'd lie to you? A couple of extra twenties is not the same as a thousand-dollar money order. We probably could've given it to you if you'd asked, though."

"I wasn't about to ask my sister for money," she said with only a hint of defiant pride, "but I've certainly been praying. I guess you're right, that my prayers have been answered. And I'm very grateful."

When Jake came home that night, I asked, "Do you know anything about the money order my sister got today?"

"Nope. Did your sister get a money order today?"

"Yes," I answered slowly. "She said they've been praying because they didn't have enough money for Doug's tuition."

Jake raised an eyebrow at me. "Did you tell her that she could've asked us for help? We probably could have come up with it."

"Yes, but she's too proud. She never would have done that."

Jake nodded and agreed, "That's what I figured."

"So . . . Natalie called to ask if I was the one who sent her the money order," I tested.

"Really?" he asked nonchalantly. "What did you tell her?"

"I told her I knew nothing about it and had nothing to do with it."

"Good," Jake said.

"But I *didn't* tell her that I suspected my husband might have had a *great deal* to do with it," I added.

Jake only watched me innocently, so I prodded, "Are you *sure* you didn't send that money, Jake?"

"Oh, for heaven's sake, Maren," he said with what I suspected was staged annoyance. "Where would I come up with a thousand dollars to just give away?" He started to leave the room, but I caught his arm. He turned back to look down at me, questioning.

I wiggled my finger, motioning for him to come closer. He moved another step toward me and leaned down to listen as I whispered in his ear. "I never told you it was a thousand dollars, Jake."

When he pulled back slightly to look at me, guilt seeped into his expression. I laughed and reached up to kiss him. "Caught you," I whispered.

"You're very clever, Maren Jantzen," he scolded close to my face. "Can't a guy get away with a little charity?"

"You shouldn't try to sneak around and do good deeds like that without letting me know," I scolded back. "So I can give you your just desserts." I pulled him close to kiss him again.

When I broke away, Jake touched his fingers to his lips and said, "Mmm . . . Maybe I'll tell you next time, after all."

I laughed and replied, "Good idea."

Jake's humble display of generosity got me thinking, and I spent much of the following day in contemplation. I pulled out the sealing cancellation forms while the children were all in school and started to fill them out. I had to specify when and where I was married to Ted, for how long, the circumstances of our divorce, the reason I was requesting that the sealing be annulled, any children that were involved, whether I had the opportunity to be sealed to another man, and the circumstances surrounding that. As I completed the paperwork some time later, a peaceful feeling began to settle in my heart at the prospect of being sealed to Jake.

When Ted came to get Rebecca and Trevor that night, he actually looked almost happy. "You packed church clothes for the kids, right?" he asked me. I usually packed them in a pathetic display of hope, but they usually came home untouched.

"Yes. You're going to take the kids to church?" I asked in shock. Then I silently reprimanded myself, figuring I'd probably just ruined it.

It surprised me further when Ted just smiled and said, "Yes, Maren, I am."

"Wow," I commented. "What's come over you?"

He shrugged. "I'm just . . . trying to keep plugging along on the road to straightening out my life," he admitted with a touch of humor. Then he became more serious and said, "I think it's important for the kids to go, and I guess I've realized lately that I'm actually pretty blessed. I mean, I have two great kids and . . . well, anyway, I'm going to take them."

"I'm glad," I told him sincerely. I almost felt choked up a little.

He seemed embarrassed then and said, "Yeah, well, who knows? Maybe I'll actually get over the whole divorce thing—and as long as nothing else happens to shake my faith, maybe I'll eventually make a full recovery after all."

I felt like he'd suddenly struck a giant gong in my head, and the reverberations echoed so loudly that I couldn't even think. I numbly told my children good-bye and turned to see Jake behind me. The blissful mood he'd been in recently appeared to have been chased away by storm clouds. "That was some impressive acting, if I've ever seen it," Jake muttered sullenly.

I was slightly annoyed by what he'd said, but I wasn't sure why. Not wanting to think about how complicated my life was, I simply walked upstairs in a fog and slipped the stack of forms I'd been working on that day into the drawer of my nightstand.

CHAPTER THIRTEEN

Rebecca and Trevor came home in good spirits on Sunday night, while Jake's mood remained a bit more somber than it had been recently. As for Jeffrey, I'd been hoping that perhaps his bad behavior had reached a plateau. After so many months, I'd just sort of adjusted to the new him and learned to live with it. But that theory was abruptly thrown out when his principal called one afternoon in March. "Mrs. Jantzen?" he asked. I still hadn't gotten used to the thrill of hearing that, but the feeling faded quickly as I wondered why the school would be calling me.

"Yes," I answered.

"This is Principal Buttars."

"Is something wrong?" I asked.

"We do have a little problem, actually. I've had Jeffrey in my office this morning. It seems that he started a fight with another student."

I gasped. "Is he all right? Is the other student all right?"

"They both have some scrapes and bruises. Apparently, they hit the asphalt. Other than that, they're fine."

"I'm so sorry," I apologized. "Would you like me to come and get Jeff, or call the other student's moth—?"

"I don't think that will be necessary, but I did tell Jeffrey that I'd be calling you to let you know what happened. He apologized to the other boy, and he's going to be spending recess sitting with the teacher tomorrow, thinking about how he could make better choices next time."

"Do you know why Jeff started the fight?" I asked the principal.

"He said the other boy teased him about something, so he punched him in the stomach," Principal Buttars explained.

"All right," I said, feeling discouraged. "I'll talk to him when he gets home. I appreciate you letting me know."

"No problem. If there's anything we can do here at school to help, feel free to call at any time."

"Thank you."

When Rebecca and Jeff got home, I let them have a snack and gave Jeffrey a few minutes to wind down while I got my thoughts together. Then I told him that I wanted to talk to him.

"Why?" he demanded, looking up from the Legos he and Trevor were playing with.

"We just need to have a little talk, buddy," I said. "I'd like you to come into the kitchen with me please."

He reluctantly obeyed, and we sat down at the table. "Principal Buttars called me today," I told him.

Jeffrey made no response.

"Do you want to tell me about what happened?" I asked.

He scowled and replied, "Nothin' happened."

"Jeff, the principal told me that you started a fight," I insisted carefully. "Why did you do that?"

His response was angry. "I did *not* start it! Daniel called me Jerky Jeff, so I called him Dorky Daniel. Then he started singing, 'Jeff loves Amy,' and I told him to shut up, and he said, 'make me'. . . so I did."

"You did what?" I asked.

"I made Dorky Daniel shut up," he said vehemently. "I *don't* love Amy 'cause girls are gross, and Daniel's just a stupid dork."

"How did you make Daniel shut up?" I probed.

Jeff glared at me and crossed his arms defiantly on his stomach, slouching down in his chair.

"Jeffrey?" I prodded.

"I hit him, and it's his own fault 'cause he told me to."

"Jeffrey," I questioned calmly, "when is it all right to hit someone?"

He didn't answer me.

"I asked you a question, Jeff—When is it all right to hit someone?"

"Never," he finally mumbled. Then he added, "Unless they're a kidnapper."

"That's right," I said. "So what could you do next time that would be a better choice?"

"Hit 'im again," he muttered sullenly.

"We already agreed that hitting him wasn't a good choice, Jeff. What else could you do?"

"Tell him to shut up."

"Maybe you could try asking him nicely to please not call you names or tease you," I suggested, realizing that he wasn't going to voice anything I might agree with. "You could tell your teacher, or maybe you could just walk away."

"It's Daniel's fault," Jeff argued.

I took a deep breath and forced myself to remain calm. "Jeffrey, it's not okay to hit someone. I can understand that you felt frustrated and upset, but that doesn't make what you did all right. Now you feel mad, and I'll bet Daniel feels mad. Daniel got hurt, and you got hurt too." I pointed out the scrapes on his hands and elbows. "Your consequence for starting a fight at school is that you can't play with your friends today or tomorrow. I know you're a kind person and a smart kid, and I'm sure you'll make a better decision next time . . . Do you want to talk to me about anything else?"

He stood up and hollered, "I don't want to talk to you *at all!* You're the *meanest* mom in the world, and you're not even s'posed to *be* my mom!"

It surprised me when Jake walked into the kitchen just in time to witness Jeffrey's outburst. I hadn't heard the garage door open. Jeff tried to run out of the room, but Jake caught him, saying, "Whoa there, buddy." He sat him back down on the chair and told him, "You can't talk to Maren like that, Jeff. What's going on?"

"I hate her!" Jeffrey hollered, as angry tears spilled down his cheeks. "She grounds me *every* day!"

Jake scooted a chair close to him and sat down. "That's not true, buddy. But if she did ground you today, it must be for a reason."

"She can't ground me! And I can talk to her however I want, 'cause she's *not* my mom!"

Jake looked very tired suddenly as he replied, "All right, Jeff. Maren's not your mom. But she *is* my wife and I want you to talk nicely to her."

"Well, I *won't!*" Jeff yelled. "And you *can't* make me!"

"Go upstairs to your room, Jeffrey," Jake ordered firmly. "You may come down when you're ready to obey me and be respectful to Maren."

"I hate you too!" he hollered, as he sprang out of his chair and raced furiously up the stairs, slamming his bedroom door.

We listened to him screaming, throwing things, and finally pounding his feet against the wall before Jake said to me, "I swear, I'm at the end of my rope." He hurried out of the room and up the stairs. I heard him open Jeff's door and holler, "Jeffrey Adam Jantzen, that's *enough!* You may not destroy our house!"

The other three children ran into the kitchen. "What happened to Jeff?" Lizzy asked, looking worried.

"He's just angry and upset," I told her. "He had a hard day today."

"Yeah, he got in a fight," Rebecca explained to Trevor and Elizabeth. "He got in trouble at school, and he's probably grounded, huh, Mom?"

"You don't need to worry about that, Rebecca," I said. "You just take care of yourself."

Jake walked back into the kitchen looking flustered. "Are you mad, Daddy?" Elizabeth asked hesitantly. Rebecca and Trevor looked a little worried too. Jake didn't yell very often, and I knew they'd all heard him.

"Yes, Lizzy," he responded shortly. "I'm mad. You guys go play."

They obediently scurried away as Jake dropped onto a kitchen chair. He looked at me with glassy eyes for a minute before he admitted, "I'm not even sure if I want to know what happened."

"I think I'd better tell you anyway," I told him, and proceeded to fill him in.

"What are we going to do with him, Maren?" he asked, shaking his head. "He used to be so calm and pleasant. I mean, he wasn't perfect, but he definitely had more of a tendency to be the peace-maker in tense situations rather than the instigator . . . I just can't get through to him at all anymore. He's never been so closed off, so angry and defiant. This can't all be because of Tess. She's been gone for months now . . . I must be doing something wrong."

"I don't think it's you, Jake," I said flatly. "It's me. I'm the one he's angry at. I'm just not sure if it's because of something I've done, or if he's directed his anger at his mother toward me . . ."

We sat in contemplative silence for a few moments until Jake asked me, "You ready to try taking him to counseling yet?"

I felt a twinge of guilt for not pushing it earlier myself. "I'm ready to try almost anything," I agreed tiredly.

Jake acknowledged my comment with a brief nod. Then he looked thoughtful as he absently took off his tie and suit coat, dropping them uncharacteristically on the chair behind him. He stood abruptly and announced, "I've got to get some fresh air."

"What?" I questioned as he headed for the door. "You're leaving? But dinner's almost ready! And Jeffrey's still upstairs throwing a fit. He and Rebecca have homework—"

"Do you know how many times I've taken care of everything while you were upstairs throwing up?" he challenged. "It's *my* turn to take a night off, Maren."

I was stunned and shot back, "I can't help the fact that I've been sick!"

"Neither can I!" he said, his voice going up a notch.

"Jake!" I protested, astonished at his behavior.

"I'm over the edge, Maren, okay? I've been taking care of sick, whiny, bawling children all day at work! If I have to deal with Jeff any more tonight, I'm going to lose it! And *you*. I have to take care of you, and try to read your mind, and carry the weight of all your baggage, because if I don't you'll—" He cut himself off sharply.

"I'll *what?*" I demanded.

"Nothing," he answered tersely, as he apparently thought better of walking and pulled his car keys from the rack by the garage door.

"You can't just get all mad and yell at me and leave, Jake!" I insisted. "That's just unfair and imma—"

Jake whirled around to face me and cut me off with an icy glare. "Maybe it is, Maren," he shot out. "But you know what? I'm gonna do it anyway!" He slammed the door, making me wince. Then I heard him pull out of the garage and drive away.

The children ran back into the room, with Trevor asking worriedly, "Where's Dad going, Mommy?"

I quickly composed myself and told them, "He's just taking a little drive. He needs a break. Don't worry, he'll be back."

"Is he still mad?" Elizabeth asked.

"Yes, sweetie, I believe he is," I admitted, then tried to soothe them all. "He'll probably feel better when he comes home."

Rebecca looked like she was near tears as she asked, "He's not going to get drunk . . . is he, Mom?"

"No," I answered firmly.

"Are you sure?" she questioned hesitantly.

I sighed and tried to cover my own frazzled emotions for the sake of my children. "I'm positive," I said. "Jake would never do that, Becca. He had a hard day and he's just . . . frustrated. He'll be back soon, and he *won't* be drunk. Everything's fine." I felt a twinge of resentment as I listened to myself defending Jake's behavior. I knew that everything I'd just told the children was true. I knew that Jake wasn't going to come home drunk and go on some violent rampage like Ted had. But the situation still felt all too familiar.

My resentment grew as I dealt with Jeffrey's tantrum, fed the children dinner, cleaned up, helped the kids with their homework, and got them bathed and into bed, all while fighting with nausea and fatigue.

"Are you sure Dad's coming back?" Trevor asked when I tucked him in.

"I promise, honey. Even Jake gets mad sometimes, Trev. Everything's all right."

I was surprised to hear Jeffrey sniffling from the top bunk as I climbed partway up the ladder to tell him good night. "It's okay, Jeffrey," I whispered to him, brushing his hair back from his forehead and kissing his cheek. To my surprise, he didn't resist. "Tomorrow will be a better day," I tried to reassure him.

"Did Daddy leave because of me?" he asked softly, still facing the wall.

I hesitated, not sure how to answer him. "He had a rough day today," I explained again, "just like you did. He did feel upset with you, and he was afraid that he couldn't talk to you any more tonight without getting angry. But he didn't leave because of you. He had a stressful day at work, and he's tired, and I guess he's also upset with me. Your dad loves you very much, Jeffrey, and he'll be back soon. I think tomorrow will be a better day for him too."

Jeff turned toward me, and I saw large tears well up in his eyes as he asked, "Dad won't *stay* away like my mom . . . will he?"

I put my arms around him to hug him and said, "No. He'll be back tonight, I promise."

"Are you mad at Dad?" he whispered hesitantly.

I took a deep breath and admitted, "A little, Jeff. But everything's okay. I'll get over it."

There was a prolonged silence before Jeffrey questioned, "Are you still staying here, though?"

"Of course I'm still staying here," I assured him. "You just relax and go to sleep, buddy. I'll see you in the morning."

"Okay," he mumbled with a degree of relief.

I went to soak my aching muscles in a hot bath, then went straight to bed. I was so tired that I fell asleep quickly, but woke up when Jake got into bed with me and whispered, "Maren?"

My back was to him, so I opened my eyes and looked at the alarm clock. It was only nine thirty, not even close to the wee hours when Ted used to come home. I still felt angry, though, so I closed my eyes and ignored him.

Jake scooted closer to me and touched my shoulder. "I'm sorry, Mar," he said softly.

I still didn't respond.

He sighed and kissed my cheek, saying, "Love you." Then he rolled over to go to sleep.

In the morning, Jake pulled me close to him and kissed me. I enjoyed it for a moment before I remembered the previous night and broke away. "You can't just kiss me and expect everything to be fine," I mumbled, closing my eyes and trying to go back to sleep. I knew it was still early. It was dark outside.

"I told you I was sorry last night," Jake defended himself.

"That was a rotten thing to do, Jake."

He sat up and turned on the lamp. When he didn't say anything else, I finally opened my eyes enough to squint up at him. His lips were pressed together, and he was watching me through narrowed eyes. I braced myself for his rebuttal.

After several more seconds of silence, Jake finally shook his head and looked away. He sighed and ran his fingers through his hair before he looked back at me. "You're right." He forced the words out through still-tight lips. "It was a rotten thing to do . . ." The muscles in his face finally relaxed a bit as he said more gently, "I'm sorry."

I sat up to meet his cool gaze and told him quietly, "I'm sorry I've been sick. This pregnancy has put a lot of extra pressure on you, I know. But it hasn't exactly been fun for me, either." I leaned back against the headboard and added dejectedly, "And Jeffrey has been so difficult, Jake . . ."

"I know," he agreed tiredly.

"I may be sick, but I've never just thrown my hands in the air and walked out," I pointed out, still feeling angry. I looked down at the bedspread and was a bit unnerved to see a wad of it clenched tightly in Jake's fist. But when I looked back at his face, he appeared relatively placid. I furrowed my brows at him in question.

"It won't happen again, Maren," he said smoothly.

When I didn't respond he added, "Look, this whole thing is stupid, okay? I don't want to fight with you."

I sighed and admitted quietly, "I don't want to fight with you either . . ."

As some of the anger in Jake's expression dissipated, I was surprised to see an increasing amount of inexplicable fear appear behind it. "What's wrong?" I finally asked him uneasily.

His eyes went wide in near panic at the apparent realization of what I'd read in his face. "Nothing," he insisted, then added too quickly, "I'm sorry, Maren. I won't leave like that again. I'll be here for you. I'll do whatever you need me to, and I—"

He seemed to be losing it, and it unnerved me. I touched his arm and cut him off. "Jake, calm down, okay? We're both sorry. Let's just leave it at that." I looked at the alarm clock and was relieved to find that it was only five o'clock. "I'm going back to sleep," I told him.

"Okay . . ." he agreed slowly. He turned off the lamp and lay down with me, putting his arm around me cautiously.

I didn't want to think about this most recent disagreement any more right then. I also didn't want to think about the fact that Jake's contradictory behavior seemed to be occurring more frequently lately. The whole thing was baffling to me, and I was too aware of my confusion and fatigue to feel angry anymore. At that moment, I decided to just drop it. I snuggled against Jake's chest to let him know that everything was all right. He hugged me and kissed my forehead before going back to sleep.

CHAPTER FOURTEEN

Jake was extra attentive over the next few days, and I made a bigger effort to be affectionate and appreciative. I tried not to make him feel overburdened or stressed. I let myself forget about his confusing behavior and focused on Jeffrey instead. I called Miles to schedule an appointment, but he was booked solid for nearly a month. He told me that we really needed to schedule three appointments close together, anyway—one for Jeffrey to meet him, another for him to talk with Jeffrey alone, and a third one for him to discuss his findings with Jake and me.

"We'll do whatever you recommend," I told him.

***

By April, the morning sickness was finally wearing off. There was the occasional queasy moment, but I started feeling like I could function normally again. The downside was that I felt enormous. Maybe it had just been a long time, but I didn't ever remember feeling so big this early before.

When we went in for the ultrasound, I was half expecting to find out that I was carrying twins. "No, there's only one baby in there," the technician assured me. She pointed out the baby's eyes, fingers, toes, and then the obvious. "Well, there's no mistaking this one," she announced.

"That's my son!" Jake beamed.

"It's a boy." I smiled up at him.

He laughed. "Yes, love, I can see that." I reached my hand up to touch his cheek.

The children were very excited to find out what the baby was. I didn't think any of them really cared one way or the other, but knowing the baby's gender made him seem more real. Jeffrey exclaimed, "Yeah! I get a brother!" I was glad to see him so happy about it.

Trevor shoved him and yelled, "You already *have* a brother!"

"Trevor!" I scolded.

I waited for Jeff to hit Trevor back, but he didn't. He only said, "I meant *another* brother, Trev. We both get another brother!"

Rebecca rolled her eyes and said, "Oh great, another brother!" She and Lizzy giggled as they all ran around rhyming, "another brother." Jake laughed and came over to hug me. I was glad to see him looking so carefree, and hugged him back.

***

I was five months pregnant then, and huge, so I gave up any attempt at trying to hide the pregnancy anymore. The first Sunday that I wore a maternity dress to church several people asked if I was pregnant. I could tell most of them had probably been dying to ask for the last month, but hadn't quite dared.

I tried to catch up with Lydia after Relief Society to attempt setting up another visiting teaching appointment, but she practically ran out of the building. Nevertheless, I decided that the Lord must have given me this call for a reason, and I couldn't give up, as tempting as it was. I decided to try the "surprise" approach and showed up on Saturday morning, unannounced. I dreaded the unofficial appointment, and spent several minutes in prayer before I left. Jake kissed me and said, "Good luck."

"Thanks," I told him. "I'll need it."

I walked around to the back of Sister Carter's house and knocked on the door of the basement apartment that Lydia rented from her. Lydia was actually there and even answered the door. I credited it to the prayer.

I took advantage of her shock and rushed into a quick and friendly greeting. "Hi, Lydia. Hey, I apologize for just showing up like this, but I felt bad that I missed you last month, so . . . do you have a few minutes?" I held up the *Ensign* in my hands, thinking that she might feel safer if she knew I had a structured lesson ready, and that I hadn't just come to shoot the breeze.

She glanced uncomfortably at my pregnant middle, and her shoulders drooped in apparent defeat. "Yeah . . ." she mumbled. "Come in." She ushered me toward a worn, comfortable sofa, and sat in a rocking chair herself. She looked nervous.

"Sister White couldn't make it," I explained.

Lydia made no comment.

I looked around me at the few rustic furnishings, searching desperately for some topic of conversation. "You like country," I observed finally.

She shrugged. "It's cheap."

I forced a smile. "Yes, I guess so . . . Did you make all of these things?" I motioned to the rag rugs and wooden decor items.

"Yeah . . ." she admitted. "It makes it feel more like home."

"Where's home?" I asked politely, as I studied an intricately woven basket on a small table next to the sofa.

"Louisiana," Lydia informed me hesitantly.

"Really?" I asked in surprise. "I never would have guessed you were from the South. You don't have much of an accent."

She watched me closely for a minute before saying, "I took voice lessons to learn to cover it up . . . I guess it just became habit."

"Voice lessons?" I echoed.

"I used to sing," she said.

I wanted to ask her more about that, but she seemed uncomfortable with the topic. Instead, I touched the basket and ran my fingers delicately over the raised woven pattern. "This is beautiful," I remarked. "It looks handmade."

"You're observant," Lydia noted in surprise, a small trace of warmth seeping into her frigid expression.

"I'm an interior designer," I explained simply.

"Oh," she commented. "I think I heard somebody say that once."

"So where'd you get this?" I asked curiously, glancing up at her. "Is it a souvenir from somewhere?"

Lydia gave a snort of dry laughter. "I suppose you could say that."

I watched her, waiting for her to say more. She seemed suddenly uneasy again and squirmed a little in her seat.

"I'm sorry," I said carefully. "I wasn't trying to be nosy."

"It's all right," she answered quietly. "It's not a big deal. It's just . . ." Her words faded as her thoughts seemed to be wandering. I noted the glassy quality her eyes suddenly took on as she spoke in a voice that seemed almost detached from her somehow. "It's from home," she stated simply. "One of the few things I have . . ."

"So you know the person who made it?" I assumed, my curiosity raised.

"I made it," she answered quietly.

"You did?" I responded, feeling impressed.

I regretted letting my surprise show when Lydia seemed to grow even more miserable. "My grandmother taught me," she evidently felt compelled to explain. "She was very talented—much better than I ever was."

"You look plenty talented to me," I remarked honestly as I admired the basket once more before I placed my hands in my lap. When Lydia remained silent I asked, "So, is your family in Louisiana then?"

"No," she answered hastily. "Grammaw's gone, and there's . . . no one else."

I was so taken aback by the harshness in her voice that I must have given her a look of alarm.

"There's no one," Lydia clarified again.

"You have no family . . . at all?" I asked in astonishment before I stopped to think.

"I'm not one of these Utah Mormons, Maren," she answered caustically. "I didn't come from some big, loving family. I don't have brothers and sisters scattered across the country. No nieces and nephews, no aunts and uncles, no cousins, no father . . . I didn't even have a mother, for heaven's sake . . . Nope, there's no big, happy, forever family here. Just me."

I could only stare at her, wondering what she might have been through. No father? No *mother*? How must it feel to be so alone? Even during my difficult first marriage I'd had parents, siblings, and children who loved me. I'd even had extended family that I could have turned to for support if I'd needed it.

Lydia was obviously embarrassed by her sudden outburst as she muttered, "So, I guess now you know why I get a little tired of my own company occasionally." She hesitated before adding, "Listen, I've got a lot to do today. Could we just get on with the lesson?"

"Sure," I agreed, wishing that I could put her more at ease. I felt a little sick at her confession and was suddenly filled with a whole lot of empathy. "The lesson this month is on faith . . ." I summed it up quickly. "Thanks for letting me in," I finished. "Is there anything you need?" And I really meant it that time.

She shook her head. "Thanks, though."

There was a sound in another room then, and Lydia opened a door off the living room as I stood to leave. Four little furballs spilled out onto the floor. I laughed and said, "Those must be your kittens."

"Yeah." She smiled.

"They're cute," I told her as I left. "See you later."

"Bye."

I thought about Lydia a lot over the next few days until my focus changed when Jeffrey's teacher called. Jeff had started another fight, and this time he'd broken the other little boy's glasses. "I'm so sorry," I apologized. "Tell the other boy's mother that we'll pay to replace his glasses."

"All right . . . Jeffrey will be missing recess this week. The principal talked with him again and warned him that he might have to have in-school suspension if he starts another fight."

"Okay," I answered, feeling embarrassed. I was thankful that the counseling session we'd scheduled with Miles was coming up soon.

Miles called me a couple of days before our appointment to get some background information over the phone. Then Jake and I took Jeffrey in with us to let him get acquainted with our counselor. We talked a little bit about some of the problems we were having, but we couldn't get Jeff to say much.

"How would you feel about coming in to talk with me yourself sometime, Jeff?" Miles asked him. "You know, your mom here came in by herself several times before your dad started coming with her."

"You mean *Maren* came in by herself," Jeff corrected him.

Miles looked embarrassed at his obvious mistake, but said calmly, "Yes, Jeff. That's what I meant."

"Why would I come in by myself?" Jeffrey wanted to know.

"Well, sometimes it's nice to have someone to talk to about things that are bothering us," Miles explained carefully. "Sometimes it can even help us think of new ways to handle things so that we can feel good about them. It's hard for any kid when their parents get divorced, and it can be a little difficult for anyone if their mom or dad gets married again, too . . . We don't have to talk about that if you don't want to, though. We can talk about anything you want. I'm a good listener."

Jeffrey thought carefully for a minute. "Do you talk to lots of kids?" he asked.

"Yes I do, Jeff. In fact, that's one of my favorite things to do." Miles leaned forward and whispered jokingly to Jeffrey, "Sometimes grown-ups get a little boring, you know? Kids are a lot more interesting."

To my shock, Jeffrey actually smiled. Then he looked concerned again as he asked cautiously, "Are you gonna tell them—" he motioned to Jake and me, "—what I say?"

"Not if you don't want me to," Miles responded.

Jeff seemed to be thinking for a long time before he decided, "I guess it'd be okay."

We brought him back a couple of days later to meet with Miles again, while we sat in the waiting room. Then Jake and I returned a third time without him.

"You both know that I meant what I said about not telling you anything that Jeffrey didn't want me to," Miles started.

We both nodded. He'd warned us of that before he talked to Jeff at all.

"However, he actually told me that it would be all right if I shared some of my insights with you."

"He did?" I asked in surprise, though I was grateful.

Miles nodded. "Most children are okay with that, once they realize that they can trust me. It's usually not too hard to convince them that their parents really want to help."

"What did you find out?" Jake asked, seeming slightly impatient.

"It took a little work," Miles informed us, "but Jeffrey did finally tell me that he's angry with his mother for leaving, and that he's angry with you, Jake, for getting married again."

"Yes, we knew all that," Jake responded. "We've talked to you about that before. And the reasons he's angry with his mother are certainly understandable. I know that shook his feeling of security. But did he give any indication as to why he's angry with me for getting married again? Maren was babysitting him for a year and a half before we got married, and he loved her to pieces. I'm sure he still *does* love her, but his aggression doesn't make sense to me. For him to be hitting other children just because he doesn't like what they say . . ." Jake's voice trailed off as he shook his head in bewilderment. "It's just so unlike him."

"It's possible that Jeffrey feels you've deserted his mother by marrying another woman," Miles suggested.

Jake looked thoughtful. "I guess that's possible," he admitted. "I suppose he was attached to her simply by virtue of the fact that she's his mother, but she never made a big effort to encourage those bonds. Maren told you that she left when he was two, didn't she?"

"Yes, and that she came back into his life when he was six, and then left again after only a few months. You've also told me that your ex-wife relinquished her parental rights."

"She did," Jake replied. "I realize that Jeffrey's young, and I admit that I rarely know what's going on in his mind anymore, but it just seems a little off that all of this would be the result of him thinking I deserted his mother. It was quite obviously the other way around."

Miles nodded. "Well, as you said, Jeffrey's sense of security has been shaken. His fear of abandonment is understandably very real. Maybe he resents Maren for taking over a large chunk of your time, or he could possibly fear that your love for her will overshadow your love for him . . . How are things going between the two of you?" We hadn't met with him alone since the last time, when we'd left his office so awkwardly.

"Things are fine," Jake answered quickly. "You know we love each other."

"Yes," Miles agreed cautiously. "But as you both know, second marriages and the struggles of blending two families are never easy. Children typically model their parents' behavior. Are you communicating well? Have the two of you been fighting often or—"

I saw Jake's jaw tighten as he interrupted him. "If we told you that we haven't had any disagreements lately, you'd know we were lying. But overall, I do think we communicate fairly well. And we certainly don't have violent fights." He looked toward me, and I nodded in agreement, squeezing his hand. I couldn't help feeling a little guilty, though, thinking that our communication skills could still use some work. I wondered if Jeffrey had picked up on that.

Miles considered Jake carefully for a minute before he said, "I believe that Jeffrey identifies very strongly with you, Jake . . . Has there been anything in your behavior recently that could have subconsciously triggered a heightened fear of abandonment in him, or invited misplaced aggression?"

"For heaven's sake, Miles!" I protested, feeling a little angry. "Jake is *not* a violent man! He's one of the calmest, most level-headed people I've ever met, and he's a wonderful father. If Jeffrey was imitating him, he certainly wouldn't be starting fights."

Jake seemed oblivious to my comment as he shook his head slowly and answered our counselor, "I don't know . . . I'll have to think about that, I guess."

"I don't think Jeffrey's problems are serious enough to require regular visits with me at this point," Miles informed us. "We don't want to traumatize him. I know you're both anxious and willing to help him. To be perfectly honest, I have a tendency to think that with time and your support, this behavior will wear itself out. If it continues much longer or worsens, we can certainly reevaluate."

"All right," I agreed.

"Thank you," Jake added as we stood to leave.

Once we were in the car, Jake just sat staring out the front windshield. I didn't want to interrupt his thoughts, so I watched him silently. "Do you think he could be right?" he finally asked, turning to look at me.

"About what?" I wondered.

"About Jeffrey's behavior reflecting mine."

"Of course not, Jake! We could probably work on communicating a little better, but you've never been violent or aggressive. You're quite possibly the calmest, most patient man I've ever met."

"I punched Ted," he muttered dryly. "I gave him a bloody lip because I didn't like something he said."

"But the children don't know about that," I pointed out. "Besides, that was different. You were trying to protect me."

"When Jeffrey got in trouble at school a few weeks ago," Jake recalled, "I yelled at him. Then I yelled at you, and then I took off."

I sighed and admitted, "That did upset Jeffrey. He asked if you were going to stay away like his mother did, but I told him you'd never do that. I'm sure he knows that, Jake."

"Maybe . . ." Jake said in a tone of self-reproach. "But my behavior was out of line."

"It was understandable," I reassured him. "We all get mad sometimes."

"I wonder if Jeffrey really does think I deserted his mother . . . ?" Jake said distantly.

"How on earth could he possibly think that?" I asked, astonished.

"Well . . . he was so small when she left the first time, and this time . . . He's too young to really understand it all even now. You can't exactly explain to a seven-year-old that his mother had an affair, although there was certainly more to it than that."

"Jake, you're the parent who's here for him. You've always been here for him."

"Yes, but that doesn't lessen the fact that he lost his mother."

"That's not your fault," I told him again.

Jake turned to look at me and said, "I've told you, Maren, that many of the problems in my first marriage *were* my fault."

"Like what?" I challenged. "You mean you got mad once in a while?"

He gave a humorless chuckle and said, "You know it went far deeper than that. I've told you about it."

"Oh, Jake!" I said, beginning to feel frustrated. "No divorce can be blamed entirely on one spouse, but it's not your fault that Tess prefers being a party animal to being a mother. There's nothing more you could have done with that situation. And I don't think you're doing your children any favors by wallowing in guilt."

Jake narrowed his eyes and suddenly gave me a reproachful look. He opened his mouth to say something, but then clenched his teeth and looked away. After watching out the side window for a few moments he turned back and said quietly, "Let's go home."

When we were about halfway there, I told Jake, "I'm sorry for saying that. I obviously have no room to talk. I'm not sure why you haven't pointed that out yet, but I know it's what you're thinking."

"Yeah . . ." he mumbled halfheartedly. "Sorry too."

I sighed and looked out my window, hoping that things wouldn't have to get worse before they got better.

My fears were soon justified. Jeffrey came home from school very grumpy on a Tuesday afternoon and refused to read to me or do his worksheet. After several attempts to reason with him, I finally gave in later that night. "Okay, buddy. I'm not going to argue with you. You're welcome to go to your room instead. Feel free to come out when you're ready to do your homework."

A familiar shadow fell over his face as he hollered, "I hate you!"

Jake walked in from the family room, where he'd been reading to Trevor and Elizabeth.

"Jeffrey, go to your room please," I instructed.

"NO!"

"Jeffrey, I really don't want to carry you upstairs, but I will if I have to," I warned.

"You most certainly will not," Jake told me, glancing at my protruding stomach. Then he turned to Jeff and said, "But I will."

Jeffrey tried to run, but Jake caught him and carried him upstairs. Jeffrey kicked and screamed the whole way, and true to form, the other children came running to observe the scene. When Jake came back downstairs, Elizabeth asked him timidly, "Daddy, what's wrong with Jeff?"

Jake sat down on the stairs and looked at her. "I wish I knew, sweetie," he finally answered sadly.

"Did you spank him?" Trevor asked with wide eyes. I didn't believe in spanking, but unfortunately, Ted did.

"I never have yet," Jake responded, but then he looked up at me and added, "Maybe I should try it."

Just then there was a huge crash from Jeffrey's room. Jake jumped to his feet and bounded up the stairs, taking them two at a time. The children were close behind him, and I brought up the rear.

The dresser was laying facedown. The lamp and the pictures that had sat on it were strewn all over the floor, some of them broken. Jeffrey stood looking at the mess, obviously afraid.

"What happened?" Jake demanded.

The fear in Jeff's face was quickly masked with obstinance. "I pushed it over," he said.

"How did you manage to do that?" Jake asked.

"I was climbing up the back of my bunk bed, and I kicked it . . . It just fell over."

"You guys go downstairs and play," I told the other children.

"I don't want to!" Lizzy insisted as she began to cry.

Trevor looked upset as he protested, "That's my room too! Jeff just smashed up our dresser and made a huge mess in our room! That's not fair, Mom!" He pushed past me into the room and picked up the broken clay pencil holder he'd made in preschool. "You broke it!" he hollered at Jeff.

Rebecca became indignant at the sight of her little brother's distress. She put her hands on her hips and said, "You're a brat, Jeff! You're a spoiled brat!" I wondered where she'd heard that expression, but then assumed it must have been at school.

"Rebecca!" I warned. "That's enough."

Trevor ran to me, crying, and held up his broken work of art. "I don't wanna share a room with Jeff anymore, Mommy!" he cried.

I bent to hug him and said, "Maybe we can make another one, Trev."

"You can share my pencil holder," Elizabeth offered. "I made one too."

"I don't wanna share yours," Trevor grumbled. "Yours is pink."

"That was very thoughtful, though, Lizzy," I told her.

Jake knelt on the floor in front of Jeffrey and took his shoulders into his hands. "Jeff, what were you thinking?" he asked urgently. "That dresser could have fallen on you and hurt you very badly."

"Nuh-uh," Jeffrey protested. "I wasn't on the floor. I was climbing up my bed."

"Nevertheless, it was a very dangerous thing to do," Jake insisted. "And look at what you've done! This has all got to stop, son. You cannot continue to behave this way."

A hint of remorse broke through Jeff's rebellious facade, and I saw his bottom lip quiver.

"I love you, Jeff," Jake told him firmly. "Maren and I both love you very much, but *this has got to stop!*"

To my surprise, Jeffrey crumpled in his arms, sobbing.

"It's your turn to be first in the bathtub, Trevor," I quietly reminded him. "Rebecca, you go downstairs and finish your homework. Elizabeth, you make sure your toys are cleaned up. It's bedtime." I ushered them away, and closed Jeff's door to leave him alone with his father.

CHAPTER FIFTEEN

After everything was cleaned up and everyone was calmed down, we had family prayer and sent the children to bed. I put a load of laundry in and found Jake sitting on the family room couch, staring absently into space. I sat down close to him and stroked his hair. "You did a good job with Jeff tonight," I said.

Jake gave a dry laugh and muttered, "Well, that's a nice change."

"Jake, you're a very good father. Jeff's just . . . struggling right now. That's not your fault."

Jake shook his head as though he was trying to figure something out. "I guess for some reason I thought that taking him to counseling would fix the problem. There must be something more that I can do . . ."

"Come to bed, honey," I urged. "We're both exhausted. Maybe we'll be able to think more clearly in the morning." He reluctantly followed me up to bed.

The following day was Wednesday, so Jake let me sleep in and got Jeffrey and Rebecca off to school. I didn't feel nearly as queasy when I got up and was surprised that an extra hour of sleep could make a difference. "Bless you," I said to Jake when I finally made it down to the kitchen. Then I smiled and asked jokingly, "Dare I ask what Rebecca's hair looked like when she got on the bus?" I knew he'd had to deal with Elizabeth's hair alone for nearly four years, but she was blessed with her mother's thick, sleek auburn locks that needed little more than combing once a day. My daughter, on the other hand, was cursed with my fine, blond tresses, which required a great deal more coaxing.

A worried look crossed Jake's face as he asked, "Was I supposed to comb her hair?"

I felt my eyes open wide, and Jake laughed. I slugged him playfully, saying, "I can't believe I fell for that."

"I didn't even try to mess with the curling iron," he confessed. "But I *did* manage to brush her hair and put it in a ponytail. It's mostly straight, and her ponytail holder matched her outfit. I think she'll do."

"Thank you," I said. "That extra hour did wonders for my stomach."

"You know, Mar, I've been thinking . . ." Jake began, as I poured myself a glass of orange juice and sat down to join him at the table. "Maybe we've been going about this all the wrong way."

"Going about what all the wrong way?" I asked.

"This whole thing with Jeffrey, and all the stress and everything."

"So, what do you think we ought to do differently?" I questioned.

"Well," he began, "I think we've done just about everything within our physical power. We've tried nearly every parenting tactic in the book. We've been to see a counselor. We've talked and analyzed and studied and pondered . . ."

"Yes," I prodded. "And?"

"And I think that now it's time to turn it over to the Lord," Jake answered with humility. "He's the only one who really knows what's going on in Jeffrey's head, the only one who understands what he needs from us . . . Do you think you're up to a temple session today?"

I smiled. "I think that with a little faith I could probably make it through without throwing up. I always do."

"Good. I know you can't fast, but I'm going to. If you'd be willing, I'd like us to spend some extra time studying the scriptures and praying this morning. Then I'd like to squeeze in a trip to the temple this afternoon while Lizzy and Trevor are at preschool." I hadn't seen so much hope or peace in Jake's expression for weeks. "And then," he continued, "I think we just need to have the faith that the Lord will help us get to the root of what's bothering Jeffrey, and help him work through it."

"That sounds like a marvelous plan," I agreed happily.

He smiled and replied, "I'm glad you think so."

In the temple, I tried to concentrate on the ceremony and Jeffrey, but I found thoughts of Lydia crowding into my mind. I felt annoyed with the distraction and tried to push the thoughts away, but they refused to budge. I thought it was too bad that Ann wasn't there. She would have known exactly what to say, and how to befriend Lydia to find out what made her tick.

I was startled at the abrupt realization that although Ann wasn't there, she'd been a perfect example of a true friend when she had been. She had befriended me at one of the lowest times of my life, when I was going through so many struggles in my marriage to Ted. I was sure that I hadn't been the most pleasant person to be around at the time, but Ann had seen good things in me anyway, and even helped me begin to see some of those things myself. I thought of the many acts of service Ann had performed for me and what a charitable person she was. She'd even tried to befriend Tess, for heaven's sake.

The idea crossed my mind that perhaps I could do something to carry on in Ann's absence. I'd actually felt remorseful when I finally talked to Tess just before she'd moved back to New York. I wished then that I'd taken Ann's advice and made a better effort to be kinder to Tess. Although I admittedly still felt angry at Tess for the choices she'd made, and for the repercussions I was dealing with as a result of them, I did feel sorry for her.

The thought occurred to me that I'd developed a lot of empathy for Lydia too, after I'd found out a few things about her. I felt bad for judging her harshly in the beginning. I'd seen her perform several quiet acts of service, if I stopped and thought about it. And she was often holding a baby at church that wasn't hers. I also knew she did a lot of extra things to help Sister Carter, her landlady—I'd heard Sister Carter talk about it. The thought also occurred to me that Lydia went to church every week. She'd also gone to most of the singles activities when I'd been going to them, and I assumed that she still was. I was painfully aware of how lonely I'd felt after Ted and I separated and then divorced. Being single in a family-centered church was a difficult thing to be, I knew. Even when I was going through that, though, I'd had my children, and I knew that I'd received the blessings of a temple sealing. I decided to make a bigger effort to befriend Lydia, not just to meet the minimum visiting teaching requirement.

Sitting with Jake in the celestial room after the temple session, I considered sharing my thoughts with him. But then I decided to keep it to myself. I knew he was concentrating on his son, as he should be.

Jake and I whispered to each other for a minute, mostly about our hopes and concerns regarding Jeffrey. Then we spent a few more moments in silence, each of us saying a prayer in our hearts for understanding and direction. The peaceful feeling I'd had lingered with me for the rest of the day.

I was surprised by how quickly our faith and prayers were rewarded, though I didn't recognize it as a blessing right off. It was only two days later, a rainy Friday afternoon, when the telephone rang. I'd just come in after dropping Trevor and Elizabeth off at preschool. "Mrs. Jantzen?" the voice on the other end asked. I was alarmed at the urgency in her tone.

"Yes?" I asked quickly.

"This is Mrs. Wright, Jeffrey's teacher."

"Is something wrong?" I questioned, an all-too-familiar feeling of dread settling in my stomach. *What did he do now?* I thought to myself.

"Jeff had an accident on the playground a few minutes ago."

"An accident?" I asked in surprise. I didn't have time to be grateful that he hadn't started another fight before panic set in.

"Yes. He fell from the top of the monkey bars. I think he'll be all right, but we're quite sure that his left leg is broken."

"Where is he?" I had to get to him, fast.

"The principal drove him to the hospital. He was in a lot of pain. We didn't want to make him wait for you to get here. I hope that's all right." For a moment, I wished they'd taken him to Jake's office instead. But then I decided the hospital might be better, after all. He'd probably be more cooperative for someone else. If he was in a lot of pain, and Jake tried to cast his leg, he might fight him.

"Thank you," I said. "I'll meet him there."

I snatched my purse from the closet and ran, not even pausing to get my jacket. I called Jake on the cell phone while I was driving, praying that Jeffrey would be all right. It made me sick to think of the pain he was in, and I drove faster in spite of the wet roads. I must have sounded panicky to Jake because he said, "Slow down, Mar. I don't need you getting hurt too. I'll meet you at the hospital."

The woman at the emergency room desk gave me a room number and pointed down the hall. "There's a nurse with him," she told me. I could hear Jeff crying from the lobby as I ran awkwardly toward him. When I got close enough to hear what he was saying to the nurse, I stopped.

"Mommy! I want my *mom!*" What was I thinking, running to him? He didn't want me. I couldn't give him what he wanted, who he needed. I felt sick.

Jake came running up behind me, and I pointed to Jeff's room. Jake's eyes met mine when he heard Jeffrey, and he looked up at the ceiling as if to question God. He touched my arm, then walked into the room. "Hi, bud. Trying to be Superman again, were you?"

"Ah, so this is your little superhero then, Dr. Jantzen?" the nurse inside the room asked. "I should have seen the resemblance. Dr. Thompson will be in to cast his leg in a minute. The X-rays just came back."

"Thank you," Jake told her. "I assume you've already given him something for the pain?"

"Yes, about five minutes ago." She bustled out of the room and patted my arm before heading down the hall.

"I want Mom!" Jeff yelled. I stood outside his door, trying to compose myself.

"Honey, Mom's not here," Jake answered softly. I peeked in to see him hugging his son, while trying not to bump his splinted leg.

Jeffrey hugged him back and cried more quietly. "Why? I want her. Where is she, Dad? Can't you ask her to come?"

I felt anger at Tess well up in me again. Jeff knew where she was. She was in New York, where she'd been for months. He hadn't asked about her for a while, but surely he hadn't forgotten that.

Jake cleared his throat and said, "I'm sorry, buddy, but I can't ask her to come. She's gone."

"Gone where?" Jeffrey demanded fiercely.

I wondered if he'd hit his head when he fell, too. Or maybe he was just confused because he was still in shock. I supposed that Jake was thinking the same thing when he answered calmly, "She went to New York, Jeff."

Jeff pushed Jake away with surprising force. "She *left?* This is all your fault!" he hollered. Jake looked stunned as his small son accused, "You *made* her leave! I knew you'd make her leave!"

Jake moved toward him and said, "Jeffrey, calm down. I'm here. I'm not going anywhere."

"I don't want you! *I want my mom!* Why did you have to marry her? That's why I *didn't* want you to marry her! I *knew* you'd make her leave, just like you made my first mom leave! *She* said it was all your fault! And it was, 'cause you kept fighting with Maren, and now you made her leave too! I hate you, Daddy! I *hate* you!"

My heart lurched as I grasped what he meant. I stepped farther into the room and moved toward him. Jeff saw me and relief swept over his little face. "Mom!" he cried. I went to hug him, and he whimpered, "You didn't leave?"

"No, of course not, sweetheart," I soothed. I held him to me and cried silently as his sobs subsided. I looked at Jake over Jeff's head and saw tears in his eyes too. I had been very wrong. We had both been very wrong. The source of all Jeff's worry and resistance was suddenly very clear. I felt awful for not seeing it earlier, but relieved and over-joyed to finally understand.

"Are you gonna leave, Mommy?" Jeffrey sniffled.

I looked down at his sweet face, at the innocent, loving little boy I'd begun to think we'd lost for good. "No, Jeffrey, not ever. It's not Daddy's fault that your mom left, buddy. That was her own choice. I'll never do that. I love your dad with all my heart, and I love you and Lizzy, too. I would never want to be away from any of you. I'll always be here for you, I promise."

Jeffrey squeezed my neck with one arm, keeping his other arm on the examining table for balance. He finally relaxed in my embrace, and I knew that he was mine, after all.

The pain medication seemed to help Jeffrey a lot, but it made him tired. He fell asleep on the way home, and Jake carried him up to the guest room. When our other children arrived, we told them what had happened, and instructed them to be quiet so Jeff could rest. They all wanted to see him, but he didn't wake up until after they were in bed. When Jeff did wake up, he just cried and said that his leg hurt. Jake gave him a priesthood blessing while I held him. When Jake had finished praying, he said to his son, "I love you, buddy."

Jeff yawned and leaned against me. "Love you, Daddy," he mumbled. I knew that Jake understood Jeffrey's anger during his earlier outburst, but I still detected a degree of relief in his expression when he heard those words.

As soon as the next dose of pain medication washed over Jeffrey and he'd fallen asleep, Jake and I went to our room and knelt to say a prayer of gratitude together. "I can't believe it was that simple," Jake said when he'd finished praying. I could only agree.

Over the next few days, Jeff was in a lot of pain, but then he slowly started improving. He practiced getting around on crutches so he could go back to school soon. In the meantime, I helped him with his schoolwork to ensure that he wouldn't get behind.

Jake worked the night clinic at the pediatrics office on a Friday night, two weeks after Jeff's accident, and came home late. I was watching the news on the family room couch, a pillow behind my aching back, when he came in. "Hi, love." He smiled a tired smile at me as he walked into the kitchen.

"Hi." I smiled back and started to get up. "I'll warm up some dinner for you."

He crossed the room quickly and touched my shoulder. "No, you stay there. I'll get it myself." He gave me a quick kiss of greeting.

"Thank you," I answered him gratefully. I knew he didn't expect me to get dinner for him, but I felt like I should, especially after he'd worked so late.

Jake heated up his meatloaf and potatoes and came to sit by me on the couch while he ate. "How's Jeff doing?" he asked.

"Lots better," I answered. "He's getting pretty good on those crutches, and it doesn't seem to hurt so much anymore if his leg gets bumped or something. I told him that I thought he should go back to school on Monday. Do you think he's healed enough to handle it?"

Jake nodded with his mouth full, and I laughed at him. After he swallowed, he said, "Yes, he should be. How are *you?* You look exhausted."

"I'm a little tired," I confessed.

"It's been hard on you, having to take care of Jeffrey these last couple of weeks," he said. "I'm sorry. Thanks for taking such good care of him."

I touched his shoulder. "Jake, he's my son too. It's no different than if Trevor had been the one to break his leg. Especially after . . ." I got choked up thinking about it. ". . . after he asked for me in the hospital and called me 'Mom,' after I realized why he'd been so upset about us getting married. I can't believe I thought it was because he didn't love me all this time."

Jake gave me an empathetic smile and said, "I should've known. I should have taken time to get to the root of what was upsetting him, instead of assuming that I understood. It certainly all makes a lot more sense now."

I nodded and continued, "Since that day in the hospital, I've finally felt like everything's going to be okay with our kids. I know things aren't going to be all sunshine and roses from here on out, but I'm greatly relieved. I was so worried over Jeff. It's nice to finally feel like he accepts me as his mother. I didn't think it would be so important to me, Jake. I thought I could handle it if Jeff and Lizzy always thought of me as Maren, but I couldn't. I don't want them to forget their real mother or to think that she doesn't love them, in spite of her choices, but I do want them to accept me as their mom, too. I'll be raising them for many years to come. I'll be the grandma to their children. I want them to love me."

Jake set his empty plate on the coffee table and reached up to rub my neck. "They do love you, Mar. You're the only real mother they've ever known. And they couldn't want for a better one."

"Maybe Jeff and I needed this time together." I told him the thought that had crossed my mind more than once. "I think it's done much for both of us to heal the pain and misunderstanding of the past few months. Jeff has acted very differently toward me since his confession at the hospital. It's like he's finally let me in."

Jake smiled and nodded in agreement. Then he looked at the pillow behind my back. "Does your back hurt?" he asked.

"It's been throbbing all day, actually," I confessed wearily.

He raised his eyebrow at me. "Are you all right? Have you been doing things you shouldn't?"

"No, Dr. Jantzen. I haven't been lifting any children or moving any furniture. It's just daily stuff. I did mop the kitchen floor. I guess that wasn't good."

"No more mopping then," he ordered playfully. Then he continued seriously, "I'll do that for you, Mar, and anything else you need me to. I want you to take care of yourself. You tell me what you need me to do, and I'll do it."

"You're too wonderful to be true," I told him gratefully.

He smiled. "Turn around. I'll rub your throbbing back."

"Bless you." He worked his strong hands along my back for several minutes, easing the tension out of stiff and tired muscles. "I can't even tell you how good that feels," I murmured. When I was just about to doze off, I stood up and said, "Let's go to bed. Thanks for the massage. My back feels much better."

"You're welcome." He smiled a mischievous grin. "Want to race up the stairs?"

"You must really need a self-esteem boost, huh?" I laughed. Then I added teasingly, "I could still beat you at jumping fences."

"Maybe." He smiled. "But I'd be there to catch you, just in case."

The picture that sprang into my mind of him catching me as I toppled belly first over pasture fences was too much. I sat on the stairs and laughed until I cried. "You okay, Mar?" He laughed at me laughing.

"It's just hormones," I justified. When I took a breath, I finally told him, "You're so adorable and so funny." I sighed happily. "I never thought I'd feel so carefree again after all the years in darkness. You light up my whole world, Jake."

"I do?" He smiled like a delighted little boy.

"Yes, but now I can't get up. I'm afraid you'll have to carry me up the stairs."

"If you insist, my lady," he replied with mock gallantry.

He scooped me up, and I protested quickly, "I was only joking, Jake! Stop! Put me down! You'll hurt yourself." He ran up the stairs, kicked our bedroom door shut, and kissed me until I had to hush up.

"We're already here, Mar—you can be quiet now." He smiled and put me down gently. "And I'll have you know that it will be a sad day when I can't carry my wife and baby up the stairs." He flexed his biceps and grinned at me.

"Would you look at that body of steel?" I teased him, grasping one of his arms with both my hands. "I'm sorry I underestimated you, honey. Tomorrow night I'll let you carry me up in the armchair."

He laughed. "Whatever it takes to get you up here with me. I can't go to sleep without you, ya know."

I smiled at him and went to brush my teeth. I could see Jake changing into pajamas in our bedroom from the bathroom mirror. He looked up and caught my eyes, mouthing the words, "I love you." I blew him a toothpaste kiss, and we both laughed again.

After we read scriptures together and had gone to bed, I sat staring into the darkness and thinking. The contrast of all that my life was now, compared to what it had been only a year ago, was amazing. I suddenly thought of Lydia, going to bed alone in her empty basement apartment. I really had no idea what that must feel like. I'd guessed before that she was somewhere in her early thirties, which meant she'd probably been alone for a long time. I'd only been twenty years old when I married Ted, and after we divorced I'd had children to keep me busy. I was suddenly filled with sympathy, and though I'd temporarily forgotten my resolve to befriend Lydia in the face of Jeff's accident, now that he was doing better, I decided maybe it was time to visit her again.

The following day was Saturday, which I knew would be the best day to catch Lydia at home. So I baked brownies and arranged some on a plate for her that afternoon. I checked on the children, who were soaking up the bright spring sunshine in the backyard, and then found Jake putting fertilizer on the front lawn. I told him I had an errand to run and asked if he'd mind watching the kids, appreciating how refreshing it was to know that he really wouldn't.

"Of course I don't mind, love," he told me, then eyed the plate of brownies in my hand. "Whatcha doin'?" he asked, giving me a sly grin.

"Nothing," I answered innocently.

Jake leaned closer to me and whispered, "You're up to something, aren't you, Mar?"

"I'm just going to visit Lydia," I said, trying not to sound defensive.

"You're taking this visiting teaching stuff pretty seriously, aren't you?" He looked amused.

I poked a finger at his chest and reminded him, "It's your fault that Lydia and I got off on the wrong foot anyway, remember?" Then I turned more serious and told him, "I've just been thinking about Ann a lot. I'm sure I wasn't the most cheerful company when she first befriended me. I needed her desperately, though."

Jake nodded in understanding as I kissed him good-bye and started down the sidewalk.

"Don't go soft and bring home any kittens!" he called after me.

Lydia looked pretty surprised to see me again, so soon. I felt a little uneasy, but I thought of Ann's incredible self-confidence and undaunted enthusiasm and I forced myself to smile. "Hi, Lydia," I said cheerfully.

"Hi," she answered haltingly.

"I just baked some brownies and thought you might like some." I held the plate out to her.

She slowly took the offering. "Thanks."

"How are you doing?" I asked her.

"Fine." Lydia hesitated a moment, but then pushed the door open further. "You wanna come in for a minute?" she offered.

"Sure." I smiled.

Three little kittens ran toward the door, meowing as we walked in. "Wow, they've already grown," I observed. "Weren't there four of them, though?"

"Yeah, I gave one away."

"One down then," I remarked.

She actually laughed as she invited me to sit down. "Can I get you anything?" she asked.

"No, I'm fine."

"To tell you the truth, I'm getting more attached to them every day," she confessed, picking up a kitten to cuddle it. She shrugged then and said, "Maybe I'll keep the rest of them. I don't have anyone else to take care of." She sounded more wistful than bitter. I didn't know how to respond.

"I guess you've got your hands full, though," Lydia commented. She hesitated a moment before asking, "When's your baby due?"

"August second," I told her quietly, feeling incredibly blessed at that moment, but also feeling guilty for having so much that she did not.

Lydia nodded as her eyes filled up with tears, but she quickly looked away. She took a moment to regain her composure and then told me, "Listen, I'm sorry for giving you the cold shoulder all those months, Maren. I should have taken the time to get to know you better. I appreciate your efforts to be nice to me. I'm sure that hasn't been easy for you. You probably felt as horrified as I did when you found out that you'd been assigned to be my visiting teacher."

Lydia looked mildly distraught at what she'd just said, like she wished she could snatch the words back. But I laughed. I couldn't help it. She watched me laughing for a moment before the corners of her mouth twitched up and she laughed too.

"Yeah," I admitted. "I was pretty horrified . . . But it hasn't been such a bad thing, after all."

"No," she agreed. "I . . . Well, I guess I have a tendency to drive people away sometimes. In some ways, I suppose I feel safer being lonely—I know what to expect." Her icy exterior seemed to have melted completely in the face of humility. "I guess I'm just . . . jealous of you. Life just seems so unfair sometimes, you know?" She looked up at me, and her eyes were glistening.

I nodded with a degree of understanding, but I was feeling a new level of awareness regarding the unfairness of life—one that I couldn't relate to.

Lydia sighed and told me, "I guess I just want what you have—a family, a good man who loves me . . . I've almost given up, though."

"Don't give up," I told her, then shared some of my own experiences. We visited a few minutes longer, and then I took my leave.

"Thanks for coming, Maren," Lydia said genuinely.

"You're welcome," I answered with a smile.

When I got home, I found Jake in the backyard with the children this time, hoeing up the flower beds to get them ready for spring planting. "Hi, handsome," I said as I reached up to kiss him.

"I'm glad to see you didn't forget where we live," he teased. "I was beginning to wonder."

I smiled and shook my head at him. When I made no further comment, he finally prodded, "Well! How did it go?"

"Good," I answered him honestly.

"I'm glad," Jake told me. "Lydia'd be lucky to have a friend like you."

"Oh, and I brought home a kitten," I added.

"What?" he asked in mild alarm.

"Gotcha." I laughed.

Jake pointed a warning finger at me, but then he laughed too.

CHAPTER SIXTEEN

I was feeling tremendously better as I approached my sixth month of pregnancy. Jeffrey had gone back to school, also feeling greatly improved. As far as my efforts with Lydia were concerned, I was surprised at how easy it was to build a friendship with her. The two of us began talking and even doing things occasionally, and I found myself enjoying her company quite a bit.

Jake and I decided to host Easter at our home. I was delighted to feel well enough to do it. The only dark spot in the excitement I felt was that Ted and I had agreed months earlier that he could have Rebecca and Trevor for the holiday. However, since Ted had backed out of what we'd agreed to for Christmas and taken the children then, it seemed only fair that I ought to have them for Easter. Ted had remained fairly agreeable recently, but I still worried about starting a fight. I didn't voice my concerns to Jake, knowing full well what stand he'd take on the issue.

I decided to try the peaceful approach first. When Ted dropped the children off the last weekend before Easter, I told them to go play with Lizzy and Jeff. Jake was upstairs, so it was just Ted and me there in the foyer. "I know we agreed several months ago that you could have the kids for Easter," I told Ted, "but since you took them for Christmas, I'd like to keep them for this holiday."

"You get them every other day," Ted said evenly. "I only get to see my own kids two weekends a month, Maren. I have to work every day—as you know," he put in sarcastically. "So it seems to me that on the rare occasions when I actually get a holiday, I ought to get the kids."

I bit my tongue and forced myself to remain calm, trying to think of what to say to convince him without a fight. "But with this being their first year living together, and with both of our families coming, I'd really like Rebecca and Trevor to be able to celebrate Easter with Jeff and Lizzy."

"It's not like they're real brothers and sisters, Maren," Ted answered quickly, eyes sparking.

"But they are, Ted," I insisted softly.

"I'm their father, Maren. I'm their family, whether you like it or not—not your precious Jake and his kids."

I closed my eyes and took a breath. "I know you're their father, Ted. They love you very much, and I know you love them." He seemed to soften a little bit. "Jake is good to them, though, Ted. He's part of their lives, and our four children are very close. It's going to be difficult for them to spend this holiday apart, especially when four of their grandparents are going to be here."

Ted grunted and glanced away before asking, "And what about next year, Maren? You'll tell me they don't want to be separated then either, and you'll have a baby besides."

"I won't argue next year," I promised. "I'll take Christmas then, and you take Easter."

Ted chuckled dryly and shook his head. "Maren, Maren . . . You always did look so pathetic when you're pregnant."

I wanted to snap back at him, but I saw the sadness in his eyes, and didn't.

He sighed. "All right, fine. But I'm taking them the whole weekend next year, no arguing. And I get Thanksgiving next year, too. I don't want you bawling that you have to give them up for both holidays."

"Thank you," I told him quickly. I was so relieved that I almost hugged him, but decided to just squeeze his arm instead.

"Okay, okay, that's enough," he muttered as he yanked his arm away and hurried out the door.

Jake came down the stairs and asked, "What was that?"

"Oh, I was just talking to Ted about Easter."

"You did tell him that we're keeping the kids then, right?" Jake asked me in a tight voice.

I looked up at him and swallowed hard. "Right."

Rebecca and Trevor heard Jake and came running from the family room to greet him. "Dad! I missed you!" Rebecca exclaimed.

Trevor threw his arms around him and said, "Hi, Daddy!"

Jake bent down to hug them both. "I missed you guys too. I'm glad you're back. Did you have fun with your dad?" They nodded and told him what they'd done over the weekend.

"And Dad took us to his church again!" Trevor said.

"Does he take you all the time now?" I asked. They nodded, and I felt grateful.

***

Our families arrived on the Saturday before Easter. Jake's parents flew in from New York, and mine drove down from Idaho. Natalie and Douglas came over, too. They were holding hands and looked content, although Nathan was a little fussy. "How're you doing?" I whispered to Natalie.

She gave me half a smile and answered, "A little better."

Our children were thrilled to see their grandparents—especially the Jantzens, whom they hadn't seen since the wedding. Jake's parents usually called every Sunday and made a point of talking to each child for a few minutes so the children felt close to them despite the physical distance that separated them.

Jake's mother hugged me when they arrived. "Aren't you blossoming, Maren dear? I can't tell you how badly I've wanted another grandchild. I just can't wait for this baby!"

My dad wasn't as gracious. "Well, you're just about as big as the broad side of a barn, aren't you now, honey?" he said, kissing my cheek. "This boy's gonna be a football player!"

Natalie playfully pushed him aside. "Don't tell her that, Dad! You know how Maren gets all emotional when she's pregnant. You'll have her bawling all over the place. This is her fourth baby, you know. Things get stretched out, I'm sure." Then she added quietly, as if he needed reminding, "She is over thirty."

I had to laugh at the way Natalie wrinkled up her nose and said "over thirty," like I might as well be ninety. I thought about how sensitive I'd been over remarks like those in my earlier pregnancies. This time nothing anyone said really bothered me. As I was thinking, Jake walked by me with his parents' suitcases and brushed a kiss across my cheek. "I think she's the most beautiful woman in the world," he said as he winked at me.

It suddenly hit me that he was the difference. He wasn't lying when he said that he thought I was beautiful. He really thought that. It hadn't occurred to me before then how his love and devotion cushioned me from the world. I had never imagined that I could feel beautiful at six months pregnant, but at that moment I did. I felt a peaceful realization of how comfortable I had become with Jake, how safe I felt. The thought made me feel strangely vulnerable, and frightened me a little. I thought of the sealing cancellation papers I'd stuffed in my nightstand drawer, and some little voice inside me whispered that I'd better deal with them—soon.

The Easter holiday passed quickly with a blur of family, smiles, laughter, and love. Jeffrey received plenty of attention over his broken leg, and everyone signed his cast. On Sunday, Mom and Dad went to church in Natalie's ward, but Jake's parents came with us. "I suppose we ought to go to church on Easter," Beverly conceded, but she seemed a bit reluctant.

When they asked if there were any visitors in Sunday School, Jake introduced his mother and father, stating that they were here from New York. The Sunday School teacher, Brother Smith, said warmly, "Welcome, Brother and Sister Jantzen." Jarold and Beverly looked a little uncomfortable, but they both smiled and nodded. "So, how large an area does your ward in New York cover?" Brother Smith asked brightly.

Jake cut in with a polite explanation. "My parents are not LDS."

"Oh!" Brother Smith looked flustered. "Forgive me. Well, we're happy to have you." He quickly got on with his lesson, but the color didn't leave his cheeks for several minutes.

On the way home, Jarold asked jokingly, "So, do we look like Mormons?"

"Yes, actually," Jake replied, cracking a slight smile. "Just think, you're already halfway there."

Beverly made a noise of indignation. "Why does everyone here just automatically assume that we're Mormons?" she asked. "It gets very annoying, Jacob. I don't think I'll go to church next time we come."

"Now, dear," Jarold soothed, "there's no harm in going to church with the kids. Some of what they preach doesn't seem to be so far-fetched."

"You could be a Mormon if you wanted to, Grandma," Elizabeth pointed out with five-year-old enthusiasm, nestled between her grandparents on the front bench of the van.

Beverly looked at her granddaughter with fondness and inquired with only a trace of annoyance, "And why would I want to be a Mormon, sweetie?"

Lizzy smiled up at her and answered, "So you could be with us forever."

Beverly's eyebrows went up in surprise, and Jarold gave his wife an amused look. She patted Elizabeth's knee and forced herself to say kindly, "Well, that's a nice thought, now isn't it?"

Jake's parents flew out on Monday morning, and my parents left for home later that afternoon. It was somewhat of a relief to have the house back to ourselves. In bed, after Jake and I had finished reading our scriptures together, he pulled me into his arms and kissed the top of my head. "You know, it's nice to have our families here," he commented. Then he added jokingly, "But it's even nicer when they all go home."

I laughed in agreement, resting against his chest for a few moments, just relishing the peace and quiet. "Remember when we went to the *Phantom of the Opera* last year?" I asked him tiredly as that pleasant memory drifted into my mind.

"Yes," he said. "What made you suddenly think about that?"

"I just happened to pull the dress you bought for me to wear to it out of the closet tonight. I was looking for my black maternity dress and grabbed the wrong one."

"Ah . . ." he answered. Then he said teasingly, "You lost that bet, didn't you?"

"Technically, yes," I replied slowly. "And I was supposed to wear my old dress from college as my penance. But you bought me a new dress anyway, so I think I actually *won* that bet, wouldn't you say?" I sat up to give Jake a smug look.

"Oh, you wish," he laughed. "Actually, everything worked out to my complete satisfaction. You see, my whole motive was to have an excuse to take you on a date, without actually having to *call* it a date because I thought I might scare you away. I *wanted* to buy you a new dress. You certainly needed one. I would've bought you one either way. It worked out nicely, though, that I was able to make it look like it was your idea."

I gave him a playful shove and said dramatically, "Oh, you're so sneaky, Jake! I had no idea!"

He laughed again, more softly, before he said, "You really didn't, did you? There I was, hopelessly in love with you, thinking it was written all over my face . . ." His words faded and then drifted back as he whispered ardently, "You were so breathtaking in that dress that night . . . I wanted to kiss you so badly, but I was terrified. I thought you were trying to tell me that you would never care for me again as anything more than a friend." He brushed my hair back and touched my face.

"Too bad I can't fit into that dress, now that you know we're more than friends," I teased. "I'd put it on for you, and we could reenact it."

Jake laughed and slid his fingers into my hair. "You know I'll always love you, Maren," he whispered. "Always and forever . . ."

I felt a sudden twinge of uneasiness, but tried to cover it with humor. "Are you sure about that?" I asked with a slight tease in my voice. "That's a long time, Jake."

He saw past my attempt to make light of his confession, and looked at me with surprise as his tone turned serious. "Are you still afraid, after all this time?"

I was a bit unnerved by his comment and looked away.

"Maren?" Jake prodded gently. "Do you really doubt that I love you?"

"No," I told him with less than absolute assurance.

When I met Jake's gaze again, he gave me a tender smile and whispered, "Are you afraid to kiss me now?"

I smiled and leaned forward to kiss his soft lips. I entwined his thick, black hair around my fingers and held him to me tightly as I kissed him so he couldn't get away.

***

I hadn't been asleep long when the phone rang. I answered it in a hurry, feeling worried. It was Natalie. "Maren?" she said with a shaky voice. I could hear Nathan screaming in the background. "I'm sorry to call so late. Did I wake you up?"

"No. What's wrong?"

"Nathan's been screaming for hours. He's burning up. I've been thinking of taking him to the hospital, but . . . well, we don't have insurance. Do you think Jake would look at him for me?" she asked with an edge of desperation.

"Of course," I said firmly. "Come right over."

"Thank you." The relief in her voice was evident.

I hung up and explained the situation to Jake. "Why didn't she call me sooner?" he asked. I shook my head.

Jake swung his legs over the edge of the bed and instructed, "Call her back and tell her I'll come to them. They certainly don't need to be dragging a sick baby clear across town."

I chastised myself inwardly for not thinking of that and quickly dialed Natalie's number. After several rings, I finally gave up. "They must have already left," I told Jake. "There's no answer."

He got dressed and went for the black leather doctor's bag he kept in the top of our closet. I'd been grateful that he was old-fashioned that way more than once. I watched him rummage through the contents, apparently searching for something. He finally pulled out a little bottle and peered at the label, sighing with relief.

I got dressed and followed Jake downstairs to wait for my sister. I heard Nathan wailing on the front porch before Natalie even knocked and hurried to open the door. My sister looked like she was ready to collapse. She had dark circles under her tear-filled eyes and was struggling to hold onto her writhing baby. I took him from her and motioned her inside.

"Thank you," Natalie whispered to Jake.

"You should have called sooner, Natalie," he told her gently. "We're family."

"That doesn't mean I need to take advantage of you. But at this point, I'm desperate."

"Where's Doug?" I asked, when he failed to appear in the doorway. I'd assumed that he was getting the diaper bag or something from the car and would follow Natalie in.

Natalie shook her head as the tears began to spill. "I don't know. He went to the library to study early this afternoon. He said he couldn't concentrate with Nathan screaming. I kept waiting for him to come home so he could go to the store for me. I didn't want to take Nathan out like this. But Doug never showed up."

Jake and I exchanged concerned glances, but didn't say anything. I just held Nathan while Jake looked at him. He reached a hand inside the baby's shirt to rest it on his chest and furrowed his brows. "When did you last give him something for this fever?" Jake asked Natalie.

"I haven't given him anything!" Natalie cried. "I told you I was waiting for Doug to come home and go to the store to get some Tylenol. How could I take him like that?" She gestured toward her hysterical baby.

"All right," Jake responded calmly, though he looked worried. He retrieved a sample of Infants' Motrin from his bag and patiently coaxed Nathan into swallowing a dose from a dropper.

"Can he take that?" Natalie asked in near panic. "I thought babies had to have Tylenol."

"Yes, he can take it," Jake reassured her. "It'll bring his fever down faster than Tylenol will."

When Nathan began screaming harder, Natalie burst out, "What's wrong with him? He's been sick before, but he's never been this bad!"

"Hold him like this, Mar," Jake instructed before he answered Natalie. I obediently turned Nathan toward me and held him tightly against my chest. "I'm betting it's an ear infection," Jake informed my sister. "I'll let you know in just a second." He looked in Nathan's ear and let out a long breath. "Oh boy, little guy," he muttered. "No wonder you're screaming."

I turned the baby's head and struggled to hold him still while Jake checked his other ear, then looked at his throat. "Ouch," he mumbled.

"What?" Natalie asked, reaching for her baby. "Here—let me have him."

"Both ears are definitely infected," Jake told her. "And his throat looks terrible. It's probably just due to drainage from the ear infection, but it's gotta hurt . . . Is he eating?"

"Not very well," Natalie responded weakly. "But I think he's had enough to keep him from getting dehy—"

I was startled to hear the phone ring again. Jake answered it and announced that it was Douglas, as he held the phone up for Natalie. She shook her head and said, "Tell him I can't talk right now."

Jake looked surprised, but obeyed. Then he managed to get anesthetic drops into Nathan's ears while Natalie held him. "Let me hold him, Natalie," he offered, and she was apparently too tired to argue. Jake held the baby to his chest, rocking him gently until he started to calm down a little.

Natalie collapsed on the couch and asked wearily, "What now?"

"These drops should numb the pain in his ears and help him calm down," Jake told her quietly. "Hopefully the Motrin will kick in soon and bring his fever down so he can sleep. We need to go get a prescription filled for him. There are a couple of pharmacies around here that are open late."

Natalie nodded. "I'll take him and go get it." She glanced from Jake to me before asking hesitantly, "Do you think Nathan and I could come back and stay here tonight?"

My eyes darted to Jake's face before I said slowly, "If you want to, Natalie . . . Is everything okay?"

She turned on me and snapped, "No, Maren, it's not! It's bad enough that I'm going to be up with Nathan again all night, but if I have to endure one more night of Doug complaining that he can't get any sleep, that he has to go to work in the morning, and that I'm not keeping the baby quiet—I'm going to scream! If I had any money, I'd go to a hotel, but I don't. I'll stay in the basement so Nathan won't keep your family awake, but please don't kick me out," Natalie pled with Jake and me. "Please let me stay. Please."

"Of course you can stay," I assured her. "And you don't have to sleep in the basement. You can stay in the guest room on the main floor. The kids'll sleep through anything."

"Thank you," she whispered tearfully.

"Tell you what," Jake said. "I'll go get the prescription. You stay here and get some rest, Natalie, and Maren can help you with Nathan." Jake looked at me pointedly and added, "But don't overdo it, Mar. I'll be back to help as soon as I can."

"I'll be fine," I reassured him. "You're the one who has to go to work in the morning."

For a moment, Natalie looked ready to argue with Jake, but logic apparently won out. She only nodded gratefully at him. Jake handed Nathan to her, still whimpering, but gradually improving. "Here," I offered, "Let me take him. I'll rock him, and you lay down on the couch for a little while, Nat." I caught the spark of an argument in her eye again and insisted, "Natalie, just let me hold him. You look like you're ready to drop."

Her eyes welled up with tears once more, and she simply handed him to me. I wrapped him in his blanket and moved to the rocking chair.

Natalie was asleep before Jake was even out of the garage. I wondered if her baby's illness had come on slowly, and how many sleepless nights she'd had before this one. I felt full of empathy, remembering all the nights I'd spent up alone with my own children. Nathan snuggled up against me as his breathing eventually calmed down and then grew rhythmic. I kissed his little head and sat rocking and thinking for a long time until Jake returned. He managed to get Nathan to swallow a dose of antibiotics without fully waking him up. The baby sighed and went back to sleep. I nudged Natalie awake and escorted her to the guest room, where she climbed into bed with her sleeping son. "Come and get me if he wakes up again," I told her. "Let me help you so you can get some sleep." She only mumbled something incoherent and rolled over.

Natalie stayed all night and through the following day. She borrowed a change of clothes from me and made no mention of leaving. Doug had called the night before after Natalie had fallen asleep, and I was left to make the awkward explanation of Natalie's decision to stay the night. I tried to make it sound more like it was motivated by a desire to stay close to Jake's professional care, but I could still sense the hurt in Doug's voice as I said good-bye.

By the time Jake got home from work that evening, Nathan was greatly improved. As I was making dinner, Jake pulled me aside and asked, "What's going on with your sister?"

I gave him a helpless look and whispered, "I don't know. I don't think she plans on leaving today, anyway."

Jake looked concerned and said, "What do you think we should do?"

"What can we do?" I asked him. "I can't make her leave. She's my sister."

"I know, but she's got to realize that she can't just hide out here forever. That's not fair to Doug."

"Maybe things will blow over after a couple of days, and she'll go home," I responded. "Maybe she wants to be sure that Nathan's doing well enough to sleep through the night so he won't keep Doug up."

Doug called during dinner, but Natalie refused to talk to him again. "She's being awfully childish," Jake told me as we got ready for bed that night. "Maybe you should talk to her tomorrow, Mar."

"All right," I agreed.

The following afternoon, I confronted my sister. "It's not that I don't like having you here, Nat," I started, "but what are you planning on doing? You can't avoid your husband forever, you know."

Natalie looked at me and responded tiredly, "I'm thinking of leaving Doug, Maren, but I'm just not sure what to do."

"Why would you leave him?" I asked in shock.

She shrugged.

"Is there something you're not telling me?" I questioned.

Natalie shook her head. "No. There's no big, awful thing, Maren. I just feel . . . empty."

"Maybe he does too," I pointed out.

She gave me a skeptical look.

"Does he go to church with you?" I asked.

She nodded.

"Does he do the things he's supposed to?"

"Yes, Maren." Natalie sounded annoyed now.

"If he's hurting you, or cheating on you, or committing a serious sin, that's one thing, Natalie. But if he loves you, and he's living right, and he's trying, that's another. I think you should talk to him. Don't you think you at least owe him that?"

She didn't have much time to think about it since Doug showed up during dinner that night. When Natalie heard him at the door, she fled to the guest room and refused to come out. "Look," Jake said to me, "I'll take Doug for a drive and see if he wants to talk or anything. You stay here and see if you can talk some sense into your sister."

I turned a video on to keep the kids busy and went to talk to Natalie, but I didn't get anywhere with her. After a few minutes, I heard Jake come home and usher Doug into the family room. Then he knocked on the guest room door. "Come in," I called.

Jake pushed the door open and found Natalie and me sitting on the bed. He walked into the room, closed the door, and leaned against it. I shook my head at him to indicate that I hadn't gotten anywhere with Natalie. Apparently deciding to take matters into his own hands, Jake addressed my sister. "Maybe I'm out of line here, but I've got to say something, Natalie."

She looked up at him expectantly.

"I know what it feels like to be where Doug is," Jake began. "Believe me, the poor guy's in a very difficult position. He has a wife and baby whom he can barely manage to support, even though he's working himself to death. He's got to get through school if he's going to be able to take care of his family, but he can't get through school if he doesn't keep up with his assignments. He feels additional pressure and stress because he has a sick child, and he can't even afford to buy medicine, let alone take him to the doctor. He knows his wife is exhausted, but he doesn't see how he can possibly hold down a full-time job, keep up with school, and still be home to help with a sick baby. He's just trying to survive and do the best he can until he can get to a better place. He loves his wife and son more than anything in the world, but he doesn't know how to make them see that. He's afraid that his wife might not love him because he can't give her everything he'd like to right now, and all he can do is hope and pray that they'll make it." Jake paused and added, "I realize that you're in a difficult position, too, Natalie but you and Doug can get through this if you work on things together." Natalie's eyes teared up as Jake added, "He really wants to see you."

Natalie hesitated, but then nodded her head in agreement. Jake and I left the room, and Doug went in to talk to Natalie. When they emerged half an hour later, Natalie still seemed reluctant, but she gave me a quick hug and left with her husband.

Jake shook his head, looking worried, and observed, "I hope they'll be all right."

"They will be," I said firmly.

CHAPTER SEVENTEEN

I felt increasingly better through the longer, warmer days of May. I was looking forward to having the children home for the summer, and to the baby who would be arriving before it was over. I started walking around the neighborhood sometimes instead of on the treadmill in an effort to tone things down as I got further along in my pregnancy.

Jake and I continued going to counseling appointments once a month, but we didn't take Jeffrey in again. His whole attitude seemed to have changed since his accident. He was back to himself, and I was deeply grateful.

I was also making real progress in my friendship with Lydia. I asked her about her singing when I visited her that month.

"I used to be pretty good, actually," she confessed modestly. "But I haven't really practiced in years."

"Why not?" I asked.

Lydia sighed and admitted, "I once dreamed of being a professional singer. I never wanted to be famous or anything, just to make a difference somehow by sharing my gift with others. It's just one of many dreams I've long since given up on."

I felt empathy welling up in me. "What other dreams have you given up on?" I asked gently.

A few tears suddenly spilled down her face, and she wiped them quickly away. I was surprised at how easy it had been over the past several weeks to get past her toughened exterior to an apparently tender heart.

"I think I've given up on ever getting married or having children," Lydia admitted sadly. "And I suppose I've also given up on really trying to make friends or get close to people."

"But you have lots of friends!" I protested. "And there seem to be plenty of men interested in taking you out."

"Yeah, but I keep them at a distance," she admitted. "I guess it's hard for me to trust anyone."

"I can understand that," I said sympathetically. "But you can't give up, Lydia."

She tilted her head for a minute, as if pondering something, and then decided to change the subject. The conversation went on, but it left me wondering during the days that followed what she'd been thinking.

***

The first Wednesday in June, I had a sudden urge to finish some spring cleaning before the children got out of school for the summer. Jake humored me and agreed to help me clean out all the cupboards and closets, dust the blinds, wash the curtains, and pack away all the winter clothes I'd never gotten around to moving. We'd been working very hard all morning. When Jake returned from dropping Trevor and Lizzy off at preschool, he kissed me and suggested, "Why don't you lie down for a few minutes? I'll keep working."

"I will in a minute," I promised. "I'm just going to finish cleaning out this last cupboard."

He shook his head and scolded, "Mrs. Jantzen, you should do what the doctor tells you to do. You're looking a bit pale." He gently touched one hand to my round stomach and brushed a lock of hair behind my ear with the other. The baby kicked suddenly, in response to his touch, and we both laughed.

"See? He agrees with me," Jake said. He leaned down to speak close to my stomach. "Tell your mommy that she needs to rest, buddy." The baby kicked again, making me wince.

Jake looked at me with concern.

I patted his cheek. "Don't worry, I'll lie down. Just give me a minute, Doctor."

He sighed and picked up a box of sweaters to carry down to the basement. I stretched to reach a glass on the top cupboard shelf, which wasn't easy with my belly in the way. I felt a cramp in my side and pulled my arm back down to push against it. Then, without warning, my water suddenly broke. I felt sick at the gush of fluid. It was way too early. I wasn't even thirty-two weeks pregnant. I didn't dare move. I felt glued to that spot on the floor. "Jake," I called softly. Another gush of fluid prompted me to scream, "JAKE!" I felt terrified. I thought I might pass out. I held on to the counter to steady myself.

He came running up the stairs, calling, "What is it, Mar?" Then he reached the kitchen and saw me. I was too afraid to look down and see the amniotic fluid that still should have been protecting my baby for two more months. How could my body fail me like this? I looked at Jake and watched his handsome face turn ashen. I knew he didn't have a weak stomach—he was a doctor. He must have been afraid. "Oh, Maren . . ." he whispered as he ran toward me. He put one arm around my waist and the other on my arm. "You need to lie down—fast," he urged.

"Why?" I asked. "Is it that bad?" I could tell it was from the look on his face. I was too scared to cry. He threw a blanket from the family room chair over the couch and helped me to lie down. Then he knelt next to me and brushed my hair back from my forehead to press the back of his hand against it.

"It's not that early, is it?" I asked. "The baby will still be okay?"

"Maren, lie flat on your back and don't move," he instructed firmly. I could tell that he was trying to stay calm, but there was an urgency in his voice that terrified me. He was so emotional as a husband that the doctor in him couldn't take over. That was a bad sign. *Why won't he tell me the baby will be all right?* I wondered.

"What's wrong? What are you going to do?" I asked.

"I'm going to get you to the hospital as fast as I can."

"The children. What about when the children come home?" I reminded him.

He shook his head. "I'll worry about that in a minute, Mar. I have to take care of you first."

He called an ambulance. I heard him talking to the dispatcher on the phone in a low voice. "Look, you don't need to tell me what to do—I'm a doctor. Just get here fast."

When came back to me, I asked, "Can't you just drive me? I don't want to go in an ambulance, Jake. I'm okay." But as I said it, I knew that I wasn't. The shock had worn off enough for me to realize that I was having contractions, hard contractions.

"Call Natalie," I told him.

He breathed a sigh of relief. "I forgot about Natalie." He ran to call her, then hurried back to me and looked down at the couch. I knew I was still losing fluid fast. I could feel it, but I thought my body would keep making more until the baby was delivered. Wasn't that how it worked? It didn't explain why I was beginning to feel so weak and dizzy, though.

A look of pure terror washed over Jake's face. I'd never seen him look like that. It scared me. "Honey?" I whispered in alarm.

"I need to give you a blessing, Mar." He gave me a quick priest-hood blessing, praying urgently for the baby's life, and mine. *Mine?*

I sat up and looked toward the kitchen, and then I understood. It wasn't amniotic fluid. It was blood . . . everywhere . . . deep red blood. Jake pushed me back down, but it was too late. I'd seen it. "Jake, you have to clean it up! The kids can't come home and see that!" I suddenly felt hysterical.

"Maren, it will be cleaned up before the children come home. I promise you." I saw tears in his eyes as I heard the sirens.

I touched his face and whispered, "I love you."

"I love you too, sweetheart. Everything's going to be all right."

I was too weak to talk anymore. Jake picked me up and hurried to meet the ambulance crew before they could get to me. He laid me down carefully on the stretcher, and someone put an oxygen mask over my face. I felt consciousness slipping away from me, though I struggled to hold on. I couldn't see Jake. I whispered his name. I didn't know if it was the oxygen mask that made my voice sound distant or the fog that was creeping into my mind. I looked at one of the EMTs and asked, "Where's my husband?"

"Honey, I'm here." He was standing above me and reached down to touch my face. "I have to drive the car to the hospital in case they have to move you. I'll be there in just a minute, okay?"

"Don't let me lose the baby, Jake," I implored him. "I can't lose the baby . . . It's just like it was with Ashlyn." I couldn't shake the terrible memory of losing my first baby shortly after birth.

He leaned over me. "Good heavens, Maren! Has this happened before? Why didn't you tell me?"

I shook my head. "It wasn't this bad. I didn't start bleeding until after I was already in labor, at the hospital. I didn't bleed this much, and she was only two weeks early. They told me it was a fluke. I never expected it to happen again, but this is worse." I tried to stop crying and keep talking. "I can't lose another baby, Jake. This can't happen again. Please."

"Maren, it will be okay." Jake touched my face and tried to reassure me. "You just hold on, love. I'll see you in a minute." He squeezed my hand, but I was too weak to squeeze back.

The ambulance drive was a blur. I remembered them rushing me into a room where nurses took off my dress and put a hospital gown on me. My doctor was already there. They were hooking me up to monitors and wires and tubes. I was still fighting to stay awake. One of the nurses told Dr. Stewart, "She's dilated to a four and having contractions."

"My baby. Is the baby all right?" I asked a nurse standing near me.

She finished connecting the monitor and smiled. "There's his heartbeat," she said.

I cried with relief, but I was still terrified. I turned to my doctor and asked, "How bad is it?"

He looked at me seriously and replied, "I'm concerned, Maren. You're losing a lot of blood. Hold on a minute, I'll be right back." He patted my arm and went out, closing the door behind him. I was glad that at least he hadn't lied to me. The nurses went out in a flurry after him, saying something about making sure the delivery room was ready, just in case.

I prayed silently, *Please let the baby be all right. Please.* I could feel blood pumping out of me with what seemed like every heartbeat. My own body was working against me, against my baby, and I could do nothing to stop it. I felt trapped and scared. I sat in deathly silence for several long moments, with only the sound of my baby's heartbeat to reassure me.

I was thankful to finally hear Jake's voice just outside my door, but he didn't come in right away. He stayed outside, talking with Dr. Stewart. From what he was saying, I was certain that he assumed I couldn't hear the conversation, but I heard every word. "What are you going to do, Paul?"

"I think the smartest thing would be to start a magnesium drip immediately and see if we can get her stabilized."

"She's already lost one baby. She's terrified of losing another one," Jake said softly. "But she's losing so much blood." I heard the fear in his voice, the torment.

"Jake, you know how big a difference two weeks will make for that baby. Even two days would be a blessing. That would be time enough for the steroid shot to speed up his lung development."

"I know, I know! But, Maren! She's got to be okay. You've got to stop that bleeding. Can't you just do an emergency C-section?"

"You know I can, Jake," Dr. Stewart answered. "Is that really what you want me to do? You'd be taking a big risk with your baby. We'd have to life-flight him right out of here. He'd have to get up to the children's hospital immediately. Of course, you know all that. You've seen enough of it firsthand."

"I can't lose my wife, Paul. I'm not going to watch her bleed to death, not even for our baby!" I could hear him clearing his throat, apparently trying to choke back emotion. It made me cry harder. "She's got to be all right. Please."

"Jake, try to calm down for a minute and think like a doctor instead of like a husband. If we can get her stabilized and stop the bleeding, it will be better for both her and the baby. We'll monitor her very closely, and if anything changes, we can still do an emergency C-section within minutes." Dr. Stewart paused for a few seconds and then said, "What would you tell a patient?"

Jake was silent a for a moment before he told him, "You *promise* me you'll deliver the baby if I ask you to. I'm staying with her every second."

"All right, Jake."

Dr. Stewart came back into the room with my husband right behind him. "Where are the nurses?" Dr. Stewart asked me in surprise.

I shook my head weakly. "They said something about making sure the delivery room was ready."

He muttered something under his breath and punched the button on the wall twice. Two nurses bustled in. "I want Mrs. Jantzen started on a mag drip immediately," he ordered. "And don't leave her alone again until she's stable."

A nurse squeezed a syringe full of clear liquid into my IV. It stung. Jake leaned over to kiss me as soon as he could get to me. "How are you, love?" I tried not to wince at the blood stains on his shirt—obviously the result of picking me up.

I managed a smile as I replied, "I've had better days . . . but I'll be all right now that you're here."

"Yes, you will," he said firmly. "I'll make sure of that." Then he said to the nurse attending to me, "She's going to need a steroid shot right away for the baby's lungs and a dose of antibiotics to prevent any infection."

"All right, Dr. Jantzen," she acknowledged. She looked to Dr. Stewart for confirmation, who nodded at her. The next few minutes passed in a haze, but I gradually became aware that the contractions had stopped and the bleeding had slowed down.

I heard Jake ask, "Did you take a blood sample yet to see if she's going to need a transfusion?"

"No, but we'll do it now that she's stabilizing."

I struggled to keep my eyes open. "I can't stay awake," I mumbled.

Jake kissed my forehead. "It's okay now, Mar. You sleep. I'll be right here."

I kissed his hand that held mine and pressed it to my cheek. He suddenly broke into tears and leaned over to rest his forehead on mine. "Don't you ever, *ever* leave me, Maren," he told me fiercely. "I could never go back to living without you."

It took great effort to lift my other hand, especially with the IV in it and all the tape and tubes, but I managed to tangle my fingers in Jake's hair and hold him to me. "I'm not going anywhere, Jake," I whispered. "I'm okay. Don't worry." He kissed my lips, sore from my biting down on them, and I drifted into sleep.

When I woke up, everything was blurry. I tried to make my eyes focus, but I couldn't. I could see that clear liquid was still dripping through an IV into one arm. My other arm was connected to a fuzzy tube filled with dark fluid. Jake was holding that hand. He looked fuzzy too. "Hi," he said, and smiled.

I squeezed my eyes shut for a minute and opened them again, but something was still wrong with my vision. "I can't see right," I mumbled.

"I know, Mar. It's the magnesium."

"What's it . . . for?" My brain felt cloudy too. I had to struggle to put my thoughts into words, and I still wasn't sure if they were coming out right.

"It acts as a very strong muscle relaxer. It stops labor. Unfortunately, it also affects your other muscles, including your eyes."

"Is that why I feel so . . ." What was the word? "I can't . . . move very well," I whispered, struggling to sit up.

Jake gently put a hand on my shoulder to hold me down. "Maren, you need to lie still. It's best for the baby, and for the blood transfusion. I know you feel weak. It's partly the IV, and partly the loss of blood. You're going to be okay, though." He touched my cheek and smiled at me, which was comforting, but it would have been more so if I could have seen his face clearly.

"I feel awful," I complained.

He nodded in sympathy. I tried closing my eyes again, but then I felt like I was spinning, which was even worse than the poor vision. I glanced around the room. It looked like a watercolor painting that someone had washed over with a wet brush—everything ran together. It made me nauseated. I tried to think about the baby and realized that I could hear his heartbeat on the monitor. "The baby's going to be all right?" I asked Jake.

"Yes, he's going to be fine."

"Thank goodness," I whispered. I felt irritated with all the tubes and wires that were connected to me. "How long does it take to get the . . . blood?" I couldn't remember the word for it.

"You mean the transfusion?" Jake asked.

I nodded.

"You're almost finished, just a few more minutes. You've been hooked up for five hours."

I felt queasy. "I lost that much blood?"

He cleared his throat and nodded. I couldn't tell for sure if his eyes were watery or just blurry, but I guessed he was probably too choked up to answer out loud.

"Is this going to be okay for the baby?" I asked.

"Yes, Mar." I didn't know why I felt like I had to ask him about everything. I knew he would make the best decisions concerning the baby and me. He knew what he was doing.

I suddenly noticed the ugly blotchy stains on Jake's shirt again and panicked. "The blood, Jake! The kids! You have to go home and clean it up!"

He stroked my hair back from my face and said, "Shh. It's taken care of, Maren."

"Did you go home then?" I wondered why he hadn't changed his shirt if he had.

He shook his head. "No. I called Natalie and she said the emergency crew that came to the house actually cleaned up a lot of it. She mopped the floor, just to make sure, and she was even able to get the stains out of the couch with the upholstery attachment on the carpet cleaner. She seemed fine, and the kids are home with her and safe."

I sighed with relief and then wondered aloud, "Have you been with me this whole time?"

"I haven't left your side . . . Did you think I would?"

"No . . ." I whispered. I remembered spending long, lonely hours in the hospital both before and after I'd given birth the first three times. Ted always managed to be there for the births themselves, but he had better things to do than sit in a hospital room with me, even after Ashlyn died. He'd just left me there to mourn alone. When I'd finally gone home, he'd acted as if everything should be back to normal, like I'd never even been pregnant. Not only was I grieving for my daughter, but I was trying to recover from seventeen hours of labor and a very difficult birth. I had felt lost in a chasm of loneliness so deep that I couldn't see daylight . . . Feeling overcome with gratitude now, I lifted Jake's hand and held it to my heart.

He leaned over to hug me through all the paraphernalia, pressing his cheek next to mine. I kissed his hair. He smelled so good, so familiar, so comforting. I prayed silently to thank God for my husband, for his presence. When Jake pulled away I could see the concern in his eyes, even if they were fuzzy. Only then did it occur to me how much he'd been through that day.

I struggled to lift a hand to his face. "Are you all right?" I asked.

He nodded as he took my hand and kissed it, swallowing hard.

"Jake?" I prodded. "How do you feel?"

He looked down at me again and chuckled softly. "Using my own tricks on me, are you?"

I smiled. "Yes, I guess I am. So . . . tell me." I felt my thoughts becoming slightly more clear and wished that I could see Jake's eyes in clear focus while I listened to his words.

"I feel relieved, Mar, but my heart's still racing. The only other time I can remember being so afraid was when I pulled you out of that river and you weren't breathing."

I nodded in understanding as I recalled the incident.

Our conversation was interrupted when a nurse entered the room. She checked all the monitors and my IV, then announced, "It looks like you're done." She disconnected the empty tube that had fed blood back into my body, flushed my IV with saline solution, and capped it off. "Will you be staying tonight, Dr. Jantzen?" she asked.

"Most definitely."

"I'll have them send a cot down, then."

"Thank you," he told her as she left.

I felt touched again at Jake's devotion, that he would stay there with me all night when he could be home in a comfortable bed. "Thanks for being here," I told him. "It means so much to me just to have you here. There's nothing worse than being in the hospital alone."

"Were you in the hospital alone?" he asked sternly.

I sighed and looked away, wishing I hadn't said that.

I watched Jake clench his hands into fists and stand up. "He left you alone in the hospital to—what?—to go get plastered?" he asked vehemently.

When I hesitated to answer, he laughed humorlessly and muttered, "Of course he did." Then he walked over to the window and leaned on the sill to look out at the deepening sunset.

After several long, quiet moments I said, "Jake?" He was still silent. "Jake, I'm sorry I brought that up. It's not important. What's important is that you're here now."

"Sometimes I just feel so *mad*, Maren. I wish I'd known what you were going through before I married Tess. I would've come and taken you away. I feel angry that you married that loser in the first place. It's made things so much more complicated."

I was stunned to hear him say that. "But, Jake, we've both said that we went through so much growth, and received many blessings as a result of that decision—"

"Was it as a result of it, Maren? Or was it just in spite of it? Maybe God simply found ways to bless us in the circumstances we chose because we were living right."

"I . . . I don't know." My brain was already cloudy without adding more confusion on top of it. Why was he acting this way now? I wanted to cry but I couldn't muster the strength.

He turned around and walked back toward me. "I'm sorry, Mar. It was just the second time I've almost watched you die. Thank heaven I'm a doctor, or I probably would have lost you the first time. And this time . . . watching you bleeding and being powerless to even do anything about it . . . When I came upstairs and saw the blood, it was like I felt the life draining from my own body."

I reached for Jake's hand and squeezed it with the little bit of strength I had left. I struggled to keep listening to him, but his voice gradually faded away as sleep overtook me again.

Somewhere in the middle of the night, I woke from a groggy sleep to the distant sound of a telephone ringing. "Hello?" I heard Jake whisper urgently.

I opened my eyes and turned toward him, but I couldn't see his face in the dark. *Please don't let anything be wrong with the children,* I prayed.

"Mom?" Jake asked then, a hint of relief in his voice. He added with a trace of humor, "Don't you know it's still the middle of the night here?"

I barely had time to be grateful that everything was all right before Jake's tone was overcome with worry again. "What's wrong?" he asked. There was a long pause before he said softly, "Oh, no . . . What happened?"

He was quiet for several moments, apparently listening to her before he went on, "How's Dad? . . . Well, that's understandable, I guess . . . But it's not forever, Mom. There's so much more hope than tha—" I heard Jake sigh, and assumed that his mother had cut him off with a mild reprimand.

"I'm sorry," he said. "I just wish the two of you knew what I know. There's so much comfort in it . . . No, I'm afraid there's not any way that I can come right now. I do have to stay here . . . I know you do . . . I'm so sorry, Mom . . . Yes, she's all right for the moment. I assume it was Maren's sister you talked to? . . . She's with the children for now, anyway . . . I'm not sure what we're going to do . . . Depending on how things go, we might take you up on that—if you're both up to it after all this."

I tried to figure out what was going on, but my thoughts were still painfully slow. I heard Jake clear his throat after a few more moments in silence. "Honestly, I don't think I've ever been so frightened," he said softly. "But I just have to put my trust in the Lord . . . He can, though, Mom, and He does . . . On the contrary, this is the best time to hear it . . . All right. I'll tell her. And the same to you and Dad . . . I wish I could be there . . . Yes, I'll keep you posted . . . Love you too. Bye."

"What happened?" I asked when he'd hung up.

Jake quickly turned on the nearby lamp and observed, "That woke you up. I'm sorry."

"What happened?" I repeated.

"My uncle, my dad's brother, had a heart attack earlier tonight . . . They just lost him."

"Oh, Jake, I'm sorry. How are your parents doing?"

"They're taking it pretty hard, I think. But then they believe they'll never see him again." Jake looked pensive for several moments before he clenched his hand into a fist and said with gritted teeth, "It's so *frustrating* to have the gospel, to know the truth and enjoy the comfort it provides, and not be able to share it with my own family. If they would just quit being so blind and stubborn. The answers are right in front of them, but they refuse to see them." I could see the bleakness in his expression, and I reached out to touch him, wishing there was something I could do to comfort him.

"Were you close to your uncle?" I asked gently.

"Yeah," Jake replied somberly. "He was still single when I was little, and I hung out with him a lot. He took me to baseball games, and movies, and . . ." Jake's voice trailed off, and he leaned forward with his head in his hands for a minute.

I tried to stroke his hair, but couldn't reach that far with everything I was connected to. I squeezed his arm instead. "I'm sorry, honey," I told him.

When Jake finally raised his head and looked at me, he observed, "At least I can do his temple work now. I think he'll accept it on the other side."

I squeezed his arm again in a gesture of comfort as Jake stared into space.

When he returned to the present, he seemed to remember, "Oh, Mom said to tell you that they're praying for you, and they love you. She also offered to come out here and stay with the kids if we need them to. I told her we might be in need of some help if they're up to it after the funeral and everything."

"Maybe you could go for the funeral," I suggested a bit reluctantly. "Maybe you could fly there and back in the same day or some—"

"I can't leave you right now, Maren," he interjected. "I wish I could go, but I can't. It's as simple as that. I'm sure my uncle will understand, and I know my parents do."

I felt incredibly relieved by his words, though I did feel bad that he would have to miss something so important to his family because of me.

Jake leaned over to kiss my forehead and whispered, "Go back to sleep." He turned off the light, but he didn't lie back down. I sensed his sadness, as I could feel him staring into the darkness for a long time. I finally reached for his hand and held it until I fell asleep.

The next morning Dr. Stewart walked into my room. Everything still looked blurry, and I felt groggy and sick. "Now that we're sure the bleeding has stopped, we'd like to transfer you to the university hospital, Maren," he told me.

"All right," I agreed. "So, are you going to let my husband drive me or what?"

"Actually, no," he answered hesitantly. Jake squeezed my hand from the chair beside me. "Your condition is too serious. You could begin bleeding again without warning at any moment. We'd like to transfer you by helicopter."

I felt mildly alarmed. "Helicopter?" I'd never been in a helicopter before.

"It's the fastest way to get you there," Dr. Stewart explained. "You'll have a nurse and a neonatal specialist with you, in case something should happen on the way. You'll be there in less than ten minutes."

"Why do you have to transfer me? Can't I just stay here so I'm close to home and to the kids?"

"If your baby is born before thirty-four weeks gestation, we're not equipped at this hospital to give him the care he'll need. If we move you now, your baby will be in much better hands if something happens and you have to deliver early."

I sighed, not looking forward to being moved or to taking my first ride in a helicopter in my present condition.

I looked toward Jake again, and he nodded. "He's right, Maren."

"All right," I conceded a bit hesitantly.

"They'll be here to get you in a few minutes then," Dr. Stewart told me. He smiled and patted my hand. "Don't worry," he said. "It's not that bad." He winked at me and left.

I tried to distract myself from my anxiety by turning my thoughts to other things. I thought about my children and suddenly realized that I hadn't even asked Jake about them. "Are the kids all right?" I said to him. "You've talked to Natalie, haven't you?"

"They're fine," he reassured me. "Natalie and Doug are there. Your parents are coming down today to stay with them as long as we need them to. I called the office and told them that I won't be in for a while. The other doctors will cover for me. I talked to all four children last night and told them that you'll be fine and that we love them."

I nodded. "And what's going on with me? What is all this anyway? What was that shot for the baby's lungs? What's going to happen? How long do I have to have this . . ." I motioned to the IV and the fluid that was making me feel so awful, ". . . stuff?"

"The bleeding was caused by a placental abruption. It's when the placenta tears away prematurely. Obviously, it didn't tear away completely. In fact, they did an ultrasound and the size of the tear is actually relatively small. It's scabbed over now, so you're temporarily out of danger. But because there is damage, you need to be on strict bed rest to prevent it from tearing away any farther."

"Why did that happen? Did I do something wrong?" I dreaded the answer, but I added hesitantly, "Was it the exercising?"

He shook his head. "I don't know, Mar. Even Paul's baffled, and this is his area of expertise. The exercising itself shouldn't have been enough to cause it, especially since you started slowing down and taking it easier. And you'd been working out before you got pregnant. I suppose it could have aggravated an existing condition, but you don't have any of the risk factors for it. It usually happens in older mothers, or in patients with very high blood pressure. Sometimes using drugs can create a sudden rise in blood pressure and cause an abruption. There's no reason why it should happen to you, but it sounds like you had a similar occurrence with your first pregnancy. It's likely that it was the same thing. Once you've experienced it, you're at a much higher risk for a recurrence in a subsequent pregnancy."

"So, if we have another baby, this might happen again?"

He nodded quietly. "If it's happened twice, it's a very big risk. Actually, we're very fortunate this time. It most commonly occurs in the second trimester, and the baby very often dies." We were both silent for a moment.

"But, Jake," I said, trying not to get too emotional. "There were two children in my dream. I saw two. Why would God make me go through this if we're supposed to have another ba—?"

Jake touched my cheek. "Maren, let's worry about getting this baby here before we start worrying about another one, okay?"

I gulped down a sob and nodded. When I could talk again, I asked, "And this baby—will the shot help him enough?"

"It's a steroid that will speed up his lung development. That's the biggest concern at this stage. The maximum benefit is between two days and two weeks after you receive the shot. By thirty-four weeks the baby will likely be able to breathe on his own without a ventilator," he explained. "It would be good for the baby if you could make it that long, Mar, but you have to stay down, in the hospital. If you start bleeding again, they'll probably deliver the baby immediately. They should take you off of the magnesium once you make it to forty-eight hours after the steroid dose." He paused before adding, "I know you're not thrilled with the idea, but I think it's wise to move you while you're still on the medication and stable."

"Can't you take me to the other hospital?" I pled halfheartedly, thinking that if I was temporarily stable, I ought to be able to withstand a few minutes in the car.

"It could take an hour that way instead of ten minutes," Jake pointed out. Then, after a pause, he shook his head and whispered hoarsely, "No, Maren. I won't take you. I won't risk your life."

I only nodded. He stroked my hair and asked, "You okay?" as if trying to change the subject.

I couldn't help laughing at the question. "Besides the fact that I'm scared to death about our baby, I apparently have a life-threatening condition, and I'm on medication that might make me throw up at any minute, you mean?" I asked teasingly.

A grin chased away the shadow of worry on Jake's face. "Yeah," he agreed with a wave of his hand. "Besides all of that."

"I'm starving," I admitted. "But I know I can't eat until they're sure they won't have to do an emergency C-section, so I'm trying not to think about it."

Jake gave me a sympathetic smile. "I'll meet you up at the other hospital as fast as I can," he told me.

I thought about how selfish I'd been over the last few hours. I remembered our other four children. "Go home first, honey," I said. "Go check on the kids, take a shower, even rest if you need to. I'll be all right."

"No, I'll go straight to the hospital."

I reached up to touch his cheek. "You've been here with me this whole time, Jake. I'll be fine alone for a few hours. The children need to see one of us, at least, and know that everything will be all right. And you need to take care of yourself, too. You should pack some things to bring back for us, anyway."

"Are you sure?" he asked.

"Positive. Tell the kids I love them and I'll be home as soon as I can."

"All right," Jake agreed a bit reluctantly. He waited until I was ready to go and helped wheel me down the hospital corridor. When we reached the exit that led to the waiting helicopter, he kissed me good-bye. "I'll see you in a little while," he promised.

I closed my eyes and tried to remember the feel of his kiss. During the helicopter ride, I thought of Jake and of our baby. I attempted to overcome my apprehension by willing myself to another place. I didn't open my eyes until I was safely on the ground again being wheeled to another hospital room.

CHAPTER EIGHTEEN

I didn't like this hospital. The one closer to home had felt much more soothing. There had been soft lights and carpeting and pictures on the walls. Jake practiced at that hospital, so a lot of the staff knew him and had been extra attentive. Here, I was just another number. Everything was white, bright, sterile, and hard. The fluorescent lights glinted off the shiny tile floor, making my eyes ache. A nurse came in to start new IV drips, and then I didn't see anyone for a long time. I was so hungry that I felt like I was going to throw up. I started to feel even dizzier and weaker than I had before and wondered if the nurse had put me on a higher dose of magnesium. I tried to watch television, but all those colors swimming across the screen churned my stomach. I couldn't focus my eyes enough to read a book or look at a magazine. I tried closing them, but felt like I was being sucked into a whirlpool.

Finally, I just lay there, thinking about the baby. It was the only thing I could do. I wondered what he would look like, who he would be. I thought of my other children at home and of Jake. Where was Jake? How long had I been there? I had lost all sense of time.

After what seemed like hours, a medical student finally came in to check on me. "Please," I begged him. "Can't you turn down the dose? I feel so sick."

"We need to do everything we can to prevent labor starting again," he said mechanically.

"Look, this is my body, and I'm telling you that I've had enough. I ought to have a say in my own medical treatment. Please turn it down—just a little."

He patted my arm and said, "Mrs. Jantzen, you don't know what you're saying."

I wanted to slap him, but he was so hazy that I couldn't even tell where to strike. "Where's the phone? I want to call my husband."

"I'm sure he'll be here when he can. You're in good hands," he replied, then left.

I certainly didn't feel like I was in good hands. The poor substitution for a real doctor that I'd just seen looked to be barely out of boyhood. How could he possibly know what he was doing? And I hadn't seen anyone else for hours. I couldn't take any more. I started to cry, alone in my cold, horrible room. I wanted Jake. I searched for the phone, and to my dismay, I found it several feet away. I didn't think I'd have the strength to get to it, even if I hadn't been imprisoned by a tangled mess of tubes and wires. I wished that I could think clearly. If I had been myself, I would have marched out there and told them what was what, but I felt too fragile and confused to take any sort of action. I said a silent prayer for strength. *Please, Lord, I don't think I can take much more. Help me to be strong for the baby. Help me to make it through this, and please let the baby be all right. Please.*

Much later, a technician came in with the familiar assortment of needles and vials. "Oh, no," I moaned. "You're not going to take my blood?"

He laughed. "I'm afraid so." I failed to see the humor.

"If you do, if I have to see even one more drop of blood, I'm going to be sick. Please don't take it right now."

"Sorry, but it's doctor's orders, ma'am."

"Well, it's my body, and my orders are get out!" I felt completely perturbed. I couldn't take care of myself, and everyone seemed to be working against me. I wished desperately that I could make my mind function normally. Even my thoughts swirled sickeningly, just out of my reach.

"Look, lady, I have to follow the doctor's instructions, and the doctor wants a blood sample."

"What doctor? Is my doctor even here?"

"No, the floor doctor's in charge of you right now. This will only take a minute." He pulled out a syringe. I knew there was no way that I could see any more blood without becoming ill.

"Get out!" I yelled at him. I could not believe this place. I was trying to figure out how I could disconnect my IV and run when Jake walked in.

"Hi, honey," he said sweetly. Then he turned to the technician to ask, "What's going on?" I figured he must have heard me.

The technician complained, "I'm supposed to take a blood sample from your wife, doctor's orders, and she won't cooperate."

I was so relieved to see Jake. I didn't think I'd ever felt so glad to see anyone in my life. He came to sit by me on the bed. "Make him go away," I pled.

Jake looked at the technician and said, "You heard the lady. Thanks for your efforts, but she'd like you to leave now."

"Look, the doctor said—"

Jake smiled and said, "Doctor . . ?" He waited expectantly for a name.

"I haven't even seen a doctor since I've been here," I informed him, before the technician had time to answer. "Only medical students."

Jake looked down at me and then back up at him. "You may tell this mystery doctor, who hasn't even taken the time to talk to my wife in the twelve hours since she's been here, that we've respectfully declined your request to provide him with a blood sample right now."

He shrugged, picked up his carton of vials, and left.

Jake put his arm around my shoulders. It felt so good to lean against his solid chest. "Where have you been?" I cried. "I've been waiting for you all day. They still won't let me eat or drink, they turned up the medicine, I'm so sick I want to die, and no one will listen to me." I couldn't remember ever feeling so ill or so helpless.

"All day? It's been like that all day?" he asked. I sniffled and nodded. "But I tried to call you, Mar. I called to check on you twice because the children needed me for a while, and they told me you were resting."

"Resting? They hardly even looked in to see what I was doing! It wouldn't surprise me if they didn't even know my name!"

"You really haven't seen a doctor all day, Mar?"

"Nope. No one. Unless you count all those obnoxious med students who keep asking me the same questions over and over again and then ignoring everything I tell them."

"Hey," he protested jokingly, "I used to be one of those obnoxious med students."

"That's not even funny, Jake."

His tone became more serious as he asked, "Are you sure you didn't fall asleep or—"

"I wish I could have!" I told him. "Every time I close my eyes I feel like I'm going to die. Look, I feel weak, and confused, and no one has listened to me. Don't you patronize me, too! I'm not stupid. It's just this terrible, horrible drug. Is this what it feels like to be on drugs? You'd have to be crazy to want to feel like this."

"I'm sorry, Mar. I know you're not stupid. I'm going to go take care of this right now. I'll be right back."

"Hurry," I implored him. "Don't leave me here again."

"I won't."

Five minutes later he walked back in with a distinguished-looking man who was tall with gray hair. "Mrs. Jantzen," he said, "I'm Dr. Marsh. I apologize for the confusion. It's been a very busy day. I thought my head resident had been keeping an eye on you, and he apparently thought the same of me. With everything that's been going on today, I'm afraid we didn't communicate as well as we should have." I didn't answer him. "At any rate," he went on, "I will personally see that your needs are taken care of right now. A nurse will be in to check on you shortly, and I'll go have a look at your chart."

"Thank you, Doctor," Jake said.

He nodded and walked out.

The nurse asked me some questions and told me that I hadn't dilated any further. I was still at a five. "Do you need anything?" she asked.

"She needs something to eat," Jake told her.

"I'm sorry, but that's just not a good idea until we're certain she's out of danger."

"She's pregnant and she hasn't had anything to eat for a day and a half," Jake retorted, obviously becoming annoyed. "That's long enough. She should at least be able to have some crackers and juice."

"All right," she sighed, her irritation all too apparent.

"And I want this mag drip turned down. She doesn't need to be on a dose this strong," Jake insisted firmly. All I could think was, *Thank the Lord for my husband.*

"She's on the dose the doctor ordered," the nurse told him curtly.

"Yes, well, he's supposed to be looking at her chart for the first time today, and I'm sure he'll agree. Even if he doesn't, I want it turned down. Either you can do it, or I'll do it myself. She doesn't need to be this miserable."

The nurse looked down at her clipboard in a huff, evidently searching for my name. "Look, Mr. . . . Jantzen, I'm sure it's difficult to see your wife in this condition, but it's necessary for the baby."

"Actually, it's *Doctor* Jantzen," he replied coolly. "I'm a pediatric surgeon and more than qualified to make a call on what's best for my baby and my wife." I'd never heard him throw the fact that he was a doctor in someone's face, but I could see how angry he was, and quite frankly, I felt grateful.

"Oh!" She was obviously shaken. "Well then, I'll see what I can do, Doctor."

"Stupid bunch of morons," Jake muttered when she'd left. "This is supposed to be the best hospital in the state, and they don't even know who their patients are! I can't believe they've had you on this dose all day! No wonder you're sick." He studied the medication dripping into my IV and adjusted a knob. Then he walked around to look at the monitors I was attached to. He picked up my hand to check the tube they'd closed off and left in my vein after the blood transfusion. When he seemed satisfied, he sat down in the chair next to me and held my sore hand.

"I'm so sorry, Maren. If I'd known, I would've come right up. It was just that the kids . . . and they told me you were resting . . ." He shook his head. "I can't believe they told me you were asleep! I should have insisted that they ring your room."

"It's not your fault," I said. "I'm just glad you're here now."

"I won't leave again," he stated firmly. "You should start to feel a little better within a half hour or so."

"Thank you. Are the kids okay?" I asked.

He nodded. "Your parents are with them now, and they're all thrilled to death. When I got there this morning, Natalie's baby was sick. He had a fever, and they'd been up with him all night."

"Again?" I asked, feeling concerned. "Is Nathan all right?"

"He will be, but he has another ear infection. At this rate, he's headed for ear tubes for sure. Anyway, I checked him and gave them a stronger prescription than last time. I also told them to go apply for Medicaid in case he has to go to an ENT. When I called up here and they said you were all right, I told Natalie and Doug to go home and take care of their baby. I stayed with our kids until your parents got there. The children were a little upset because the baby had been crying all night, and Natalie was exhausted."

"I'm sorry for getting upset with you," I said, feeling incredibly guilty in light of what he'd just told me. "I'm glad you stayed there. That was more important. I'm an adult."

"If I'd known, I would have found someone else to leave them with."

"No, I'm sure they're upset enough. I'm glad you stayed with them today. I would have felt terrible if you'd left them to come up here under those circumstances."

We were both silent for a moment until I asked, "How are Natalie and Doug doing?"

"They seemed to be getting along pretty well, actually. Doug looked a lot happier than he did the last time I saw him."

"Well, that's a relief," I said.

He smiled, thinking. "The kids and I had fun. We painted the baby's room."

"You painted the baby's room?"

"Uh-huh. I knew you wouldn't be able to do it now, and the kids thought it was great. They're really excited about the baby."

"The kids helped you paint?" I asked incredulously.

He laughed. "I know what you're thinking. Don't worry. They didn't ruin the carpet, no one has blue hair, and it actually turned out pretty neat. It's a little different than you'd planned, but I think you'll like it."

"Wow." I smiled at him. "I'm impressed." I paused and then noted, "At least I think I'm impressed. What did you do to it?"

Jake laughed. "I'm afraid I can't tell you that, love. I promised the kids that it could be a surprise for when you and the baby come home."

"Oh, boy," I mumbled good-naturedly.

The nurse came in with some apple juice and soda crackers. Nothing had ever looked so good. I thanked her. She looked at the knob on the IV and then raised her eyebrows at Jake. "I see you've taken care of that." She actually smiled. I couldn't believe it.

Jake smiled back and read her name tag. "Yes, I did. Thank you, Phyllis."

"Well, it looks like you're in good hands, Mrs. Jantzen, so I'll be back to check on you later," she told me as she left.

"You certainly have a way with people." I looked at Jake. His eyes weren't so blurry anymore.

"What do you think it is," he teased, "my good looks or my sunny personality?"

"I think it's your incredibly humble attitude."

He laughed and kissed my cheek. "I'm sure you're right."

Jake had brought pictures for me from the children, which he stood up on the table next to my bed. My eyes filled with tears, just thinking about them. I missed them terribly. I wanted to go home and hug all four of them. I prayed that this whole ordeal would be over soon—for all of us. Phyllis came back in around ten o'clock. "I'm not supposed to let husbands stay overnight, you know," she said to Jake as she handed him a blanket and a pillow. She didn't appear so harsh then. In fact, she looked almost grandmotherly with her silver hair and kind eyes. I guessed she'd probably had a long day. "The chair folds out," she advised with a wink. "It's not comfortable, but it is a step above the tile floor."

"I'm grateful to you," Jake told her. "You have a good night, Phyllis."

"Same to you both." She patted my leg and added, "Good luck to you, dear. I trust you're feeling better?"

I nodded.

"Good then. I hope everything goes well."

The next morning, another doctor came in. "I guess we could turn off the magnesium now," he offered.

"Oh, could you?" I asked. "I'd be thrilled to be done with this horrible stuff."

He was younger than Dr. Marsh and not as serious. He chuckled. "I've never tried it myself, but I'm told it's not very pleasant."

"That's an understatement if I've ever heard one," I muttered.

He turned off the drip and put a plug in my IV tube. "You ought to be feeling better in an hour or so. The nurse should be in soon, and you may have breakfast if you feel up to it."

"Thank you."

Jake came out after taking a shower in my bathroom to find me eating breakfast and smiling. "Good morning." He grinned at me.

"Come over here," I instructed. "I haven't been able to look into your eyes for two days."

He sat down on the bed and kissed me. I studied his face, his newly shaved jaw, his freshly combed hair. He was wearing light khaki slacks and a pale green shirt that was one of my favorites. "What, no tie?" I teased him. "You think you can just lounge around here all casual like that?"

"I tried to get a hospital gown to match yours, but they were all out," he quipped.

"It's so good to see your face clearly again." I touched his smooth cheek and kissed him. "You're a very handsome man."

"No wonder I'm so in love with you," he said. "Besides being beautiful, sweet, and funny, you're also a shameless flatterer."

They let me get up to take a shower later in the morning. After that and doing my hair and makeup, I felt one hundred percent better. "I feel like I'm back in the world of the living," I told Jake.

"I'm glad," he remarked happily. "Well, we have lots of time now. What do you want to do?"

"Did you bring a card game or something?"

"Yes, I think there's one in the suitcase."

"Before that, maybe we should think of a name for this baby." We'd put it off, thinking we had several more weeks to decide.

"Okay, what do you want to name him?" Jake asked.

I sighed. "I still can't think of anything I really love."

"Maybe we'll have to wait until we see him," he suggested.

"Maybe you're right," I agreed.

CHAPTER NINETEEN

By the end of my first week in the hospital, I thought I would go mad. I felt fine after the magnesium wore off, but I had to stay in bed. I missed the children so much it hurt. I talked to them on the phone every day, but it wasn't the same as being with them. Jake brought them up on Sunday, and I hugged them, kissed them, and soaked up every word they said. Jake's parents came to take them back to our house. They'd flown in to take a turn with them, and my parents had gone home to check on the farm. "Are you sure you're up to this?" I'd heard Jake ask them over the phone from my hospital room. His parents had assured him that they were. They said they'd done everything they could for his uncle's family and, with the funeral over, they thought they could use a change of scenery. They also noted that a visit with their grandchildren might help to soothe their grief and lift their spirits. I felt despondent after the kids left with them and didn't hide it well.

"It's all right, love. You'll be coming home soon." Jake tried to comfort me.

"I want to come home now. My other children need me too. I feel fine."

"I know," he sympathized. "I'm sorry."

When the doctor came in that day, I asked her to let me go home. "Please," I pled with her. "I can rest at home as easily as I can here."

Her reddish-blond hair looked like it had been wrapped too hastily into a tight bun. She removed her tortoiseshell glasses to scrutinize me. "Mrs. Jantzen, are you aware of the seriousness of your condition?"

"Yes," I answered. I was so tired of being treated like a child in this place.

"You realize that at any time the placenta could tear again? There would be no warning. You could bleed to death in a very short time."

"There's not much risk of that if I'm on bed rest, is there?"

"Bed rest reduces the risk, but it's still a very big risk. Placental abruption can be life threatening to both the mother and the baby. If I were to release you, I would be putting your life at risk, as well as that of your unborn child."

"But I have children at home who need me," I argued, almost tearfully.

"Right now, this baby needs you even more. We'd really like to see you make it to at least thirty-four weeks."

"All right," I mumbled in defeat, but when she left the room I turned to Jake and begged, "Take me home. Please take me home, Jake. You're a doctor. You can watch me."

"I'm not an obstetrician, Mar. And I wouldn't take you home even if I were. It's too risky."

"Jake, please! I'll be fine. I can vegetate at home just as easily as I can here!" I wanted my baby to be safe, but I just couldn't see the point of lying around in the hospital when I could be lying around at home.

His expression was filled with sympathy as he said firmly, "I can't, Mar. You need to be here."

I turned away from him. I thought perhaps he was right and I did trust his judgment, but I still felt upset.

Jake went back to work that week. He couldn't take an indefinite amount of time off, so we decided it would be best for him to work while his parents could be there, and while I was stable. We didn't know what the future held, or how much leave he might need to take later on. Though I realized it couldn't be helped, the days were far worse without him.

Natalie came to see me briefly here and there, when she could leave the baby with someone and get away. She assured me that he was recuperating from his ear infection again. "How are things going?" I asked her. "You're not still thinking of leaving Doug, are you?"

"No, things are okay," she said. "I guess I'm just learning to accept the fact that Doug can't do everything I'd like him to right now. I know that he has a good heart, and he loves me. He works hard for us, and I appreciate that. I've made a couple of friends in the ward, other wives who are staying home with babies. We get together once a week or so, and I talk to one or the other of them on the phone here and there. It helps."

"I'm glad," I told her.

"Yeah, me too. I just wish it was easier to get through this phase of life. In fact, I don't think I'd mind skipping it altogether."

"If you did, you might miss a good opportunity for you and Douglas to grow together," I pointed out.

Natalie smirked and commented sarcastically, "It's so nice to have a big sister who already knows everything."

I felt sheepish at her remark. "I'm sorry, Nat," I said honestly. "I suppose hindsight is twenty-twenty. Got any suggestions for me?"

She smiled and answered, "Just a little bit of your own advice. I know you're in a rotten situation at present, and it's not your fault, but you could try counting your blessings. You have family on both sides who are willing to help. You have a loving and supportive husband, even if he can't be here twenty-four hours a day. Maybe you should stop feeling sorry for yourself and use all this glorious time to your advantage, rather than wishing it away."

I raised my eyebrows at her. "Like how?" I asked.

"Read, or cross-stitch, or write poetry, or make a baby quilt. Or just sit and listen to your own thoughts for a while. That's got to be pleasant in and of itself after being with four kids every day. What would you love to sit down and work on in the middle of the day, but you never do because you always have to clean, or cook, or take care of kids, or fulfill some other obligation?"

I considered her words thoughtfully for a minute before saying, "Maybe I'll have Jake bring my scrapbook supplies up. I could catch up on those. And actually, now that you mention it, I think I would enjoy making a baby quilt. I suppose I could do that by hand. I don't have anything better to do. If I gave you some money, would you have time to go to the fabric store for me and pick something out?"

Natalie smiled and answered, "I'd love to. It'll give me something to do."

I handed her some cash from my purse and instructed, "Get double. Maybe I'll make one for Nathan, too. Or maybe I'll get it started and let you finish it."

"That'd be great, Maren."

"And thanks for the advice," I added good-naturedly.

Natalie grinned and told me, "Anytime."

***

The next day she brought me some adorable pieces of fabric, and Jake brought my box of scrapbook supplies up after dinner. He usually went home after work to see the kids and eat dinner, and then came up to the hospital. He stayed as late as he could, but they wouldn't let him spend the night anymore. Sometimes there was another female patient in my room, so husbands couldn't stay. I realized that it was probably better for him, but it was still difficult for me. The worst times were when I shared a room with a new mother. Someone else's new baby would wake me up all night. I wanted my baby. I wanted to take him home and be back with my family.

Two weeks after I entered the hospital, when I was two days short of being thirty-four weeks pregnant, I started having a few random contractions again early in the morning. I called Jake and told him that he'd better see if he could skip work and come early, just in case. The contractions stopped, so I got up to take a shower and get ready for the day. I was just getting back into bed when Jake got there.

"What are you doing up?" he asked.

"Taking a shower," I answered.

"Maren, you should be in bed if you're having contractions."

"They stopped."

He shook his head. "Do I have to watch you every second?"

He was teasing, but his comment only served to agitate me anyway. "I just want to have this baby and go home, Jake. I can't take this hospital anymore!"

He sat up on the bed and put his arms around me. "I know it's hard, Mar, but it won't be much longer."

Nothing happened the rest of the day, but Jake stayed anyway. I finished one baby quilt while I talked to him, and got started on the other one. He filled me in on what I'd been missing at home and how things were going at work. By evening time, I was having some contractions again. When the doctor came in, I told her. She looked at the monitor and said, "The monitor's not picking up anything. They must be pretty mild."

"So, you're not going to do anything?" I asked.

"No. If your body goes into labor again, it's probably for a reason. The steroid shot should have helped your baby's lungs quite a bit, and you're almost to thirty-four weeks. At this point, I'd feel better about delivering the baby early rather than risking any more bleeding."

I prayed silently after she left. *Heavenly Father, I don't think I can take much more of this. My biggest concern is my baby's health, but if he'll be all right, then please let me have this baby and get it over with. Only if the baby will be all right, though. Please.*

By the time Jake was supposed to leave, my back ached terribly. The nurse said the monitor still wasn't indicating much activity, but I felt uneasy. Jake called his parents to check on the children and told them he'd be staying with me that night. When I complained to the nurse again, she asked me if I'd like to take something to help me relax and go to sleep.

"Is that a good idea?" I asked her.

"I think it's a very good idea. You need to get some rest, and it's time for your husband to go home," she added tactfully.

I gave him a worried look.

"I'm not going anywhere tonight," Jake told her.

"Now, Mr. Jantzen, you know the policy on husbands staying overnight."

"There's no one else in her room right now."

The nurse, Leeann, prodded again, "Yes, but we never know when we might need the room. Labor-and-Delivery is almost full."

Jake's tone became more serious. "Maren says she's having contractions and something just doesn't feel right. I don't want to be a pain, Leeann, but I feel strongly that I need to stay with my wife tonight."

She shrugged her shoulders in defeat. "Well, I'm not going to try to bodily remove you, but I can't guarantee that no one else will."

Jake smiled and said, "I appreciate that."

After she left, I asked Jake to give me a blessing. He blessed me with strength and peace, told me that the baby would be healthy, and promised me that I would recover completely from my ordeal. I already felt pretty much recovered. I thought maybe the promise referred to emotional healing.

"Thanks for staying with me," I whispered to Jake.

"You're welcome, love," he whispered back. Then he kissed my forehead and suggested gently, "You should get some rest."

The medication was already making me sleepy, so it didn't take me long to drift off.

CHAPTER TWENTY

I could feel the terrible throbbing in my back as it almost pulled me out of sleep, but I kept fighting the pain and drifting back into unawareness. I felt wet, too, but I wasn't ready to wake up and face it. Finally the pain was so intense that I opened my eyes. I slowly realized what was happening again. "Oh no," I whispered into the darkness. I rolled onto my back, but it hurt so much that I couldn't stay that way. I remembered that lying on my left side was the best position for the baby, so I moved my huge body painfully over. Jake was sleeping in the chair next to my bed, and I touched his shoulder. "Jake?" I whispered.

He started awake. "What? Are you okay?"

"Call the nurse, please," I told him. I couldn't twist around to look for the button.

He pushed it and then turned on the little light over the bed. "What's wrong, Mar?"

I grimaced as I felt another contraction coming. He gave me his hand, and I squeezed it hard. The contraction had barely subsided before another one began. "Oh, Jake, this is bad," I moaned. "I need an epidural fast—before it gets worse."

The nurse came in and asked, "What do you need?"

"I'm having contractions," I said through gritted teeth. "Bad contractions."

She looked at the monitor. "Nothing's showing up on the monitor."

"Well, maybe you should check the darn monitor then!" I growled at her. "This is my fourth baby—I know contractions when I feel them!"

She pushed on the monitor cord and moved the Doppler device down on my abdomen. I felt a bitter triumph at seeing the huge peak printing out.

"Oh," she remarked. "I guess you are having contractions. How far apart would you say they are?"

"About that far apart," I answered sharply, pointing to the next peak printing out on the red-lined paper.

"Oh!" The nurse looked alarmed. "Are they all that close together?"

"Yes! Look, I'm not a fan of natural childbirth. Could you please get the anesthesiologist down here? *Now!*"

"Of course. I'll call him and the doctor."

"Call him quickly, because I'm also bleeding again."

She rushed out of the room and Jake flipped on the overhead light. "You're bleeding again?" The color fled from his face.

"Jake, I'll be fine." I tried to give his hand a light squeeze, but ended up nearly crushing it instead as another contraction came. I could still hear the baby's steady heartbeat on the monitor, and I thanked God silently.

The younger doctor came into the room to check me. Jake glanced down at my legs and then looked away. "Pretty bad, huh?" I asked him. I knew it was. I could feel the blood pumping out of me again, but this time the contractions were so painful that worrying about the bleeding was secondary. Jake just stared at me with glazed eyes and didn't answer.

"Please," I pled with the doctor, "I need an epidural."

"The anesthesiologist is on his way down, Mrs. Jantzen," he answered. "I know you're in a lot of pain—just try to stay calm."

He looked at the nurse who was scribbling on my chart and said, "She's dilated to a seven. Wait. Actually . . . almost eight." Then he turned to Jake and informed him, "She's changing very quickly. We're going down to delivery right now."

"No, no. You don't understand," I protested. I wanted to cry, but it hurt too much. "I need drugs!"

The doctor gave me a sympathetic look. "I'm sorry, Mrs. Jantzen, but it's too late for that. You're going to have to do this the old-fashioned way."

I grabbed Jake's arm. "No. No, Jake, no. You've never seen me in labor before. I'm a wimp. I can't do it. Make them give me drugs—please."

"Can't you give her a dose of Demerol or something?" he asked the doctor, in a voice almost edged with panic.

Dr. Billings, I finally read on his name tag, nodded to the nurse who quickly squirted the contents of a syringe into my IV. As far as I could tell, it didn't do anything.

"Do you feel like helping us wheel this thing down?" he asked Jake.

Jake nodded. "Whatever you need." His face was still pale as he pulled the blankets over me and squeezed my hand. I started to feel weak, like I had before, as they rushed me down the hall. I wondered how much blood I was losing and how fast.

Outside an official-looking door, a nurse threw Jake a mask and gown and told him to scrub up. Inside the delivery room, everything was quickly prepared before Dr. Billings said calmly, "Okay, we're almost ready to start pushing, Maren."

"I can't do this," I insisted. I hadn't known that it was possible to feel so much pain. With every contraction I could feel the blood pumping out of me, and I thought I would die. The realization did hit me, though, that I wasn't dead. The pain was worse than I had ever imagined, but I was living through it. I wondered why on earth any woman would choose to go through this if anesthesia were an option. "How do women survive this?" I wondered aloud, before I sucked in my breath sharply. "I never knew it was this bad."

"Actually, it's usually not," Dr. Billings explained. "You're having titanium contractions. Your body's in trauma, so you've gone into extremely hard labor very fast, and the contractions are much worse than they would be in a normal delivery, even at this stage. It's your body's way of getting the baby here as quickly as possible so the bleeding can be stopped."

"Lucky me," I mumbled feebly, but then grimaced again.

Jake came in and took my hand. "You're going to be all right, Maren." He smiled at me. I tried to focus on his face.

"Okay, let's get this baby here!" Dr. Billings said cheerily. I wanted to smack him.

The nurse attempted to coach me through breathing and pushing, but I couldn't follow her. I remembered the pushing, but I'd never had to breathe through this much pain before. I clutched her arm in panic. She pried my fingers off and put them on the bed rail. I crushed Jake's hand and pushed as hard as I could over and over again, fighting against pain too excruciating to even allow room for tears. After what seemed like forever, I began to believe that death would be a welcome release, and I felt my mind getting foggy again. Everything around me began to slowly fade away, until I couldn't see anything but the bright overhead lights. I closed my eyes and gave up. "I can't do this. I just can't," I whispered. I felt so weak and hopeless that I didn't even cringe at the next contraction. I just let it wash over me, squeezing blood and draining life from me. I could almost feel myself slipping away and I had no will to fight it.

Jake put his face next to mine and whispered urgently, "You have to do this, Mar. You have to. It's the only way out. You've got to get that baby here so they can stop the bleeding." I didn't answer him. "Maren?" he said softly. I still couldn't will my eyes to open. I was swallowed up in a scarlet sea of pain so deep that I couldn't even feel it anymore.

I heard a loud beep, and Dr. Billings's voice floating toward me from somewhere far away. "Her blood pressure's dropping way too low!"

I was barely aware of someone shaking my shoulders, and Jake's voice calling to me, "Maren!" He shook me again. "Maren, please. *Please.*" The next plea seemed to be directed toward the doctor, *"Do something!"*

"The baby's moved too far down the birth canal," I heard Dr. Billings's distant voice again. "If we put her under and try to do a C-section now, we could lose them both."

I was vaguely aware of a flurry of activity in the room as a rough cheek was pressed next to mine, and tears trickled down to my neck. "Please, Lord," I heard Jake's voice whisper. "Don't take her. Please don't take her. I'll do anything." I felt fingers pressing against the artery in my throat, and then arms wrapping tightly around me. *"Maren!"* he whispered fiercely in my ear. "You can't leave me. You *can't.* We're not even sealed . . ."

His words jolted something in me, and I found my will to live. We weren't even sealed. I had to get through this. I tried to force my mind back to the room, to make my eyelids open.

There were loud beeps and someone was shouting orders, but the only thing I could focus on was Jake's voice. "Please, baby. *Please,*" he sobbed into my neck. "Don't leave me . . . I need you."

My brain finally connected to my body, and I forced my eyes open. I still felt incredibly weak, but I knew I had the will to get through it. I turned to brush my lips over Jake's brow. He lifted his head to look at me, and then laughed and cried and kissed me. "Thank you, Lord," he whispered near my ear. "Thank you." He pressed his mouth over mine, then told me, "I love you, Mar. You can do this. I'll help you."

I managed a faint smile, and Jake kissed me again.

The nurse shooed him out of the way and thrust an oxygen mask over my face, saying, "Her blood pressure's still far too low." I appreciated not having to make such an effort to breathe.

Dr. Billings patted my arm and said, "You're a trooper, Mrs. Jantzen. We can have this all over with in a couple of minutes. Are you ready?"

I looked to Jake for strength, and then nodded at the doctor.

Jake took my hand again and whispered, "Here we go, love." He watched the monitor, and when the next contraction came, he leaned close to me and said quietly, "Look at my eyes, Mar. Look at me. Take a deep breath . . . Good. Now breathe out and push."

I did what he told me to. I squeezed my eyes shut and pushed. Then I looked at his face and breathed and pushed again and again.

"We're almost there!" the doctor encouraged.

I was afraid my strength would falter before I made it through, but I managed to push three more times. "It's a boy!" Dr. Billings announced.

"Why doesn't he cry?" I whispered, suddenly aware that I hadn't heard the familiar sound. I shifted my head to look at him. I didn't have the strength to sit up.

Dr. Billings held up the baby and the nurse suctioned out his nose and mouth. I held my breath until my tiny son parted his lips and let out a squeak. I felt tears of joy and relief drizzle down my cheeks and into my hair.

"I'm sorry, but you can't hold him yet," Dr. Billings said. He handed the baby to the nurse, who quickly passed him through a window to another nurse. I knew they'd have to check him in the intensive care nursery to see if he needed help to breathe or with anything else. They'd already told me what the procedure would be if he was born early.

I looked toward the window in awe. It was so amazing seeing that little baby. But I was so afraid that he would die. I kept thinking of Ashlyn's weak little cries and the doctor handing her back to me, saying, "I'm very sorry, but she's not going to make it. You'd better say your good-byes." I shuddered at the memory.

Jake kissed me. "You did it, Mar." He smiled at me through his tears. "I knew you could do it."

I felt so frail that I thought I might faint, but I whispered, "Go with the baby."

He shook his head. "No, love. I think I'd better stay with you." I could see the concern in his expression.

"Please, Jake," I insisted. "He needs you."

He hesitated. "Are you sure? Are you all right?"

"I'm fine, honey. Go with the baby." I could hear the urgency in my voice. I somehow felt that his presence would give our son strength, like it had given me.

He turned to Dr. Billings. "You can stop the bleeding, right? She'll be okay?"

"She's going to be fine," he promised.

"Jake," I pled.

"I'm going, Mar." The nurse pointed out the way and he ran down the hall.

Dr. Billings said, "We're going to give you some Pitocin to make your uterus contract back down quickly, so you don't have any more major bleeding. I'm also going to give you some pain medication because it's going to hurt."

"All right," I managed to whisper before everything went dark.

My next awareness was sunlight filtering into my room. I felt a warm peace wash over me and strength returning. I couldn't remember where I was for a moment after my eyelids fluttered open, but then Jake squeezed my hand, and I turned to look at him. "Good morning." He greeted me with a smile, and I smiled back. "How are you?" he asked as he gently brushed my hair back and pressed a tender kiss to my lips.

"Fine," I whispered. "You?"

He chuckled, but I saw moisture in his eyes as he whispered, "I'm wonderful . . . and you're the most beautiful thing I've ever seen."

I suddenly remembered where I was and what had brought me there. I sat up too quickly, and would have fallen back against the bed if Jake hadn't caught me. "Careful, love," he said as he held me with one arm while he pushed the button to raise the head of the bed with his free hand. "You need to take it easy. You've been through quite an ordeal."

"The baby, Jake." I took hold of his arm. "How's the baby?"

He smiled and reassured me, "He's fine, Mar. He's wonderful." I sighed with relief as Jake stated proudly, "He has blue eyes."

I gave him an amused look and whispered conspiratorially, "All babies have blue eyes, Jake."

"Yes, but his are going to stay blue," Jake insisted.

Even though it hurt, I couldn't help laughing at him. "That's a bold prediction, Dr. Jantzen. Didn't they teach you about recessive genes in medical school?"

He laughed too. "I knew they'd be blue, Mar. It's just . . . seeing him. It's amazing. He's real. He's ours."

He sat down carefully on the bed, and I smiled and threaded my fingers through his, making him wince. I glanced down at his hand and saw bruises. "Did I do that?" I asked in alarm.

He laughed once more, softly. "That's quite a grip you have there. Remind me not to ever mess with you."

"Oh, Jake, I'm sorry. I didn't even realize . . . Why didn't you put my hand on the bed rail like the nurse did?"

He leaned over and brushed a lock of hair behind my ear. "Not hold your hand through that? You needed me, didn't you?"

"You're the only thing that got me through it," I whispered, hearing the emotion in my voice.

He cocked his head and smiled down at me with an expression of tenderness. His eyes were filled with emotion, and he finally said simply, "I love you."

"I know." I smiled back.

He laughed. "Well, that's a relief!"

"And that's why I'm still here," I added softly.

Jake's expression turned abruptly sober. He drew me quickly into his arms, holding me to him fiercely, as though he feared I might slip away. He buried his face in my hair and kissed my head. I tried to reach my arms up around his neck, but it was too painful. Instead, I curled up in his arms and rested against his chest for a long time.

"So, are they going to let me see the baby?" I asked finally, still leaning against my husband. "I want to hold him. They haven't even told me how much he weighs, or what's going on, or anything."

"He weighs exactly five pounds," Jake reported.

"Really? He felt more like nine."

"I'm sure he did. Maybe it's good that he didn't go full-term. Five pounds is good sized for a thirty-four week baby. He's eighteen inches long. He was born at three thirty-three—that's kind of neat, huh?" I laughed. "He started breathing on his own right away, no ventilator. They didn't keep him in the intensive care nursery, but he's in the intermediate nursery. They want to watch him closely. He'll probably have to stay here at least a few days. I'll go back down in a minute and try to convince them to let me bring him to you."

"Thank you," I said.

"So, how are you feeling, love? You never really answered me. That was pretty exciting, wasn't it?" His attempt at humor didn't disguise the concern in his voice.

"I feel like I've been run over by a train," I laughed weakly. "But I'm alive, and we have our baby, and I love you, and I feel very happy."

"Me too."

I untangled myself from Jake's arms and looked back at him to say, "Okay, Jacob, now go use your gift of persuasion and bring me my baby."

"I'll do my best."

He returned a few minutes later, followed by a nurse wheeling a bassinet. "They wouldn't let me bring him without an escort," he explained.

The nurse grinned and pointed a finger at him. "Now, we need him back in half an hour, Mr. Jantzen, don't you forget. That's all the bending of the rules that I can allow." Then she turned to me and said, "He's a fine, healthy baby, Mrs. Jantzen. He's doing very well." She scooped up the tiny bundle and placed him in my arms.

"Thank you," I whispered. She left us alone, and I stared in awe at my baby. He was so tiny. He had miniature fingers and long, dark eyelashes. I took off his little cap and gasped, "Look at all his hair!" I looked up at Jake. "I didn't think he'd have any hair at all being this early." I stroked his downy little head. "It's as dark as yours. I hope he looks just like you."

Jake just stood watching me with the baby, smiling. I patted the bed next to me. "Come sit by us," I invited him.

He sat down again, gently. "I'm afraid of even bumping you after all you've been through."

"Actually, I feel a lot of energy coming back already," I told him. "Did I sleep long?"

"About six hours—long enough for another blood transfusion."

"Another one?" I asked quickly. I was aware of the IV with clear solution dripping into it once more, but the tube in the other hand was still capped off. Or maybe it was just capped off for the second time.

"I'm afraid so," Jake answered seriously. "This time was worse than last time. If I'd taken you home, Maren . . . If you hadn't been in the hospital when this happened . . ." He let his voice fade away, but I caught his implication and swallowed hard.

"I don't feel nearly as weak as I expected to," I observed when I found my voice. "Especially if I lost that much blood again."

"I think perhaps you've just been very blessed," Jake offered quietly. "I know I have."

I smiled, remembering the blessing he'd given me earlier. "I think you're right."

Jake put his arm around me and we sat marveling at the little miracle we'd created. He let out a tiny sigh, and his small chin quivered. I squeezed him to me gently. "I can't believe I missed the first six hours of his life," I said sadly.

"But you'll have many years to make up for it," Jake answered pointedly.

"Yes," I agreed. "And he had you with him, didn't he?"

Jake nodded. "I stayed with him until they were certain he was out of danger. After that, I went back and forth between the two of you about every half hour or so. I was so worried that something would go wrong with one of you while I was with the other. I can't tell you how wonderful it feels to sit here and hold you both."

I turned to smile up at him and kiss him. "So, I guess we'd better decide on his name now, huh?" I said, as I turned back to gaze at the baby. "What do you think?"

Jake shook his head. "I've been thinking about that for the past few hours while you were sleeping, but none of the names we've considered seem to fit."

A sudden thought came to me and I asked, "What was your uncle's name? Your dad's brother?"

His eyes went wide as he grasped my implication. "Jason," he responded simply.

"Really?" I asked in surprise.

"Mmm-hmm."

"I thought that tradition of names starting with 'J' was an oldest son thing," I told him.

"Nope. They've been doing that for four generations. I just happened to be an only son of an oldest son."

"Huh," I commented. "I never knew that. We never even considered any names that started with 'J.' I just assumed that Jeffrey was your oldest son, and that was that."

"I thought you just didn't care to keep it up," he observed.

"Why wouldn't I want to keep up your family tradition?" I asked in surprise.

He shrugged. "I don't know, Mar. I guess I've just learned to give in over the years to keep peace. I took a stand over Jeffrey's name, even though Tess wasn't thrilled with it. I figured I didn't need to push it again. Honestly, it would mean a great deal to me if our son's name carried on my family tradition. I think it would mean a lot to my family too, especially since my uncle only had three daughters."

"Me too," I agreed. "And you know, your sons will be the first generation to be raised with the gospel. You did that for them." Jake smiled and I added, "What about his middle name?"

"We could name him after your dad," Jake suggested.

"Jason William?" I asked. "Do you like that?"

He looked thoughtful for a minute. "I'm not sure. I haven't thought about it at all. Do you?"

"I think so. Get the baby name book out of the suitcase. Let's see what Jason means."

Jake went to get the book and flipped through the pages. "Jason," he read when he'd found it. "Greek. It means *healer.*" He looked up at me and smiled.

"I like it a lot now," I decided. "It's perfect for us." I looked down at my baby and thought of all the healing that had come into my life and Jake's. Our son was a perfect symbol of that, of repairing our broken lives, of blending our two families into one.

Jake closed the book decidedly and came to sit by me again. He lifted our baby from my arms and said, "Hello there, Jason William Jantzen. How do you like your name?"

Jason let out a tiny squeak, and Jake took it as a sign of approval. He grinned broadly at me, making me laugh.

"I think I've gotten used to it already," I told him.

CHAPTER TWENTY-ONE

I stayed in the hospital for four days. I was informed that it was their policy to closely monitor premature babies—regardless of their condition—so they wouldn't let Jason come to my room again. I spent most of my time holding him while sitting on a padded rocking chair in the nursery. I was grateful that a good deal of my strength seemed to return quickly, though I did still feel tired and a little weak. I didn't get very much rest because I couldn't bear to leave my baby. I felt anxious to recover quickly, however, knowing that the other children were really missing us. Jake took more time off work, trying to balance his time between being home with them and being at the hospital with Jason and me. He often told me to go back to my room and rest while he stayed with the baby, but I rarely did. It was too hard to leave them both.

When Jason was four days old, I had to check out of the hospital. Leaving him there that night was one of the hardest things I'd ever done. Jake and I kissed our tiny, sleeping baby. Because he was too tired to wake up and eat, his blood sugar level had dropped, so they'd inserted an IV in his arm several hours earlier to feed glucose into his body. The nurse on duty smiled sympathetically and said, "Don't worry. We'll take good care of him. We'll call you if anything changes."

I left the hospital with empty arms, but it was nothing like the ache I'd felt when I left the hospital without Ashlyn nearly eleven years earlier. This time I knew my baby would be coming home soon, and I had the comfort of a loving husband's arm around my shoulders. It was a shock to walk out into the balmy June night after being locked inside for nearly three weeks. I breathed in the warm night air and was reminded of the joy of being alive.

There was a banner across the house that said, "Welcome Home, Mom!" The children had colored all over it. They were still up and rushed at me when we opened the door. Jake stepped in front of me to block them from tackling me. "Whoa there, guys! Hey, Mom's pretty sore. Just come and hug her very gently. No jumping on her for a while."

They timidly approached to hug me. My stomach was almost flat again, thanks to the medication they'd given me to help my uterus contract back down quickly, but I realized how sore my entire body was as I bent to hold the children to me. I felt tears on my cheeks as I kissed their four little faces and told them how much I loved them.

"What's wrong, Mommy?" Trevor asked, a worried look on his innocent face.

"Nothing, sweetie. I just missed you all very much. I'm so glad to be home with you."

After the excitement of having me home wore off, they all started asking about the baby. "When's Jason coming home? When can we see him? Tell us what he looks like again, Daddy!"

I felt so happy to be home, and yet I felt despondent at not having my baby with me. Jake's mother put her arm around her son and offered, "Why don't you go take care of your wife? I'll read the children a story and get them ready for bed."

I wanted to cry with relief. As much as I wanted to be with my children, I was just completely exhausted. "Thank you," I whispered.

She patted my arm. "You get all the rest you can, dear, before that sweet little one comes home to keep you up all night." I knew she was right, but I couldn't help wishing that he *was* home to keep me up all night.

Jake kissed his mother on the cheek and said, "Thanks, Mom." Then he picked up my suitcase and followed me up the stairs, his hand resting gently on my back. He closed the bedroom door and took me in his arms. I leaned against his chest and closed my eyes, breathing deeply to inhale his clean, soothing scent.

"Oh, I'm glad you're home, Mar," he told me. "The house doesn't feel the same without you here."

"Me too," I whispered, trying not to let my voice betray my mixed emotions.

Jake heard it, though, and understood. "Don't worry, sweetheart. We'll have him home soon." A few silent tears squeezed out, but I didn't answer him. "It feels so wonderful to be able to hold you close again," Jake whispered. It did feel nice to lean next to him without my stomach separating us, but I was acutely aware of the emptiness in my womb, and in my arms.

"What can I do for you, Mar?" Jake asked me.

"You know what I'd love? I just want to take a long hot bath and soak my aching body."

"That's easy enough," he laughed. He went to start a bath for me, and I sat down to pull off my shoes and socks. It felt strange to see my feet again.

Jake held my hand while I stepped into the oversized bathtub. A look of pain crossed his face as I grimaced, trying to ease my sore body down. He sat on the edge of the tub to touch my cheek and look into my eyes. "Maren, I'm so sorry you've had to go through so much to get this baby here. I can't believe how sick you were for so long, and then the early labor, and the bleeding, and the time in the hospital, and the delivery . . ." His voice cracked, and he looked down at his hands, twisting his platinum wedding band for a minute before he looked back up at me.

I rested my hand on top of his, on the edge of the tub, and said quietly, "I'd go through it all again to get our baby."

He was silent for a minute, as I searched his face. The fear in his eyes was evident, and I could see him struggling with whether or not to tell me how he felt. "I'm not sure that I can watch you go through it again, Maren," he finally admitted softly.

I leaned back against the tub and covered my eyes with the back of my hand, all the pain and discouragement rising to the surface. I couldn't stop the tears. Truthfully, I didn't know how I could go through this again, either, but I knew there was another baby. I pictured my tiny son and imagined denying the last baby I'd dreamed of the right to be born to us, denying myself the opportunity to witness the miracle of bringing another child into the world.

"Maren, I'm sorry." Jake knelt down and reached over the tub to try to pull me to him.

I pulled away from him as the hurt turned to anger. I felt an extreme need to avoid the anguish that this conversation was heaping on my already-strained heart. "I can't talk about this right now," I cried. "Just go away."

"I'm not going away, Mar. We can talk about this later. It's not important right—"

I interrupted his words with a quiet, but firm, "I didn't just go through seven months of torture for something *unimportant,* Jake."

He defended himself humbly, "That's not what I meant."

I shielded my eyes and leaned back again. "Just go away," I said.

"You're not being fair, Maren." He was right. I wasn't being fair. But at that moment, I didn't care. Everything I'd suffered during the past weeks and months seemed to be suddenly racing toward me at once, threatening to overtake me and crush me if I didn't run.

"I just want to be alone, Jake," I pled softly. "Please. Go away."

I heard him go out and close the door. I sank down into the hot water and tried to forget about everything.

I knew I'd slept late when I woke the next morning to bright summer sun streaming through the blinds. I thought of Jason and jumped out of bed too quickly. I regretted it after pain shot through me. I walked more slowly into the bathroom to take a pain pill and get ready to go to the hospital. I was curling my hair when Jake knocked on the bathroom door. "Come in," I called.

He set a glass of juice on the counter for me. "Good morning." He smiled tentatively, almost as if he feared my reaction. I felt bad for being ornery with him the night before, but chose to ignore the subject for the moment.

"Good morning." I smiled back. I could see our bedroom reflected in the mirror. He'd made the bed.

He relaxed a little after my response and put his arm around me. I turned to look at him. "I'm sorry I upset you last night. It's way too soon to talk about that," he said.

I felt upset all over again. "Jake, I know there's another baby."

He looked at me quietly, not saying anything.

"I've told you about my dream. You believe me, don't you? You were there."

"Yes, Maren, I believe you."

"I saw two children—a boy and a girl."

"I know." He stood looking at me, his arms still around my waist.

I rested my palms against his chest and searched his face. "Can you possibly imagine how painful it is to have you tell me that you don't want another baby, when I've just been through all that I have to get *this* baby, and I know there's another one?"

"I didn't say that I don't want another baby, Maren."

"You said that you didn't know if you could watch me go through this again."

"Yes, I did."

"Well, isn't that the same thing, then? I know I'll be sick again. I'm always sick. And there's obviously a big risk of a placental abruption and premature labor again."

"Yes, there is."

I made my hands into fists against his chest, but he still held me. "Jake, don't do this to me! I need you! I need your strength! I'm scared to death to get pregnant again, but I know there's another baby."

"And I need you, Maren. You nearly died. Do you realize that? I almost lost you . . . forever." He stopped to wrestle with emotion for a moment before going on. "I'm still trying to cope with the terror of almost losing you *and* our baby, and you're asking me to think of going through it again!"

"I'm sorry," I told him more calmly. "I know this whole thing has been very difficult for you, but you're the one who brought this up, not me. I certainly don't want to get pregnant any time soon, but you can't tell me already that you won't let me have another baby."

"I didn't say that either, Mar."

"Oh, you're infuriating, Jacob!" I pushed on his arms, but he kept them around my waist. "Let me go! You can't stand there with your arms around me and talk to me like this! You just keep dancing around everything. Why don't you be more specific about what you meant?"

He pulled me to him more tightly, though he was careful not to hurt me. I pushed against his chest, but I was no match for his strength. "I won't let you go," he said firmly. "I will not be shut out. We're in this together." I stopped resisting him and let my hands lie still against his chest. I could feel his heart beating fast under the soft cotton of his shirt. "What I said, Maren, was that I didn't know if I could watch you go through all this again. I don't doubt the truth of your experience. I doubt my own strength. This is something we're going to have to work through together, and it's going to take some time."

"All right," I conceded, feeling a degree of comfort in his words.

He looked into my eyes for a moment and then pressed a gentle kiss to my lips. When he pulled back, I smiled at him.

"Oh, I almost forgot about those four little monkeys downstairs!" Jake suddenly remembered.

"Your parents will watch them," I said.

"No, I sent them to the hospital this morning."

"You did?"

"They wanted to see the baby, and I wanted someone to be with him. I didn't want to wake you up or leave you, so I sent them."

"Oh, good." I breathed a sigh of relief.

"Anyway, the kids sent me up here to see if you were recovered enough to come see their surprise, and I'm afraid I got a little side-tracked."

I laughed. "I still have to finish my hair. Go tell them I'll be done in five minutes, okay?"

"Yes, ma'am." He tipped an imaginary hat to me and left.

When I opened the bedroom door a few minutes later, all four children were sitting in the hall waiting for me. "Mom!" they all shouted. I hugged and kissed them all again.

"So, do I get my surprise now, or what?" I asked.

Jake was standing in front of the door to the baby's room, holding it shut and grinning. "I don't know, guys," he teased. "Should we let her have it?"

"Yes! Yes!" they all shouted. He opened the door and waved us in. I sucked in my breath. He'd painted three walls baby blue, like we'd planned, but the fourth wall was different. It was painted with a fresh coat of white paint, and covered with perfect little handprints in pastel colors.

"Mine are the green ones!" Trevor said proudly.

"And mine are blue," announced Jeff.

I looked at Rebecca and she volunteered, "I did yellow."

Lizzy stood smiling shyly at me. "Let me guess," I said. "Elizabeth's are pink?"

She giggled. "Yep!"

"And whose idea was this?" I asked curiously.

It was unanimous. "Daddy's!"

I smiled at Jake. "It's perfect." Then I looked at our children and said, "I love it! Jason is so lucky to have such wonderful brothers and sisters."

The new crib was set up with its blue and yellow bedding, and Jake had bought a rocking chair to put in the corner. I opened the dresser drawers to find all the baby things I'd bought or pulled out of storage washed and folded. "I have the most wonderful family in the world," I told them all, and meant it.

I tried to relax and not worry about Jason that morning as I read stories and played games with my other four children. I wanted them to know how important they still all were to me, especially since Ted was coming to get Rebecca and Trevor for the weekend. "Will we be back before Jason comes home?" they wanted to know.

"I think so," I said wistfully, wishing that he could come home sooner.

I knew that Ted was aware of what had happened. He'd taken the children one weekend while I was in the hospital. Still, it surprised me when he arrived to pick them up and looked at me with concern. "You okay?" he asked, when Rebecca and Trevor went to get their things.

I managed to disguise my shock and answer, "Yes. Thanks."

"You don't look so good," he observed, but it seemed more compassionate than cruel—another shocker.

"I've been through a lot, Ted, but I'm okay. Childbirth is never easy."

"No, I guess not. And the baby's okay?"

"He's still in the hospital, but he's all right."

Ted nodded slowly before the children reappeared with their arms loaded. "Let's go, Daddy!" Rebecca urged, tugging on his arm.

"Okay, Bec," he responded, turning to go.

"What was that?" Jake asked, stepping into the foyer from the kitchen after the door closed.

"What was what?" I wondered.

"Since when does Ted care if you're all right?" he asked bitterly. Then he added, "Let alone when a child that isn't even his is all right."

I shrugged, too tired to comment or defend Ted.

Jake's parents returned after lunch, and we went to the hospital. They'd warned us that Jason had jaundice and had been placed in an incubator under ultraviolet lights. He looked even tinier stripped down to his miniature diaper than he had wrapped in blankets. His eyes were covered with a foam mask to protect them, and we could see his small chest moving rapidly up and down with every breath. They only let us take him out to change and feed him every three hours. It was getting harder to get him to eat. We would coax and coax just to get a few swallows down him. He only wanted to sleep.

"Is he going to be all right?" I asked Jake, feeling incredibly grateful for his profession at that moment.

He sat down next to me and gave my shoulders a reassuring squeeze. "Yes, love. Just remember that he should still be sleeping away peacefully inside of you for six more weeks, getting everything he needs with no effort. He's early, that's all." He paused for a few moments before adding, "Though he might need to have a feeding tube if he doesn't start eating better soon."

That sounded bad. "What's that?"

"They run a tiny tube in through his nose and down his throat to his stomach. That way he can be fed without waking up."

"No! That sounds awful. That'll mean he has to stay longer!" I protested.

"Sometimes a couple of days of that will give them sufficient nourishment so they can start waking up and eating better on their own," he explained gently.

"I want him to go home, Jake," I said.

"I know. So do I."

"If you told them that you're a pediatrician, maybe they'd let us take him home."

Jake shook his head sadly. "I'm afraid that won't make much difference, Mar. I don't practice at this hospital, so no one here knows me. I suppose I could get someone to come over from the children's hospital and vouch for me." He let out a long sigh. "But honestly, I don't think that would persuade them either. He's not completely out of danger yet, and I don't have any of the equipment at home that they have here. They'd just tell us that it's too risky, and they'd probably be right." In a gesture of comfort, he urged my head to his shoulder and kissed my hair.

We stayed until almost midnight. Before we left, they let us take Jason into an empty room that was normally reserved for nursing mothers so Jake could give him a blessing. His gentle prayer for our son brought me some peace, as well. Even though things seemed difficult at the moment, I knew that we'd been greatly blessed and that we would be taking our baby home before too long.

CHAPTER TWENTY-TWO

The Saturday after Jason turned two weeks old, Jake and I knelt in prayer before going to the hospital. When he'd finished praying, Jake stood up and held his hand out to me. "Let's go get our son and bring him home," he said.

"Jake, you know they won't let him come home yet. He's still on a feeding tube, and he's lost eight ounces. Yesterday they said he could be in there until his due date." I felt discouraged. Four more weeks of this and our family was going to fall apart. Jake had gone back to work again that week, unable to take any more time off. His parents couldn't stay any longer and were going home the next day. My parents said they'd come back if we needed them to, but I knew how difficult it was for them to leave the farm, even for a couple of days—something always seemed to go wrong when a hired hand was left in charge. I didn't know how I was going to take care of my baby in the hospital and my other four children at home.

"Have a little faith, my love," my husband responded to my worries.

We kissed the other children good-bye, and Jake picked up the diaper bag and car seat to take with us. I wanted to have faith, but I didn't want to get my hopes up only to have them shattered.

At the hospital, Jake carried the car seat up to the nursery. I raised my eyebrows at him, but he just winked and smiled. When the head pediatrician walked in for her daily visit, Jake stood to meet her. We'd never really had much interaction with her, except for her looking down her nose several times to explain the situation to us as though we were children. More than once, she had repeated to us that we simply had to wait for our baby's nervous system to develop, and told us that it was so much better for him to be there with six to ten other babies, supervised by one very qualified nurse, than at home with two parents who loved him.

Jake held his hand out to her. "Good morning, Dr. Johnson," he said brightly. I just smiled and shook my head to myself. I supposed he might as well try.

"Hello, Mr. . . . uh . . ."

"Jantzen," he filled in for her. "Jacob Jantzen."

"Yes. And how is your little one doing?" she asked in a patronizing tone.

"About the same," he answered, knowing full well she had no idea what that meant. "He's still on a feeding tube, still not gaining weight, still not very responsive . . ." I didn't think he was making a very good argument for taking our baby home, but I didn't say anything.

"Well, these things take time," she began. "We're simply waiting for a nervous system to develop. There's not much to be done, except to give him close, qualified supervision."

"I couldn't agree more," Jake answered cheerfully.

She seemed a little taken aback by his enthusiasm and looked up at him over her wire-rimmed glasses. "Yes. Well, I'm glad you agree."

"Oh, I absolutely do. Which is why I've decided to take him home today."

"Excuse me?" she said, looking confused.

"We've ascertained that he's out of danger at this point," Jake reminded her. She nodded slowly, her brows still furrowed as he continued, "And as we've said, he's been here more than two weeks now with no real progress. Certainly he'd be under better care if he could be supervised by his parents, and a qualified doctor at home."

She laughed haughtily. "Well, yes, that would be ideal."

Jake went on, "Especially if that doctor had only him to attend to every night, and not several other babies as well."

She gave him an annoyed look. "Yes, that would be very nice, Mr. . . . uh . . ."

"Jantzen."

"Yes. That would be very nice if it were possible, Mr. Jantzen. Unfortunately, there are far too many babies here, and far too few doctors to provide twenty-four-hour, one-on-one care. And as for physicians making house calls . . ." She obviously found the idea so ludicrous that it didn't warrant a response, and snapped her clipboard closed as if that were the end of this frivolous discussion.

"Precisely." Jake smiled. "Which is why I've decided to take him home."

Dr. Johnson sighed and took off her glasses. "Mr. Jantzen, I'm sure you'd make a very good attorney. But this is a waste of my time."

"Perhaps I would." He grinned. "However, fortunately for both of us, I happen instead to be a pediatrician. That relieves you of the burden of wasting any more time on my son. I'll be taking him home where I can focus my complete attention on him, and only him, at least fourteen hours a day. He'll also have the benefit of being in a loving home with his mother and father, an environment which I feel confident will be much more conducive to his well-being. Now, what do I need to sign?"

"You're a doctor?" she asked suspiciously.

"Yes, ma'am. Feel free to call the licensing board and check for yourself. I'd appreciate you leaving whatever paperwork I'll need to fill out while you're doing that, though. We'd like to get him home as soon as possible."

I buried my face in Jason's blanket so Dr. Johnson wouldn't see me laughing. I couldn't believe this man I'd married.

"Well . . ." She hesitated and looked around the nursery. There were eleven babies at present and two nurses. "I suppose we *are* a little crowded."

"Thank you. I appreciate your understanding," Jake said. Then he turned to me. "Why don't you get Jason's things ready to go, love? I'm sure the paperwork will only take a minute." He took the baby's chart off the hook by his bassinet. "I'm assuming you'll want his vitals before we go?" He pulled his stethoscope from his pocket and listened to our baby's chest. He wrote something down on Jason's chart and then picked up the tiny blood-pressure cuff hanging over the bed. Then Jake proceeded to weigh him, take his temperature, and record what I'd just given him through a syringe in his feeding tube as a bewildered Dr. Johnson rummaged through a file at the nurses' desk looking for the papers she needed. She handed them to Jake a little begrudgingly. He jotted a couple of things down, signed his name, and said, "It's been a pleasure. You'll have a free bassinet in five minutes."

I bundled my now four-and-a-half pound baby into his car seat with a blanket rolled under his little bottom, and another one rolled up and over his head and shoulders to make him fit snuggly against the newborn headrest. He looked like he could drown in that tiny car seat. I tucked a blanket around him and picked the seat up to carry him outside. Jake scooped up everything else and took my arm. We left quickly before Dr. Johnson could get her wits about her and change her mind.

Once we were safely inside the elevator we both started laughing. "Oh, Maren!" Jake said. "It was worth all those eight years in medical school just to have that one moment! I get so irritated with those doctors who get so high-and-mighty they think they're above the people they serve, and forget all about what they went into it for."

"I can't believe you," I giggled.

He put his arm around my shoulders and hugged me. "Let's not forget who really let us take our baby home. I told you to have a little faith."

"Yes, you're right. I'm very grateful to my Heavenly Father for my baby, and for my husband."

He was still kissing me when the elevator doors opened. An elderly man shook his head and chuckled as he hobbled into the elevator and we walked out. "Those were the days," he said to Jake. "Enjoy it while you've still got it, son."

Jake humored him with a smile and a good-natured, "Thank you, sir. I will."

As we walked out to the car I told him, "You'll always have it—even when you're ninety-nine."

He threw his head back and laughed. The music of it filled my heart with joy. Then he wrapped his arms around me, car seat and all. "Just as long as I have you, my love. Just as long as I have you." He covered my mouth with his in one long, sweet kiss before he took us home.

Jake proudly carried Jason into the house in his car seat and announced from the foyer, "Hey, everybody, we've got someone here we'd like you to meet!"

Our four children came running from various corners of the house, bursting with excitement. "They let you bring him home?" Beverly asked in wonder as she nudged her way through the crowd of noisy children to peek into the car seat and smile.

"How on earth did you manage that?" Jarold questioned, peering over his wife's shoulder to look at the baby as well.

"Your son is a very smooth talker," I bragged.

Jake just gave a modest shrug, and both of his parents laughed.

We made our way into the family room, where each of our four children took a turn holding their baby brother. Their little faces were all beaming. "He looks like me," Jeffrey announced in a proud seven-year-old voice.

I smiled. "Yes he does, like you and your dad. Isn't he beautiful?"

Trevor scrunched up his face and said, "He's not beautiful, Mom. He's handsome."

"That, too," I laughed.

Rebecca stroked Jason's dark little head, and Lizzy kissed his tiny pink cheeks. The children took turns holding him off and on until dinnertime. We bribed them with holding him again if they all took their baths and got ready for bed quickly. Jake's parents were only too happy to watch their newest grandson while we saw to the task. Then everyone passed him around while we read bedtime stories, and Jake held him while he offered our family prayer, expressing gratitude for the blessing of having our baby home with us.

We set the alarm clock when we went to bed since Jason still wasn't waking up to eat. We would have to make ourselves get up every three hours to watch his formula slowly drip from a large syringe and through the tube into his stomach. When I finally woke up, I could see a hint of dawn seeping through the blinds, and I panicked. I'd slept all night! I hadn't gotten up to feed my baby! What kind of mother was I? I was exhausted, but that was no excuse.

I sat up quickly to check the cradle and saw Jake sitting next to it in the rocking chair. He was wearing burgundy pajama bottoms with a white T-shirt and holding Jason wrapped in his fuzzy blue blanket. Jake was rocking and singing very softly as he held up the nearly empty syringe and watched the last of the formula drip into Jason's feeding tube.

I sat quietly watching him for a minute before he looked up and smiled. "Good morning," he whispered.

"What are you doing?" I asked him, smiling.

"Taking care of our baby. What does it look like I'm doing?" Amusement flickered in his eyes.

I sighed happily and leaned back against the headboard. "It looks like you're trying to worm your way even deeper into my heart, which I didn't think was possible."

"Oh, you noticed. I thought I was being sneakier than that," he said slyly.

I sat there for several minutes after Jake had finished feeding Jason, content to just watch my husband holding our baby. He rocked him and watched him quietly until his eyes took on a glazed expression. "What are you thinking?" I finally asked.

"I'm just so grateful," he told me. "I know it's only a technicality, but it'll be such a relief for me once we're sealed. After everything we've been through over the past few weeks, I'm just going to feel a whole lot better when that's taken care of."

I suddenly felt ill.

"Did Bishop Rowley give you any indication as to how long the process might take?" Jake asked, looking up at me with anxious eyes.

I swallowed hard and shook my head in the negative.

"Oh well," he said good-naturedly. "I guess that's not important."

I gave him a halfhearted smile before I glanced down and fidgeted with the bedspread, twisting the velvety fabric in my hands while I wrestled with my emotions. I knew I had to discuss this with Jake soon, but I simply didn't have the emotional strength to tackle it at that moment. Instead, I sank back against the pillows and pulled the covers tight around me. I turned away from my husband and my baby, and lay staring at the wall.

The entourage of well-worn thoughts that was constantly present at the back of my mind pushed its way into conscious awareness. I wanted desperately to be sealed to Jake, but how would Ted react to such a request? What if I undid all the progress he'd made? How could I face Rebecca and Trevor with that? What about Ashlyn? And now, what about Jason?

I squeezed my eyes shut and fought desperately against the onslaught of agonizing questions until I managed to force them all back into a dull ache in the pit of my stomach. I found that I was suddenly grateful for the bone-deep exhaustion that had plagued me for the previous weeks, as it lulled me back toward the welcome oblivion of unconsciousness.

***

Later that morning, I found Jake and Jason downstairs, along with everyone else. I was filled with a combination of guilt and gratitude when Jake kissed me and said, "Good morning, Mar."

The morning was a bustle of activity as Jake's parents were getting ready to return home. At one point, Rebecca impulsively threw her arms around Jake's mother and said, "I'll miss you so much, Grandma!" I felt touched by how well our two families had bonded already.

Early that afternoon, I was trying to clean up the lunch aftermath when Jake came into the kitchen. "What are you doing?" he demanded, but his tone was one of concern, not reprimand.

"I'm just cleaning up a little," I told him. "You go relax with your parents. I'll be there in a minute."

"No." He swept me out of the kitchen with one strong arm. "You go upstairs and feed your baby—It's been three hours. I'll handle the kitchen."

"Jake, you should visit with your parents before they go. You can feed Jason down here while you do that."

"I can visit with them just as easily while I'm cleaning the kitchen as I can while sitting on the couch. Now go." He kissed me, and I obediently started toward the stairs. "Hey, kids, I could use a little help in here," Jake called. When he got no response, I heard him announce into the family room, "Let me rephrase that—anyone who helps me clean up the kitchen can come with me to take Grandma and Grandpa to the airport!" I heard shouts and squeals, and I figured he'd be getting some help, after all.

Jarold and Beverly knocked on my bedroom door a few minutes later. I had just finished feeding Jason and was holding him up to my shoulder, patting his back. "Come in!" I called.

"We just wanted to kiss the baby one last time, while the other children are occupied," Jake's mother said.

"Good idea." I smiled. "Why don't you sit down? I'll let you hold him."

Beverly sat on the edge of the bed and I carefully handed my baby to her. She kissed his cheek and cooed at him. Jarold sat down in the rocking chair to watch her.

"I can't thank you enough for all you've done," I told them.

"We're just glad to spend so much time with our five wonderful grandchildren," Beverly answered.

"And thank you for adopting my children as your grandchildren too." I said.

Jake's mother kissed Jason again and observed sadly, "It breaks my heart to leave them. This little one will grow so fast, we might not recognize him when we come back."

Jarold gave her a tender smile and observed, "I guess we'd better come back soon then."

"Please do," I invited. "You're always welcome."

Elizabeth appeared in the doorway a few minutes later, breathless from running up the stairs. "Come and see the kitchen, Grandma!" she implored. "We cleaned it up so fast that you didn't even get to help!"

Beverly laughed and said, "Are you finished already? I was going to come back down and help."

"Come and see!" Elizabeth prodded again, reaching for her hand.

"All right, sweetie. Just let me give Jason to your mommy first." It took a moment for me to realize that she'd just called me Elizabeth's "mommy." I leaned back against the headboard and smiled.

Jarold stood up and told his wife, "Give him to me, dear. 'Mommy' gets to hold him all the time."

"All right." She handed the little bundle to her husband. "Be careful now," she admonished gently. "He's awfully tiny, and—"

Jarold shook his head good-naturedly and cut in. "I think I can manage, darling. It won't be the first time I've held him. And I did have two children of my own, if I recall correctly."

"So you did." She smiled and kissed him. Then she hugged me and told me good-bye before following Lizzy out of the room.

Jake's father sat back down and cradled Jason against his chest, swaying slowly back and forth in the rocking chair. I watched the laugh lines that crinkled around his eyes when he chuckled at Jason's tiny hiccups, and I smiled at the glimpse into my husband's future.

"You know," Jarold observed carefully after watching his grandson for several peaceful moments, "there's such a wonderful feeling in your home . . . I've almost begun to wonder if there might actually be something to this church that Jake's been trying to convince us of all these years."

I felt my heart pound as I answered him. "There absolutely is. You can find out for yourself, you know. God will answer anyone who asks."

After a few seconds of silence, his eyes narrowed, and he asked almost in surprise, "You really believe that, don't you?"

I blinked back the tears that rose in my eyes with the confirmation. "Yes," I answered quietly. "I really do."

He watched me for a minute, seeming hesitant to voice what he was thinking.

"Do you want to ask me something else?" I finally inquired, after several moments of waiting.

"Pretty *and* perceptive," he said jokingly. "Actually, I can't help wondering, Maren—What if you'd lost this little guy?" He looked down at Jason to hide the moisture in his eyes. I didn't know if it was that thought, or the memory of losing his brother so recently that had brought such emotion to the surface. Jarold took a moment to compose himself and then met my gaze again. "Would you still believe in your church then? Would you still believe that God answers prayers?"

It suddenly occurred to me that he didn't know I'd lost a baby already. I'd assumed that Jake had told his parents, but then I guessed he'd never had a particular reason to. I forced away the knot in my throat to say, "Losing a child is the most difficult thing in the world."

He nodded and agreed, "I can imagine."

"I don't have to imagine," I replied carefully. "I know firsthand."

His eyes went wide with a combination of interest and compassion as he waited for me to continue.

"I had complications in my first pregnancy similar to the problems I had with Jason," I explained. "Although Ashlyn was only born two weeks early, she lived just a few hours. She'd be almost eleven now."

Jarold didn't even try to hide the tears in his eyes after that. His empathy sent a few tears cascading down my cheeks, as well. "I didn't know," he said quietly.

I shrugged. "I don't know why I just assumed that Jake had told you. I've faced a lot of trials in my life, Dad," I continued, "but none so terrible as burying my baby daughter. I didn't have the comfort or support of a loving husband at that time either, which added to the pain and discouragement. And I can't lie to you—I did turn bitter for a while. I was so angry at God. I even quit going to church. After several months in agony, though, I finally realized that I'd cut myself off from the only true source of comfort. I turned back to God. I went back to church, and to the temple. I humbled myself and prayed for strength to keep breathing."

My father-in-law reached over to squeeze my hand as I wiped away more tears. "I still miss her every day," I confessed, "though there is some healing that takes place with the passing of time. But honestly, my faith is the only thing that got me through it. With Ted's drinking, and losing my daughter, and the depression that followed, I sometimes wonder if I might have become suicidal if I hadn't turned back to God. I've come to accept the fact that the Lord knows more than I do. I don't understand why my daughter wasn't permitted to stay on earth, but I have the faith to accept the fact that there is a reason, that God loves me and knows what He's doing. I know the truth, Dad. I *know* the gospel is true. There's an immense amount of comfort in that knowledge because I understand that life goes on beyond here. Ashlyn is alive and well and happy somewhere else, and I have the promise of being reunited with her someday."

"Because families are forever?" Jarold asked seriously.

I nodded. "And in answer to your question," I responded with heartfelt sincerity, "if I'd lost Jason too, I would have been devastated. I would have been heartbroken at losing another child. But I would *not* have turned away from God again. I would have prayed continually for peace and strength, and I would have gotten through it. I'm blessed with a loving husband now, which might have made it a little easier. Even though I know it would've been very difficult, I also know that I would have been reunited with Jason someday as well, and that I could have survived losing him if it had been the will of the Lord. I'm immensely grateful that it wasn't, though."

"So, you think my little brother lives on somewhere else?" Jarold asked.

I leaned closer to him and answered firmly, "I *know* he does. And like I said, you can know too. You can pray and ask the Lord to answer your questions, to give you peace and comfort. He will, Dad. You don't have to take my word for it, or Jake's."

Jarold meditated thoughtfully for a bit, his face mirroring Jake's sparkling eyes and sweet smile. "I just may look into that, Maren," he said finally.

After a few more moments in contemplative silence, Jarold sighed and got to his feet. "I suppose I'd better get downstairs and help load up the car," he acknowledged a bit reluctantly. He touched Jason's little head before he handed him to me and kissed my cheek. "I enjoyed our talk," he told me.

I smiled and answered, "So did I."

Jake ran up to check on us before he left. "You'll be okay?" he asked.

"Yes. I'll be fine."

"Okay, then. I'm taking all the kids with me—all except this one, that is." He planted a kiss on Jason's cheek. "I'll be back soon." He reached over to kiss me too.

When he pulled back, his eyes searched mine for a minute. I pushed away the guilt and confusion left over from a few hours earlier to touch his face, and smile. "Bye," I whispered.

CHAPTER TWENTY-THREE

Jake went to work the following Monday, and things returned to normal—as much as possible, anyway. I sensed that Jake felt guilty returning to the office again and leaving me to deal with everything at home alone, but I also knew that he simply couldn't take any more time off.

It was a challenge taking care of a premature baby, in addition to four other children. I felt constantly tired, but I was so happy to have Jason home with us that it was easy to overlook that. It helped that it was summer, and the kids spent a lot of time outside in the backyard.

We didn't want to take Jason to church for a while. Jake said that any little germ could send him back to the hospital. It was hard to turn away the ladies from the ward who wanted to see him, but the thought of having him in the hospital again was enough to make me assert myself. "I'd love to let you see him, but he can't be around anyone who's not family for a few weeks, doctor's orders," I told everyone.

I did cave on my conviction once, however, when Lydia came to see me. I couldn't bring myself to turn her away. We sat in the living room and visited for a few minutes. When I volunteered to go get Jason, she said, "Oh, I'd love to see him . . . but you probably don't want a lot of people around him. I won't be offended if you'd rather that I waited until he's a little older."

"Are you healthy?" I asked her. "No colds recently or anything?"

"No." She shook her head firmly.

"Well, he is almost four weeks old . . . and I'd like you to see him, Lydia. I'll go get him."

"You're sure?" she asked.

"Yes," I told her. "You can wash your hands in the bathroom down the hall, if you don't mind."

"Nope, not at all."

Lydia seemed awestruck when I placed my baby in her arms. "He's so tiny!" she exclaimed. "I've never held a baby this new before."

I just smiled and let her enjoy it.

"Gosh, he sure looks a lot like Jake, doesn't he?" Lydia observed.

"He does," I agreed.

After talking about the baby a little more, and sitting for several moments in comfortable silence, I inquired, "So, are you doing anything fun tonight?"

"I have a date with Glen, actually," she admitted, looking up at me.

"Have you gone out with him before?" I asked, knowing that he'd obviously been interested in her for several months.

She shook her head. "I didn't date anyone for a while. I just felt too discouraged. After all that time I wasted being hung up on—" She cut herself off as a blush rushed into her cheeks.

The moment was awkward for both of us, but I knew that it was likely worse for her. I figured there wasn't much point in trying to ignore it, and decided that maybe it would be easier for her if it was out in the open anyway. "On Jake?" I asked her softly.

"Yeah." She gave a nervous laugh, and then told me awkwardly, "I'm sorry, Maren. I didn't mean to say that. I was just—"

"It's all right," I told her, then added with an understanding smile, "He's easy to get hung up on."

She smiled back. "I guess so . . ."

"I'm sorry if that was difficult for you," I felt compelled to say.

"I got over it," she assured me. "And since we're on the subject, I want to apologize again for being so rude to you all that time. You know, I've been making more of an effort to reach out to people since we talked last, and it's really making a difference. Thanks for helping me to get past my hang-ups."

"I don't think I did much," I said truthfully. "But you're welcome."

Lydia looked down at my baby again and her eyes filled with tears. "You're so lucky, Maren," she said. "You have a beautiful family, and a husband who loves you and lives the gospel . . . I'm sorry. I suppose I'm still a little envious. I just hope you realize what you've got."

I felt my own eyes fill with moisture, and I looked away from Lydia. I thought about her words. She was right. I was tremendously blessed. I had beautiful children, and a wonderful husband. So, why did I hesitate being sealed to him? I felt terrible, suddenly, and was relieved when Lydia rescued me from my thoughts by continuing more cheerfully, "Anyway, Glen's asked me out a few times, and I've always told him no because I felt like . . . Well, I just felt a little tired of the dating game for a while. He seems like a really nice guy, though, so I finally said yes this time. I figured if he was going to make the effort to keep at it, the least I could do was agree to go with him sometime. I don't know if anything's ever going to come of it, but I guess you can't have too many friends."

I nodded in agreement and assured, "You'll have fun."

"Thanks." She grinned. "I think I will."

***

By the time he'd been home for two months, Jason had doubled his weight and looked like a normal, healthy baby. Our other children couldn't get enough of him. I'd healed from my whole ordeal much sooner than I'd expected to. I knew it was a blessing, but I also gave a lot of credit to Jake for helping me so much.

Gratitude filled my heart every time I looked at my family, and I knew that life was good. Lydia's confession of envy kept coming back to haunt me: *I just hope you realize what you've got.* Jake didn't bring up the sealing issue again, but I knew that was because he assumed it was being taken care of. I tried to think of a way to explain my feelings to him, as well as the fact that I hadn't turned in the cancellation request yet. The dilemma was constantly at the back of my mind, but I put off dealing with it. Eventually, though, I knew that I was going to have to face it, make a decision, and accept the consequences. I included my concerns in my daily prayers, but it didn't seem to help.

Ted's attitude remained more agreeable, and from what I could tell, he seemed to be regaining his testimony. Rebecca and Trevor were closer to him than they'd ever been. His progress only served to make my decision more agonizing.

One Sunday in late August, Jake told me that he had an appointment with the bishop. "Uh-oh," I told him teasingly. "What do you think they're going to ask you to do?"

Jake smiled, but he seemed slightly uneasy. "I don't know." He shrugged.

When he came home, I asked, "So, what's your new calling?"

He looked deeply at me for a few moments, almost as if he was searching for something. I tilted my head in question, and he looked away. "I'll talk to you about it later," he told me.

I gave him a strange look, wondering at his somber tone.

Jake put on a smile and visited pleasantly with the children and me through dinner. I still sensed something brewing inside of him, though. By the time we went to bed, he seemed to be caught somewhere between volatility and despair, and I was fast becoming swallowed up in a deep sea of foreboding.

"So . . ." I began dubiously. Whatever it was, I didn't want to talk about it. But I was afraid that Jake was going to explode if we didn't get it over with soon. "We obviously need to talk about something."

Jake sat on the bed and stared at me. For the first time, I noticed that he appeared not just angry, but deeply wounded, as well. "The bishop didn't ask to talk to me," he explained evenly. "I asked to talk to him."

"Why?" I wondered aloud before I took time to think. The simple question ignited a fuse, and a time bomb began ticking in my head.

"I had some specific questions that I wanted to ask him about the sealing issues and some of the doctrine surrounding them—he answered them. Then I asked him how long we could expect this process to take, and whether he thought we could be sealed on our first anniversary. He told me that *once you turn your cancellation request in,* it could still be several months, and that at this point, even if you got your papers to him right away, we most likely wouldn't make it by then."

I felt my throat constrict as breathing became more difficult.

"So, Mar," Jake said coolly, "what I want to know is *when*, exactly, were you planning on getting around to this?"

"Well, I . . . I'll get to it, Jake. I mean, I wasn't planning on having the baby two months early, and it's definitely thrown me off. I just haven't had time. I haven't been able to even think about anything else lately."

"Neither have I," he told me pointedly.

"Look, Jake . . ." I started wearily. I felt completely exhausted suddenly, too emotionally drained to deal with this. I opened the drawer to my nightstand instead, and sifted through the contents until I found the papers that Bishop Rowley had given to me. I thanked the Lord that I had filled them out all those weeks ago. "Here." I handed them to Jake. "Take them over to the bishop right now, if you want to."

Jake took the forms from me and studied them. He went through the pages—to see if they were really all filled out, I assumed—and then looked at me. "You had them ready?" he asked, faltering, apparently needing verbal confirmation to back up what he could see.

"Do they look ready to you, Jake?" I responded curtly. I wasn't consciously trying to make him feel as though he were in the wrong, but I was overwhelmed with a combination of guilt, anger, confusion, and despair—and it was simply more than I could handle.

Jake glanced at the forms again, then leaned back against the headboard and covered his face with them. He finally let out a long, low breath and laid the stack of paperwork on his own nightstand. "I'm sorry," he said without looking at me.

I knew he shouldn't be apologizing to me, but I couldn't have confessed my true feelings to him even if I'd wanted to—I hadn't even straightened them out completely in my own mind.

Jake glanced uneasily at me, and it made me feel sick. I wanted more than anything to just take him in my arms and explain everything I felt to him. But I simply couldn't do it. In that moment, I was filled with self-loathing. I felt completely powerless. "Good night," I mumbled tonelessly and rolled over to feign sleep.

Jake turned off the lamp, but then just sat there in the darkness for a long time. I could feel his troubled thoughts, and they tore at my heart. It seemed like hours before I finally fell asleep.

In the middle of the night, I woke up to the familiar sight of Jake sitting in the rocking chair, feeding Jason his bottle. My heart softened at the scene, and I simply wanted to be close to my husband. I crossed the room to stand behind him and began rubbing his shoulders as he gently held Jason up to burp him. After several moments, Jake seemed to finally relax some. "Ahh . . ." he sighed at last. "That feels good, Mar."

"You got up with him again." I stated the obvious.

"Mmm-hmm," Jake mumbled sleepily.

I kissed the top of his head and kept massaging his shoulders. Jason slept contentedly against his father's chest, his little fists drawn up under his chin. "Why don't you ever wake me?" I asked. "I can get up with him. You have to go to work in the morning."

"You have to work too," Jake pointed out. "Why would I wake you? You're exhausted. You've hardly been able to rest since you had him. You never really even had time to recuperate from childbirth, and this particular one was much more harrowing than normal. Besides, he's my baby too."

I was so tired from my restless night that I rambled on without thinking. "I always got up with the babies . . . I don't think Ted got up in the night even once, ever."

I felt the muscles in Jake's shoulders grow instantly tense again. He kept rocking silently for a minute before he said, "What's my name, Maren?"

"What?"

"My name. You do remember it?"

"Of course I do. Don't be ridiculous."

He set the empty bottle on the nearby table and carefully placed Jason in his cradle. Then he came around the chair to take hold of my upper arms. I could see his face in the lamplight as he insisted quietly, "Say my name."

"Jake—" I started to protest.

He shook me, very gently, but it still shocked me. "My name, Maren. Say it," he ordered.

"Jake, you're scaring me. You're acting like—"

"Like who? Like Ted? I'm acting like Ted?" He put his face close to mine, and I could see fury in his eyes. He never got angry enough to scare me. He'd never been unkind to me, but I felt a growing uneasiness. "Maybe that's what you want! Is that what you want, Maren? If I knocked you around a little bit, would that make you happy?"

"What are you talking about?" I asked, feeling disconcerted. "Of course not!"

He let go of my arms and turned away from me to run his hand through his hair. He took a deep, agitated breath before turning back to me. "Maren, you've been divorced for over two years now. We've been married nearly ten months. Do you have any idea how many times a day you throw that name silently at me?"

"No, I—"

"When are you going to let him go?" He threw his hands in the air for emphasis. *"When?"*

"Jake, I have let him go."

"No, Maren, you haven't!" he insisted vehemently. "Every day I hear 'Ted this' and 'Ted that'! I am continually compared to him. Every time I do something nice for you, or even just something that any decent husband should do, I'm slammed into the brick wall of 'Ted didn't do that,' like there's something wrong with me for doing it, or that you don't believe that's who I really am! And on the rare occasions when I get angry, you try to tell me that I'm acting like Ted! I . . . am . . . *not* . . . TED!"

He clenched his hands into fists at his sides and then said more quietly, "I wanted to be him. For ten years, I would have killed to be him, Maren. I tried to be everything I thought you'd seen in him, hoping it might somehow fill the hole in my heart and make me whole again without you. But now that I know who Ted really is, and what he put you through, I thank God that I'm not him. I will never be him. I would do anything to stop myself from being like him in any way."

He paused for a minute, and I saw his shoulders slump as he lowered his voice again. "I'm doing everything I can think of to be a good husband to you, Maren. I love you more than I think you can even comprehend because you lived so long with a selfish son-of-a—" He stopped himself and chuckled humorlessly. "There. I almost acted like him again. With every thought or feeling I have, I'm compelled to stop and think, 'Wait . . . am I being like Ted?' And yet I hear so much about him, I have to wonder if it's easier for you to accept a drunk abuser than an imperfect man, who, nevertheless, tries his best to love you and your children and honor his priesthood in the hope that he might someday be worthy of your complete love."

"Jake, I do *not* want to be with Ted," I insisted quietly.

"Then why do you throw him between us all the time?" he demanded. "And why do you want to be sealed to him instead of me?"

"I filled out the request, Jake—" I started to say.

"You've had months to turn it in, Maren, and you *haven't!* And what's worse—you let me believe that you had!" Electrical daggers shot from his eyes straight into my heart as he glared at me. After a few moments of painful silence, despair seeped into Jake's expression, overtaking the anger. "I don't understand, Maren," he muttered. "You told me the problem was with Tess, but my sealing to her was voided out months ago."

I fought back tears and replied steadily, "Maybe I have responsibilities to Ted, Jake. I made mistakes in my first marriage too, you know. He's making progress. Do you have any idea how bitter it could make him if I ask him to break the sealing? He might never come back to the Church! If he gets angry and volatile about the whole thing, that's simply going to cause more problems for us! And what about my children? They're too young to be included in any kind of decision now, but how will they feel when they're older and they understand that I broke my sealing to their father?"

The look of astonishment on Jake's face was growing increasingly more intense, so I took a deep breath and said, "There are plenty of factors to consider besides Tess—"

"Are you telling me," Jake hissed, "that this whole thing . . . is about *Ted?*"

I struggled for words. "I . . . I want to be sealed to you, Jake, but I'm so confused! It all just seems like such a complicated mess, and I can't talk to you about any of it because you get so upset every time I—"

"And why is that, Maren?" Something seemed to snap in him, as his eyes seared into my soul. *"Why* do you think this whole thing makes me so upset? . . . I'll tell you why! Because on the same day that I'd planned to propose to you for a year—and you had led me to

believe that you would accept—you ripped out my heart, threw it on the ground, and said, 'I've decided to marry Ted.' *Ted.* Ted, Ted, Ted! And that's all I've heard since! I listened to it for months after we were married and never said a word, even though you complained ceaselessly to me about all the repercussions we had to deal with because of Tess! Well, *excuse me* for making the mistake of trying to find a life without you when that was the only option you gave me! I can't believe you're demanding my sympathy when this whole 'complicated mess' is *your* fault in the first place, Maren! And I *really* can't believe you're still so enmeshed with your sick ex-husband that you're more concerned about rescuing him from his own well-deserved consequences than you are about us!" Jake paused long enough to take a breath, then lowered his voice to speak with barely contained fury. "I've been running in second place to that moron for too many years, Maren, and I *will not* be in second place anymore!"

The tears came hard and fast, and I felt ill. I sought in vain for words that might somehow undo what I'd done. I could see the agony coiling around him, suffocating him . . . but I was powerless to change it. Jake grabbed hold of me like a drowning man, and searched my face desperately. I didn't know what he was looking for. I tried to twist free of him. I knew it was illogical, but my mind suddenly swirled back to the panicked fear I'd felt so often with Ted.

"Let go of me!" I hollered as I pounded on his chest. "You have no right to treat me this way! I won't live in another marriage being treated this way! *I won't!*" I felt trapped—like I was being sucked back into a raging tempest that I'd thought was far behind me. "I will *not* live with Ted, Jacob, and you're acting just like him!"

He seemed stunned by my words and released my arms quickly, but then caught me around the waist. I could feel his hot breath in my face, but his eyes weren't full of hate like Ted's used to be. They held only unbearable pain—pain that I realized had made him snap, pain that I had caused. "Say my name, Maren," he insisted fiercely. *"Say my name!"*

"Jake!" I screamed in his face. "Jacob Adam Jantzen!"

"And yours. Say yours," he ordered.

"Maren," I whispered.

"Maren what?"

"Maren Jantzen. Maren *Jantzen*. I'm your wife. I'm *your* wife, Jake," I said more quietly. "I know you're not Ted. I thank God you're not Ted."

"Do you?" he asked cynically, but there was a desperation in his expression. He let go of me suddenly, and held his hands up as though they'd been burned. He seemed to be teetering on the edge, and I felt frantic to pull him back.

I forced myself to calm down. "Jake," I urged him quietly, "come back to bed." I tried to take his hand, but he pulled it away.

"I can't, Maren," he said gruffly. "I just can't."

I felt anger rising in me again as he moved toward the door. "Fine!" I hollered after him. "Why don't you just leave! Go ahead and wimp out, and leave me here to deal with all this alone! You're being a selfish fool, Jake!"

Jake whirled around and shot back, "One more thing, Maren— I'm not perfect! And I'm tired of trying to pretend that I am! Maybe sometimes I *am* a selfish fool! I've been putting on this show for months because—because I've felt so much pressure to make up for all the pain you went through in your first marriage. I have to constantly prove myself to you, so that maybe—just *maybe*—if I can manage to be flawless, you'll eventually come to realize that you can trust me and get over the garbage from the past. I'm human, Maren, okay? You have to allow me some space for error here!" Jake lowered his voice then and said fiercely, "And I have *never* left you alone! I'm not going to a bar to drink myself into oblivion, all right? I'm going to the guest room! And if you don't like it, maybe *you* should leave! You're good at that—remember?" I watched Jake slam the door and went back to bed, too angry to cry anymore.

I got up early that morning to feed Jason, and then went downstairs to start breakfast for my other children before I woke them up to get ready for school. I was grateful they'd started back the week before. My head ached, and I still felt full of anger. I was grating cheese for omelettes when Jake came up behind me. I could feel his eyes on me, but I didn't turn around. He hesitated, then touched me on the shoulder. "Maren," he said softly.

I shrugged his hand off and ignored him.

Jake sighed loudly and mumbled, "We've got to find a way to get past this."

"Why don't you just keep shouting at me and then taking off?" I shot out. "That seems to be working great."

His voice was filled with both irritation and exasperation, but he seemed to be attempting to stay calm. "Maren—" he started again.

"Just go to work, Jake," I told him.

"Fine," he responded after a pause, then left.

I went through the morning routine mechanically and sent Rebecca and Jeff to the bus stop. I didn't have the energy to even pretend to entertain Trevor and Elizabeth, so I turned the TV on for them before I went to take a shower. I got ready, fed Jason again, and kept myself busy with housework and laundry. I was afraid that if I stopped moving, I'd sink into unbearable depression and never be able to get back up again. I hadn't felt so discouraged since I'd been married to Ted.

After I got Trevor and Elizabeth on the afternoon kindergarten bus and put Jason down for a nap, I wandered into my bedroom, thinking that I'd lie down and hope my headache went away. The dam of emotions that had been building up for so many days and weeks refused to be held back any longer, though. I buried my face in my pillow and sobbed for what seemed like hours. Much of the anger and anguish that I'd been harboring washed slowly away with the tears, and I felt humility trickling in to replace it.

I suddenly realized that I hadn't been doing this the right way. I couldn't just ask the Lord to tell me what to do. I needed to make my own decision, and then pray for confirmation that it was the right one. I slid to my knees beside my bed to pray. I'd prayed over this before, I knew, but this time was different. For the first time, I was able to truly open myself up and pour my heart out to my Father in Heaven.

I told the Lord that my deepest desire was to be sealed to Jake, which meant that I would have to attempt to have my sealing to Ted canceled. I explained that I felt it was the right thing—and was surprised to find that I truly did—but I expressed the concerns that I had to Him as well. I told God of my faith in Him, and in His ability to make everything work. I asked that I might feel peace in my decision if it was right.

I didn't know how long I prayed before I was interrupted by the doorbell. I tried to ignore it, but after it rang several times, I gave up and went to answer it. "Natalie!" I exclaimed in surprise.

"I knew you were in there somewhere," she told me. "Did I wake you up?"

"I wish," I mumbled. "What are you doing?"

She looked pensive. "I don't know. I just . . . felt like dropping by. Sorry I didn't call first." I didn't tell her that I probably would have told her not to come if she'd called. I decided that a little distraction would be a welcome reprieve, and invited Natalie in. After some lighthearted conversation she finally said, "You look good. Are you feeling okay?"

I was surprised at the concern in her tone and told her, "Yes, I feel pretty good, actually." I realized suddenly that we hadn't had a real one-on-one conversation since I'd had Jason.

"How's Jake doing?" she asked me.

I gave her a strange look and answered slowly, "Okay . . . Why do you ask that?"

Natalie probably looked more serious than I'd ever seen her as she scrutinized me. "You should have seen him, Maren," she finally said.

"What?" I asked her, not sure what she was referring to.

"When you were first in the hospital, and Jake finally came home to stay with the kids because Nathan was sick, he just looked so worried. And I went up to the hospital right after Jason was born— did you know that?"

I shook my head in the negative.

"I didn't think so," she remarked. "Jake probably didn't think to tell you with all the stress he was under at the time. I made him promise to call me as soon as you had the baby, no matter what time it was. Since Mom's so far away, I wanted to be there for you. I guess he waited until he was sure that you and the baby were both going to be all right, but then he called to tell us. It was . . . I don't know— maybe five in the morning? We're so close to the hospital, that I came right over. I waited as long as I could, but you never woke up. I finally had to go home and take Nathan so Doug could get to class."

I gave her a confused look, not sure what she was getting at.

"I know Jake went back and forth countless times between you and the baby," Natalie told me. "The poor guy just looked completely exhausted. But when he was with you . . . the way he looked at you . . ." Natalie's eyes grew misty as she said, "He just sat there, holding your hand and watching you sleeping. I tried to get him to go eat breakfast, or just take a break for a minute while I stayed with you, but he wouldn't go. The only thing he would leave you for was to check on Jason."

I felt a lump forming in my throat as Natalie continued, "He's just so completely in love with you, Maren. I think he'd do *anything* for you."

"Why are you telling me this?" I asked hoarsely, wondering if the timing was divine intervention, or simply coincidence.

"Because you've been so concerned with saving my marriage, while you continue to sabotage your own. You've told me to consider Doug's feelings, and his struggles, and appreciate what a good man he is, in spite of his imperfections . . . and it's helped, Maren. I know he's doing the best he can, and I really do love him. I've also come to realize that marriage requires some sacrifice from both parties, and it's easier to give things up for Doug when I look at all he's doing for me. I'm grateful for your insights and your advice. But how do I hold a mirror up to you, and tell you to put some of that to use in your own life?"

My thoughts still felt a little hazy, though I sensed that Natalie had touched the tip of something I needed to uncover. "I know you're still struggling with the sealing issue," Natalie continued. "The thing is though, Maren, I can't figure out why." When I didn't respond, she asked, "Have you talked to Jake about this whole thing—I mean really, honestly talked to him?"

"I've tried," I admitted tiredly. "He doesn't understand, Natalie. It just hurts him."

She shook her head in bewilderment. "You're really going to give up being sealed to a man who loves you with his whole heart and soul, just so your ex-husband won't be ticked off?"

"It's not that simple, Nat—" I started, but she cut me off.

"Why? You have two choices here, Maren—Ted or Jake. You know darn well who you want to be with, and you also know—intellectually anyway—that you can't control another person's behavior . . . so why is it hard?"

I sat rolling her words around in my head for a minute before I finally asked her seriously, "When did you grow up?"

She laughed a little. "You're well aware of the fact that I've grown a lot because of my own struggles this year," she told me. "But looking in on someone else's life gives you a different perspective too, you know? Especially when it's someone you love."

"It's not just Ted, Natalie," I confessed to her after a moment's hesitation. "What if Rebecca and Trevor hate me later on for breaking my sealing to their father?"

Natalie scrunched up her face and said, "Remember when you first started getting counseling, right after you kicked Ted out?"

"Yes."

"I still remember, Maren, when you told me about your first couple of sessions, and what you were beginning to learn about recovering from an abusive marriage. What did you tell me the first rule of recovery was? . . . It seemed like that sort of had to be your mantra there for a little while, to give you direction."

I rummaged through the files in my mind, but it didn't take me long to get to that one. *"What's best for me will be best for everyone,"* I said, quoting what Miles had told me in those early weeks. "Wow . . . I'd forgotten about that."

"Well, there you go," Natalie told me brightly.

"But what if being sealed to Jake isn't what's best for me?" I said slowly, more to myself than to my sister. Natalie just stared at me for a moment, apparently bewildered.

"What if it's not what's best for Jake?" I continued verbalizing the thoughts that were slowly making their way through my brain. "Maybe Jake's too good for me, Natalie. What if I don't deserve him? What if I wake up one day, and he doesn't love me anymore? What if this whole fairy tale is just too good to be true, and I suddenly wake up from my dream . . . and I'm not sealed to anyone and I've lost everything?" I felt something erupt inside my chest, and rush through my body, making me gasp as a fresh wave of tears came. I thought of Lydia telling me how lucky I was, of Natalie telling me how wonderful Jake was, of Mandy raving about his charm, and my parents in awe of his goodness. "Why me?" I cried to my sister. "Why would Jake love *me*? What if he decides I'm not worth it, and leaves?!"

Natalie's eyes teared up too as she witnessed this transitional moment for me—one she'd advised me to consider months ago, I suddenly remembered. "There are a million reasons why Jake loves you, Maren," she told me gently. "But individually, they don't matter that much. It's all of those little things put together that make you who you are. Jake loves you because you're *you*. Do you think you're any less wonderful than he is? You deserve a righteous husband who loves you, Maren. Your confidence and self-esteem have improved so much since you left Ted, but it looks like you still need to come to grips with the fact that you're a daughter of God, and a woman worthy of love."

"Yeah." I wiped at my eyes, then started to laugh. "I'm sorry for being a baby," I apologized. "It's been a rough day."

Natalie smiled and said, "I just want you to be happy, Maren. Honestly."

"I know you do, Natalie . . . And I'm glad you're my sister."

"Thanks." She smiled.

"And I think you just answered my prayers," I added.

CHAPTER TWENTY-FOUR

When Natalie left a few minutes later, I went straight for the phone to call the executive secretary for the ward. I told him that I needed to make an appointment to meet with the bishop right away. "It's kind of important," I added.

"All right, Sister Jantzen, we'll squeeze you in tonight. Would six thirty work?"

"I'll make it work," I promised before I hung up.

I wanted to talk to Jake more than anything—to apologize for hurting him, for getting angry, and for taking so long to find my faith. I wanted to tell him about my experience, confess my massive dose of self-awareness, and convey my decision to him. But I knew I couldn't do all that over the phone. I would have to wait until I could see him.

When Jake still wasn't home by six o'clock, I called his cell phone. He didn't answer. I was disappointed, though not terribly surprised. I knew it was his turn to be on call that week, and that it wasn't unusual for him to have to stop by the hospital or stay at the office a bit later on those days. A rather nasty thunderstorm had blown in that evening, as well, and I knew the abrupt change in weather would add time to Jake's commute home.

Not wanting to miss my appointment with the bishop, I called Lydia and asked if she could come stay with the children until Jake got there. The kids had grown fond of her by then, and she happily agreed to help out. I told her where I was going, but didn't give her any details. "Jake should be home anytime," I said. "But I don't think I'll be too long if for some reason he's not."

I drove to the church house slowly on the wet roads. Bishop Rowley welcomed me with a smile and a firm handshake, offering me a chair right away. "How are you, Maren? And how is that new little one?" he asked, concerned. I hadn't talked to him personally since Jason's birth, having stayed home from church with my baby for several weeks. Still, the ward had been generous. We'd received count-less offerings of dinners, unsolicited plates of food, and invitations for our older children to go to neighbor's homes to play.

"We're both doing very well, thank you," I answered. "And the ward has been great."

"Good," Bishop Rowley responded. "And how are you and Jake?" I wondered if he was concerned about our relationship, having talked with Jake the day before.

"Jake and I are very happy," I answered honestly. But then I briefly explained the situation to him. "So, I want to be sealed to my husband," I finished. "I'd like to give you my paperwork to request a sealing cancellation, and get the ball rolling."

Bishop Rowley smiled and promised, "I'll get it rolling right away."

"Thank you." I smiled back. I felt like a huge weight had been lifted from me.

The rain had let up some by the time I left, but the roads were still slick. I was glad that I only had to drive a few blocks to get home. To my chagrin, Jake wasn't there yet. I wanted so badly to see him, to hold him. "I thought Jake would be home by now," I apologized to Lydia, noting that it was after seven thirty. "Did he call?"

She shook her head. "Nah, but don't worry about it. We had fun, didn't we, kids?"

"Yeah!" all four children answered in unison. They were eager to tell me about the games they'd played with Lydia, but I felt distracted by sudden worry. Jake had never come home so late without calling.

Lydia apparently sensed my concern and handed Jason over to me. "Why don't you call him?" she suggested. "I'll take the kids upstairs and get them ready for bed . . . Oh, and I think Jason's ready for a bottle."

"Thanks," I mumbled. I called Jake's cell phone again, but got no response. I distractedly punched in the phone number for his office, not really expecting an answer this late in the evening. I was surprised to hear a feminine voice greet me with, "Valley Pediatrics."

"Trina?" I asked after a pause. I felt a degree of relief. If the receptionist was still there, maybe Jake had needed to stay later than usual to attend to something urgent.

"That's me."

"It's Maren. Late night, huh?"

"Yeah. With the rainstorm and that terrible accident and everything, I figured I might as well stay and catch up on some paperwork instead of sitting in traffic for two hours."

"What accident?" I asked curiously.

"Oh, didn't you hear? There was some big accident on the freeway around five thirty. I guess the storm came in so fast that it caught a lot of people off guard."

"So is Jake still there too?" I asked hopefully.

"Nope. He left a long time ago—before it even started to rain. It was a little after five, I think."

"Oh," I mumbled, trying not to sound too disappointed. "Well, did he say he had to go over to the hospital or anything?"

"No. In fact, he was in quite a hurry to get out of here. I don't know where he was going—I assumed he just wanted to get home."

"Okay. Thanks . . . Be careful going home," I added.

"I will. Bye."

I fixed a bottle for Jason and went to the family room to sit in the rocking chair and feed him, feeling troubled. Lydia came downstairs a few minutes later and announced, "Well, I put the kids in bed, but I can't guarantee they'll stay there. I thought I'd worn them out pretty good, but they all seem to have caught a second wind."

I smiled. "They have a tendency to do that."

Lydia threw herself down on the couch and gave an exhausted sigh. "I don't know how you keep up with them, Maren."

"Sometimes I don't," I admitted jokingly, trying to distract myself from my worries.

"So did you get ahold of Jake?" Lydia inquired.

I shook my head. "He didn't answer his phone."

"Did you try his office? He ends up working late once in a while, doesn't he?"

"He's not there either. The receptionist said he left a long time ago."

"Oh. Well, I'm sure he'll be home soon then."

"Probably," I agreed halfheartedly.

"You don't sound too convinced," Lydia observed. "You wanna fess up to what's bugging you?"

I laughed a little before I admitted, "We had a fight last night. Maybe he took off somewhere to be alone for a while . . . I just hope he comes home soon."

"He will," Lydia stated matter-of-factly. "Jake doesn't seem like the type to hold a grudge."

"Not usually," I agreed. "But I hurt him pretty badly, I think. I mean, he was already hurting. He's been hurting for months. And then he tried to make up with me this morning before he left for work and I told him to go away." I felt an ache in my throat and fought against the tears.

Lydia nodded her head in understanding. "Well, maybe he did need some time alone then. He'll come home though, Maren. You know he can't live without you. He loves you to pieces."

"I know," I muttered as my voice cracked. "That's part of the problem."

Lydia gave me a strange look, but then attempted to lighten things up with humor. "Your perspective on adversity might be a little twisted, Maren. You see, most women would consider it a *good* thing if their husbands worshiped the ground they walked on."

I laughed and wiped away a couple of tears that escaped down my face. "You've really come out of your shell, haven't you?" I asked her teasingly, trying to think about something else.

"I already told you that." She smiled. "And I thanked you for helping me with it, too—didn't I?"

"Yes." I laughed a little. Then I furrowed my brows and voiced another troubling thought. "Jake's receptionist also said there was a big accident on the freeway . . ."

"Yeah, I managed to catch that on the news while you were gone," Lydia told me. "It happened right by our exit. They said the accident was huge—a rollover, and several cars piled up because of the rain . . . I'm sure he's not in that, Maren," she said firmly. "But maybe he's stuck on the freeway because of it. Now that's a realistic possibility."

"Maybe," I agreed. "But if he was just stuck in traffic, he'd call me on his cell phone. He won't even answer his phone." I shook my head in bewilderment. "It can't be good either way, Lydia. Either he's in that accident, or he's too angry to come home."

"I'm sure he's fine, Maren," Lydia attempted to reassure me. "Do you want me to stay and keep you company until he gets here?"

"No, but thanks. You've got to work in the morning, and I should go to bed early anyway. I'm pretty worn out."

"Okay," she agreed. "Call me if you get lonely."

"I will. And thanks for staying with the kids."

"Anytime," Lydia responded as she got to her feet. She nodded toward my sleeping baby and said, "I'll show myself out. See ya later."

"Bye."

I laid my head back against the rocking chair and sat rocking and thinking for a long time. I thought the kids must have fallen asleep, because I couldn't hear them stirring. I knew there wasn't much point in going to bed myself, however. I wouldn't be able to sleep anyway. I felt heartsick and just ached to share my news with Jake. I wanted to tell him how sorry I was, and how much I appreciated him. I chastised myself for being so cold that morning. *I should have apologized to him then,* I thought. I said a silent prayer for his safety and asked that he would arrive home soon.

***

I woke with a start from a bad dream and shook my head groggily. I was shocked that I'd fallen asleep, and glanced at the clock on the mantle. Ten forty-five. *Ten forty-five!* I got to my feet quickly, though I was careful not to wake Jason who slept on peacefully in my arms. I hurried up the stairs and laid him down gently in his crib. Then I ran down the hall to my bedroom. I switched on the light. The bed was still made. I went downstairs to check the guest room, just in case, but Jake wasn't there either.

Having fallen asleep, I'd never checked on our older children, so I hurried back up to peek into their bedrooms. After I'd been assured that all four of them were sleeping soundly, I wandered back out to the hall and sat at the top of the stairs, staring down into the entryway. I tried not to overreact, as I considered where Jake could possibly be. I wondered if he would actually spend a night away from home at a hotel or something. Could he be that angry with me? Only the night before he'd told me that he wouldn't leave. I considered Lydia's theory and questioned whether he really could have been delayed by an accident on the freeway. But surely even a multi-car accident couldn't shut down the freeway for five hours. If it was that bad, they would have found a way to reroute traffic and get things cleared up.

My heart sank at the obvious conclusion, and I prayed silently again, *Please bring him home safely, Lord. Please.* I hurried into the kitchen and searched frantically through the phone book for the number of the local hospital, wishing that I'd succumbed to paranoia and called them hours earlier. The line was busy for several minutes, but I kept punching the number in over and over again, feeling a rising panic. When I finally got through to a tired-sounding operator, I blurted out, "I need to see if my husband's there, if he was involved in a car accident. His name's Jacob Jantzen. J-A-N-T-Z-E-N."

"Just a moment, please," the operator said mechanically. I heard the tapping of fingers on a keyboard, and then a pause. "There's no 'Jantzen' listed," she finally told me.

"He's a doctor," I pointed out hopefully. Perhaps she would recognize the name then. "He practices there. Maybe the EMTs didn't know his name," I suggested, trying to stay calm enough to speak. "If he was knocked out, or couldn't tell them for some rea—"

The woman on the other end of the phone line sighed and said in a dull voice, "Ma'am, with that freak thunderstorm we had tonight, there've been more accidents than I can count. And then there was that pileup on the freeway right close to here . . . At this point, we've got so many unidentified patients I don't even know where to start. I'd suggest you call back in the morning. Maybe some of the chaos will have died down by then."

"In the morning?" I asked incredulously.

"I'm sorry, ma'am. I wish I could help you." I heard a click and then the hum of a disconnected phone line.

I replaced the phone on the receiver numbly as my mind began to race. Surely God wouldn't take Jake from me now. He wouldn't require me to raise five children by myself. He wouldn't leave me here to agonize for the rest of my days that my last words to my husband had been in anger. He wouldn't sentence me to the torture of knowing that because of my hesitation, and lack of faith and insight, I had deprived myself of the blessing of being sealed to my husband, and consequently deprived myself as well of the comfort that ordinance might have brought me in Jake's absence . . . would He?

I fell to my knees and prayed. First I begged for Jake's life, for his safety. I pled with God to return him to me, well and whole. Then, after several minutes of desperate supplication, I prayed for the strength to accept the will of the Lord, whatever it might be.

Finally, a gentle feeling of peace rushed over me again. I was reminded of the similar feelings I'd had that afternoon after I'd talked to Natalie, when I had finally discovered what had been holding me back and had been able to turn over to the Lord my concerns about being sealed to Jake and all the uncertainties surrounding that desire. If I had the faith that God could take care of Ted and Tess in the hereafter, if I believed that He could make it possible for all of us to be with our children if we earned that right, then I had to believe that there would be hope of being with Jake. I pictured a loving, omnipotent Heavenly Father, who understood all of my worries and heartache, who knew me as an individual, and who knew what would be best for me.

I felt a firm conviction that if I had to raise these children alone, I could do it. God would help me. Oh, I didn't want to! . . . But if He required it of me, I would do it. And I vowed that I would not give up hope that the Lord would allow Jake and me to be together, even if the ordinances could not be taken care of in this life. I thought of all that God had seen me through and knew that He had never deserted me. My Heavenly Father loved me, I realized, just like Jake loved me. I remained on my knees for what seemed like hours, praying for continued peace and comfort. *Have faith, Maren,* I told myself over and over again. *Have faith.*

My face was still buried in my arms when I heard the grandfather clock in the foyer strike midnight somewhere off in the distance. I wondered if I'd fallen asleep, and dreamed that I heard the far-off sound of the garage door opening. I knew I must be hovering somewhere between consciousness and unconsciousness when I sensed Jake's presence in the room.

"Maren," he whispered.

A sob escaped me, and then another, and another. I didn't dare lift my head, afraid that the hallucination would evaporate and leave me empty and alone again.

"Oh, baby . . ." His arms came around me, pulling me onto his lap as he sat down on the kitchen floor. "Come here, Mar . . . All I want to do is hold you."

I looked up and touched his face. "You're all right!" I choked on the words through my tears and threw my arms around him. "I love you, Jake. Oh, I love you! I'm so sorry."

"I'm sorry too, love. I prayed all day, Maren. And I know that everything will be okay somehow. God will make everything work. I'm just not going to worry about it, and I'm not going to pressure you anymore." He pulled back to look at me and said, "Okay?"

"Okay," I agreed as I wiped at tears.

"Mar," he said tenderly as he helped me brush tears from my face. "I'm sorry I hurt you so badly. I didn't realize . . . Why are you crying so hard?"

"You didn't come home! There was a bad accident on the freeway close to our house, and you didn't answer your cell phone. Trina told me you left hours ago. I was afraid that you were hurt or—" I gulped down another sob and finished, "or worse. I just kept thinking that if you died, and we weren't sealed . . . and I was so mean to you this morning, and—" Emotion overtook me again, and I pressed my face to his shoulder.

"Didn't someone call you?" Jake asked in surprise as he squeezed me close again.

I could only shake my head in the negative.

"Oh, man," he muttered. "I'm so sorry, sweetheart. I asked one of the nurses to call you. I just didn't have time."

I pulled back to look at him again. For the first time, I noticed that he was wearing green doctors' scrubs instead of the shirt and tie he'd left in that morning. I crinkled my brow in confusion.

"Let's go sit on the couch," he suggested tiredly, "and I'll tell you what happened." There were dark circles under his eyes, and his expression was one of complete exhaustion. Something else was there, too, though I couldn't quite put my finger on it. Was it hope? Peace? A little of both, perhaps. I followed Jake into the family room and sat down close to him.

"Yes, there was an accident," Jake told me. "If I'd left five minutes earlier, I would have been right in the middle of it." I gritted my teeth. "It was bad, Mar," Jake mumbled. His mind seemed to be wandering as he glanced down for a moment, but returned to the present. "Anyway, I did what I could to help."

I nodded. Of course he did. Of course he would have stopped to help. I should have thought of that.

"It took a couple of hours to get everything cleaned up," Jake went on. "By the time I got back to my car and made it off the freeway, the hospital was paging me. I'd been in such a hurry to get home to you that I accidentally left my cell phone at the office."

"That's why you didn't call me," I realized.

"Yeah. I couldn't call the hospital back either. The page was urgent, so I didn't waste time looking for a pay phone. I just drove straight there. It was a mess, Maren. There were so many injured people, so many children . . ." Jake stopped to press a thumb and forefinger to the bridge of his nose. I stroked his hair and waited for him to go on.

When he looked back at me he explained, "They were terribly shorthanded with everything they had to attend to. I think they paged every doctor who was on call. Anyway, the chief surgeon asked me to help out. They know I'm a surgeon, too, even though I've been sticking mostly to general pediatric practice. There were a couple of kids in bad shape, and not enough doctors to handle it all. One little boy had a ruptured spleen and we had to go right in. I didn't even have time to think about anything else. On my way down the hall, I asked one of the nurses who knew me to call you for me and tell you where I was. I guess she probably got caught up in something urgent and forgot. By the time I was able to get away, it was so late that I just came home."

"Are you all right?" I asked with quiet empathy for all he'd been through that night.

He only nodded.

We both sat in silent contemplation for a few moments. Gruesome images kept flashing through my mind of all the death and injury that Jake had likely witnessed. Even though taking care of such things was his job, I knew he didn't deal with that on a daily basis. I thought it must have been very difficult for him. In an effort to turn my thoughts to something less troubling, I focused on a more mundane issue. "Did you bring the clothes home that you wore to work this morning?" I asked Jake, thinking they were likely wet and dirty if he'd been out helping accident victims in them. "I could hurry and get them in the washing machine so they won't be stained."

Jake gave a humorless chuckle and said dryly, "They're history, Mar. I ripped my shirt up to make bandages, and everything else is covered in mud and blood and . . . I just threw them away."

"Oh," I mumbled, rebuking myself for being so naive.

"Speaking of all that," Jake went on, "I cleaned up as much as I could at the hospital, but I think I'll go up and take a shower."

"Okay," I agreed. Instinct told me that I should just let him go to bed after that. He was obviously overcome with fatigue. But then I thought of how I'd suffered all day because I hadn't apologized to him that morning. The thoughts and feelings I wanted to share with him seemed too pressing to wait any longer. "I know you're tired, but could we talk for a few more minutes after you take a shower?" I asked him. "There's something I want to tell you—something important."

He raised a curious brow but agreed, "Sure, sweetheart."

I got ready for bed while Jake was in the shower and was waiting for him when he came out. He sat down beside me on the bed and I took his hand. "I gave my sealing cancellation request to Bishop Rowley tonight," I told him right off.

"You did?" he asked in surprise.

I nodded. "I wanted to tell you so badly that I almost called you this afternoon, but I knew I couldn't tell you over the phone. I've wanted to be sealed to you all along, Jake," I clarified. "But I finally realized what's been holding me back, and that allowed me to get past it and find my faith."

Jake shook his head. "Maren, don't do this because of my behavior last night. Please. That won't happen again. I let myself get out of control. I was completely out of line."

"Maybe I needed to hear some of the things you said last night, Jake," I told him honestly. "I've gone through some deep introspection today. You know, I let Ted hurt my self-esteem a lot. I stayed in a bad situation for ten years. I let myself lose sight of my own worth. I blamed myself for everything, and let myself get to a place where I didn't feel worthy of love. I thought I'd overcome a lot of that by the time I married you, but I guess that much of the insecurity was still there. And getting pregnant triggered it all over again—being pregnant is a very vulnerable place for me. I suppose that's because it's always been so difficult for me, and because I felt even more rejected and unloved during my pregnancies with Ted."

I took a breath and exposed my whole heart to him. "I didn't realize until today that I haven't truly felt worthy of your love. I've questioned your love and commitment, because deep down, I didn't really believe that I deserved it. I haven't fully been able to accept the fact that I really am a daughter of God, that you truly love me, and that I deserve a good, faithful husband—until today. It's been difficult for me to accept love and service from you, and to realize that I'm not putting you out or being a burden. I don't think I've truly believed that you love me, Jake. I know you've tried to prove it every day, but I just . . . had to get to a point where I could accept it, I guess. Anyway, I know you love me, and I know you love our children. When you told me last night that you've been trying to show me that I can trust you . . . Well, I know that I can. I do trust you, and I'm sorry I've made you feel like I didn't. I'm sorry you've had to work so hard, but I'm grateful."

"Wow." Jake looked deeply at me for a long moment, and then glanced down at my hand in his. "Since we're on the topic of introspection," he started carefully, "I guess I should confess my insights into myself as well."

I laughed softly and squeezed his hand. "Shoot," I told him, imitating his macho voice.

Jake laughed too, but then his tone turned serious. "You know how Miles asked me if I'd done something to model misplaced aggression or a heightened fear of abandonment to Jeffrey?"

I nodded.

"I know it doesn't make sense, Mar, but honestly . . . all these months I've been terrified on some level that . . . I mean, I think I've just been scared to death of messing up somehow. I told you that I felt like I needed to be perfect so you'd quit comparing me to Ted, but I've also felt like I have to do everything perfectly so you won't . . . leave me again." Jake took a deep breath and finished, "There. I said it. I've been afraid of losing you, Maren. I denied it to myself for months, but I think I must have reflected that insecurity to Jeff somehow. For a long time, he was afraid of you leaving as well—and he assumed that it would be my fault if you did."

"Jake . . ." I said softly. "I'm never going anywhere."

"I think I know that now," he told me. "Did I ever tell you that I love you?"

I smiled. "Not recently."

"Mmm. I'll have to remedy that." He slid an arm around me and pulled me close to kiss me.

The sound of Jason crying broke us apart. "I'll go get him," I said. "Good night."

"No, let me get him, Mar," Jake protested as he stood up. "I can sleep in tomorrow—I'm going in to work a little late. I want to see him."

"Okay. You get him and I'll get the bottle," I offered.

I went downstairs to fix a bottle and came up to find Jake carrying Jason with him to check on the other children and give each of them a kiss. "Are you sure you want us all forever?" I asked him teasingly when he appeared in the hallway. "This is quite a brood."

He laughed and assured me, "You'd better believe it."

I then turned my attention to my baby and stroked his cheek. "It's unbelievable how much he looks like you," I observed contentedly.

Jake grinned and joked, "I'm assuming you think that's a good thing?"

"There's no more handsome man on earth, Prince Charming," I assured him.

He pulled me close with his free arm to kiss me again. "Ah! You've finally recognized me! . . . And you told me you didn't believe in fairy tales."

I laughed. "I don't. I just believe in you."

CHAPTER TWENTY-FIVE

On a blistering Wednesday afternoon a few days later, Jake answered the doorbell. I assumed it was a salesman at that time of day, but peeked into the front hall to find out. It was Ted. I didn't know how he'd known what day and time to come to find us both there. Maybe the kids had told him. At any rate, there he was, green eyes flaming. "I need to talk to you," he demanded of Jake. Then he looked toward me and added, "Both of you."

"Come in," Jake offered hesitantly. He waved his hand toward the front room.

I sat down on the couch, holding Jason in his blanket. Ted sat on the edge of a chair, and Jake sat down next to me, putting a protective arm around my shoulders. I could feel the tension in his arm, though I couldn't see it in his face. "What can we help you with, Ted?" Jake asked.

Ted angrily pulled a folded paper from his shirt pocket and waved it at me. "What is this?" he demanded.

I leaned closer to study it as he opened it and held it out for me. My heart started to pound. I hadn't expected him to receive the papers so soon. "I believe it's the form for you to respond to my request to have our sealing broken," I said smoothly. Jake squeezed my shoulders.

"Why would you do this, Maren?" Ted questioned urgently.

I looked to Jake for strength and then turned back to him. "Because I want to be sealed to Jake, Ted."

"You're choosing to spend eternity being the other woman in his brothel?" Ted snapped.

Jake said quietly, "Ted, I would hope that we could discuss this reasonably. I'd hate to have to ask you to leave. But if you're going to come into my home and talk to my wife, I'm going to insist that you treat her with the respect that she deserves."

"Your wife?" Ted narrowed his eyes. "She was *my* wife until you stole her away. In God's eyes, she still *is* my wife."

I saw the hint of a wince on Jake's face before he spoke again. "Perhaps it's the other way around. You stole her from me. I loved her before she even met you."

"All right, look," I interjected, "this is ridiculous. I'm not some object. I'm a grown woman and I've made my own choices."

"Whatever," Ted said, annoyed.

"And as far as God's eyes," Jake began, "I think that God can see our hearts. God saw how you treated Maren when she was your wife, Ted, and although I wasn't there, I've seen enough to know that it wasn't pretty. I love Maren, and I do my best to treat her well. God can see that, too."

"Yeah, you're real spiritual for a convert," Ted spat, like it was a dirty word. "Did you forget that what God binds on earth is bound in heaven? You two are not bound."

"But we want to be, Ted," I said softly. "That's why I filled out the request."

"What about the kids, Maren?" Ted shot out. "Did you ask the kids how they feel about this?"

"Ted, this is an adult decision. Including children in it would simply be inappropriate."

"*Inappropriate?*" he jeered. "How do you think it's going to work in the next life if you break up our family?"

"Ted," I said quietly, "*You* broke up our family . . . and I don't believe that God will keep my children from me in the next life if I live obediently in this one."

"Oh, but you believe that He'll take them from me?" His voice was heated.

"I didn't say that. I believe that we'll be rewarded according to the lives we've led. God wants us to be happy. He'll find a way for both of us to be with our children if we both earn that. Do you think that our children would be happy if they were torn from one of us?"

"What about Ashlyn?" Ted said more quietly. "We're supposed to raise her in the next life. What about her?" That was probably the first time I'd even heard him speak her name since the day she was born and then died.

"Ted, I can't believe you're even talking this way after all the years you spent in open rebellion against God! I know you've been going to church and making progress, but do you really even believe in the gospel?"

Ted's voice was angry as he said, "When did I *ever* tell you that I didn't believe in the gospel, Maren?"

"You mocked me for going to church, for reading the scriptures, for trying to teach our children the truth. You broke the Word of Wisdom continually, and—"

"Did I *ever* say that I didn't believe the gospel was true?"

"Ted! You—"

"Did I, Maren?"

I sighed. "No, you didn't, but—"

"I made a million mistakes, I know," he interrupted, but the anger quickly turned to remorse. "I'm sorry, Maren. I really am sorry. I'm sorry I made it hard for you to live the way you should have. I'm sorry I screwed up. Yes, I rebelled. I even questioned. But in my heart, I've always known that it was true. I spent two years of my life preaching it, you know."

I watched him in stunned silence before admitting, "I know . . . and I don't have all the answers. I don't know for certain how everything will work out in the next life. But I'm putting my trust and faith in my Heavenly Father. I don't want to see you suffer. I honestly don't. I would love for you to be happy. I'm sure that God can work all that out. For my part, though, I know that the best thing for me is to be sealed to the husband I love and want to be with." I looked up at Jake.

Then I turned to see—to my surprise—not anger, but sadness in Ted's eyes. "You don't love me then, Maren? Not at all? Does ten years and three children mean nothing to you?"

It would have been easier if he'd yelled. I struggled to find my voice. "Ted, I'll always care deeply for you. I'll always pray for your happiness and inner peace. There were good times, I know, but I can't deny that you put me through an incredible amount of pain and misery. You were unwilling to change. I'm sorry if this hurts you, but Jake is the man I want to be with. I've felt happiness and love with him that I never knew before. I want to be sealed to him."

Ted stared out the window at the bright summer sun, and then turned back to us. "What if I refuse to give my consent?" he challenged.

"Then it will make the process harder, but not impossible," I answered him. "And even if you could prevent us from being sealed in this life, it wouldn't change the way I feel. I love Jake. I want to spend forever with Jake. You don't just automatically 'get' me in the next life, even if our sealing still stands. If I live worthily, I believe the Lord will allow me to be with the man I want to be with."

Ted pounded a fist against the arm of the chair as he groaned in frustration.

"Ted," I said softly after a brief pause, "I tried everything during those ten years, and nothing worked. You've made incredible progress since I left. It's probably the best thing that ever happened to you. Please, Ted, let me go."

He looked up, and I was astonished to see moisture in his eyes. "I love you, Maren," he admitted, to my shock.

"Then let me go," I whispered. "It's the only way we'll ever find peace, either one of us."

He chuckled dryly. "I don't know what it is that you've got, Jake . . ." he muttered.

To which Jake replied softly, "I know you don't, Ted. You never did. But I do know what I've got." He looked down at me as he hugged me to him. "And that's the difference."

Ted just sat looking at both of us, stunned. Finally, after several long moments, he said, "So, you're really happy. You both really love each other and this isn't going to end?"

We looked at each other, and then nodded at him.

"I guess there's not much point then. I'm done." He stood up to leave. I didn't ask him whether he would give his consent right then, and truthfully, I wasn't really worried. One way or another, everything would be all right. I was sure of it. And Ted would be all right, too, if he chose to be. It was such a relief to finally be able to accept the fact that things were in God's hands, not mine.

"Good-bye, Ted," I said.

"Bye, Maren." He left quickly without looking back.

Jake stood in the doorway, watching long after he'd driven away.

I finally touched his arm and asked, "What are you thinking?"

He glanced down at me before gazing back out the door. I was surprised at how readily he admitted, "That for the first time in thirteen years, I actually feel sorry for him. I've hated him, Maren. All this time, I've been harboring envy, and rage, and hatred toward Ted. I don't know if I even consciously realized it until now. I think that over the years I've blamed a lot of my trials and problems, and even my mistakes on him, because he took you from me and ruined my life.

"Of course, that's not really true. I made mistakes all by myself, without help from anyone. You made your own decision about who to marry, and I survived without you. Don't get me wrong. I love you deeply, Mar. But my life wasn't ruined. I'm glad you're here now, but I may be stronger than I ever gave myself credit for. Maybe I really hated myself for not doing something differently all those years ago. Or maybe Ted was just an easy scapegoat for my own deficiencies. You know when I hit him last fall? I did want to protect you, and I hate to admit it, but I almost think I hit him more for me than for you. So, there's my 'misplaced aggression.' How's that for enlightenment?"

I just watched him, gently bouncing Jason so he'd stay asleep.

"It's odd," Jake began again, "But he suddenly doesn't seem like the monster I've thought he was. I've only been hurting myself by hating him. He never should have treated you and your children the way that he did during those painful ten years. That's inexcusable, and I'm not trying to trivialize it. But there must be some good in him somewhere if he can find the strength to start back from where he's been. I'm going to be more decent toward him. He's right. I've been a jerk."

"Wow," I breathed. "You've certainly improved with the open-and-honest thing. And you're not a jerk, Jake. You're a good man. A very good man, in fact." I started walking back toward the family room to check on the children in the backyard. "I'm a lucky woman," I mused as I glanced out the kitchen windows.

"Well, not *that* lucky," Jake contended as he joined me at the window. He lifted Jason from me and went to put him in the baby swing in the family room.

I followed after him and he turned around to tell me, "You'd be luckier if you had a more sensitive, understanding husband . . ."

"Oh, no." I started to back away from him.

"One who wouldn't give in to the temptation to tickle you all the time!" He laughed a deliciously evil laugh as he caught me and wrestled me to the floor, where he sent me giggling and squirming across the rug to the fireplace. Then he paused to take me in his arms and kiss me.

"Still think you're lucky?" Jake asked me with a broad grin.

"Absolutely," I answered breathlessly, as I reached to deliberately mess up his hair.

"No, not the hair!" he protested theatrically. He growled at me and kissed me once more before he jumped up and ran away.

***

I came upstairs a few minutes after Jake did that night and checked on all the children before going to bed. I planted kisses on five sleeping heads as I thought of all that I had to be grateful for. I walked into our bedroom, expecting to see Jake, but didn't. I glanced back out in the hallway to assure myself that all the lights were turned off. "Honey?" I called softly, stepping further into our room.

I barely had time to gasp before the door was swept shut, and I was in his arms. "You were hiding behind the door?" I laughed, trying to slow my racing heart.

"I just wanted to catch you by surprise." He grinned.

I laughed again, more quietly. "Well, you certainly did."

"Do you still want to be with me forever?" Jake whispered ardently in my ear.

"Like you can't imagine," I whispered back. I looked into his eyes as anticipation rushed through me. "How can you make me feel this way every time?" I asked him softly.

He drew out a long, sweet kiss before he answered, "I was just wondering the same thing."

"I'm so happy, Jake," I told him. "Now if I could just get Ted to cooperate and speed things up with getting our sealing canceled, then—"

Jake touched a finger to my lips and whispered, "Shh. Don't worry about that, Mar. Have faith, remember? We already decided this. Everything will be fine. Besides, we have forever."

The passion I felt with him had become almost as familiar as breathing, and yet the wonder and power of it still left me in awe every time. I felt overwhelmed with the fresh realization of how much he loved me as he pulled me close to kiss me again.

Later, as my husband held me tightly and brushed his lips over my brow, a sudden twinge of doubt tugged at me again. "Jake?" I asked. "What if they won't grant my sealing cancellation? What if—"

"Then God will work it out somehow," he answered confidently. "I'll simply go to Him and explain that I've done my best, that I'm so in love with you that I can't possibly live without you—which He already knows, of course—and then I'll plead with Him for divine intervention. If we do everything we can, Mar, if we earn the privilege of being together, then God will grant us that. I'm sure of it."

I sighed and kissed his shoulder, squeezing him to me. "I'm sure too," I told him. Then I reached up to kiss his lips once more before I fell asleep in his arms.

CHAPTER TWENTY-SIX

Jeffrey and Rebecca were both going to turn eight in September, within a week of each other, so we spent several family home evenings discussing their upcoming baptisms. One night, Jake showed them how they would stand in the water, where to put their hands, and how to plug their noses. He practiced dipping them back, so they'd know what to do when it was time.

They asked a long list of questions, and then Jeff said, "You're going to baptize me, right, Dad?"

"That's right, buddy."

Rebecca went over to put her arms around Jake's waist and asked, "Will you baptize me too, Daddy?"

There was a sudden silence. We hadn't discussed this yet. I hadn't talked to Ted. I had no idea whether he was worthy to baptize her. "Becca Bug," I told her, "that's something your dad might want to do for you."

"I don't want him to," she said. "I want Jake." She looked up at Jake, who picked her up and held her to him.

"Sweetheart, I would love to baptize you," he answered her. His softened attitude toward Ted showed through as he added, "But you know, your dad might be planning on that. That's something that I think you should discuss with him first. You can tell him how you feel, but I think you should ask him how he feels about it, too."

"Okay," she agreed as she pushed her small arms around Jake's neck.

As October approached, and Rebecca and Jeffrey's baptism date drew nearer, I asked my daughter, "Have you talked to Daddy about baptizing you?"

"No," she said hesitantly. "I still want Jake."

"I know you do, sweetie," I told her sympathetically. "Do you think you can talk to Dad about it and explain how you feel to him? Or do you need me to talk to him for you?" I offered. I knew the children felt much more comfortable around Ted than they used to, but I wondered if she might be afraid to discuss this with him.

Rebecca mulled it over for a minute before she said, "I can talk to him."

"It might be a good idea to do it soon, Becca," I suggested gently. "It's only a couple of weeks away."

"Okay," she agreed.

The following Sunday evening when Ted returned with Rebecca and Trevor, he asked me if he could talk to Jake and me again for a minute. "Sure, Ted. Come in," I told him.

Trevor hugged him and said, "Bye, Daddy!" before he ran to find Jeff, but Rebecca stood holding his hand.

I called to Jake in the family room, "Honey? Could you come out here for a minute, please?"

He walked into the front hall, carrying our happy, chubby baby. "Hello, Ted." Jake held out his hand and Ted shook it hesitantly. "Good to see you again," Jake said genuinely.

"Look at our baby, Daddy." Rebecca pointed Jason out to Ted. "Isn't he cute?"

Ted smiled. "He sure is, Rebecca."

"Let's go sit down in the front room," I suggested. "Becca, why don't you go play now?" I assumed that Ted wanted to talk more about our sealing annulment.

"Actually, I'd like her to stay," Ted said.

I was surprised, but agreed, "All right."

Jake and I sat on the sofa, and Ted sat in the armchair, pulling Rebecca down to sit on his knee. "Rebecca and I were talking about her getting baptized next month," Ted began. I could see him struggling with emotion. "And, uh . . ." He stopped to clear his throat. "Well, she told me that she'd like you to baptize and confirm her, Jake." I could see how painful this was for Ted, and I was in awe that he would humble himself so much on behalf of his daughter.

"How do you feel about that, Ted?" Jake asked sincerely.

Ted smiled at Rebecca and then answered, "Well, I'd like to do it for her, of course. But the most important thing is Rebecca's happiness. It's her baptism, after all, and she should be able to choose who performs the ordinances for her." He cleared his throat again and swallowed hard a couple of times. "She uh, she uh . . . she loves you, Jake." He seemed to be struggling against inevitable tears. "I know you've been a good father to my children," he admitted. "Much better than I ever was." He quickly wiped away a few drops of moisture that escaped down his cheeks. I couldn't remember ever seeing Ted cry before. "So, will you do it for her?" he asked Jake brusquely.

"I'd be honored, if you're sure that's what you want," Jake answered softly, his eyes glistening as well.

Ted nodded. "I want my little girl to be happy. She shouldn't have to pay for my mistakes."

Rebecca threw her arms around Ted's neck and said, "Thank you, Daddy!" He smiled at her, and she skipped out of the room.

My own eyes were certainly not dry as I remarked, "That was a very noble thing to do, Ted."

He chuckled humorlessly and said, "You know what the funny thing is? This would have been the first time I was actually worthy to perform an ordinance for one of my children."

"Really?" I asked.

"Yeah. I realized that because of my choices, I lost everything I loved. I lost my wife, I lost my children, I lost the Spirit. I know I can't get you back, Maren, but I do have my testimony back. Maybe in time, I can win my children back too."

"Your children both love you very much," I told Ted earnestly.

He nodded. "I know that. I'm a lucky man. The only thing that's ever brought me happiness is living the gospel, and part of that means loving my children more than myself. I meant it when I said I still believe in the gospel, Maren. I really screwed up in walking away from it."

I just watched him quietly for a minute, not sure what to say. I finally extended an invitation to him. "You will at least come to the baptism, won't you?"

"Of course I will, if you'll let me."

He stood to go, and Jake put in, "I think I owe you an apology, Ted. I believe I *have* been a bit of a jerk, and I'm sorry about . . . well, I shouldn't have hit you that day last year. I apologize."

Ted just stared at Jake, looking bewildered for several seconds. Then he composed himself, and said simply, "Thanks for being willing to do this for my daughter."

Jake nodded and Ted left quickly.

Later that evening I asked Rebecca, "What did you tell Daddy about wanting Jake to baptize you?"

She shrugged. "I just told him that I wanted Jake to do it."

"What did he say?" I asked, knowing I really shouldn't pump her for information, but feeling both concerned and curious.

"He asked me how come I wanted Jake, and I told him I just did. Daddy asked me if I love Jake more than him, and I told him no. I love them both."

"Then what did Daddy say?" I pried.

"He told me that he wanted to baptize me, but that I could decide. So I asked him if he'd be mad if I wanted Jake. He said he'd be sad, but not mad. He said if I wanted Jake to baptize me, it was okay."

"And you told him you did?"

"Yeah. And then Daddy told me he's sorry for the bad things he did. He said I'm lucky to have such a good mom, and that Jake's not really a jerk."

"He said all that?" I asked in surprise.

She nodded and asked, "Can I go play now, Mommy?"

"Yes, go ahead." I smiled and shook my head, marveling at how far we'd all come.

***

I didn't think that October could have started out any more beautifully. It was usually a month that I dreaded, but the weather was warm and welcoming that year, and life was too good not to enjoy it. The leaves were barely beginning to turn, and everything just seemed beautiful. I had hope of being sealed to Jake someday. I was happy to see Ted's progress. Trevor and Elizabeth were both enjoying kindergarten, and Jason was growing beautifully. There were still challenges, but I looked forward to settling into a more relaxing year than the previous one, and was anticipating the coming holidays.

The second Saturday in October, our families crowded into the small Relief Society room. It was the first time Jake and I had everyone there together. My parents, and brother and sister, and their families came. Jake's parents were there. Tess's mother came, and was actually pleasant. Ted's parents, his brothers, and their families were there, and Tyler and Lydia both attended the occasion, as well. Everyone that was there was at peace. There were only smiles, and kind words, and tears of joy.

Jake sat between Rebecca and Jeffrey, dressed in white. Ted sat on Rebecca's other side in a gray suit, his hair neatly combed. There was a degree of serenity in his expression, something I hadn't seen in years.

After the short program—which included a beautiful vocal solo by Lydia—Jake baptized Jeff and then Rebecca. Ted looked almost teary-eyed as he observed the scene.

I met Rebecca in the dressing room to help her dry off and change into her lavender dress. I took the white bow out of her French braid and changed it to a matching lavender one. "You look beautiful, sweetheart," I said as I hugged her. "I'm so proud of you."

"Am I done, Mommy?" she asked hurriedly. "I need to talk to Dad before I get confirmed."

"What? You don't want to talk to me?"

She shook her head and smiled. "Thanks, though, Mommy. Love you."

"Love you too, sweetie."

She ran to find Jake. I followed her back to the room and watched her sit on Jake's knee to whisper in his ear. He smiled at her and nodded. She threw her arms around his neck and kissed his cheek. Jake turned to smile at me, and my heart fluttered seeing him in his suit with his freshly combed, damp, black hair.

Rebecca ran over to Ted then, and whispered something to him. He looked at her incredulously, and then held her to him tightly. I wondered what she'd said.

Trevor asked me if he could go sit by his dad, and I said yes, not sure which dad he meant. He sat next to Ted. Rebecca took her seat on Jake's left side. Everyone was back, and Bishop Rowley resumed the meeting. We listened quietly as Jake confirmed Jeffrey. As I watched him giving Jeff the gift of the Holy Ghost, and promising him future blessings in his life, I was filled with peace.

Just after Jake said, "Amen," he looked at me and smiled. He hugged Jeffrey to him, then shook his hand, along with all the other men who had stood in the circle.

Bishop Rowley announced, "And finally, we have Rebecca Saunders, who will also be confirmed by her stepfather, Jacob Jantzen."

Jake cleared his throat and went to whisper something to the bishop. Then he sat down and Bishop Rowley said, "My mistake. Rebecca will be confirmed by her father, Ted Saunders."

I tried not to gasp as Ted stood up and took Rebecca's hand. He showed a slip of paper to Bishop Rowley, then led our daughter to the chair at the front of the room. I reached over to touch Jake's arm on the front row. He shrugged his shoulders, as if in awe himself, before he got up to join the circle.

Ted's words were clear and steady as he blessed his daughter with a firm testimony, a love for the Lord, and a desire to always do His will. His voice cracked once or twice as he prayed for her. Afterward, he hugged Rebecca to him and blinked back tears. She hugged Jake and her grandfathers and uncles. Then she ran to hug me, and I asked her what had happened.

"I don't know, Mommy," she said. "After Jake baptized me, I just felt like my dad should get to confirm me. I didn't want Dad—Jake—to feel bad, but he said it was fine, and I think it made Daddy happy." She smiled.

"Yes, I think so too, honey." I kissed her sweet, young cheek.

Ted shook Jake's hand and told him, "Thank you."

"It was Rebecca's idea, Ted. I just wanted her to be happy."

Afterward, everyone came to our house for dinner. The day was surprisingly warm, so we set the tables up in the backyard rather than in the house. After dinner, I sat under a tree feeding Jason his bottle. Ted brought a chair over and sat down next to me. "Maren, tell me something."

"What's that?" I asked him.

"Did you tell Rebecca to ask me to confirm her?"

"No, Ted, I didn't."

"Did Jake then?"

I shook my head. "It was her own idea, on the spur of the moment. She told me that she just felt like you should do it." I smiled at him.

He smiled back, and I caught a glimpse of the man he'd been when I'd first met him. His eyes weren't filled with hate anymore. "You're doing a good job with the kids, Maren, you and Jake. I never appreciated how much you did."

"Thanks," I said softly. "And you're doing a pretty good job yourself these days, you know?"

He looked away and tapped his fingers together.

"How are things going?" I asked him.

"Pretty good, actually. I started going to some of the singles activities."

"You did?" I asked in surprise.

"Yeah," he admitted. "I've been working on myself for a while, and I decided maybe I'm ready."

"Good for you," I answered genuinely. "It'll probably be good for you to socialize a little."

"I guess it couldn't hurt," he agreed. "Well, I suppose I'd better go talk to my family. Thanks for inviting everyone."

"Of course I would invite everyone. You're Rebecca's father, and your family's her family."

"I know, but after everything I've done, I wouldn't blame you if you—"

"Ted," I interrupted him. "What's past is past. Let's just concentrate on moving forward."

"Yeah . . ." He got up to leave, then hesitated for a moment, shoving his hands in his pockets. "Look, Maren," he finally said, "I'll, uh . . . Well, what I mean is . . ." He cleared his throat a couple of times and then finished quickly, "I'll give my consent. You can be sealed to Jake. You're right. If it's not what you want, then . . . Well, anyway, I'll do it, so it'll speed up the process for you, and . . . that's it, I guess. See ya." He hurried off before I had time to react, leaving me in shock.

Lydia came to sit by me a moment later and waved a hand in front of my face. "Earth to Maren," she said jokingly.

I managed to respond with a faint, "Hi," as my mind returned to the present.

Lydia made faces at Jason until he laughed, then looked around and sighed. "This is incredible, Maren," she observed. "Do you know that?"

"What's incredible?" I asked her, feeling puzzled and still a bit distracted.

She held her arms out for emphasis and exclaimed, "Your family! Look at all these people! Your parents are here, and Jake's parents, and Ted's parents. Most of your brothers and sisters are here with their kids. And if you start to count all the people from the ward who showed up, there must be dozens of people here, maybe more, all to see one little boy and girl get baptized." She turned to look at me and demanded, "Don't you realize how extraordinary that is?"

"Well, the support from the ward is nice, though not a huge surprise. And to tell you the truth, I guess I just take it for granted that our families will come to everything."

"You can say that again," she muttered.

"What?" I asked, not sure if I'd heard her right.

"You definitely take it for granted," she clarified bluntly. "You have no idea how lucky you are, Maren. Know how many people came to my baptism?"

"No, how many?"

"Five. The missionaries who taught me, the bishop of my ward, and the couple whose home I took the discussions at. I barely knew any of them. And growing up, there was my grandmother and me. That was it. For Christmas and Thanksgiving and birthdays, there were only the two of us. Once in a while we got together with a few people from our church, and they were nice, but they were nothing like the friends you have in the neighborhood and in the ward."

I looked around me with a different perspective and admitted, "We *are* very blessed."

"Yeah, you are," she agreed emphatically.

"These people are all your friends, too, Lydia," I pointed out. "The people from the ward, I mean. And my family's adopted you. So has Jake's."

"I know." She smiled. "I have to admit, I've been surprised at how kind people have been since I started to reach out a little more. All this time, I thought I was being shunned by them, but maybe it was more the other way around."

"Things are improving for you, aren't they?" I observed.

"Yeah. Now, if only Prince Charming would appear on my doorstep . . ."

I watched to see if she was serious, but she looked at me and laughed. "Aw, let him take his time. I'm busy anyway. Besides," she added slyly, "Glen's a pretty nice guy." I smiled and then Lydia noted, "Oh, there's Sandy! I need to talk to her. We're on the activities committee in the singles ward together now. I'll see you later, Maren."

"Bye." She started away and I called after her, "You did a great job singing today!"

She turned around, smiled, and waved at me before a couple of other people stopped to compliment her, as well. She really had come a long way.

Jason had finished his bottle, so I stood up and went to find my husband, anxious to share my news with him.

He was in the kitchen, cleaning up. He'd taken off his tie and suit jacket. His shirt sleeves were rolled up, and his top buttons were undone, but he only looked all the more handsome to me. He glanced up and smiled. "Ah, there's my beautiful wife." He beamed at me, then came around the counter to kiss me. "I wondered where you were."

Jason gurgled, and Jake kissed his cheek. "And my baby, of course. I didn't forget you, bud." Jason smiled at him, and little dimples appeared on his chubby cheeks.

"You did a great job today," I told him.

"Thank you," he answered. "I was pretty proud of Rebecca. How about you?"

I nodded. "I think that was a good thing for both her and Ted. Thanks for being so supportive of her and her decision."

"You're welcome," he said as he wrapped his arms around me.

"Guess what?" I asked him, trying to keep my excitement in check.

"What?"

"Ted just told me that he would agree to cancel our sealing so that I can be sealed to you."

He tilted his head, studying me. "Don't toy with my emotions, Maren," he warned, only half joking.

"I'm not," I reassured him. "He really did."

"Are you sure?" he asked.

I nodded.

"Did he mean it? You think he'll honestly do it?"

"Yes," I told him. "I do."

"Oh, Maren," he whispered. "If he really does . . . that will speed the whole process up."

"I know." I smiled at him. "How long do you think it will take, though?" I asked.

"I don't know." He laughed. "I don't care. It doesn't matter. We'll wait as long as it takes. You're mine, either way, Mar—no matter what."

That night, we sat in the family room visiting with Jake's parents before they had to leave in the morning. "There certainly is a nice feeling among all these people," Beverly remarked to Jake and me. We exchanged knowing glances, and I smiled to myself, recalling that Jarold had made a similar comment to me a few months earlier. I'd decided to hold off telling Jake about that conversation, waiting to see if anything would come of it, and not wanting to get his hopes up in the meantime.

"So," Jarold started. "What if someone had some questions about your church? How would they go about getting the answers?"

Jake stared at his father. "You're not saying what I think you're saying . . . are you?"

Jarold glanced at Beverly and replied with a grin, "Nope."

Jake cracked a smile and responded, "Well, *if* a person had questions, and *if* they didn't, say . . . know anyone else to ask, they could always look up The Church of Jesus Christ of Latter-day Saints in the phone book. Or, if they happened to be staying in Salt Lake, they could go to the Temple Square Visitors' Center. They might even want to consider asking their son to track down a phone number for the missionaries in their area. I'm sure he'd be happy to do it for them—if he was a member, of course."

"Really?" Jarold asked as Beverly smirked at him. "How interesting."

Jake spent a bit of time on the phone in our bedroom that evening, and I saw him slip a folded piece of paper into his father's shirt pocket when he told his parents good-bye.

"Wow," I said to him after they'd gone. "Do you think they'll really call the missionaries?"

Jake gave a happy shrug and said, "Who knows? But at least they're finally thinking about it. That's big progress."

"Yeah," I agreed, smiling to myself.

***

Jake and I met with Bishop Rowley the end of October to discuss what we could expect when my sealing cancellation came through. He told us that he would like to interview each of us and give us the necessary recommends, "just in case" it didn't take too long. Jake didn't see the bishop wink at me as we left his office.

CHAPTER TWENTY-SEVEN

Jarold Jantzen called Jake a few days later. I recognized his voice over the cordless phone as they talked. When they hung up, Jake said, "That was my dad."

"Yes, I know." I smiled, feigning complete innocence. He didn't seem to suspect that the phone call had been at my request.

"They're coming to look at houses next weekend. He says they're here so much now, they might as well move when he retires."

"You'll like that, won't you?" I asked.

"It'd be great." He smiled.

"Did they say anything about the missionaries?" I asked him.

Jake grinned and replied, "Not yet. But they're close, Mar, don't you think?"

I was happy to agree with him. "Yes, I do."

"Anyway," Jake went on, "Mom and Dad said they'd love to watch the kids overnight while we go away for our anniversary. What do you think?"

I threw the dish towel I was using over my shoulder and put my arms around him, smiling at how well my plan was working. "Mmm. That sounds wonderful. Let me plan it though, okay?"

He looked surprised, but agreed, "Well, if you insist, my dear."

"I do." I kissed him again.

On the morning of our first anniversary, we had breakfast with the children and Jake's parents, then got ready to leave.

"Wear a suit, will you, honey?" I asked him sweetly.

"All right. What are we doing?"

"I'm not telling. This whole weekend is a surprise."

He raised his eyebrow at me and went to the closet. He pulled out his dark gray suit, held it up, and asked, "Is this one all right?"

"That one is wonderful." I smiled at him. "Will you zip this for me?" I turned around and held up my hair while he zipped my blue dress, the one I'd worn on our wedding day.

"I'm assuming you're being sentimental, and that you'd like me to wear my blue tie to match you?" He smiled.

"Would you?" I asked. "I love how it brings out your eyes."

"Anything for you, love." He was obviously humoring me.

We kissed the children good-bye, hugged our baby, thanked Jake's parents, and went out to the car. Our suitcase was waiting, already packed.

"See you soon!" Jake's dad gave me a conspiratorial look before closing the garage door.

"How would you feel about me driving?" I asked Jake.

He shrugged and replied, "Whatever makes you happy." He walked around to the driver's side and opened my door for me.

He gave me several curious looks as I drove south on the freeway, toward our temple. When I finally pulled into the parking lot in Provo, he said, "Ah. The temple. What a wonderful idea, Mar." He pulled me into his arms after he opened my door for me. "I can't believe we've only been married a year," he whispered. "It seems like we've been together forever."

I smiled at the implication he was missing and kissed him. As we walked across the parking lot, Jake said, "So, we'll do a temple session, and then . . . what?"

"You're very sneaky," I observed, "but I'm still not telling." I paused before adding, "Oh, and by the way, we're not doing a regular session."

"We're not?" he asked in surprise.

"Nope. I actually signed us up to do sealings."

A look of dismay crossed his face, and he tugged on my hand to hold me back. "You did?" he asked when I stopped to meet his gaze.

"Is that all right?" I asked him, trying to look worried.

"Um . . . sure, Mar. That's a nice idea."

"What's wrong, Jake?"

He sighed and ran those long, graceful fingers through that thick, dark hair. His wedding band glittered in the autumn sunlight. Oh, how I loved him! "It's just—"

"Just what, honey?"

"It'll just be hard to go through that ceremony with you on behalf of someone else, that's all."

"I know," I agreed with empathy.

"I guess we should do it, though," he admitted reluctantly.

I could see Jake struggling with his thoughts as we resumed walking. His brows were furrowed, and his look of concern deepened with every step. Just before we reached the temple doors, he hesitated. I took the opportunity to pull him aside, moving a few feet away so we wouldn't be conspicuous. I met his expectant gaze with a smile and whispered, "I almost forgot to ask—Will you marry me?"

A grin finally broke through his mask of apprehension as he pulled me close to give me a brief kiss. "I already did that once, remember?"

"I remember," I assured him. "And it was very nice, but I've decided that I'm actually rather fond of you and . . ." Jake watched me with amusement as I went on, "I was thinking we ought to make it a more permanent arrangement."

"What?" he asked, a little baffled.

"It just seems like such a shame to let something so wonderful end after only one lifetime," I told him lightly. "So, I want to know if you'll marry me again—forever, this time."

"What are you saying?" he whispered, looking mystified.

"I told you, silly. We're here to do a sealing for a very important couple. The bride specifically requested *you*. You're the man she wants to be with forever, you know."

Realization crept slowly across his face. "Us? This is for *us?*" he asked in amazement.

I nodded.

"But has your sealing to Ted been canceled? You didn't even tell me?"

"Bishop Rowley was very sneaky, wasn't he?" I remarked with amusement. "I told him I really wanted to surprise you for our anniversary if I could, and he was able to help me arrange it."

Jake pulled me into an iron embrace. "Maren," he whispered. "My sweet Maren. Oh, I love you!" He relinquished his hold on me to look into my eyes and kiss me.

"Is that a yes?" I asked.

He threw his head back and laughed. Then he hugged me and kissed me again. "Yes," he answered firmly. "Most definitely, yes."

We entered the sealing room to find all of my family waiting for us. Jake and I knelt across the altar from each other as we were pronounced sealed for time *and* all eternity. After the ceremony, Jake kissed me tenderly and then held me to him as we both wept.

When Natalie and Douglas came to hug us, Natalie had tears running down her cheeks, but she gave me a triumphant grin. "I'm glad you finally got your head on straight," she whispered to me.

I laughed softly and hugged her back. "So am I," I agreed. "Thanks for the help."

They told us that we could have a few minutes alone in the celestial room, so I followed my husband down the beautiful, serene hallway. We sat together on a velvet sofa, his arm around me, my head on his shoulder. "Maren, this is the most wonderful gift in the world. I can't think of anything that would have been better."

"Really? Not even if we still went away overnight after we have lunch with our families?"

"Okay, that will make it better, but this . . . You're sure about this, aren't you?"

I laughed softly. "It's a little late if I'm not." Then I laid my hand against his cheek and whispered, "Jacob Adam Jantzen, I've never been as sure of anything in my life as I am of you."

He took my hand and kissed it, looking into my eyes. "You're finally mine," he whispered. "Nothing and no one can take you away from me again."

I smiled at him and contemplated how happy I felt, until one tiny thought tugged at my heartstrings. I hesitated to voice it, but then did it anyway. "Jake . . . I know this may not be the best timing, but being here in the temple, so close to heaven, I just can't help thinking that there's still another baby for us."

When I dared to meet his gaze, Jake looked away for a moment and squeezed his eyes shut. "Maren," he whispered, as though he was struggling with some inner argument. He finally sighed and looked back at me. "The thought still frightens me, Mar. I just . . ." He shook his head. "I just don't think we can make a decision about that yet. I think we need to give it a year or two."

I nodded and smiled, trying to swallow the knot in my throat.

Jake's expression turned more tender as he tilted his head and watched me. "We'll pray about it, Mar. Not yet, but when it's time. I promise we'll pray about it, okay?"

"Okay," I agreed, feeling a degree of relief. I couldn't ask for more than that. I rested my head on his shoulder again and enjoyed a few more peaceful moments.

"I guess we should go, hmm?" Jake finally asked softly.

"I suppose we'd better. Everyone will be waiting for us."

He took my hand as we left, and held it until we parted at the dressing rooms. We met our families outside on the grass. "Congratulations, son," Jake's father said, as he and Beverly hugged him. Jake's mother wasn't crying this time. Instead, she looked truly happy for us.

"Thanks," Jake told them. Then he cracked a smile and asked, "So, are you gonna come back and go inside with us someday?"

His parents were both speechless for a few seconds until Beverly finally remarked, "Well, I guess anything's possible, isn't it?"

The children pounced on us then, begging to go to lunch. "All right, all right," Jake laughed, as Trevor almost knocked him down on the grass. He picked Trevor up with one arm and Elizabeth with the other, and started toward the van. I hugged Rebecca and Jeffrey to me as Jake announced, "Let's go!"

"Don't forget Jason!" Rebecca reminded me.

"Of course we didn't forget Jason," I assured her, and went to retrieve my baby from my dad. Jason grinned to show his one tooth, and then promptly tangled his fingers in my hair, yanking hard enough to make me whimper.

Jake chuckled as he came to untangle the plump little fingers, then he kissed them. "Be nice to Mommy, sweetheart," he whispered teasingly. "You're going to be with her forever, you know."

He took Jason from me to buckle him into his car seat as the other four children pushed past him to pile into the van. "Stay right there, guys," Jake instructed. "We'll be back in just a minute." He closed the door and took my hand.

"We'll keep an eye on them," my dad offered from behind us.

"Thanks," Jake told him.

"Where are we going?" I asked as we started across the parking lot.

"I thought we'd walk up the hill to our tree," he told me.

I followed him to the top of the grassy hill next to the temple, to the place where I'd told him good-bye more than thirteen years ago, to the place where he'd proposed to me fourteen months before this day. Jake took me in his arms and kissed me until the world started to spin. Then he held me to him and sighed contentedly. When he pulled away he had a mischievous grin on his face. "Want to race down the hill?" he challenged.

"Jake!" I laughed in protest. "Besides your obvious advantage of height, I'm wearing hose and heels!"

His grin widened, and he leaned close to whisper, "Are you chicken?"

I raised my eyebrows at him. Then I kicked off my shoes and bent to pick them up. I barely had time to catch the look of astonishment on his face before I took off down the hill, his laughter chasing after me. I ran as fast as I could with my skirt in the way, and would have slammed into the fence if Jake hadn't jumped in front of me. "That was close," I said breathlessly after he'd caught me. "For a minute there, I thought you were going to let me hit the fence."

"Maybe you'd better slow down a bit next time, love," Jake advised. "I'm getting old, you know."

I smirked and told him teasingly, "I will say one thing for you—you definitely keep life interesting. How long do you think you can keep that up?"

He grinned and replied, "Well, we've got forever to find out, so I guess we'll see."

I smiled at the thought as I bent down to slip my shoes on, then stood up and paused to watch my husband. When he met my gaze, I looked into his deep blue eyes and knew that I could see forever. The prospect of spending eternity with this man filled my heart with joy.

Jake held his hand out to me, eyes dancing with amusement, and said, "This is the part where we're supposed to waltz across the parking lot, right?"

"Too bad it's filled with cars today," I quipped.

"Yes, too bad." He winked at me and shrugged. "Oh, well. I guess we'll have to come back later tonight, when it's empty."

"I suppose so," I agreed.

"Or we could try dancing around the cars," he teased.

"Whatever you think, honey," I teased back. I glanced toward the crowded parking lot, amused at the thought of trying to maneuver our way through it with any degree of grace. Then I thought of our five rambunctious children waiting for us in the van, and paused to soak in the last few peaceful moments before we returned to them. I stood gazing up at the temple and the expanse of blue sky beyond it until Jake interrupted my thoughts.

"It's beautiful, isn't it?" he commented.

I turned to see him watching me and asked coyly, "What's beautiful?"

He pulled me close to kiss me once more and whispered, "All of it."

"It certainly is," I whispered back.

He extended his hand to me again and flashed that sweet dimple in his right cheek. "Shall we go get started on forever?"

I smiled and slipped my hand into Jake's, content to follow him wherever he might lead me.

About the Author

Candie Checketts has been writing for as long as she can remember and usually has multiple works in progress. Feeling driven to surpass mere personal enjoyment in her writing, Candie hopes to offer a new perspective on some important LDS issues. *Always and Forever* is her second novel in this venture.

Candie is a graduate of Utah State University. She holds degrees in elementary and early childhood education, and enjoys working with children. Candie currently lives in Riverton, Utah, with her family.